# MY KIND OF *Trouble*

ELLE MACDONALD

My Kind of Trouble
Book 1 in the Falling in Freymoor series



Cover design by: Authors Aura Design
Edited by: Scribbling Crow Ink
Formatted and proofread by: Samantha Simpson Editorial

ISBN: 978-1-0682838-0-2

*To anyone who has ever had to start over and feared that doing so would break them. It's okay not to have all the answers right now. Trust that the best is yet to come!*

## NOTE FROM THE AUTHOR

My Kind of Trouble is for the most part a light and fluffy romance. That being said, as with any work of fiction there may be some sensitive topics covered inside that could be triggering for some readers.

Whilst for the best experience I recommend going into this book blind to avoid spoilers, please put yourself and your mental wellbeing first.

There is a full content warning page at the back of the book for those who wish to use it.

I hope you enjoy this story and the characters within it as much as I do. And I would love to hear your thoughts on Goodreads if you find the time.

# Chapter 1

## Noa

'We need to talk' has to be one of the most foreboding conversation starters known to man. And right now, Noa was living in the aftermath of it.

If there was an opt-out clause you could take once they were spoken, she would have eagerly done so.

But, unfortunately, no such luck.

'Noa, I don't think this is working. We're not the same people we used to be, but that's okay, you know? We've both grown, as we should do, but we've grown in completely different directions, and I think we both know it,' Lucas had replied to her simple question of 'Shall we start that new documentary on Netflix?' Noa then choked on her forkful of spaghetti she now wished she hadn't gone to the effort of making.

Sitting crossed legged on their sofa, she tried to remember to breathe as her mind scrambled to get a grip on what the hell was going on. The thin layer of dust that covered their living room side table felt like it taunted her in that moment, because hadn't that been his job this week? *Figures.*

Her eyes narrowed into slits at the offending particles that felt far more significant than they probably were.

She fixated on anything but the fact that her boyfriend was currently giving her his best breakup speech.

Had she entered some form of alternate reality? Should she search the flat for hidden cameras? Because this could not be happening.

Slowly putting her fork down, she turned to stare at him like he had grown two heads, blinking rapidly, like it would allow her to clear the nightmare and be transported back to before Lucas had opened his mouth to speak those words.

However, it seemed that this was, in fact, happening, and there was no way that he could take the words back.

Lucas looked completely unruffled, like he'd had all the time to prepare for this, and that hurt. His curly blonde hair remained in exactly the same style he'd had since they were twenty-two years old—short on the sides and shaggy ringlets on top. His face was clean-shaven, and the bridge of his nose was slightly crooked from an old rugby injury he'd experienced when they were at university.

Physically, everything about him looked so familiar and yet, at the same time, she didn't recognise the man in front of her.

Noa struggled to find an appropriate response as she stared at him, her brain short-circuiting. Instead, she just sat there, mouth gaping like a goldfish.

'Don't look at me like that Noa, you know I'm only saying what we're both thinking but have been too scared to put a voice to for months. We can't do this anymore. It's not fair on either of us. We deserve to be the best versions of ourselves, and you know as well as I do, that we're not doing that right now. I'm just sorry that I had to be the one to say it.'

She had gone mute. Simply no words came to her mind, something that often happened when she was faced with confrontation. Avoidance of difficult conversations had always been her preferred method of managing these kinds of situations. But it seemed, despite her best efforts, that she had been unable to outrun her relationship problems, as here they were, having clearly caught up with her. Brushing them under the carpet to handle later was no longer an option, and Lucas was not messing around.

But had things really been that bad?

This all felt like it was coming out of nowhere. Okay, yes, she knew they had both been distant lately, often more interested in their own lives as opposed to prioritising the one they were creating together. There were times they argued because Lucas had seemed unsupportive or uninterested in her dreams, or because he accused her of expecting too much. And, yes, she knew she was in her own head a lot and he found her anxiety and the constant reassurance she needed sometimes hard to handle. Well, actually, the word he had used was 'exhausting.' But those weren't reasons enough to break up, were they?

They just needed to talk things through. They could work it out. You don't throw away six years of a relationship just like that. They could form a plan to fix what was broken, and it would all be okay. She needed it all to be okay.

Being plunged into the unknown had always been overwhelming to Noa in a way that she found difficult to navigate. And not in a this-is-a-rather-annoying-inconvenience way, but in a bury-yourself-under-the-covers-and-hide-from-the-world-for-weeks way. It was why she liked to plan every aspect of her life, as a way of avoiding this exact scenario. So, she needed to get a grip on the situation before her life spiralled in a way she was not ready for.

Her fluffy tortoiseshell cat, Tinkerbell—or Tinks as she liked to call her—brushed through her legs, moving in a figure of eight as if in silent support, encouraging her to deal with this head-on.

God, adulting was hard sometimes.

'We—we can fix this. I—I can try harder. Let's just take a minute to figure this out and not jump into anything without thinking it through.'

'I'm not jumping, Noa. This has been coming for a long time. We aren't each other's people and I'm tired of trying to force us to be. I think one day you will realise that and probably thank me. Don't get too worked up over this, I promise it is the right decision.'

She tried her hardest not to scoff at his words. The audacity.

Why did he always think he could dictate how she should or would feel? Like her emotions were an inconvenience for him to manage in order to make his own life easier. He'd always made her feel that way and she hated it.

She thought her expression was still vacant, but whatever Lucas saw on it softened his tone as he began to talk to her like a scared animal he didn't want to spook.

'Noa...' he whispered.

But that snapped her out of it. She had too often felt like a burden to those around her.

Fragile Noa Drake who was always too close to breaking. Noa, who people had to tiptoe around or risk triggering an anxiety spiral that they would then be forced to support her through. She was sick of feeling that way and so, in that moment, she decided she wouldn't anymore.

Or, at least, she would remove from her life someone who actively made her feel that way.

If Lucas didn't want her, then she sure as hell wouldn't be talking him into it, and she would be strong enough to walk away before he witnessed whatever breakdown would inevitably come next. Her and her 'big feelings,' as he often referred to them, would not be his problem anymore.

She would deal with it on her own, because he had never actually been much good at emotionally supporting her anyway. It had just taken this one lightbulb moment for her to realise it.

With a newfound determination, she knew what she had to do next and where she needed to do it. And it certainly was not here.

She turned one last angry glance his way, determined to at least get the last word, before snapping, 'You're right. God, how rude of me Lucas. Thank you. Thank you for opening my eyes to the comfortable life I've been unknowingly living. I'll be sure to send your thank you note in the post when I leave.'

And with that, she slammed the bedroom door so it rattled on its hinges and began to pack.

# Chapter 2

## Noa

Undulating hills surrounded Noa in all directions. There was nothing but several shades of greenery as far as the eye could see, only broken up by skipping lambs and the occasional clusters of daffodils well within bloom—a sign that spring was underway.

Surely, there was no better time to start afresh than in the season known for its resurgence of new life. It was the season colour finally broke through from the gloom of winter, but Noa wasn't feeling much of a sunny disposition right now.

At twenty-eight years old, she never thought that she would find herself newly single and driving back to her parents' house. She had a plan for her future but, funnily enough, this was not it. She couldn't help but think that life had a warped sense of humour and that she was currently the punchline in some sardonic joke. Noa flexed her fingers on her steering wheel to release the pressure from her white-knuckle grip.

She tried to focus on her surroundings, grounding herself in the moment, to avoid the cascade of negative thoughts and worries that would only serve to overwhelm her. She already couldn't shake the feeling that she was making a mistake and would regret not fighting harder for her relationship.

The winding country roads came to an end as the sign welcoming her to Freymoor gave way to a mix of paved and cobbled streets. She had always felt like the hills protected her sleepy hometown, cocooning it at the foot of their slopes. A far cry from the chaotic city streets of London, where she had spent the last eight years.

Locals waved eagerly at her through her window as she passed them by, clearly more enthusiastic than she was to see her back home. Freymoor was one of those places where everyone felt like more than just a familiar face, and where the gossip mill was even faster than the internet speed. So, she knew that her arrival would be the talk of the town by the evening, and the idea of her failures being small town tittle-tattle elicited an uneasy feeling in her stomach.

Ignoring it, Noa wound down her window as she drove down the familiar cobbled street that led to the place she once called home, and now would again. She took in a deep breath and let the cool, fresh spring air fill her lungs, reminding her she certainly was not in the city anymore. Somehow, that thought settled her. There was something about the countryside that soothed a part of her whenever life felt too heavy. Everything felt slower and less chaotic in Freymoor, and she needed that now more than ever given her whole life had just gone up in flames.

*Dramatic? Maybe.*

But she felt like she had earned the right to be a little dramatic.

She'd wanted to move back here with Lucas one day, but had soon buried that idea with a few other things on her 'to do' list, under the sacrifices-she-was-happy-to-make-for-him pile. It was funny thinking of those things now. She doubted that list ever ran both ways, but she would pull it out once she got settled and start crossing them off one by one. Doing so would probably be very therapeutic under the circumstances, like claiming back something she had lost. She mentally applauded herself for the head start she had unknowingly given herself by returning home.

*Silver linings.*

There was no time like the present to start a '30 before 30' list after all and, with no other solid plans in her future, maybe it could be a way of really turning her breakup into something positive. That ought to motivate her to really give it a good go too. Nothing motivated her quite like the power of putting pen to paper and creating tasks for herself. It had been an ongoing joke in her family growing up; she'd constantly left scraps of paper and rambling lists around the house, and it drove them all crazy. Just as the recollection of her family began to calm her racing thoughts, she was jolted back to reality when a ginger ball of fluff shot into the road, causing her to slam on her breaks. The piercing screech of metal on metal reverberated through the car and Tinks mewled in the back seat, clearly less than impressed by the disturbance. Now, it wasn't only her thoughts that were racing, but her pulse thrummed so intensely she had to slow to a crawl as she tried to gather herself. A panic attack was not on her bingo card for today and every tiny disruption or stimuli threatened to tip her over that edge. She was a raw nerve, and it was clear the next few days were going to test her coping strategies.

The ginger cat now sat preening itself on the kerb, looked completely unfazed by the war currently raging inside Noa. She couldn't help but think that the near miss was a sign—from who she didn't know—that she had made a mistake and that this journey home was the wrong one. But there was no going back now. Overanalysing would get her nowhere.

Trying to drown those thoughts out, she turned up the volume on her car's old speaker, the tinny sound of *The Greatest Showman's* 'From Now On' filling her ears. She braced herself for the tears she was sure would fall soon enough.

*They should, right?*

Six years of her life and the future she had once planned for, now nothing but a distant memory. And yet, all she felt was numb. Like the last forty-eight hours had been nothing but a fever dream, or a few chapters in the latest book she was reading—*The Third Act Breakup*—and everything was going to be okay again soon. Well, that settles it, she was definitely in the first stage of grief alright: denial.

And if denial was what kept the overwhelming anxiety she felt when anything big changed in her life at bay, she was all for it. In fact, she could stay here in that bubble forever, quite blissfully ignoring the shitty situation she had now found herself in. The car rocked, her suspension being pushed to its limits as she directed it over the cobbles that paved the way to her family home.

Noa tried to centre herself, to push down the rising sense of panic gripping her chest. She focused on the light smell of pollen in the air and the newly-planted hanging baskets which lined the stone-built terraced street—the sign of new beginnings. She concentrated on the hum of her engine as she pulled to a stop and on the bright green door, now chipped and peeling from years of slamming and heavy rainfall in this northern town. The sight had her making another mental note to apologise to her parents for those moody teenage years when she got a chance.

The door's stained-glass panel had always been one of her favourite features of their house. It was like her very own 'welcome home' sign that stood out from the rest on the street. The side of her mouth tipped up into an almost-grin at the sight of the plain glass squares in the corner, a stark difference to the vibrant patterns surrounding it. A memory arose from the depth of her subconscious, of a much younger Noa and her brother, Ryan, when he had kicked a ball through the glass during a game of dodgeball. The wrath of their father had scared them half to death—a side of him it took a lot to unlock—and their mum had refused to replace it to match the rest because she'd said that it would only happen again. Turns out, she wasn't wrong.

Her brother was a human tornado, always had been. And he had never been one to simply walk through life, more like hop, skip, and jump with a crash landing.

He was fun-loving Ryan. What she would do to steal a bit of that for herself right now, to not take life too seriously and just take her current situation in her stride. She knew that's what he would do.

Unlike Noa, Ryan hadn't wandered too far from home when he'd moved out. Still sitting in the car outside her parents', she glanced to the bottom of the street. There, she could see his small inconspicuous cottage, tucked behind overgrown green shrubbery, a huge opposition to her brother's exuberant energy. She'd made fun of him endlessly at first, teasing him for being too chicken to fly too far from their parents' nest. But who was laughing now?

The slamming of a car door, followed by loud greetings between neighbours, halted her trip down memory lane.

Noa turned to her cat, eagerly meowing to be let out of her cage where she sat on the back seat.

'We're back where we started, Tinks,' Noa whispered to her feline companion with a deflated sigh.

Tinks had always been Noa's emotional support animal and had moved out with her when she was twenty and it seemed the two of them had come full circle together. It was hard not to feel that heavy sense of failure and somehow, despite her grounding techniques, her mind still wandered to forty-eight hours before.

Lucas's 'we can still be friends' still rang on repeat in her head, along with him calling her 'irrational' as she packed her bags to immediately flee the scene of their breakup.

They didn't call it fight-or-flight for nothing. And irrational or not, she'd chosen flight as she hightailed it out of there.

Noa shook her head to rid herself of the hazy memories. In less than twenty-four hours, she had called her mum, quit her job, and driven halfway across the country back to her parents' house where she now sat paralysed by the gravity of what she had done. Again, maybe that was a dramatic reaction, but if after six years her relationship truly was over, then why delay the inevitable, right?

Whilst for some people a move like this might be as insignificant as changing a pair of socks, to Noa it felt like she was free-falling with no one waiting to catch her. It was like being on a fairground ride when the carriage suddenly drops, taking her stomach with it, except the ride doesn't end, and neither does the sensation that comes along with it. She had never been an impulsive person. It simply wasn't in her makeup. Maintaining control and acting according to a well-established plan had always kept her anxiety at bay. The closest she had ever come to an impulsive decision was when she'd decided to use a semi-permanent box dye to turn her hair Rhianna red at eighteen.

So, maybe this rash decision should be concerning; the personality transplant was what they would probably reflect on later as the beginning of her mental breakdown. When she left for university and her career eight years ago, relocating hadn't felt like a big deal. But now, retreating back to her old life with no master plan, did. There was no goal she was chasing. And that made her feel dizzy.

But when Lucas ended things, there was a voice inside her head telling her that she had to get out of there—it hurt too much not to. She couldn't breathe in that flat they shared so many memories in, a constant reminder of the future she had lost. And she couldn't process her emotions with him there either. So, here she was, in a place she had always imagined herself returning to, yet the circumstances couldn't be further from the plan she had envisioned. It made it impossible to know whether she should be grateful for the push that brought her back here or wallow in fear and heartbreak.

It was a battle in her brain, a dichotomy of emotions, and it was exhausting.

Whilst she too, knew her and Lucas had grown apart as of late, she really thought the conversation was coming where they'd talk about how they could work through it. But, it seems, they truly had been on different wavelengths. Or maybe denial really was her go-to coping mechanism.

She'd talk to her therapist about that later.

With that thought in mind, Noa took one more deep, soothing breath, opened the car door, and let her feet hit the pavement to make her way to the old terrace house. For the first time in her life, Noa's family home, did not fill her with comfort. The sudden realisation that this was not just a vivid dream, but real life, sunk in. Had she made the right decision?

She didn't get a chance to dwell on that too long as the door flew open and she was enveloped into her mum's arms, her floral scent making Noa feel at home. She was then clumsily tackled to the floor by her not-so-gracious older brother. With a playful huff, she shoved him off and got to her feet.

The smell of her mum's home cooking coated her nostrils and pulled her through the house and into the family kitchen. The room was dimly lit by candle and firelight. It had historically been a cardinal sin to turn on the 'Big Light' in their house. Her mum had always thought it gave their home a friendly and cosy feel compared to harsh artificial light, and right now Noa couldn't agree more. Wood crackled and popped in the log burner, a comforting soundtrack that made her want to curl up with a book and get lost in a fictional world for a while. But, no matter how much she tried to ignore it, she knew that this was not just another story. This was real life, and she certainly was not getting her happily ever after.

# Chapter 3

## Noa

After what felt like hours of countless trips traipsing all of her worldly belongings from her car up the two flights of stairs to her single box room, Noa stood there, looked around her, and took it all in.

'Well, this is cosy,' she muttered to Tinks who had quickly settled under the radiator on a pile of old blankets. The purring bundle of fluff was a true constant in Noa's life, which was something she valued now more than ever. She'd also become a good listener over the years. God only knows Lucas had rarely listened to her ramblings the way Tinks always had.

In fact, there was only one other person who had listened to her, truly listened and saw her, the way her furry companion did. But she ruined that relationship years ago. With a heavy sigh, Noa picked up her cat and snuggled into the fur at her neck, letting the soft rumbles of her purrs ease all her worries.

'We only need each other, don't we Tinks. Us against the world,' she rambled, 'And definitely no men allowed.'

Tinkerbell purred louder at that, and Noa decided she had already started to go mad. Although, some might say that boat set sail years ago.

Surveying the hoard of boxes and bags, Noa knew what she needed to do next. *Home sweet home*, she thought as she pulled out her various photo frames from the boxes on her floor and hung them in a random pattern on her wall using the self-adhesive strips her brother had brought up for her. He had always known her so well, and he knew Noa never quite felt at home until she had her photographs hanging and her books and trinkets on the shelves. As if she had conjured him, the broad-shouldered man that her once gangly and always goofy older brother had turned into appeared in her doorframe. He looked so different since the last time she saw him. Sure, they had talked on FaceTime, but seeing him in the flesh she was reminded again of the passing of time. And of how much she had neglected her family over recent years.

She wanted that time back.

But, knowing that wasn't a miracle she could just manifest, she knew she could only move forward and nurture the relationships that had always been there. And always would.

She had clearly put too much energy into the wrong place, and she wouldn't do that again.

'Why do you look so constipated? If that is your thinking face, then stop—we don't want the wind to change and for your face to stay like that,' Ryan remarked, laughing at his own crappy joke.

'Jesus, I don't come home for a few months and you turn into Dad. Has anyone ever told you how much you sound like him? Be careful Ry, you'll have the receding hairline next!' she threw back, knowing just the thing to say to rile up her big brother.

'Take that back or I'll remind you that you have just become a spinster overnight.'

The comment should have hurt or acted as a stark reminder of the shitstorm that she found herself in, but instead, she felt nostalgia wrap itself around her body as the familiar interaction with her brother made her feel even more at home. It made her feel that, maybe, no matter how much time passed or what happened, she would always have this place. Have this. A brother who knew her well enough to know when she needed sibling ribbing and banter over sympathy. A family that loved her enough to take her in at moment's notice and make sure she had everything to make her feel comfortable. She might feel lost in a storm, but that had to be enough for now. She would lean into it the best she could to make the most out of a bad situation.

Ryan winked at her as he bounced himself on top of her unmade bed, not a care in the world for her belongings that went tumbling to the ground with the motion. She sighed heavily and bent to pick them up before standing and faking a scowl in his direction.

He shrugged innocently at her, his eyes mirroring that of a sorry puppy, a very good comparison for Ryan.

Her brother was a hard person to stay mad at. He always had been. And he had always known it, too. The shit-eating grin that he was currently sporting told her that was yet another thing that hadn't changed.

'You know, I was going to tell you how much I missed your ugly face, but I don't think I'll bother now.'

Ryan waved her off, his dark curls falling into his eyes as he shook his head.

'I missed you, too, squirt,' Ryan said, pulling her into a noogie that she had to wrestle herself out of. It felt like old times already.

'You need a haircut,' she barbed, attempting again to lighten the mood before she joined him on the bed, folding her legs under herself. They both fell into easy conversation, catching up but also skirting around any difficult conversations, and Noa felt grateful for that.

Ryan told her all about a project he was currently focused on to become the pastoral lead at the school he worked at, and that he was running against a guy who cared so much more about the status than helping the kids.

Her heart swelled at how caring her brother was, and she was suddenly hit again by how much she had missed him.

After a while, Ryan looked around and gestured to the mess around them—unpacked cases on the floor, books piled high out of boxes.

'You need a hand?' he asked.

'No, I'm good,' she shook him off. Keeping busy was a much-needed distraction. 'I guess I should start getting used to doing things on my own.'

Ryan frowned and she didn't know what she had done to put it there until he said, 'You know that's not true right?'

Noa didn't reply, so he continued, 'You'll never be on your own, Noa. We have and will always be here to support you. And before you say anything to the contrary...' he rolled his eyes, as if exasperated by something she hadn't yet said. 'That does not make you less of a "badass" or "independent woman" as you and Tes like to call it. It makes you someone who has their own team on their side, and sometimes it takes one. A 'badass woman' would know that.'

He had shocked her to silence because, yes, that was exactly something she would have said. And was definitely something she was still thinking, because she wanted to prove to herself that she could do this on her own, like it would mean that she had won the breakup or something. She didn't want to let her brothers' words sink in because that meant changing the mindset that currently held her together, but she didn't want to argue with him either. Instead, she just pulled him into a hug before responding with a, 'Thank you, Ry, but I think I need to be alone to think right now.'

And, with that, Ryan moved to make his way back downstairs.

As he reached the door, he turned to look at her, his expression thoughtful.

'So, hey, I know you don't want to talk about it right now, but I'm here if you ever want to tell me what happened.'

'I know.'

She gave him a soft, grateful smile.

'And you know I'd do anything for you right? If we need to hurt someone, I'm your guy. Whatever you need, I'm there. Escape guy? Help hiding a dead body? I think I've watched enough CSI to pull it off.'

Noa chuckled at that, but she knew he meant every word. She moved off the bed and hugged him in response. He smelt woodsy and like home.

Tears pricked behind her eyes as the whole interaction started to overwhelm her. She pulled away, allowing him to retreat again.

He was at their parent's house to welcome her home, but was also staying for their Friday night dinner tradition. One that they had lived by growing up and that her parents and Ryan had kept up after she had left. She promised that she would be down to join them later.

But, first, she had to make this room look less like a bombsite and more like a safe haven.

So, that is what she did. She set to work on the task of decorating her little room until it felt like hers again. Her clothes could stay in her suitcases for now; maybe it would prepare her in a way for the travelling which she planned to do and had mentally placed at number two on her '30 before 30' list on her long drive home. She really ought to write this stuff down before she forgot. Once all her photos, trinkets, and rugs were in place, Noa unpacked her books onto the bookshelves her dad had put up for her the moment he found out she was coming home. In her time away from home, Noa had become a well-established editor, meaning her book collection had reached all new extremes. There was no way her old bedside bookcase would have housed what she often referred to as her 'emotional support books', and her dad had known that. He had listened when she spoke about them, and he observed her life and cared about her passions. The song 'If He Wanted to He Would' rang in her head as she thought of her dad doing this for her. A song lyric that her best friend, Tes, had regularly reminded her of during those long phone calls, late at night, where Noa had moaned about Lucas's lack of effort in their relationship. Another glaring reminder that maybe she had chosen to ignore the signs of her impending breakup, as opposed to them not existing.

*'Are you even listening to me?'*

*'Sorry what?' Lucas mumbled with a vacant expression that had Noa's hackles raising. He turned away from her before she could even answer, going back to flicking the buttons of his PlayStation controller. Clearly the game was way more important than whatever conversation she wanted to have.*

*She'd been excited to come home and tell him about her new editorial project at work and how it had given her some inspiration to finally start writing something of her own. But Lucas barely managed to feign interest, and her own excitement wavered along with any motivation she'd found to make her childhood dream a reality. So, back in the box it went.*

As she snapped out of her daydream, or nightmare she realised now, Noa started to carefully unpack her various candles and trinkets that had somehow doubled in volume since she left Freymoor. Handmade marketplaces truly were a dangerous place for her, especially when left alone with her thoughts every weekend whilst her now ex-boyfriend went out with his friends. Because, of course, an invite for her would have been too much to ask. She remembered feeling so wracked with nerves on those evenings. Her mind was her own worst enemy at times and, with Lucas too distracted in his own world to consider that, she was left wondering 'why'? Was she no fun anymore? Too much to handle? Did his friends not like her?

'Well, I guess I don't have to worry about that anymore,' she said on a half-laugh, half-sneer to her empty room. Even Tinks had gotten bored of her pity party now.

Once she finished, she wiped the sweat that glistened on her forehead away with the back her hand and sighed with the relief she felt. She could do this. So, with her bed made, her things mostly unpacked, and a huge sense of accomplishment, Noa decided that was enough for one day and finally made her way downstairs to face the music that was her family. She loved them and all their craziness, but she was clinging on to her sanity by a thread and had been proud of how well-functioning she had been since arriving home. And she feared that seeing them again, seeing her mum's sympathy-filled eyes, being wrapped in the safe embrace of her dad's arms, and answering the twenty questions that were sure to come might just tip her over the edge. She wasn't ready for the fall just yet. As she shuffled down the stairs, Tinks playing dangerously at her feet, the sound of her dad's familiar deep and rumbling laughter, and her mum's screeches in mock offence at something Ryan said filled her ears. As she listened, her heart started to thaw for the first time all day. These were her people, and she could face anything when she had them. She took the last step and rounded the corner for all three sets of eyes to fall on her and, suddenly, the loud hustle and bustle of the kitchen fell silent.

'Wow, you should see all your faces right now,' Noa said, trying to lighten the mood. 'What's up? What did I miss?' she joked, casting pleading eyes at Ryan.

Luckily, it didn't take long for Ryan to catch on to what Noa was putting down: she really didn't want to do the whole sympathy thing.

'No, I was just wondering how long it would take for this catastrophe...' he said pointing in an aggressive circular motion in her direction '...to look presentable, so that we can go and have some much-needed sibling time at The Brew tonight. I've not seen you in so long and, I have to say, I'm feeling extremely hard done by.'

Noa looked down at her holey black leggings and her threadbare jumper that read 'in my cowboy romance era', ripped at the sleeves and with a huge coffee stain down the front, and she rolled her eyes.

'Yes, you're right, I can see how this could be a good time for a "woe is me" moment for you.'

'Thank you, it's about time I get some recognition around here,' he nodded with the straightest, most serious facial expression she had ever seen her brother wear.

He was trying to be serious, but the way his mouth pulled up in the corners gave him away. Ryan was the most playful, easy-going person she knew, and she had always wished that, one day, his laid-back outlook on life would rub off on her. But, unfortunately, she was still as rigid as ever. This was something she really wanted to work on and now, when life was so up in the air, felt like the perfect time.

'It's open mic night,' he added, still trying to sell a night out at The Brew to her. 'You know you can't miss the opportunity to see Old Man Albert hog the stage and sing himself into a drunken stupor.'

Well, he was right, there. She could confidently say that was something she had missed and could definitely help lift her out of her current funk. Old Man Albert was a Freymoor attraction they could sell to tourists at this point. He had been born, lived, and would die in their small town, and was a huge personality here. He loved to spend every moment he could serenading the townspeople who loved him and would get away with stalling the stage for hours because almost everyone had a soft spot in their heart for him. His performances had to be one of the best parts of open mic night at The Brew—if you ignored the fact that his words became progressively more incoherent as the night went on and that he absolutely could not sing. He was what people meant when they talked about small town charm.

Noa must have been smiling at the thought of a night spent at their local bar, like old times, because Ryan bumped her shoulder before saying, 'Go on, you know you want to,' with a wink.

Once again, her brother knew how to help pick her up when she was down.

Noa and Ryan were only two years apart in age, so growing up they had been the best of friends. They'd done everything together, and people had often commented that they were more like twins than siblings since they were notoriously joined at the hip. It wasn't just them, though. Her best childhood memories often took her back to a time when the two of them and their respective best friends, Alex and Tes, spent most of their time together. Nights camping in the garden, and Sundays watching movies and playing boardgames.

She loved those memories. She missed them.

But Noa had ruined that, with a secret that had forced her to pull away from the group to keep it.

Ryan never questioned it, probably assuming that it was nothing more than the physical distance between them since she'd moved away for university.

But, she'd always known it was more than that.

She was beyond grateful for her relationship with her brother and the comfort he brought her because she needed him right now. He was fiercely protective, and she knew that there was nothing he wouldn't do for her. As kids, Ryan went through a hard time in school, and Noa thought it was that experience that had made him so protective over the ones he loved, as if he felt he could shelter them from going through similar experiences. It hadn't hardened him like it could have though, and he had always been the biggest softy around. Ryan was caring to a fault and the definition of charismatic. He somehow always found a way to be everywhere all at once, helping everyone with that boyish grin on his face. There was once a photo of him on the town's WhatsApp group watering Mrs Finch's tulips, which had ended in a string of requests from the rest of the town's OAPs to help with their own. He was always helping Sarah Kingsley with the heavy lifting in the book shop and he just enjoyed looking out for people. Ryan had one of the biggest hearts she knew. The biggest mouth, too, but that was just unapologetically Ryan.

He was Freymoor's golden boy for that reason and, boy, didn't he know it.

Getting to spend some quality time with him felt like another silver lining in her breakup, and she would take as many of those as she could find. Otherwise, she'd be forced to think about the uphill battle ahead of her, and that felt too hard to even consider.

So, taking up her brother on his offer, she decided that maybe a Ryan-shaped distraction was exactly what she needed. She just hoped his offer only applied to the two of them. Although Ryan loved to socialise, Noa had survived enough reunions for one day, and there was one encounter in particular she hoped to avoid for a little longer.

# Chapter 4

## Noa

As Ryan and Noa made their way into The Brew, a sense of nostalgia hit her all at once. This was the place she had come to during her rebellious teenage years when she was under age, and it was the only place in town lenient enough to look the other way. She'd had her eighteenth birthday here, and the whole town had turned up. Freymoor was good like that. It had a sense of community like nowhere she had ever been before. As much as she'd first wanted to lock herself away at her parent's house and throw away the key, when her brother had suggested coming tonight, she'd thought maybe unlike denial, distraction could be a healthy coping mechanism. Thinking back to that birthday put a smile on her face. Her brother was going through his 'I'm going to be in a rock band' phase at the time and had eagerly volunteered—pushed may be more accurate—to make this event his first *'gig'*. Let's just say this dream fizzled out by the end of the year, but the mohawk took slightly longer to grow out.

The Brew was the favourite go-to joint in their small town that didn't have another good bar for miles. It was one of those places where regulars had their own seats they would sit in time after time, and tabs could be left open for weeks on end. The definition of the quintessential small-town vibe.

Now, everything on the inside looked... different. It still felt warm and inviting—unequivocally Freymoor—but there were subtle changes that highlighted the passing of time and the fact that, as much as she thought it would, the town she grew up in had not stood still since she left it. Her heart ached at the thought of what else she could have missed, a pang of sadness settling in her bones. The once-shaggy-looking interior had been replaced to give it a much more upmarket feel. The sticky vinyl floor was now lined with deep Mahogany wood, which matched what looked like a hand-crafted bar and bar top. The dingy dance floor and DJ booth had been swapped to an intimate band-stand and multiple sofas dotted around, encouraging people to chat and enjoy the atmosphere.

*This must have happened when the new ownership took over*, she thought.

Ryan had mentioned something about it, but she had been so wrapped up in her own dramas following an argument with Lucas at the time, and she clearly hadn't been listening. She recalled there was something about The Brew becoming run-down and the owners becoming too old to maintain it. She was sure they had run into financial troubles, but that was the extent to which she had listened before Lucas had stood with his hand on his hip, waiting for her to get off the phone so they could finish their disagreement. Also, in her defence, Ryan was like an overgrown toddler and spoke a mile a minute sometimes. She couldn't be expected to remember every word that came out of his mouth.

'What you having?' Ryan asked, nodding over to the crowded bar and draping a heavy arm over her shoulder, temporarily shaking her out of her daydreams.

'Oh, you tell me. Whatever's good these days... and locally brewed, obviously. You know I prefer it to the imported stuff,' she feigned cheerfulness, not wanting her brother to jump into protective mode.

So, as Ryan took off toward the bar, Noa returned to her trip down memory lane as her eyes cast over the surrounding space. The pool table where her dad taught her to play pool, the dart board where she'd beaten Ryan on her twentieth birthday— he'd insisted he'd let her—before she'd gone on to get a very wavy level of drunk in a celebration of said big victory. As her thoughts spiralled, she realised that this was the very same night she lost her virginity to... Noa very quickly cut off that train of thought. It felt wrong to think of it, to think of him in Ryan's presence.

But, despite her best efforts, self-preservation did not win, and she was tossed back into the memory of her twenty-year-old self.

*'Shit, shit, shit,' Noa thought as she frantically tried to grab her clothes from where they decorated the floor around the bed.*

*Alex's mum always worked every hour of the day, and it had seemed to work in their favour as they'd fumbled into the house last night. But now, she wished there had been someone to talk sense into her and stop her idiocy.*

*Someone who would have reminded her that this was not just anyone that she was about to lose her virginity to, but her brother's best friend.*

*For so long, she'd ignored any whisper of a connection between her and Alex.*

*She'd plastered on her friendliest smile around him, reminding herself of the not-so-subtle warnings her brother had drip-fed them over the years. Yet, in one drunken night, she had torn down any flimsy barriers she'd kept between them.*

*Shit, shit, shit.*

*This time she was sure she'd spoken the words aloud as she heard rustling from over her shoulder, evidence of life from the bed.*

*She closed her eyes, hoping that if she couldn't see him then he, too, couldn't see her attempt at a discreet escape.*

*How would she explain this?*

*'Where are you going, Trouble?' a gravelly voice asked. Her heartbeat picked up, and—were those butterflies? No!*

*No, no, no.*

*She had to get out of here before salvaging their friendship became impossible and the risk of causing a rift between Alex and Ryan became inevitable.*

*She turned to look at Alex then.*

*He was twenty-two to her twenty and was just starting to fill out in all the right places. His defined pecs were on display over the covers and a light dusting of chest hair decorated them in the centre, evidence that Alex was not a boy anymore.*

*He was a man.*

*And, like a man, he could make his own decisions. That's exactly what last night was.*

*The rational part of Noa's brain should have known that. But Noa was a perpetual overthinker, and rational thinking often took a back seat to 'worst-case scenario'.*

*And, right now, that worst-case scenario playing on repeat in her head, was the one where her lust-infused decision could very well lead to the downfall of Ryan's and Alex's relationship.*

*She didn't know if she could take that. Even if a part of her was curious to explore what last night had meant.*

*She had to protect that friendship because, for years, her family had been more like a second family to Alex, and that wasn't something worth risking.*

*Her brother was protective to a fault, and no relationship brought a guarantee. Everyone went into it risking their hearts. But this wouldn't just risk their own, and she knew that, if something went south between them, Ryan would always take her side.*

*As she stood almost catatonic, staring at him, Alex reached out to grab her arm. She suspected he knew she was deep in her thoughts and, as he often did, was likely trying to pull her out of the place she had gone to.*

*He was good at that.*

*Looking into his warm eyes she felt lucky that her first time had been with someone she trusted and felt safe with.*

*But it wasn't enough to make her question the words she spoke next as the fear took over.*

*'We need to keep this between us,' she blurted. Alex reared back like she had shot him before schooling his features.*

*She saw it then. That expression he had been wearing before was hope, and she had just crushed it.*

*'I'm leaving for university. There is no need to complicate things with you and Ryan. If you are worried he will find out, I won't say anything if you won't...'*

The sound of the microphone squealing jarred her from the memory. A memory she had buried to keep her own guilt at bay. And, when she had met Lucas at University, she hadn't needed to think about it, because she had moved on, and it was truly in the past. But there was something about being in this place that unearthed it. The Brew was a reminder of that night.

A reminder of him.

The pact that they made that night to pretend like it never happened was the only secret her and her brother had ever had between each other.

She'd left for university that month, so what good would it have done to blow up Ryan's friendship, with his best friend no less, and then leave him alone as she started a new life across the country? No, she stood by it and maintained that it was the right decision for all involved. He and Ryan had remained friends and lived out their playboy life styles together, and she had moved away and moved on. She wouldn't feel bad for that. It was a one-night stand, with too many beers on behalf of both parties that would never be repeated. If she was honest, she doubted he—who's name felt too dangerous to even think about—would even remember it now. Not after the stories she'd heard from Ryan about his escapades over the years and the many notches he now had under his belt since that night. Besides, losing him from her life had been an easier transition than she'd expected. It wasn't like she had seen him since.

Not until—

A throat cleared behind her. Noa turned and quickly felt like all the air had been stolen from her lungs, the bar suddenly too hot, as her eyes caught on a pair of rich amber ones not three feet away from her. Eyes that had always reminded her of the leaves on the trees in her favourite season. Eyes that she had worked so hard to forget so that they wouldn't be her undoing.

Eyes that could not be mistaken as belonging to be anyone other than him. Ryan's best friend. And the one she'd pushed away. Alex Fletcher.

# Chapter 5

## Alex

Tucked in the corner of The Brew was what Alex had renamed 'The Cosy Corner' after he'd added a leather sectional sofa and several wingback chairs. He'd felt it took the bar from small-town-dive to country-core and gave customers an area to feel more relaxed and laid-back when they spent their evenings there. But, right now, as he sat in that very spot, Alex felt the opposite of relaxed. He filled salt and pepper shakers, gripping them like they were solely responsible for his bad mood.

The door rattled with the sound of another customer entering the crowded bar. Alex's head whipped back and forth with every patron who entered, his eyes flying across them like a man possessed. You'd think he'd be thrilled seeing more happy customers flock in for open mic night. It was one of his busiest nights of the week, not a spare seat in the house, and just nine months after he'd taken over this place. He should be proud. But all he'd felt the entire night was on edge.

His closest friend—well, more like family if he was honest—Ryan, had called him last night. He'd rambled on and on for an hour about how his sister was moving home after almost eight years away chasing her dreams. Eight years since she'd left this town and never looked back… since she'd left him.

Alex didn't hear much after that. His ears had rung, and his mind had wandered back to the night of her twentieth birthday, like it always did whenever he heard her name. Usually, it was regarding some achievement she'd made in London or about a flying visit that he would somehow manage to avoid. His best friend never did question him about his random and weirdly-timed doctors' appointments, but this time she, apparently, planned to stay.

He'd done an impressive job so far, but he couldn't avoid her forever it seemed. Their paths would soon cross again, and he wasn't sure what that would do to him considering how he'd reacted to the mere mention of her name, how his heart sped up and his hairs stood on end. He could only surmise it would not be good.

What spell had she cast on him that, after all this time, he couldn't shake the ache in his chest when he thought of her? That he couldn't look around rooms, including this bar that he'd given a complete revamp of over the past year, and feel like he was surrounded by the ghosts of their younger selves.

The corner booth, where a naive version of himself had sat, staring into the eyes of a girl he thought might just give him a chance. The small patch of floor space in front of the bandstand where they'd swung around, happy and dancing with friends. But all he'd seen was her.

Alex snapped his head away, forcing his eyes to stop their travels before they sent him any further down memory lane. Because it was a slippery slope, and he knew it.

Last night, when Ryan said he was bringing Noa to the bar to 'get her mind off things', Alex quickly developed a plan. If all his efforts to avoid her failed, he would simply act... detached. Unfazed. Like this was no different to any other day. He'd be the perfect portrait of the town fuckboy. Yes. He could do that, couldn't he?

She'd no doubt heard of his reputation around town. Ryan wasn't one to keep his mouth shut, after all, and the two of them kept no secrets.

Well, except one.

It's not like it was that far from the truth anyway. Alex wasn't ashamed that he enjoyed the company of a woman in his bed, but that's all it ever was. He just couldn't find it in him to commit to one for longer than a few nights. He had never wanted to, not since Noa. Now, he was a no-strings-attached kind of guy. It was easier that way. That way people couldn't leave him like they'd always had a habit of doing. He'd learnt that at a young age thanks to his dear old dad. Or, technically, just his sperm donor, for all he'd been involved in Alex's life. Noa knew this about him, too, and he would charm the pants off as many women as it took to make both her and him believe that he simply didn't care.

You never know, maybe he would have some fun trying. He loved to fuck, so this didn't sound like the worst plan in the world. And, luckily for him, owning a bar in a town that attracted tourists meant beautiful women were never in short supply. So, there was nothing in his plan that could go wrong. And, in the end, maybe that one night eight years ago, and the decade of memories before that, really would mean nothing.

The dartboard currently hanging across the room taunted Alex with the memory of Noa and him huddled under it before he asked her to come home with him. Damn his wishful thinking.

A short blonde walked past him then, drawing his eyes in her direction with the clicking of heels on the varnished wood floors. The slick mahogany that now covered The Brew triggered memories of his fingers tangled in glossy brunette waves—a dangerous train of thought he cut short before he got lost in the memories again.

He refocussed himself on the woman clearly vying for his attention. She was pretty in a way he would usually be attracted to when he wasn't so distracted. He hadn't seen her before and presumed she was another tourist. She strutted toward the bar, waggling her fingers in a seductive wave as she went past the booth. But, at the batting of her fake eyelashes, all he could do was compare them to a natural beauty who, once again, took over his thoughts. Alex ignored the blonde, slamming his hands down harder than strictly necessary as he moved to standing, his frustration simmering and threatening to boil. He needed to get himself together.

Maybe he'd see Noa, the spell would be lifted at last, and he could finally move on with his life. Maybe her time away had changed her. Maybe she wasn't the stunning and completely magnetising girl he remembered, the girl who he'd feel safe to bare his soul, to spill every secret about his messed-up life as a kid knowing she'd never judge him. No, that was then, and this was now. All he needed was to see her and he would realise that.

He kept that thought at the forefront of his mind as he busied himself wiping tables, whistling along to 'Piano Man' currently being sung by his regular, Albert. He smiled at a group of older women who owned businesses around town. Sarah Kingsley, the owner of the local bookshop, gave him a warm smile back as the other women enjoyed the music.

Watching them holler enthusiastically at Albert as he swung his hips back and forth on stage made Alex laugh, and his chest suddenly felt lighter again.

This town had always been here for him through the good and the bad.

But as the sway of rich mahogany hair caught his eye in his periphery—the same shade of mahogany as his newly refurbished bar—that thought caught in his throat. He cleared it with a cough, and she turned to look at him, her beautiful bright blue eyes locking with his. Her glossy and perfectly plump lips dropped open, and it was then that he knew he was well and truly fucked.

With nothing but a curt nod in her direction, he turned quickly on his heel, making a beeline for the safety of his office—somewhere Noa Drake was not.

Since that awkward face-to-face, Alex had been working or maybe just hiding in the back office for the last hour. But he knew he couldn't hide in there forever. So, he ventured back out into the main bar area with hopes of finding the blonde he'd ignored earlier to sweet-talk her into forgiving his rudeness. He needed to find a way to put some space between him and Noa without making things so obviously awkward, a way to stifle his thoughts and keep a purely platonic relationship with her for fear of being a shitty friend.

Guilt gnawed at him. He knew he was already a shittier friend than Ryan deserved for the less-than-savoury thoughts he was having about his best friend's sister since she'd stepped foot in his bar an hour earlier like she belonged there. Not only that, but for the secret he'd kept from him for all these years. He'd always wanted to come clean to Ryan about what happened that night but, despite Noa's insistence to keep it a secret hurting him, he respected and cared for her too much to break that promise.

He also knew Ryan would read him immediately and know that he'd wanted it to be so much more than one night. He couldn't have risked that.

Ryan had warned Alex off his sister when they were teens, early on in their friendship, and he wasn't naive enough to think Ryan would jump up and down with joy at the prospect of him and his sister.

They'd also both entertained their fair share of women over the years, with Alex earning his reputation as a non-monogamist. Ryan had made comments in jest about 'pitying the girl who tried to get him to settle down', and despite the joke in which they were intended, they'd made it perfectly obvious how Ryan would feel if he thought he was ever pursuing his little sister.

Ryan was more like a brother to Alex, his parents like second parents, and that alone made her off-limits. He just wished his dick, and more importantly his heart, would get that very important message.

The Drakes lived across the street from Alex growing up. His family life was never like the other kids in school. His dad knocked his mum up when she was seventeen, after only a few months of them dating. His mum said he tried to stick around but, in the end, he just wasn't cut out to be a dad. When Alex was five, he just left, like it was a fucking opt-out programme.

Alex was an angry kid, and on the nights where his mum had to work late or leave early before school, Ryan's family took him in. They made sure his belly was full and gave him a place that felt like home, like the normal family life he had always craved. Whether it was out of pity or not he couldn't find it in him to care, because it was better that than face being alone. Better that than to face the heavy sense of rejection that his dad had left him with. Those scars ran deep and had often caused him to lash out, drink too much, smoke too much, and find himself in places he had no business being. But the Drakes never judged him or wiped their hands of him, despite how often he pushed them to, as if testing them to reinforce his belief that people just didn't stick around. Instead, they gave him the space he needed whilst making sure he knew he always had a safe place to come back to.

Besides this, amongst all the darkness, the anger, and hostility that often felt like it could swallow him whole as a lost teenage boy, Noa Drake was always the light in the dark. Even at his worst, she'd been there for him. Even that night, when he was seventeen, when he'd thrown a plate across his kitchen at his mum. Alex had asked if she could help him find his father. She'd just looked at him, with a pitying look that he hated and made clear his dad didn't want to be found. He'd seen red, letting anger win out, and he'd run, hiding in a tree house in the park down the road. His mum must've called the Drakes, because Noa found him. She'd known he'd be there and had looked up at him with understanding in her eyes—not pity, not fear. When she reached out a hand for him to come down, he couldn't help but follow. As he landed back on solid ground, she smiled and he thought, maybe, he wasn't such a terrible person. He'd internalised his dad's downfalls over the years, letting them seep into his psyche, convincing him that he could not be much different if the same blood ran through his veins. But she made him believe he was more, that he wasn't his dad. He couldn't be if someone like her could look at him like that.

He doubted she had ever known she did that for him and that just her smile could set his whole chest on fire. He'd spent his teenage years in absolute awe at how she radiated such a carefree aura, a hopefulness, and a sense that everything could be better.

When he was around her, everything felt lighter. A calmness would wash over him, and after the day she had found him, he often hung around at their house on days that Ryan wasn't in, just to be close to her, to bask in that aura whenever he could.

He'd worked hard to hide those feelings. Until one night, when he had dared to believe that maybe he wouldn't have to anymore. But he wouldn't be that naive again.

Like a bucket of iced water coming down on him, Alex was ripped from his wandering thoughts the moment Ryan patted him on the shoulder, and he worried he had spoken his thoughts out loud.

'Hey man, where's your head at tonight?' Ryan asked on a laugh. 'You not gotten laid recently or what? You seem so uptight.'

Alex quickly feigned a strangled laugh and, with a quick flick of his wrist, gave his best friend a whack on the head with a bar towel to distract him.

'Owwww,' Ryan grumbled.

'I have more success with the ladies than you ever could, and you know it. Now stop pestering me. I've got work to do, and you've got a sister to save,' he shot back at him, pointing at where Noa stood with a crowd of nosy locals surrounding her.

They never could read when to stop with the twenty questions in this town. And, because no one could mind their own business, the return of Noa Drake would be like headline news.

Ryan rolled his eyes, just like his sister always did, and walked toward her. As he disappeared from view, a perfectly manicured hand tapped impatiently on the bar from a few seats down, pouty lips and scowling eyes directed his way. Deciding he was up to the challenge of winning the blonde beauty he had likely pissed off earlier, he headed in her direction. She stood with Suzie, a woman who had been trying her chances with him for years. And tonight, he might be able to look past his rule against flirting with locals. Because, if her friend decided to hold a grudge, he would happily take her brand of distraction.

Keeping himself busy proved to be a fruitless task. After the blonde left with a group of her friends, Alex began wiping down the already-spotless bar. He'd absent-mindedly wiped the same spot for at least ten minutes, likely just wearing down the wood more than cleaning it at this point. Suddenly the deep brown of the wood rippled and swayed, and he realised his eyes had involuntarily found Noa's perfect waves again without his permission. It was instinctive, like any control he usually had was completely gone.

It was always that way when it came to Noa. It was that way eight years ago, when he'd thought all his Christmases had rolled into one and that she'd finally noticed him as something other than Ryan's tag-along best friend. And clearly, not much had changed now. Back then, he'd thought they'd finally moved past that into something more. He was wrong. And when the lights came on after one of the best nights of his life, and she looked at him with those steely eyes and made him make that pact, he had agreed. He hadn't fought it, not when the last time he'd asked someone to stay, he'd watched the back of his dad's head walk out the door.

As much as he'd known that swallowing his feelings and watching her leave would be hard, asking her to stay only to watch her leave anyway would be crushing. It would risk reinforcing the voice inside his head that had been there since his dad left, the one that told him he wasn't worth sticking around for. Fear stopped him from finding out if that was true.

So, he knew that he had to turn it off. And he had. For the past eight years, he had done everything he could to avoid thinking about her. And he had been successful... for the most part. He purposely filled his days with work and his nights with whichever gorgeous woman crossed his path that day. He was the one in control, always. He liked it that way—no, he needed it that way.

But now, she stood in his bar. Her rich, chocolate brown hair tumbling over her bare shoulders in waves, settling over her strapless orange playsuit that accentuated her every curve. She wore barely any make-up, which meant the freckles painting her face were on full display. She was perfection personified, and she was here in his bar threatening to ruin him again. And the thing that terrified him the most? He might just let her.

# Chapter 6

## Noa

Noa stood in the family kitchen that had barely changed since she was a little girl. Her bare feet padded on the same taupe-coloured linoleum floor as she pulled a mug from the cupboard and put it down on the oak countertop. The kettle whistled, sounding like nails on a chalk board in Noa's fragile state. She turned off the hob, poured the boiling water into her cup, and let the smell of bitter instant coffee soothe her. She hoped that this would be the miracle cure for the world's worst hangover she was sporting this morning. It was almost noon and the throbbing between her temples had still not subsided thanks to her brother's bad example and far too many IPAs last night.

*God, why did she drink so much?*

To forget about her problems and how much her life has spiralled in the last three days was the obvious answer. Oh, and to dull the annoyance she felt that Alex didn't even seem to acknowledge her existence, never mind her return to town. They were friends once. Or so she had thought. As much of a friend as you can be with your older brother's annoying best friend who enjoys teasing you and behaves like an overprotective caveman. The second brother you never asked for. She swore one of Alex's and Ryan's favourite past times growing up was to scare off any boy who even looked her way, and she never knew which one of them was worse than the other. Their childhoods had been intertwined in one way or another. Alex spent most of his time at their house, usually scowling and cursing. Always angry, but never at her. For her, he just used to save his most elaborate, exasperating pranks and incessant teasing, which annoyed her to no end but, at least, she felt like he cared in some way.

But Alex also had a softer side, and he had always been able to show it around her. It often made her feel lucky, like they had a connection that he only shared with her. Like the time she had found him practically buzzing with hurt and anger in a tree house the three of them had once found near the woods. She'd gone to look for him, hoping she would find him there. She knew it was a place only they would know about and he would likely feel able to hide out in.

After seeing how broken Alex looked when she arrived, the hurt his dad had caused when he left and continued to cause now—well, she hated him for it. A man she had never met, but wished she could, just to tell him what a mistake he had made.

She'd had to fight to hide that anger, needing to be there for him through this but, to her surprise, the moment he saw her he softened. His eyes warmed like she was the only person he wanted to see.

Last night, though, he was cold. His features were hardened and completely stoic. He looked at her with the same indifference he'd often offered the rest of the world growing up, like she was just another random person and their history was non-existent.

It hurt.

The anxious part of her brain had spun into overdrive, questioning her ability to judge people. Had she gotten it all wrong? Could she trust her instincts anymore? First, she'd misread—or just simply missed—the signs with Lucas and, now, Alex had treated her like a stranger. Was it something about her that made her merely a short-term option? But, the more she let the 'what ifs' snowball, the more her hurt merged into anger.

Because *fuck them*.

Fuck Lucas for not communicating and wasting her time. And Alex, well, she guessed the rumours were true, the towns biggest fuckboy really had earned that title. Not only did she get little more than a nod here and weird eye contact there, but he'd also spent the whole night flirting with Suzie Whitehead when he wasn't in his office, a girl Noa had never gotten on with in school. Had it not been for that fact, Noa might have considered that Alex was just busy with the bar and that she was overreacting. Because second guessing herself was kind of a hobby at this point.

She didn't expect a welcome home party to be thrown in her honour. She didn't know what she was expecting. It wasn't like they had seen each other since getting naked together eight years ago. And now, after the way he had reacted last night, Noa couldn't help but think it had been intentional on his part. She wasn't sure why, whether she had hurt him then, or whether it was the opposite and that night genuinely meant nothing. Maybe he'd actually been relieved when she suggested the pact. She'd always brushed off his absence when she came home, but the way he had blatantly ignored her could not be brushed off.

Was a smile and a conversation in reaction to seeing her too much to ask? Clearly.

She flushed with anger. Would she have to avoid the bar now that he not only worked there, but owned the damn thing? She shook her head to erase the thoughts that filled her with only annoyance, immediately regretting it.

'Ouch,' she moaned.

Her mum came into the kitchen in that moment, her fleece dressing gown with tiny flowers decorating it wrapped around her and cinched at the waist. Her brunette hair, the exact shade as Noa's, was still a tangle on top of her head, as if she'd just dragged herself from bed.

She placed some painkillers in Noa's palm, effortlessly taking care of her like she always had.

'There you go sweetie. I hear you need these this morning,' she said with a playful wink in her direction. Noa groaned, realising Ryan had more than likely tattle-taled any embarrassing stories from last night to her mum, as always.

'Oh, we've all done it, love. Don't look so mortified. Is it really a breakup if you've not botched Single Ladies on the karaoke? It's a rite of passage into a new chapter if you ask me.

At least you kept all your clothes on, unlike Ryan when he and Melody broke up.'

Noa giggled at that, and she could feel the weight on her chest lift a little bit more. It was true that sometimes all you needed was your mum.

Like they'd summoned him, Ryan came barrelling into the kitchen and wrapped his arms around their mums' shoulders from behind, leaving a kiss on her cheek.

'Oh, you ladies are just jealous you can't get the crowd going like me. There wasn't a set of dry knickers in the house that night, and I've been fighting off booty calls ever since.'

'Ryan!' their mum shrieked, scolding him with a thump on his shoulder and an exasperated glare.

'Don't bite, mum. You know it'll only encourage him,' Noa chuckled and ducked out of her brother's arms as he came to hug her, only to see him smirking at her as he sat himself on the kitchen side.

'You know it would be boring here without me. Now, where's my coffee? I thought with having two women in the house now it would be ready and waiting. It's the only reason I'm here,' he replied, ducking before mum could launch her spoon at his head.

'Oh, it has nothing to do with revelling in my alcohol-induced misery then?'

'*That*, my dear sister, is just an added bonus.'

Noa harrumphed, but grabbed two more mugs of varying shapes, colours, and patterns to make them all a coffee. The mugs were only the start of their mum's eclectic taste when it came to their kitchen. The mismatch of colours and decorations that came with years of collected memories gave it so much heart and personality. It was almost like the space had a life of its own.

The large polka dot vase, for example, pulled Noa back to her mum, Bethan's, birthday ten years ago. Noa had been so busy, lost in the chaos of exam season, and had forgotten. Her face fell when she'd walked into a set table, gifts decorating it, ready for a celebratory meal. Without a word, the warm, firm hand of a thoughtful boy planted itself on her back. He slid a gift bag next to her, sacrificing his own gift, and saving her the mortification of having to apologise to her mum. But that boy was not the man Alex Fletcher he had become last night.

Clearly sensing a shift in her mood, Noa's mum tried to lift it, like she always did, and Noa was thankful. But the topic of conversation didn't quite work as she intended.

'I'm sure Alex enjoyed your performance,' she said, lifting her brows. 'You two always did love a Christmas karaoke competition.'

'Oh god, yes! You used to harass us all to get involved, and he was the only person who felt sorry enough for you to get on stage,' Ryan barked out a laugh at the memory.

Noa just shook her head at her brother.

'You know, you're right. Come to think of it, he was always the nicer one out of the two of you. It's a wonder we let you hang around with us at all,' Noa joked, and Ryan gave her an overdramatic pout in response.

'You know, it's comments like that that make me glad I warned Alex not to misconstrue your friendship as more than that. Couldn't have him stealing my little sister from me, could I?'

Noa blanched at his words.

She knew about the conversation they'd had because she had overheard it. Though none of them had brought it up since, it had played on her mind and fed her fears that led to her putting up boundaries with Alex for years after.

She felt irritated that Ryan would even bring it up now.

Letting that irritation slip out, she glared at her brother.

'Didn't you move out? You've spent a lot of time over here since I came home for someone who has just bought their own place.' The snarky comment came out clipped.

Noa's mum interrupted them, having years of practice at refereeing what she used to call 'sibling squabbles'.

'Why don't you go for a walk by the lake this morning? That always used to cheer you up, and the fresh air should do you some good,' she suggested, unboxing pastries onto plates on the kitchen island.

But the idea of any exercise this morning felt like Satan's idea of an introduction to Hell, and she told her as much.

Ryan's chair scraped along the floor as he pulled it out from the island, plonking himself down in front of the coffee she had set there. Noa held her head as the sound felt like it bounced off her skull, scowling in his direction, but her expression was only met with a wide, mischievous grin. Just like that, the tension broke and was replaced by light-hearted conversation over breakfast.

The morning went on much like that, and Noa realised how much she had missed this. The friendly banter and ribbing you could only get from being at home, from those you loved and who loved you. It felt as if she had never left and, despite all the years that had passed, despite all that had transpired over that last week, Noa could feel nothing but grateful looking around at her family right now.

But even with the soothing noise of the people she loved around her, she couldn't quiet the even louder one inside her head.

The anxious part of her that wanted to plan and prepare wouldn't still, and she just kept on thinking, what next?

# Chapter 7

## Noa

After a morning of catching up with her family, Noa decided it was time to stop putting off the inevitable. With a fresh cup of coffee in her hands, she pulled out her laptop to start the dreaded job search. She pulled her feet underneath her so she could sit cross-legged on the living room couch, propped up by cushions and covered by her mum's crochet granny square blankets. Comfort was key when starting the tedious task of disseminating her CV, as was having her comfort show playing in the background. Friends was both hers and Ryan's comfort show actually, and she was pretty sure her brother could recite it line for line at this point.

Scrolling through job sites, Noa began her search. She'd worked in publishing in London for the past five years after finishing her degree at University College London, but scouting the internet now, she quickly realised she didn't entirely think this through. Moving back to a small town in the middle of nowhere may not have been the smartest career move, and everything she stumbled across was either a huge step down or not in her industry in the slightest. After a few soul-crushing hours, Noa decided to call it a day and call in backup to bring her out of this job hunting-induced funk. She closed her laptop and grabbed her phone, shooting off a message to her childhood best friend, Tes.

Tes had always been one of those friends who, even when long periods passed without them seeing each other, the moment they were reunited, it was like merely a week had passed. Noa had always been grateful for their friendship, and never more so as when Tes walked through their front door an hour later without knocking, as that was never something they did, with a bottle of prosecco in her hand and a shit-eating grin on her face.

'The bitch is back!' she squealed, running over to Noa and almost knocking her to the ground as she tugged her into a hug.

She smelt like home—fresh air and a hint of pine. Noa hung onto her for dear life. Not even a mouthful of her dark hair could make Noa want to let her go.

'She is,' Noa smiled into Tes's shoulder before reluctantly letting Tes extricate herself from her grip. 'And she is very much in need of that,' Noa said, pointing at the prosecco.

Tes quickly got to work retrieving two glasses, like their kitchen was her own, and waved Noa into the lounge where the two of them snuggled into the sofa like they were preparing to put the world to rights.

Noa couldn't help but stare at Tes. This was familiar. This would never change.

Her best friend, in her classic leggings and a baggy T-shirt, black hair pulled into a high ponytail. She would always show up. Always be her safe place to fall.

When Noa moved away, they never lost touch. She still knew every little detail about Noa's life, every secret. The physical distance did nothing but prove how special their friendship was. Weekly video chats over morning coffees and Tes's bi-monthly trips to the city had been the foundation of their friendship for the past eight years. But being back with her at home made Noa's heart sing.

'Right, spill!' Tes demanded, never one to beat around the bush. 'And not the half-garbled ramblings I got on the phone yesterday. Start from the beginning.'

She interrogated Noa, seeking the lowdown on everything that had happened in the last week and how Noa had ended up back in Freymoor. Soon enough, Noa had filled her in on the entire ins and outs of her and Lucas's breakup. Or as much as she could make sense of, at least.

Tes had been Noa's sounding board on more occasions than she could count over the last year or so as she talked through her and Lucas's troubles. Even if she saw now that maybe it was Lucas she should have really been having those conversations with, Tes always gave the best advice, approaching all their conversations with a supportive, yet brutal, honesty that she was grateful for.

'So let me get this right...' Tes slurred as she stood from the sofa with her hands on her hips. 'After everything you did for that boy...' she shoved one finger in the air. 'I'm sorry, I cannot in good faith bring myself to call him a man because that would simply be a lie. But, after all you did, the sacrifices you made, the time you gave him... he just let you go.'

'He did more than that that. He as good as asked me to. I know we hadn't been seeing eye to eye as of late, and maybe we have been wanting different things, but it feels like the moment he realised that and realised he might have to make some sacrifices himself, he chucked in the towel instead of putting in the work when times got tough, you know?'

Tes nodded.

'And, don't get me wrong, I know we shouldn't have to sacrifice ourselves or our happiness for the sake of a relationship,' Noa continued, 'but the way he made it out was like this had been coming for a while. So, if he never had any intention of putting our relationship first or giving it the care it deserved, then why did he waste so much of my time by keeping me around for so long if it was so "*inevitable*", as he put it?'

Her shoulders sagged, and she huffed out in exasperation, 'I just can't believe he felt like that, you know?' Tes just stared at Noa like she had something to say, but didn't know if she should.

'What?' Noa pressed.

'Well... did you not see it coming?' Tes said. 'You told me months ago you felt like he rarely put your needs before his, and that you hadn't been on a date in almost a year. Did you question him or bring it up before now? You know I love you, but you do have a tendency of burying your head in the sand and ignoring your problems instead of dealing with them head-on. You always said communication never came naturally between you two. Are you sure you didn't just miss the signs? Did he really never try to voice his side of things and his issues, or did you just choose to ignore it because it was easier? You also told me you'd started bickering about little things all the time, so I don't think it's an altogether shocking turn of events.'

Wow, Tes really was a no holds barred kind of friend, but sometimes it really did take Noa by surprise just how honest she could be. She felt grateful for her all over again, even if a little wounded.

'Okay, so maybe I was comfortable and too scared to do anything about it, but I still think we missed a step in the breakup, you know? Like, we never even tried to make it work, we didn't talk about our issues and how we could resolve them at all.'

'There's that lack of communication rearing its head again, but maybe it went both ways. And then, one day, it just felt too late,' Tes reasoned. 'I agree, and am equally appalled that he didn't voice his concerns way sooner and given things a chance, but you were far too patient with him. But... and this is a big fat but... I know my best friend and I know you avoid conflict like the plague and will have equally allowed him to do that.'

Tes could interpret the situation so well and, as much as she hated to admit it, deep down Noa knew she was right. However, in that moment, had Noa been a dog, she would have put her tail between her legs, cowering at her friend's brutal honesty. This was why she needed her best friend at a time like this, to tell her straight what sometimes she just refused to acknowledge.

With that wake-up call probably being displayed all over Noa's sombre facial expression, Tes expertly attempted to lighten the mood by shouting a little too loudly, 'Oh, and did you not tell me he refused to use your vibrator on you when you told him you'd like that?'

She let her palm fall to her chest, feigning a look of horror.

'I'm sorry, girl, but that right there should have been your final straw! A man who finds his masculinity so threatened by a rubber toy that he will deny his girlfriend a killer orgasm should immediately be put in the bin, whether you loved him or not,' she added, holding her hands up like she was under arrest.

Noa laughed, a huge belly laugh that felt really good, as she threw a pillow at her drama queen of a friend. She was absolutely right. Lucas had often shut down her ideas to spice things up in the bedroom. And, although she knew he hadn't ever tried to deliberately make her feel bad or kink shamed, she had been embarrassed all the same. It was safe to say she had put her guard up after that and not been honest about her desires again. This girl's afternoon was everything she had needed and more, and she felt so much lighter for it.

'Oh, oh, oh! I know what you need,' Tes squealed again, jumping off the sofa and doing an excited dance like she'd just discovered the world's best-kept secret.

'Do tell…' Noa pressed.

'Well, a good dicking, *obviously*,' Tes stated so matter-of-factly. 'And from someone who knows what they're doing. A real man. You have been deprived for far too long and looking like *that*…' she emphasised the last word, waving her arms in Noa's direction. 'Well, it is simply a crime that must be rectified. My best friend is hot and deserves a man who makes her feel that way.'

Noa rolled her eyes and decided to brush her friend off.

'No, Tes, what I need is a plan. I did not just call you here to get prosecco drunk on a Friday afternoon and join Tinder. I need your help.'

Noa updated Tes on her less-than-successful job search, and then digressed into the fact that she was now twenty-eight and couldn't shake the feeling like she had just taken too many steps to count backwards in her life. She felt like, without even knowing it, she had been making sacrifices for her relationship that she was clearly just 'comfortable' in for the past few years and now, with thirty fast approaching, she just felt lost and lacking any sense of direction.

She'd done a lot of thinking over the last forty-eight hours, and Noa couldn't remember the last time her heart had felt like it beat just for Lucas, a time where she felt head over heels in love with him.

She knew she had once, but had she just been trying to make the pieces fit? Content in a life that was easy and predictable? Had she been scared of starting over and let that fear hold her back?

*Yes*! The exasperated voice in her head huffed.

After that epiphany, the realisation that she definitely wasn't getting any younger, and that she wasn't where she thought she would be at her age, had hit her like a truck over the past few days. It seemed any time she picked up her phone, her social media was concentrated with people she once knew who were now either settling down, getting married, having babies, or making big career moves, and she just didn't know where she fit into it all.

She wasn't moving forward at all. Since finishing university, she had been in the same editing role in the same city. She wasn't sure how she wanted her life to look without that.

Was she supposed to have it all together now? Because that's what her eighteen-year-old self had sat in her bedroom and imagined.

When she thought back to how she had viewed the world back then, she remembered staring at the 'grown-ups' around her and wanting to be them. Feeling in awe of how together their lives were. Being a teenager and having your life dictated by people around her, she remembered wanting the freedom they had.

But was that an illusion? Because Noa didn't feel very much like the adult she thought she'd be. She'd neglected and abandoned her childhood dream of writing in favour of security and what she thought was a guaranteed future, only to end up back at her parent's, single and fumbling through her twenties.

Recruiting her friend to help her with this felt like the best thing to do, so she continued to tell Tes all about the '30 before 30' list. She hadn't been able to stop thinking about it since her breakup, when she'd first realised how much she hadn't done yet.

She'd written a similar list when she was nineteen, dreaming of the future. She'd been sitting on the pier by the lake, the silhouette of the fells painting the horizon, when Alex sat down beside her.

*'Hey, Trouble, what you got there?'*

*She startled, her head whipping up to look at him. She'd been so engrossed in her bucket list that she hadn't even noticed him approach.*

*'Oh, it's nothing,' she said, moving to close her notebook. But he stopped her, covering her hand with his.*

*She tried to ignore how much she enjoyed the feel of it.*

*'You looked like you were lost in another world. It can't be nothing.'*

*There wasn't a hint of insincerity in his eyes as a warm smile crossed his lips, and Noa believed that he really was interested. For some reason, she'd always felt able to be more vulnerable with Alex than most people, so she handed it over to him.*

*She watched, feeling suddenly shy as his eyes skimmed the page.*

*He looked at her like he was seeing every part of her, and she squirmed at how it made her feel.*

*'You're made for greatness, do you know that?' he stated like it was the simplest of facts.*

*'Never stick to the status quo, Noa. Always keep chasing the things that make you happy. You can do everything on this list. Even if some of them might be scary, they're the things you'll look back on one day, the times you were brave, and you'll remember them the most.'*

*She nodded, but only because the lump in her throat meant she couldn't form words.*

'Earth to Noa,' Tes cut through yet another trip down memory lane as she waved her hand back and forth in front of Noa's face.

'Sorry, I was miles away. What were you saying?' Noa said, trying to shake off the remnants of the memory that had wrapped itself around her. He had told her she was meant for greatness, that she could do everything she dreamed of doing, and she wanted that to be true.

'I want to... stop feeling like a bystander in my own life and make things happen for a change,' she said, only half meaning to say it out loud. Tes looked like she wanted to burst with excitement at Noa's revelation.

'Well, that's easy then, isn't it,' she stated. At Noa's confused face, she continued, 'That's your answer. That's where we start to help you get your spark back. We make that list.'

Noa grinned at how fabulous her friend really is because, yes, that is exactly what she needed.

'And then, you go and grab life by the labia and get out there, and experience everything on that list.' Tes paused, and Noa could tell that it was for dramatic effect. Tes was so confident and self-assured. She had a theatrical flair that would bring a smile to the face of the most sullen person. Noa had always admired that about her.

'But...' Tes resumed. Before you go on any more about having your life together at thirty, I think that is an extremely outdated and overrated notion. I'm all about being happy and living your life to the fullest at thirty, and that's what this list should be about. It should in no way reflect what everyone else is doing because that's just downright boring,' she said boldly with so much gumption, chugging the remainder of her glass.

With that, the two of them set to work on the list that Noa hoped would help her find some sense of direction, a release in list form of some of the weight that had recently felt so heavy on her shoulders.

# Chapter 8

## Noa

1. Move back home to be closer to family
2. Solo travel for one month
3. Watch the sunrise from a viewpoint
4. Count the stars
5. Get kissed in the rain
6. Swim naked in a waterfall
7. Get Tinks a sibling
8. Cut back on your coffee consumption (you know it's not good for your anxiety)
9. Learn to surf
10. Go scuba-diving

11. Plant a tree (feels like the right thing to do given your list tendencies)
12. Start writing your own book, not just publishing them
13. See Taylor Swift live (dream big right?)
14. Think of 17 more things to put on this list...

As always, before she headed home, Tes had bolstered Noa's confidence with her 'there's no time like the present' speech and, now, Noa scrolled through airline websites, wanting to take action before that confidence waned.

Now that the list was done, Noa decided that, whilst on this very out of character spontaneous streak of hers that she had never before experienced in her life, she was going to take the first step toward number two on her list.

The two prosecco bottles and empty snack wrappers littering the coffee table in front of her should have been a warning not to make big life decisions. But she ignored them, wanting to break free of the restraints her tendency to overanalyse put on her, and enjoying the temporary reprieve the alcohol in her veins was giving her.

When her dad had come down to the living room earlier, he'd found her and Tes huddled on the sofa in the same spot she remained now.

'What are you two scheming about over there?' he'd asked.

'Isaac Drake, you wound me with your lack of faith. How do you know we are not just sitting here online shopping like all the innocent girls do.'

Her dad had given Tes a pointed look that said please.

'You, Tes Anderson, since we are apparently using full names today, have mischief in your bones and could talk a saint into joining the circus, so excuse me for checking that you aren't corrupting my daughter.'

'Waaaaaay too late for that I'm afraid,' Tes teased.

He'd rolled his eyes, and they all shared a laugh before Noa had spoken to him about her plans. And he supported them. Given the fact that she'd talked about travelling since being a teenager, he wasn't shocked by the prospect of it, merely by how quickly her plans to leave were coming together. Besides parties and underage drinking when she was younger and moving away from home for university—a move that was meticulously planned to a T—he said Noa was well past due for a 'wild phase' and seemed excited for her.

Considering her parents had fallen in love when her dad had hitchhiked a lift from her mum in order to get home after his own European adventures over thirty years ago, she should have expected his reaction.

So now, alone with only the sound of the log fire crackling in the background, warming the living room and lighting it in a soft amber glow, she was ready to make that jump. She resolved to take the savings she thought she'd use for a wedding or a baby at some point in the near future to finally go on that trip she'd discarded as something she'd just never do. This seemed like an altogether better way to spend that money right now. Maybe this is how she'd discover who she was now and what she'd do next.

To some, it might look like she was avoiding her problems, running away from them maybe. It's not like she'd never heard that before. But what if she was simply running toward her own new beginning. She loved the notion of 'what was meant to be would find her', but so far where had waiting around gotten her? What if she really did go out there and grab what was meant for her by the balls—or labia as Tes liked to put it? Either way she looked at it, a temporary distraction or a new start, it felt right. And it felt like exactly what she needed in that moment.

She wanted to be better at living in the moment. Maybe that was all that mattered. So, for the first time in her adult life, she didn't question it. There was no pros and cons list. No doom scrolling TikTok for all the things that might go wrong. No anxious overthinking.

She opened her laptop, and she booked the flight.

Noa spent the rest of the day planning her trip to Southeast Asia. That felt like the place that everyone on her newsfeed went when they were trying to find themselves and, if it was good enough for some of her favourite YouTubers, then it was good enough for her. She was sure she'd watched all of 'Backpacking Brianna's' videos twice over, never thinking that she'd get to go on her own adventure one day. It felt refreshing to make this decision for her and her alone and, in doing so, she felt like she had set free a part of herself that she had kept locked away, the selfish part that could put herself first and let herself grow into the person she wanted to be.

It was in doing this that she realised, maybe, Lucas had been right. Maybe they had both been stifling each other in their relationship and holding each other back from being the best versions of themselves. Maybe she had been avoiding conflict, or just hadn't wanted to see it. Realising that made her see her relationship and the breakup differently. She was grateful for the memories they had shared, the happiness they had given each other, but also the lessons that both their relationship and breakup had taught her. Thinking of it like this eased the heartbreak and grief that gripped her chest, a little, at least. Letting each other go was giving themselves permission to grow, and she would do exactly that. She still missed him, of course. They'd given each other years of their lives, but she was determined not to let that break her.

Noa planned roughly where she would visit first and the general route she might take before her mum called her down for family dinner.

Over her mum's homemade risotto, Noa decided to break the news of her upcoming travel plans to her family. In less than a month she'd be on a flight across the globe, so she guessed she needed all the help she could get to prep for it. Her dad offered to loan her his backpack and travel charger, and her mum offered some advice about where to buy the best swimsuits for 'larger-chested girls'. Ryan just sat there quiet, almost like he was sulking about something. In a way, he was so predictable, but Noa didn't bite, and she certainly didn't question him on it. She left him to have his feelings about it. She knew he would voice them eventually.

As if on cue, as Noa thanked her mum for dinner and stood up to clear the plates, Ryan looked at her and, with an overdramatic sigh, took the dishes off her and placed them on the side.

'Noa, you know I love you and I say this with only love. But you are not equipped for this. You surely cannot be considering travelling on your own,' he said. 'There is being a strong and independent woman, and then there is being downright stupid. It's not safe.'

Noa scoffed and looked her brother dead in the eye with a look of defiance. She would not back down on the first thing that had made her feel this good in a long time, no matter how overprotective he wanted to be. Whilst their close age gap had made them more like best friends than siblings growing up, Ryan still sometimes struggled to see her as anything other than his baby sister that he needed to shield and wrap in cotton wool to protect. She knew he was going to play that protective older brother card now, but she was not that little girl anymore. She was a woman, and he would just have to face it.

Her brother's experience of bullying growing up, of the harshness of the world and the hurt he had endured, had shaped him more than he would ever admit. Noa knew it was why he felt a compulsion to guard everyone around him, like he could shield them from what he'd felt. And for the most part, they all let him, knowing it made him feel better. It was unspoken knowledge within their family. But this was not one of those times. Noa needed this act of independence like she needed air.

'Ryan. I love you. But I am an adult. This is my choice to make. My risk to take. I can look after myself, okay?'

His face fell, clearly deflated and frustrated that his attempts to discourage her trip had failed.

Ryan was always the joker in the family. He was a complete goofball, as well as the biggest flirt in town. He radiated that easy-going golden retriever energy that made everybody love him. It would be annoying if she didn't love that about him, too. But it also meant that he was used to getting his way. Now, any traces of humour were wiped from his expression.

'I'm sorry Noa, but you are my little sister, and I worry. What if something happens to you and you are on the other side of the world?' He looked at their mum, as if seeking support, but she just held her hands up like she wasn't getting involved. Their dad just let out a hearty chuckle and gave his son a firm pat on the back, rising from the table.

'Well, I guess you've got this one covered son. I can retire for the night.'

That was her dad's subtle support. He had done his own travelling once upon a time, and the twinkle in his eyes as he smiled at her told her he was thinking about that. And that he wanted those memories for her, too.

Their parents had always been easy going and free-spirited, having lived a lot of life before they had kids. But it wasn't lost on Noa that both their kids had gone the complete opposite way in one way or another. Noa, with her anxiety and obsessive need to overanalyse and plan the future, and Ryan, with his need to protect those around him. Although Ryan was a lot more easy-going in his own life, being bullied in his younger years had changed him. He'd give anyone the shirt off his back and bend over backwards to help someone in need, as if he could shield the world from experiences he endured. Their parents tried not to feed into it, but it was hard for him to let go and allow Noa to make her own mistakes and endure the consequences if it came to it.

At the lack of backup, Ryan just looked around, his mouth agape in disbelief.

Noa still didn't reply, letting her brother work through his thoughts out loud, because nothing she said would do a thing anyway. She knew it because she knew him as well as he knew her, and they had done this dance a time or two before. Just like when she was twenty and he protested her move to London, right up until she was due to leave, then he finally came around to the idea.

'I—I just think, maybe, you might be rushing into this,' he started his argument anew. 'You've been home for twenty-four hours. Don't you need to wallow or something before you start making big life decisions? You know I'd come with you if

I could, but I'm up for a promotion and just can't leave right now. What about if you wait six months until after my job review, and then I could come with you? We could make it a sibling trip?'

His eyes look hopeful, a boyish smile cresting his lips like he just might have come up with a solution to solve all their problems.

'First off, I never rush into anything, Ryan, and you know that,' Noa rebutted. 'Just because this seems fast, and I have not planned it to a T, does not mean it's not something I haven't wanted to do for years. The opportunity has just never presented itself until now, when I have nothing to lose.'

She put her hand on his tense shoulders, trying to relax him and continued, 'And, secondly, I have three weeks until my flight. That's plenty of time to wallow and plan. But, most importantly, Ryan, I cannot put my life on hold any longer and, as much as I love you, I don't want you to come with me. I want to do this on my own, to do something for myself and prove to myself that I will be okay on my own. You coming with me defeats the point.'

He let out a long groan of defeat, but his eyes told her he understood, even if he wasn't happy about it. At least, she hoped he did.

# Chapter 9

## Alex

It was late on Sunday evening. Alex was locking up at The Brew and only he and Ryan were left inside. Ryan had been at the end of the bar since just after eight, like he often was on a Sunday, waiting for the early wind-down as the weekend came to an end.

Sunday evenings were when the two of them usually got to lock up together to have a catch-up over a whisky or two. Tonight, though, Ryan was being less than helpful as he sat there with his head resting on his palm, skimming through something on his phone. Alex looked over his friend's shoulder as he came to sit on the barstool next to him.

'Planning a trip, are you?' he asked, focussing his attention on his friend.

'No, no,' Ryan shook his head. 'Noa is.'

He grunted, not sounding all that impressed about it. Ryan had always been extremely protective of his younger sister, and it was one of the reasons Alex hadn't actively pursued Noa, even when she was all he'd wanted years ago. Even if they were best friends, he knew Ryan still wouldn't be grateful for a fuck-up like him dating his baby sister. Sure, he'd made something of himself now, but he still had a reputation he was sure Ryan wouldn't forget when it came to Noa.

Luckily, Ryan continued talking, not noticing that Alex's lack of response had meant he'd disappeared into his own head.

'I'm just looking at the safest hostels in Thailand so I can subtly influence her whilst still seeming like a supportive brother when it comes to these crazy plans of hers.'

Alex let out a chuckle because, from what he saw the other night, Noa was not a child anymore. No, she was definitely all woman now, and he had a feeling she could look after herself just fine. But, seeing his best friend so tense right now, he didn't say that. Instead, he decided to move the conversation on.

'Well, I, for one, can't blame her for wanting to get away. I would kill for a break right now.'

Ryan stilled, stopped his scrolling, and looked up at Alex from where he was staring at his phone.

'What do you mean? The bar's doing great isn't?'

'Exactly,' Alex said. 'It's been a long road getting here over the last year, one that has taken all my attention and time. You've been a huge help, and I appreciate it more than you know, but now that the bar has finally picked up and is doing well, it feels like the adrenaline has worn off. And I am beyond exhausted.'

When Alex bought the bar a year ago, the previous owners had almost driven it into the ground. They were on their knees financially, and had let the place go. It was almost crumbling. This had meant that Alex got it for a great price, which allowed him to put in the work to bring it back to its former glory whilst putting his own stamp on it.

Alex had always found enjoyment in giving a second chance to something that had been neglected and helping it thrive again. But he wouldn't look too deeply into why.

Such an overhaul on the bar had meant, though, that he had to close it for the first three months after taking over and, with no income coming in, he had to put in most of the work himself. And some help from the town, of course.

Freymoor was great like that. He was lucky to have so many supportive people around him. When he thought back to those long, tiring days and short, sleepless nights, he didn't know how he got through them. Saying that, it wasn't much better once he opened. With only one member of staff, and a reputation to rebuild, The Brew's reopening was just the start.

Alex looked around at the memory of it and felt a sense of pride surge through him at how far he'd come. The bar really was doing great, like Ryan had said, and all his hard work had paid off. But he was well and truly spent, and he really did need a break. He made a mental note to look into taking a trip soon—Italy, maybe, or Spain. With the new help he'd been able to take on recently, now seemed like as good a time as any. Maybe Noa was truly onto something.

Ryan pulled Alex from his thoughts with a wave in front of his face.

‘Sorry man, I spaced. I told you. Tired is my new permanent setting right now. I feel like a walking zombie some days,’ Alex snickered.

‘Well, that’s exactly what I was just saying. Why don’t you go?’ Ryan asked, waiting expectantly.

‘Go where?’ Alex asked with a furrow in his brow, evidence of his confusion.

‘To Thailand. Or not just there, you could do the whole South East Asia thing. Take back all the holidays you should have taken this year in one long trip.’

Alex couldn’t help but laugh in response to that, ‘I was thinking more like a quick vacation to Europe, Ryan. You know I can’t leave this place for too long. And being so far away just doesn’t feel right.’

‘I would be here, just a phone call away if anyone needed anything. I could keep an eye on things. Besides, you said yourself you needed a break.’

‘Because you don’t have enough on?’ Alex teased. ‘Plus, I think Bella might actually kill me, and then you, if I leave you in charge whilst I’m away.’

Bella was The Brew’s manager. Alex had employed her a few months back, and she’d been a godsend. He knew she could handle things whilst he was away, but it still felt like a big ask.

‘That’s just an added bonus,’ Ryan smirked.

‘Don’t.’

Alex raised his eyebrows in a warning at his friend, but it only made Ryan smile wider.

‘Don’t what?’ he feigned ignorance, but they both knew that Ryan was using this as an opportunity to try and flirt his way into her good books.

Alex didn't know what Ryan had ever done to piss her off, but their relationship was prickly to say the least, and he knew Ryan could never let that lie. He had a perpetual need for everyone to like him. But the more he seemed to push, his antics only seemed to irritate Bella more. It'd been interesting to watch, but was leaving them to take care of his pride and joy together going too far?

Ryan bumped his shoulder with Alex's.

'Come *oooooon*. You know you want to.'

All of a sudden, Alex's Spidey Senses tingled. Something was going on here that he was missing.

'Why are you pushing this?' he questioned.

'Well...'

Just then, a light bulb came on in Alex's head. He must have been tired because how did he not see what Ryan was hinting at until now?

'No,' he harrumphed, shaking his finger in front of his friend's face.

Ryan, truly, had lost it.

'But hear me out...' Ryan tried to argue.

But, before he could continue, Alex interrupted, 'No, no, no, no, no. One hundred times no. I am not babysitting your sister on her travels, Ryan. Have you gone completely insane? Firstly, your sister is a grown-ass woman. I don't know if you've noticed that lately, but she does not need a babysitter. And, secondly, why don't you go if you are so worried?'

With that he started to look sheepish, like he'd been caught with his hands in the cookie jar.

'Well, because when I told her I was worried and asked her to wait six months for me, she told me she didn't want to wait and didn't want me to go. And I don't know if you've noticed, but when my sister has made her mind up about something she's not going to change it. Plus, I know she doesn't need a babysitter, but have you seen some of the horror stories on the news about the young girls who go on these trips? Maybe you could just look out for her?'

Ryan was quick to add, 'Think of it less as a babysitter and more as old friends hanging out.'

Alex ignored Ryan's dramatics over the dangers of solo travel and got straight to the point.

'Then what makes you think she would be okay with me going along with her?'

'Why wouldn't she be?' he asked, pointing a stare at him. Even though he knew the question was innocent, as he continued to stare at Alex and silence wrapped around them, Alex felt his skin start to itch and feel suddenly too tight. He felt like maybe his secrets were plastered on a neon billboard across his head, which only made him start to panic.

'I... I... I... I haven't seen her in years.'

He grasped for any excuse not to do this. He felt like the guilt of the secret he'd been keeping might swallow him and his heart raced, palms sweaty. God, he needed to get a grip of himself quickly.

'And what a way to catch up,' Ryan continued persuading. 'You were like family once and I know you drifted when she left for university for whatever reason, but she's back now and maybe for good. You are my two favourite people, and you should never have drifted apart. It would be great if you could fix that. This would be a perfect way to rebuild your relationship. I know she'd like that, too. It would kill two birds with one stone for you and me and really save me a whole month of crippling anxiety.'

Alex knew a little something about crippling anxiety. He felt it any time he let someone new get close enough that their absence could hurt. He also felt it right then, as his best friend looked at him with pleading eyes. Without spilling all his secrets, which would threaten to destroy their friendship, he didn't really have another excuse he could pull out to get out of saying yes. He was backed into a corner. After all, Ryan was right. The world was a frightening place, and so many things could go wrong if she was out there on her own. Could he ever say no to protecting her?

He must have gone insane because Alex hesitantly agreed to help his friend out, to keep his sister safe whilst she travelled. For the rest of the night, he sat there in a daze as Ryan went about booking his flights and hostels. It was clear this had been premeditated as Ryan pulled out his list of Noa's plans, making sure their itineraries left no question as to whether or not Alex would be following her across the world. What had he signed himself up for? And how would he manage his plan to feign indifference around her now?

*Double fuck.*

# Chapter 10

## Noa

Noa and Tes walked side by side into the large warehouse that was their local outdoors shop. She had never been much for such activities as a kid, as her stubborn nature had made her continuously fight against anything her parents or teachers had wanted her to get involved with. So, naturally, exploring the beautiful countryside around her had been out of the question.

It seemed sad to her now that she was back and had gotten a newfound appreciation for the rolling mountains and swirling countryside around her. The vastness of it now made her feel so small in comparison, but in the best way possible, like nothing really mattered in the grand scheme of things. The thought had settled her in the last few weeks.

Freymoor was, in short, her happy place. It was a quaint little market town, home to little more than four thousand townsfolk. It was nestled in the middle of the Yorkshire fells, which painted a breathtaking backdrop to the houses and main street that sat at the bottom. It was one of those places that, if you saw it on a postcard, you would probably assume it was a figment of someone's imagination. It was so picturesque and known by tourists for both its close proximity to great walking trails and some of the most beautiful lakes in the country. Hence, with its attraction of the outdoorsy type, the town had a generous-sized warehouse to cater to all their adventurous needs.

Tes held up a giant, bright green rucksack in front of her with a huge smile on her face as they passed the climbing and camping section of the shop.

'Yes, you're right, they'll really see me coming with that,' Noa quipped, walking past her to a much more inconspicuous and less in-your-face black fifty litre rucksack.

'Well sure. That one's fine if you don't want to make a statement. But I've been a glutton for making an entrance since I brought Evie Cassidy to my cousins christening at fifteen, and I've not stopped since.'

Noa laughed as she recalled the memory. Tes unapologetically holding hands with her first girlfriend, as they sat in the crowded pews, her mum's eyes bugging out of her head. 'God, your mum's face was priceless. That was one way to come out that's for sure.'

'How do people fit all their things in such a small bag anyway?' Tes pondered, still eyeing the rucksack like she was trying to solve one of Poirot's great mysteries.

Noa picked up the black bag, trying it on and fastening the excessive number of straps in the mirror. Despite Tes's sarcasm, not making a statement was exactly what Noa was going for. Going on this trip meant that she was already massively stepping out of her comfort zone enough as it was.

'I guess we're about to find out,' she responded, shoving it into her trolley. It was clear that her dad's rucksack had seen better days when he had dragged it down from the loft, the wear and tear from his own adventures evident. Noa had decided she wanted her own, one she could pull out one day and look upon with a fondness from what it represented. Plus, the gigantic hole in the side of his, that her mum insisted she could repair, seemed like a recipe for disaster.

They continued through the shop, Noa's well-researched list in hand, because apparently her temporary spontaneous streak was just that, temporary, and she could never break the a lifelong habit. Noa could make a career out of overthinking and planning. It always helped her keep a sense of control when her thoughts spiralled. She'd struggled with anxiety her entire adult life, but after lots of cognitive behavioural therapy, established coping mechanisms, and a support network she could never quite thank enough, she was functioning and doing better than she had in years, despite recent events.

Noa's tendency to write lists for any occasion became one of those coping mechanisms after she started seeing a therapist at sixteen, when her panic attacks had first started getting out of hand. There was no big, traumatic event leading up to it like people often assumed. Just her own sense of impending doom that got worse and worse until she finally accepted help to manage it.

She was diagnosed with generalised anxiety and panic disorder, which meant she was prone to overthinking and becoming generally overwhelmed by life, and her brain often turned that into physical symptoms.

She'd learnt over the years that list-making allowed her to empty her often chaotic brain enough to think clearly and compartmentalise tasks before they could overwhelm her. Somewhere along the way, they had just become a force of habit, and probably one of her main personality traits at this point.

Looking down at her list, Noa realised how little her anxiety had reared its head over the breakup, how she had managed it using skills she had been working on for years, and a sudden feeling of pride washed over her.

Compared to when she was twenty-one, and had broken up with her first real boyfriend, Toby Crawly, who she had met at university, she was doing just fine. After he'd broken up with her over text, she'd locked herself in her room for a week, unable to quell the nausea or get out of bed. Her mum had gotten the train all the way to London after her roommate had called her, concerned with how Noa was taking it. Thinking of it like that made her feel like a whole new woman.

*So this is what people liked to call growth.* Noa smiled at herself, wondering if a pat on her own back was a step too far. Credit where credit's due and what not.

At that moment, her best friend looked over at her and, like she'd read Noa's thoughts, Tes said, 'I'm proud of you, you know that?'

'Oh, don't go getting soppy on my now. We are only two weeks in. There's plenty of time for a mental breakdown yet.

You never know, you might come around tomorrow, and I'll have shaved all my hair off.'

Noa couldn't deal with the emotional conversation she was sure was about to occur, so she tried to deflect using humour, and was glad when it worked. The last thing she needed in a town where the gossip mill worked at a frightening speed was to start crying down the camping aisle.

'Always one for the dramatics,' Tes laughed.

'Takes one to know one,' Noa wagged her brow at Tes, who just feigned a look of outrage.

'I'll have you know that I think you get it from your brother, and it has absolutely nothing to do with me.'

The two of them proceeded to work their way through Noa's list of travel necessities, filling her trolley with everything from packing cubes and microfibre towels, to travel chargers and portable lamps.

A guy who had been in their year at school was working there and helped Noa pick out the most appropriate walking shoes for steep and rocky terrain in humid climates.

'Why are you buying those?' Tes asked, completely bewildered. 'You are going to be hiking? You? Really?' She dragged out the last part.

'I should be offended.'

'Oh, hun, you forget that I was the one you hid in the toilets with at school during PE and helped you fake your period on sports day.'

'Point taken, but things change if you haven't noticed. Maybe I'll find that I love hiking and sports when I'm off finding myself.'

The words sounded like a lie even as she said them, and she could see that Tes was trying to hold in a laugh.

'Okay, I'll humour you. But if you as much as think about bringing that attitude home and trying to make me all healthy and shit, then I will revoke your best friend privileges. Hard pass on the twenties fitness trend, thank you very much'.

Noa wrapped her arms round Tes, then fixed her mouth into a straight line and gave her a serious nod, 'Aye, aye, Captain.'

Once they'd paid, it took them longer than it should have to transport Noa's purchases into her old, faithful car before they flopped into the front seats with a harrumph. Shopping was exhausting.

Noa knew she had all the gear and no idea but, if social media said she needed it, then it was probably in her back seat.

'Come on, let's go get you packed so that I can rub it in your brother's face and watch him turn as red as a beetroot. You know it's my favourite pastime,' Tes grinned.

'He was so high-strung about the whole idea when I first mentioned it, but he seems to have backed off and come around to the idea now. He's even been getting involved in the planning and booking process, asking me questions about my route. I'd go as far as to say he might actually be excited for me now.'

'Mr Overprotective is loosening the reigns? Well, that is surprising,' Tes raised her brows. 'Oh well, let's head back either way. I'm sure I can find some other ammunition to bust his ass about.'

And Noa knew she meant it. Tes had always ribbed Ryan like he was her own brother, and their interactions were always entertaining to say the least. Noa couldn't help but bark out a laugh at her friend's no-fucks-given attitude, and it felt freeing to be here laughing with her again. She knew she needed to see some of the world for herself, and she couldn't wait to start her adventure but, in this moment, she knew that this town would always be her home. When all was said and done, she would always find her way back here. But she just needed to go and find herself first.

# Chapter 11

## Noa

Noa took a long, calming breath as she stared out of the plane window, looking out at the tarmac of the runway at Manchester Airport. She'd arrived there way too early this morning, having thought being prepared would settle her bubbling nerves, and was now sat in her requested window seat. The gravity of the trip had suddenly dawned on her last night, and the butterflies that took flight in her gut had not settled since. Maybe Ryan was right, and she was not equipped to deal with this. She had never left the country on her own in her life. Arriving at the airport early had helped some. Or, maybe, it was the three gin and tonics she had been able to get in before boarding the flight as a result. Now she sat there buzzed and ready to go, but the longer she had to sit and wait for take-off, the more she could feel her booze-induced confidence wavering. Her knee bounced and she sat tapping on her armrest, becoming more restless.

The older gentleman next to her chuckled, 'You okay there, lovey? You scared of flying?'

'Something like that,' she whispered, offering him a polite smile.

'Well, listening to music always helps me tune it all out. Won't be long and we'll be in the air and the free bar will be open. If all else fails, a good few drinks should knock you out cold,' he winked at her.

As she regarded him, movement in her periphery caught her attention and a shadow seemed to be cast over their row before she heard the clearing of a throat, followed by a gruff voice. She lifted her attention to the man towering over them. Muscular, tatted arms rested on their row and that of the seats in front of them as he cast a devilish smile her way. Her stomach dropped, and any worries she had earlier were soon replaced by the overwhelming realisation of what this was.

Alex Fletcher stood in the aisle, in all his handsomeness, and there was simply no way that this was a coincidence. He and Ryan had gone too far this time. She couldn't keep her simmering anger from bubbling over. She should have realised that Ryan had let it go a little too quickly.

'I don't need a bodyguard, so you can turn right back around and head home,' she hissed, grinding her teeth.

'Sir, can you take your seat please? The doors are closing now,' the air hostess sing-songed to Alex.

Noa gaped at her, wide-eyed in horror. This could not be happening.

'What? No. He was just leaving,' she protested.

She looked at him and shook her head as he took his seat and put on his belt, folding her arms to show him just how displeased she was. No way would she let him get off lightly.

'This is just great. Fucking brilliant, actually.'

Alex didn't speak, just stared at the seat in front of him, his perfectly chiselled jaw visibly tensing. Good. She wanted to rile him just as much as she was.

'Have you lost your damn mind? My brother clearly asking you to babysit me is one thing, but you saying yes? That just goes beyond all comprehension. What were you thinking?' She shook her head. 'Wait, don't even answer that because you clearly weren't thinking or you wouldn't be here with your big man shoulders taking up all the room on the aeroplane.'

One of his eyebrows rose halfway up his forehead, clearly curious and amused.

'Big man shoulders?' he smirked at her.

It was infuriating. Yes, he had the sexiest smirk she had ever seen—eight years apart hadn't changed that—but it was still infuriating. As was having to try and hide the effect it had on her.

'Seriously? That's the part that you heard? You know, I don't remember you being this insufferable. But, I guess, a lot has changed,' she spat the last words, lacing them with the anger intended as a clear dig at the way he'd ignored her since she'd come home. And they clearly hit, because she saw him wince before he schooled his features.

His facial expression morphed into one of boredom then, or maybe it was irritation. Either way, she wanted to punch his stupid face.

'Well, to answer your question, I wasn't thinking of it as babysitting. I needed a holiday, and I heard Thailand is the place to go. So, don't flatter yourself too much. But, from what I remember, your company wasn't all that bad back in the day, so seeing as we both seem to be heading in the same direction, maybe we could enjoy it together,' was his retort, 'But I am sorry if that feeling isn't reciprocated.'

'You're telling me this wasn't a plan cooked up between you and Ryan to ruin my fun?'

'What I'm saying, is I have more important things to concern myself with than ruining your fun. Believe it or not, it is not on my priority list. I was well due a break and Thailand was somewhere on the list, so when I heard you needed keeping out of trouble, it seemed like a win-win to me,' he replied with a wicked wink and a grin. 'I got the break I needed and didn't have to listen to your brother whine about your safety for the next month. We can catch up and have some fun together, or you won't even know I'm there. You don't have to be all dramatic and get your knickers in a twist about it.'

'Dramatic,' Noa whisper-shouted, pounding her fist a little too firmly on her armrest.

'Does one of you want to swap seats with me?' the man in the middle seat asked. Noa just then realised he was there, and that he had been watching them argue back and forth as if watching a tennis match.

God, could this get any more embarrassing?

'No,' came from Noa in unison with Alex's confident, 'Yes.'

Noa just folded her arms and glared at Alex as he climbed out from his aisle seat and swapped places with the old man next to her. He took up so much space with his large frame that it almost felt like he was boxing her in.

*Not there to ruin her fun her ass*, she thought as she rolled her eyes and went back to continuing her staring out the window, resigning to ignore him for the rest of the flight. It felt like a better option than a GBH charge. A prison sentence would put a slight damper on her travels, even if she was all about trying new things at the moment.

She huffed and folded her arms, trying to make herself as small as possible so they wouldn't touch. It was only partly to avoid the static electricity she felt from the touch of his arm against hers when he'd sat down, but Alex didn't need to know that.

They spent the rest of the long haul flight in a tense silence that only got worse when they hopped onto the same coach to the same hostel. *Perfect*.

When planning this trip, spending it with her brother's best friend was not what she had in mind. But apparently, she wasn't getting much of a choice.

The last time they had spoken played on repeat in her brain, taunting her—her stumbling for her clothes at record speed, her demanding they never speak of it again.

Around and around the memories went in her brain. Alex wordlessly watched her from his seat on the coach across from her. It was like he could sense the tension radiating from her as she realised his presence brought with it a whole load of buried memories that she had tried to forget.

But, by being here, he'd made sure there was no hope of forgetting anymore. And that just made things a hell of a lot more complicated.

# Chapter 12

## Noa

After what had felt like the longest eighteen hours of her entire life, Noa arrived at the hostel and immediately all but ran from Alex's vicinity. She couldn't find it in her to be embarrassed about it because, after spending a long-haul flight in close quarters with the man who, not even a month ago, basically ignored the fact that she existed and now was following her across the world, she was exhausted. A more mature person would have known rationally that there was probably a perfectly understandable and rational explanation to this whole debacle, maybe even given him time to explain himself and have a grown-up conversation. But not Noa. She didn't want to be grown-up about it. She preferred to dig her heels in and ice him out. She was too busy being angry at him to sleep the entire flight so, now, she was ready to find out what napping in a six-bed dorm was really like. Alex, of course, had been given keys to a single room when they arrived because, of course he had. He, apparently, just wanted to ruin her trip, not get the fully authentic backpacking experience.

She scoffed at the thought as she put the key in the door that read 216. Stepping inside Noa was greeted by what she could only describe as feminine rage music and the sound of friendly chatter before five pairs of beady eyes flew to her all at once from their respective bunks. She stood frozen in her spot. Her mind went blank, and she suddenly couldn't think of a single thing to say. God, should she have created prompt cards? Suddenly, Paris Geller didn't seem quite so crazy after all, because some conversation prompts would have come in real handy right now.

Noa gave the most awkward little wave of her entire life and immediately wanted to shrivel up and die. How was she going to last an entire month of this if she failed at the first hurdle? Luckily, as she opened her mouth to finally introduce herself, a red-headed girl in a pair of pink polka dot pyjamas broke into conversation first.

'Hey, I'm Thea. We were wondering if anyone would be taking that bunk tonight. We were enjoying the girl gang vibes and were praying to the heavens it wasn't a man.'

'Not a man,' Noa chuckled, making her way over to what appeared to be her bunk, then realised she hadn't given them her name. Letting her heavy rucksack clatter to the floor she turned, 'I'm Noa. Sorry, I've literally just landed and don't feel very human right now. I'm not usually this spaced out.'

'Oh, god. The first day is the worst. Don't worry, we've all been there. I'm Lola,' one of the other girls said as she carried on applying concealer under her eyes.

As Noa looked around, she realised the girls were all getting ready and must be going out tonight. She climbed onto her bed, feeling the coil of springs digging into her thighs uncomfortably. Then the other three girls introduced themselves as Carly, Bridget, and Hattie. She recited them over and over for several minutes in her head, praying she'd remember them and not come across as completely rude. Though, in her current fatigued state, she wasn't feeling hopeful. They all appeared Noa's age and wore friendly smiles that made her feel immediately at ease.

'What are you planning on doing tonight?' the girl who had introduced herself as Hattie asked.

Noa decided she didn't have anything to lose. She needed to unload the events of the last day on someone and, despite only just meeting these girls, she felt like she could trust them. She told them about Alex—or a brief summary at least—about his reaction when she had returned home to Freymoor, and how he had shown up on her flight and was now, coincidentally, here at this hostel. She described her sleepless flight and how she had pictured her night involving a shower and a long stint in her bed.

They all looked completely hooked by her story, like it was the most interesting thing in the world, each throwing in a few 'no ways' and 'that's insane' as she spoke.

The only person she'd ever told beyond them was Tes, but the past twenty-four hours felt like it had pushed her to the end of her sanity, and she just needed to get it off her chest.

'Well, you absolutely cannot go to sleep now. It's 'how to outrun jet lag 101'. If you go to sleep now, you'll only wake in the night and your body clock will be all messed up. You should one hundred percent bin that plan and come out with us instead,' Lola insisted.

'Besides, it sounds like you could use a drink,' Carly added.

Noa just nodded as excitement bloomed in her stomach and replaced the anger from earlier. She looked around and thought maybe all was not ruined after all.

Once Noa had agreed to go out with the girls, they had continued to get ready with Noa joining in. She wasn't used to the humidity she'd experienced since arriving, so she decided to pull on an off-the-shoulder flowery dress and a pair of strappy sandals. Only struggling once to fight through the mess that was already her backpack, she'd made a mental note to ask the girls about their systems later. She had slotted into their light-hearted conversations easily and enjoyed hearing about all their travels so far. Lola was by far the most outgoing of the group and reminded her the most of Tes. Noa took an instant liking to her. She just had a warmth that drew Noa to her. Being around these girls had immediately lifted her mood.

As they headed down to the hostel bar and got caught up in happy hour, which was in full swing, Noa took in her surroundings, letting it really sink in that she had made the jump and that she was here. Even if Alex was here, too. She tried to focus on that achievement over her earlier irritation, refusing to let it ruin her trip.

She scanned the bar and its cheap and simple aesthetic that was so different to most bars and pubs in the UK. It lacked décor, the concrete floor simply covered in a wide range of seating spaces scattered around plywood tables. There were beanbags and benches and bar stools putting people on all different levels and, despite the extremely minimalist setting, the atmosphere felt electric. Freeing somehow, if an atmosphere could feel like that. Chatter and laughter could be heard in all directions, with accents from all around the world permeating the space, even above the music.

The girls took seats around a long table, then began quizzing her on Alex. They wanted to know what he looked like, particularly if he was hot, and if she thought she would have a 'steamy holiday fling' with him as Lola had so delicately put it.

Noa looked at her with an expression of mock-chastisement before Lola shrugged and said, 'What? We all know brother's best friend is the best trope.'

'No,' Noa responded. 'We both made that clear after our one mistake of a night together eight years ago. It was a one-time, never-to-be-repeated-again event, and we have barely even acknowledged it happened since.'

She rocked herself, considering her next words. She'd only ever spoken to Tes about this, but there was something really freeing about these girls being holiday friends, and it made her want to talk through all her secrets.

'Maybe that night was meant to happen, to get it out of my system, but he's a moody, arrogant, playboy these days, and I just don't see him that way. So, no steamy flings here girls. Sorry to disappoint,' she shrugged.

'So, what's the plan then? No steamy love affairs, but do you plan on at least speaking to him?' Hattie, who was the quietest of the bunch asked this, and Noa took a second to consider her response.

'You said you were friends once. Travelling can be hard on your own sometimes. It might be nice to have someone to fall back on,' Hattie continued, clearly sensing Noa's uncertainty.

'But I'm just so angry at the underhandedness of it all. I know I'm projecting it all on him when my brother is more likely to be to blame. But Alex still agreed to it. He's still here. Why do the two of them think they can control my life like that, you know?'

'All I'm saying is that I can think of a good way to work through that anger in a way that sounds a lot more fun than the silent treatment,' Lola winked, just to punctuate her point.

Thea added, 'Sometimes a man in control isn't all that bad, if you know what I mean.'

She wagged her brow before Noa brushed off their jokes.

'Guys, this is serious! I don't know what to do. I'm meant to be taking back control of my own life here.'

They all looked at her, nodding and looking deep in thought, before Lola banged on the table with a force not strictly necessary, almost spilling their fourth round of cocktails onto the floor.

'I've got it,' she slurred, looking so proud like she had just solved the Rubik's cube. Noa just stared at her before she continued. 'Well... revenge is best served by a pissed off woman. If they want to try and put you in a box and treat you like a child, then I say you let them. And by them, I mean Alex.'

She was sporting the grin of some supervillain cooking up their next diabolical plan, but Noa didn't get it yet.

'That doesn't quite sound like the trip I had in mind,' she frowned. 'This trip is supposed to be about reclaiming my own happiness and finding out what I want next from my life.'

'I didn't say that means you have to make it easy on him,' Lola winked. 'This could be so much fun for you! Make his job to "babysit" you, as you put it, as hard as possible and show him just how much you are a woman and not a child after all.'

'Lola, has anyone ever told you are an evil genius?' Thea laughed.

'Not lately.'

Noa just smiled brightly and downed her drink. Alex Fletcher wasn't going to know what hit him.

# Chapter 13

## Alex

Today was a long-ass day. Landing in Bangkok, after two very painful flights and eighteen hours later, all Alex had wanted was to sleep. The tension between him and Noa felt like a rope pulled too tight, starting to fray in the middle under the strain. It was thick and suffocating, and it had made for an uncomfortable journey, to say the least. He had huffed a sigh of relief when they arrived at the hostel and they'd finally gone their separate ways. However, as he got to his hostel room—a single because, if he was going to do this for Ryan, he was not going to sleep in a fucking dorm—he soon realised sleep was not on the cards. It seemed that their hostel came alive at night, with travellers looking to let loose. So, with the noises seeping into his room, he may as well have been sharing after all. Realising this, he took himself straight out for a stroll through some market streets. Well, 'market streets' was a big understatement for what he experienced, because these were nothing like the Sunday markets at home.

They were utter chaos as swarms of people weaved through vendors selling all manner of foods that he had never heard of in his life. His head whipped between each multicoloured stall, threatening whiplash, but he just couldn't look away. It was all so intriguing. Scorpions on sticks caught his attention, and he shivered at the prospect of their freaky-looking pincers touching his tongue. He stifled a gag, trying not to judge something before he'd tried it. After all, he'd wanted to immerse himself in a new culture, but somehow that seemed like a step too far.

Instead, despite the overwhelming choice, Alex played it safe and enjoyed the best Pad Thai of his life before heading back to the hostel. When he first arrived back, he noticed that Noa seemed to have made a group of friends. He wasn't surprised. Noa drew people in by simply just being herself. She had always had a magnetising presence, and watching her throw her head back, laughing with people she'd just met, he realised that was something that hadn't changed.

Alex settled down at a bar stool, with Noa perfectly within his line of sight, deciding to enjoy a few Chang beers before bed. Maybe that would help him sleep, at least.

The bar was basic, but lively, packed with sweaty bodies who were all mingling after their days being tourists. He didn't feel like mingling, though, and he was glad to have found one of the only corners in the bar that wasn't occupied. He would guess from the wooden furnishings scattered throughout that they'd used mainly repurposed materials and that, paired with the beanbags and pool tables, created a laid-back atmosphere. He took a pull from his beer, enjoying the mix of the bitter and sweet notes that danced on his tongue before he gulped it down.

Keeping his eyes on Noa, knowing that, for the first time in years, their proximity was inevitable, he had a feeling he was going to need more where that came from.

Another mouthful of his beer took him back to The Brew, before The Brew was even his. To Ryan venting about a guy from college who had been trying his luck with Noa. To a conversation that had put yet another brick in the wall that he and Noa had both built between each other. He'd wanted to rip it down, and the night they'd slept together he'd been close to doing so, but it turned out Noa was a better sister than he was a friend. She'd been able to do what he couldn't. She'd re-enforced the foundations with the pact and made sure that neither of them could dismantle it.

*'You know he's not good enough for her. He keeps turning up at the house at all hours, taking her out in his not-so-impressive wheels that I'm sure makes him think his dick's grown two sizes, and he flashes her with that stupid fucking grin that might have Noa fooled, but it doesn't me,' Ryan moaned as he sipped his pint.*

*'Jeeeez, man, tell us how you really feel! I know you never love the guys interested in your sister, and I kind of get it, it's in the older brother "how-to guide" and all that, but your knickers really are in a twist about this one.'*

*Noa had always been stubborn, and Alex didn't know whether Ryan had noticed, but over the years, when they'd given the guys chasing her a hard time or tried to get in their way, Noa had only been more inclined to give them the time of day. As if in protest to her brother's interfering. So, Alex had recently learnt to step back, and he would not be getting involved in anything Ryan had cooking up this time.*

*Noa had definitely grown into her own person, she was eighteen now and had plans to go off to university in the next couple of years. And, as much as Alex loathed that it wasn't him, he knew she was capable of making her own decisions and would date whoever she wanted. He just preferred not to think about that.*

*'He's pretty much dated the entire netball team and jumps from girl to girl. A bit like you, actually', Ryan said.*

*Okay, ouch.*

*Ryan must have sensed that his words hadn't landed how he'd intended them to, so he was quick to speak again.*

*'No, shit. It's not just that. He even tried it on with Melody once. The guy's a snake, and I just don't like him or want him near my sister.'*

*Melody had been Ryan's on-and-off-again girlfriend since school and, even though Alex wanted to focus on that, the idea of Ryan disapproving a guy for showing similar traits as him made his beer feel like it was starting to curdle in his stomach.*

*To add insult to injury, the next words he spoke felt like a fist in the gut and a knee to the balls all wrapped in one.*

*'Not to mention his dad has always been a womaniser. Cheating on his mum for years. The whole town knows it. I don't think Noa should be getting wrapped up in a family like that. The apple doesn't fall so far from the tree.'*

*Alex knew Ryan didn't know what he just said or why it would hurt. He was Alex's best friend in every sense of the word, but he didn't know how deep the cuts ran. Only one person did.*

*And this conversation had just made it clear that she was even more off-limits than he had ever imagined.*

*Ryan had, within seconds, fed into Alex's biggest fear that he would turn into the man his dad was just by sharing blood with him. The only person that had ever shown him he was more than that was Noa, and now Alex didn't know what to do with that.*

The sound of hooting and cheers coming from the dance floor as the song 'Pink Pony Club' started to fill the room brought Alex back to the present. The reminder of why Noa had always been his greatest desire, and yet completely out of reach, felt like he'd just ripped the scab off a cut that had just started healing, and he cursed himself for ever thinking this trip was a good idea.

It was just past midnight when Alex stepped away from the hostel bar and toward the dance floor where Noa immediately had his attention, as she always did. The way her hourglass figure was currently being hugged by that black and white flowery dress should be illegal. Her shoulders had the softest glow, the light sheen of sweat-coated skin from hours spent on the dance floor.

She looked so much more relaxed than when he last saw her. His eyes skimmed over her body, and he was drawn to her pink painted toenails. They looked so dainty and as perfect as her, sticking out of her little black sandals. She swayed her hips, drawing his attention to her toned ass, but when she threw her hair back with a laugh, he was frozen and completely captivated. Her smile really did light up the whole room, as the saying went, and he truly understood what people meant when they said that now. She was still that beacon of light she had always been, and that meant that he was in trouble.

It wasn't lost on him that 'Trouble' was the name he had always called her growing up. Part of him just loved to see her cheeks flush with annoyance every time he used it, but the other part of him used it as a reminder that he couldn't cross that line.

He'd first used it after Noa had gotten between him and Joe Rigby, who'd been goading Alex with 'dad jokes' until he snapped. Joe's dad worked with Noa's, and she'd held Alex back whilst scowling at Joe with a warning, threatening to tell his dad if he didn't walk away immediately.

The way she'd jumped to Alex's defence and then looked after him afterwards by helping him get cleaned up at her house so he wouldn't have to face his mum's questions had made him want to kiss her more than he ever had.

The way she'd shyly whispered, 'I hate him,' as she dabbed his nose. The silent understanding between them that the 'him' she was referring to was Joe made Alex want to wrap her up in his arms.

No one had ever made him feel as validated as she did. And that need to kiss her and hold her had only grown with every passing year, until her twentieth birthday when he'd lost the ability to hold himself back anymore. One lust-filled look from her, and he'd been a goner.

Now, as she swayed in time with the music, carefree and beautiful, he couldn't help but think that maybe that would still be all it took. He'd hoped she would've lost her allure over the last eight years. But she was a seductress, and she didn't even know it. She didn't need to flaunt her perfect body or use flirtatious words, because her smile was the sexiest thing he had ever seen and watching her laugh made his dick come alive.

He wanted to be the reason she laughed like that, and the thought sparked a feeling of jealousy in him that he could not explain. Right now, though, she was not with him. She was on the dance floor with a bunch of hungry pricks who did not deserve to be in her orbit. Because, as beautiful and mesmerising as she was, he was not the only one who'd noticed. How could he be?

That thought woke him up from the trance she had him in and his feet moved toward her in an instant. Because Ryan had asked him to protect her, right? That was the only reason he was there, and if he was going to do a job then he was going to do it well. That was the only reason he grabbed her hand and pulled her off the dance floor to a dark corner of the club.

He instantly knew that was a mistake the moment they faced each other. Noa was breathless from dancing and, for a moment, all he could focus on was the rise and fall of her chest, the swell of her perfect breasts. She wasn't wearing a bra, he noticed, and he couldn't miss how her nipples pebbled from his attention alone.

He mentally scolded himself for noticing and recited the line, '*This is your best friend's little sister*,' in his head five times before shaking his head and raising his eyes. He couldn't be distracted from the reason he came here. When he looked up, she was beaming at him, the rosy hue of her flushed cheeks giving away that she was slightly buzzed. Still, even in her inebriated state, he couldn't help but feel suspicious at her sudden change in demeanour. All he'd been afforded earlier was a frown. Now she looked almost happy to see him.

He decided to ignore his scepticism, focussing on what he'd come here to do. He lowered his lips and spoke in her ear, telling himself that the closeness was so that he could be heard over the music, not an excuse to get closer to her.

'You're drunk,' he whispered.

She giggled some more, so close he could feel her breath on his cheek, and she put her delicate hand on his chest. He focused on the contact that felt far more intimate than it should have, and his own breath hitched.

'Thank you, Captain Obvious. What do you want? A prize? I'm allowed to let loose and have a good time you know! Or did my brother give you strict orders otherwise?' she pouted.

Alex swallowed hard, fighting against the thoughts of what kind of prize she could offer him. He could've sworn he watched her eyes trace the bob of his Adam's apple. The air in their little corner seemed to suddenly change, feeling charged, and he cleared his throat, trying to stay on course. She'd been so angry to see him less than forty-eight hours ago, and now this almost felt like flirting. What was going on? He concluded that she must've had far more alcohol than he'd realised. Though he'd found it hard to take his eyes off her all night, so he wasn't sure how.

'You should go back to your room. It's late, and you should get to bed before you get yourself into trouble, Noa,' Alex tried to say, but it came out as more of a rasp.

Even knowing that she was drunk, he couldn't help the natural desire that he felt for her, and he could only hope that she didn't notice.

When he looked around, he discovered that without even realising, the two of them had become completely secluded in the furthest corner of the dancefloor.

'But what if I like getting myself into trouble? I've been good for so long,' she quipped, stepping even closer to him so their chests were almost touching.

*Oh no.*

The only person in trouble right now was him, and he needed to remember that. He was playing with fire. It took everything in him to step back. Her arm dropped away from him, falling to her side.

He wondered if she said that on purpose, remembering the nickname he'd given her growing up—Trouble. Did the word have their entire history playing out like a vintage film in her head? Or was that only him?

Before either of them could say more, they were interrupted. A girl with dark blonde, curly hair came rushing over to them. He'd seen Noa with her earlier, and she stood in front of them now, one hand on the curve of her hip, looking slightly scary with an amused gleam in her eyes. He got the impression that this girl made up in sass what she lacked in height.

Pulling her gaze from him, she turned to Noa, rocking excitedly on her feet.

'Hey, we are going to get going to the next bar. You coming?' she almost sing-songed.

He could've sworn that the two women exchanged a look, like they shared some internal conversation that he wasn't privy to. But before he could read too much into it, the look was gone and Noa's new friend had a maniacal smile plastered across her face.

*Weird.*

'Oh, Lola, I wouldn't miss it,' Noa said, glancing back at Alex with a look of pure mischief in her baby blues.

Well, at least he knew her name now.

Noa patted his arm and spoke again, 'Alex here is going to give it a miss, though. He was just saying how late it was and how he needed to get going to bed.'

'Oh, that's a shame. Well, night then. See you at breakfast,' Lola said, waving at Alex and pulling Noa out of his reach and back into the crowd toward the exit.

Alex just stood there, unmoving, replaying the last ten minutes in his head, and he realised keeping an eye on his best friend's little sister was going to be harder than he ever imagined. He needed to stick to his plan, but Noa Drake was temptation in its purest form. When it came to her, he was a weak man desperately clinging to his control.

# Chapter 14

## Noa

The underlying sense of nausea and drumming constantly taking place inside Noa's head had become somewhat of a trend over the past few weeks in Freymoor. But waking up now, in a stuffy hostel dorm with no air-con or drinkable water, had Noa questioning her life decisions. Maybe partying every night while away was not the way to go if she wanted to get any sightseeing done over the next month. Although, it would be a good way to drown out her dangerously sexy tag-along. Had Alex always been this good looking? She would have noticed, surely.

God, she must still be drunk having thoughts like that, because who was she kidding? She had always noticed. She'd just buried it under the guilt she carried for her brother. Growing up, Ryan had it hard at school, and he'd struggled for years to make friends. It wasn't that he wasn't the same charismatic person he is now, kids at school had just been cruel, and Ryan got the brunt of it. Noa had been so happy for him when he met Alex and, over time, having that one person seemed to drown out the noise of all the rest for him. And, one day, the bullies just stopped, likely getting bored once their words didn't seem to have the same effect as they once had. After that, Ryan's confidence grew, and his friendship group with it, but Alex had always remained the one constant.

For years, Noa thought that was the reason she felt so drawn to Alex. Because she felt grateful for him. But she knew it was more than that, and the night they'd slept together had been an accumulation of years of dangerously toeing the line between friends and more.

Ryan had made a comment once whilst the three of them watched a movie. The main character had just fallen in love with his best friend's sister, and Ryan hadn't held back on his feelings about it.

'There is definitely some rule somewhere in the best friend code that's been broken here,' he'd scoffed.

Alex didn't say a word.

And that's all Noa kept thinking about after they'd crossed that line, and why she had to be the one to make sure they didn't take it any further.

To protect their friendship.

And protect it she had, because now her brother was sending his best friend across the world to babysit her, making it hard for her to forget that night ever happened.

'Ughhhh,' she groaned, pulling her small, lumpy pillow over her head. Her throbbing head.

Despite her longing to turn back time now, last night had been fun from what Noa remembered, and she could see herself becoming fast friends with the girls in her dorm. She had to fight off a hoard of questions from a very perceptive Lola after she'd caught her and Alex in, granted, what did look like a compromising position. Noa had assured her that it was all part of their master plan to watch Alex squirm. And it had worked. Alex had likely been sent here to 'protect' Noa, or whatever else Ryan thought she needed, and she knew that didn't include getting up close and flirty with her. So, the prospect would likely be alarming to Alex if she pushed it. She'd taken a gamble, and it had worked.

She'd seen so much swimming in his eyes when she had touched him—confusion, fear, desire. Although, after being in such close proximity with him last night, she wasn't sure that he had been the only one squirming. Noa internally cringed as she thought back to the two of them alone in that dark corner of the bar, too many rum punches coursing through her veins and the thrill she had gotten from teasing him to see if she could get a rise out of him. She thought she'd succeeded until she saw him visibly shut down, his nonchalant, fuckboy persona locking back into place. It was just as well that at that point. Lola had bulldozed over and interrupted them. Just like she interrupted Noa's thoughts now, but Noa welcomed it. It meant she couldn't dwell on their weird encounter or overanalyse it for too long.

'You look like you could use an energy drink or two,' Lola pointed out in a tone that did not reflect that of someone who had sunk way too many drinks the night before.

'Was it just me who went overboard last night or what? You look fresh as a daisy, and I don't know whether to hate you for it or to hate myself.'

Lola laughed as she lunged forward, ripping Noa's tattered bed sheet off of her. The movement felt, to Noa, like her brain bounced against her skull and she couldn't help her wince.

'I just hide it well. After seven months travelling, you learn two things: one, that alternating every drink with water is a must, and two, that rotting in dingy hostel dorms does nothing but make a hangover worse. Get your game face on, missus. We have plans for today if you remember and we have to get breakfast.'

Noa groaned overdramatically, which only made Lola laugh more, spurring her on as she bounced excitedly off her bed.

Lola headed toward the shared bathroom with her toiletries to get changed, pausing to turn around and wink in Noa's direction, 'You never know, maybe Mr McHotty will be down there after all.'

Noa plastered a confused look across her face.

'Who?'

'Alex, duh. Girl that man is *fiiiiine.* I think I got pregnant just from looking at him last night. You may have made it clear that you don't want him, but who said I didn't.'

She sauntered into the bathroom with a swing of her hips and Noa fell back onto the bed, trying to ignore the sinking feeling in her stomach that Lola's words gave her. Lying there and closing her eyes, she let the darkness take her again.

Ryan:

Hey, have you landed?

Ok I know you've landed because Alex let me know you are both still in 1 piece. So maybe just ignoring me then?

I'll take that as a yes. On a scale of one to that time I got drunk and vomited on mum's new shoes and blamed it on you, how mad are you?

Noa:

More like that time you and Alex toilet-papered my college boyfriend's new car (his pride and joy by the way) so he broke up with me just so he didn't have to put up with you anymore. So yeah, not ready to talk yet.

Ryan:

Ok that's worse. But he was a tool, and I definitely did you a favour.

Noa:

Seriously? That's where you're going with this?

Ryan:

Right, not the point. I get it. I'm sorry! If it helps, Mum and Tes have both been chewing my ear off about it since you left.

That put a smile on Noa's face as she put her phone away, deciding to let Ryan stew in his own decisions a little longer. He could grovel for being such an overbearing ass.

Right now, though, she didn't want to think about it. She could barely think about putting one foot in front of the other as she dragged herself out of their room. Her head had only just stopped spinning after last night's escapades, and she was inwardly cursing herself as she shuffled along the corridor, groaning as she went.

After Noa fell back to sleep, Lola had practically hauled her out of bed and shoved her into the bathroom to get ready. Now, the two of them were making their way into the hostel reception for breakfast. It may have been late morning, but it had felt like the early hours, and she knew that both the hangover and jet lag were kicking her ass.

As they approached a long sharing table where the girls from their dorm and a few other new friends from last night sat, Noa's stomach let out a roar of protest and she flushed. Maybe it had been a good idea to come down here after all.

She inhaled her entire omelette faster than you could even say the word, then stepped out of the hostel, straight onto the busy streets of Bangkok. Thea, Lola, and Hattie had all invited her to spend the day with them and she felt giddy at the thought of having made new friends so early in her trip.

Carly and Bridget were headed to the airport this morning, having completed their month of travelling. It was a bittersweet feeling to have met such lovely people knowing she likely wouldn't see them again. They'd both been from the US, so exchanging social media accounts would likely be as far as their friendship bloomed. Such was the life when travelling, she guessed. She should probably get used to it.

As Noa stood on the hostel doorstep, everything that surrounded her felt like an attack on her senses. She didn't know what to focus on first. Her skin was damp with sweat from the permanent moisture that seemed to linger in the air in Bangkok. The humidity was stifling.

The streets were loud, bright, and busy. Shop signs blinked all around them, turning the street into a tapestry of colours that made the streets back in England look drab in comparison. It was overwhelming trying to take it all in and catalogue every detail. She didn't want to miss a thing.

They rounded the side of the hostel, aiming for a side street that one of the breakfast servers had told them would lead to a tuk-tuk hire shop. Despite the permanent blaring of horns, Noa almost jumped out her skin when a moped got too close for comfort and honked for her to move out of the way even though she was on the pavement. Her hand flew to her chest like she could calm her racing heart, and she scowled in the direction that the driver went. Lola and Hattie both chuckled.

'You'll get used to it soon enough,' Lola assured her.

'What happened to right of way?' Noa grunted, but she could see the humour in the situation.

She was such a tourist. Even having lived in a city as constantly on the go as London, she was clearly out of her depth and needed to readjust. She, suddenly, felt very grateful having these girls by her side to help her do so.

'Ha. Non-existent. It's dog-eat-dog out here,' Hattie responded.

As if understanding the comedic value, a small shaggy-looking dog with pointy ears and big, sad eyes circled around her legs. Noa bent down to stroke it when a firm hand circled her bicep.

'Don't,' a harsh, clipped voice bit out.

A familiar male voice.

She looked up slowly into eyes that reminded her of honey, but they didn't ooze sweetness right now. They held a warning.

Alex looked the opposite of impressed, and Noa moved her gaze to where he held her in place, before tugging her arm out of his grip.

'What the hell do you think you're doing?' she shot at him.

'Stopping you from catching a not-so-nice bout of rabies it seems.'

His tone sounded bored now, and it only angered her more.

'I don't know if you need to get your ears checked or something, but I am pretty sure I told you I do not need you looking after me.'

'Apparently, you do.'

Noa ignored the sniggers in the background from the girls, who were doing a dreadful job at hiding their smiles behind their hands.

She ignored that comment too, suddenly realising he had just materialised out of nowhere. Was he following her?

'Where the hell did you even come from anyway?' Irritation dripped from her words, and she rolled her eyes for good measure.

Alex just pointed his finger in the direction of the hostels bifold doors. She tried to ignore how his navy T-shirt clung to his biceps as they flexed with the motion, black ink weaving itself along his skin and disappearing under his sleeve. It hadn't been there eight years ago, and she liked how manly they made him look. However, she was mad, and if he caught her ogling him, she could kiss him taking her seriously goodbye.

They were on the street around the back of the hostel now, where the bar was located and, following where he pointed, Noa could see an empty chair and coffee cup on the bar.

Rolling her eyes, again, she said, 'Well, looks like you saved me. You can tell Ryan your job is done, and you can go back over there now.'

Instead of dignifying her with a response, Alex just looked past her this time to the girls now just openly laughing and said, 'Make sure she doesn't pet any more strays, will you? A visit to a hospital is something I could do without.'

Then, he left.

She baulked, wide-eyed, at the spot on the floor where he'd just stood, realising this was how it was going to be.

And she didn't like it one bit.

# Chapter 15

## Noa

After their run-in with Alex, it took Noa what felt like forever to steer the conversation away from their encounter and back to discussing what they were going to do with their day. The girls had turned into giddy schoolgirls over him, deciding it was 'totally hot' how he had grabbed her like that.

She just found it annoying, but whatever.

They decided to explore Bangkok by foot and just see where it took them.

'Is here okay?' Hattie asked, pointing at a kerb-side Thai café.

As seemed to be the case with most of the hospitality spots they had seen, the food was served outside. Small, red plastic chairs that barely raised off the floor were placed around plastic tables. There were no fancy frills, but the strong aromas of smoke and fragrant spices travelled from the kitchens and were enticing enough. Noa felt her legs moving without subconscious thought, as if the alluring smells were dragging her over against her will. They were shepherded over by a short and friendly man who smiled widely at them as he sat them down.

Thea's head bobbed as she said something to the man that Noa couldn't understand. Her and Lola had clearly picked up on some basic Thai whilst they'd been travelling, and Noa couldn't help but think that was impressive as shit. She'd barely been able to pass her GCSE French exam, and here they were having a conversation with a local after only a month there.

Noa's shock must have been written across her face, because Thea chuckled before explaining, 'It got boring after a while. A year travelling and visiting all these amazing countries but not being able to talk to the people in them. You find you miss out on some of the best and most authentic places when you're searching for somewhere that'll cater to our *Englishness.*'

'So, you learnt to speak Thai?' Noa concluded.

Thea beamed, a bright smile on her face that radiated pride. She had such a light bubbliness about her that melted into those around her. She nodded rapidly, pulled up the sleeves of her shirt, and picked up the menu for perusal. Bright flowers and vines painted her brown skin with a few small quotes tucked amongst them. They were fine lines and intricate. It suited her perfectly.

Noa had never been brave enough to get a tattoo. She second-guessed herself every time she considered it. But looking at Thea's now, she thought maybe she would want one just like that. Maybe she'd even add it to her '30 before 30' list.

'We found a three-day intensive course when we arrived in Thailand, so even though we aren't fluent by any means... it's enough to get by,' she added.

Lola pushed against Thea's elbow.

'She says "we", but what she means is "she". She gets by and I'm just along for the ride, because I suck. And, now, it seems you're along for it too.'

Noa couldn't help but smile at that. The way they'd easily let her into their fold like it meant nothing, like they wanted her there as much as she wanted to be.

The man who had welcomed them earlier shuffled back over with smoothies for them all, that Thea had clearly ordered, and offered Noa a warm smile as he pointed at her menu.

So far, all the locals had been so friendly, and it reminded her of how different it was in London. Before she'd left, she'd become a professional at avoiding eye contact on the tube in the mornings, like every other commuter going about their busy days.

After ordering, the girls settled into comfortable conversation. They talked about their travels so far over mango and sticky rice. Thea and Lola had met in Indonesia over six months ago. They were both on a year's travel sabbatical from their jobs in the UK and had decided to stick together. Hattie, on the other hand, was on a long holiday from where she lived and worked in Sydney. The four of them then discussed their travel plans for Bangkok and beyond.

By the time they finished lunch, Noa felt like she had a good idea of how she was going to spend the next week, at least. They all decided they were going to continue to travel together, and it surprised Noa how easy it had all been so far. Ignoring the minor Alex issue, of course. Lola and Thea still had a couple of months left of their backpacking trips, so their itineraries were flexible, but Hattie's was coming to an end after Thailand.

Before flying to Thailand, Noa hadn't thought of, or booked, anything beyond Bangkok and Koh Tao, as she was told it was best to make plans once she arrived. She was beyond glad that she had ignored the voice in her head telling her to plan every second of the trip when she booked it. Knowing she potentially had a small group to go along with made her feel a whole lot better. It helped to break down her perpetual fear of letting go and stepping into the unknown. And it reinforced the idea that good things could come from that, something that she had been trying to work through with her therapist for a very long time. She knew that she was already getting exactly what she'd hoped for from this trip and, maybe, even more. Her previous anxiety quickly morphed into excitement at the prospect of all the adventure that the next week would hold, and Noa felt like there was absolutely nothing that could ruin her mood.

After a whole day of exploring Thailand's bustling capital city, Noa practically crawled back through the hostel doors. She was exhausted in the best possible way. Today had been exhilarating. Being in a new country, with no schedule but her own, absorbing the change in culture, the scenery, and trying all the incredible food had made her feel alive in a way that she hadn't in a long time. There was no question in her mind that she had made the right decision in booking this trip, but right now she needed sleep.

She made her way through reception as she thought back on the day. They'd explored a small village community floating on stilts just above a moss green river. It started as a very serene way to start the day, even with Lola's loud and flamboyant commentary of their surroundings. But when Thea pretended to throw Noa into the river at one point, the two slipped and fell hard together in a heap of laughter. After they'd dusted themselves off, Lola insisted they visit Khao San Road next.

As they'd ambled down the famous street, Noa couldn't help the smile that took over her face the whole time she was in Lola's presence. Her bright and bubbly personality was infectious. Unlike the start of the day, when Lola's caramel curls had been tucked in a bun, they now looked wild and untameable, tumbling out of her bobble and sticking to her face in the heat. Her green eyes were almost glowing, like her character was being reflected on her face and her features. She wore a bright flowery sundress, and Noa couldn't help but think that she fit right in with the bright, mesmerising colours of the stucco buildings and signs towering over them.

Whilst Noa ogled at the living daydream, Lola had snagged her hand and easily lead them through the tight crowd and commotion of various food vendors until they arrived at a small Pad Thai cart where they proceeded to eat enough to make their stomachs hurt. She was going to put on fifty pounds if she carried on eating like she was, but she couldn't bring herself to care. The food was glorious. They'd then visited the most beautiful temple Noa had ever seen. It really was like a religious experience stepping through it. The beauty met with the quiet that surrounded the place made her mind still in a way it rarely did, and she felt so at peace. Even Lola and Thea, who'd spent most of the day acting as chatty tour guides, were silent in their reverence.

Lola had taken a natural leadership in their group and suggested most of the day's activities. Noa was filled with gratitude for all she had experienced as a result. Had she been in charge, she thought to herself with a grumble, she would have taken a much slower and laid-back approach. However, as tired as she now was, and as much as her feet ached, Noa felt fulfilled by today's experiences and was glad that she had met these people, these new *friends*, when she had.

Deep in thought on her way back, she hadn't noticed the looming giant rock planted in the middle of the walkway to her room and almost fell on her ass after knocking straight into it.

Wait. No, it wasn't a rock. Of course, it wasn't. It was Alex Fletcher.

She still couldn't believe he was here and, even though her body almost vibrated with anger at the thought of him and her brother plotting to undermine her ability to be independent, she still couldn't help but notice just how attractive he was now. She had been considering it since they'd arrived and decided that he had always been good to look at when she allowed herself to look. However, with the relationship between him and her brother, and the fact that he had practically lived at her house growing up, she hadn't often allowed it. Right now, though, she didn't know if it was the fact that the disobedient and stubborn part of her wanted to stick it to her brother, or their current proximity as Alex held her by her wrists to steady her from falling over, but she allowed herself to take him all the way in.

As she stood there ogling him, the phrase 'aging like fine wine' came to mind. She looked down at where his hands gripped her, and her gaze travelled up his inked arms. He was wearing a plain black T-shirt that clung to him, hugging his muscles in all the right places. He was a level of toned rarely seen outside of Hollywood movies, but still had some soft edges that reminded her he was human. She didn't know whether he gained his muscles from hours spent at the gym or from hard work and long hours lifting kegs at The Brew.

Noa had the sudden urge to reach out and feel his pecs, like that would answer the question. The V-cut neckline of his shirt showed off a fair dusting of hair on his chest, and she would have loved to run her nails through it. It was then that she realised what she was doing.

She was checking out Alex Fletcher.

A man that had been her brother's best friend for most of their lives. A man so off limits that she had been forced to wipe him from her memory after one electric night. Suddenly, Noa worried that he could read her every thought and she could feel her cheeks start to burn.

She had stood there silent and unmoving for almost a minute and, when she looked up to his smirking face, she didn't know if she wanted to punch him right in it or run away and hide from the embarrassment. Deciding to go with the latter option, she quickly pulled herself from his grip and bolted into her room before he had time to protest.

# Chapter 16

## Alex

Ryan:

So I have come to think you following Noa across the globe wasn't the best idea we have ever had.

I think you should have put up more of a fight.

Alex:

We? I am not even going to go there. You have made our bed and now I am the one who has to lie in it

Ryan:

She is pissed

Alex:

Oh you have noooo idea!

So far, Bangkok was not the relaxing trip Alex had imagined, and he would be sure to let his best friend know that the first chance he got. God, did Ryan owe him for this. The city was busy and chaotic, a far cry from the small town he'd come from. But it was also vibrant and exciting, bursting with life and he thought that getting out really was doing him some good. He wouldn't admit that to Ryan, though. And that's if Noa Drake didn't kill him first and dump his body somewhere along the way, which had felt extremely likely from the look she gave him when they'd first arrived.

Today, Alex decided to enjoy the bustling coffee culture that seemed to be so popular, which allowed him to escape the hectic streets for a while. He tucked into a half-inside, half-outside coffee shop and ordered a Thai black coffee, giving him some downtime to think. He needed to formulate a plan to get himself into Noa's good graces, because, somehow, he had well and truly made it onto her shit list in the last twenty-four hours. He, of all people, knew how stubborn she could be though, and he knew that getting on her good side would likely be an uphill battle.

He could think of countless examples of when he'd been on the receiving end of Noa's stubbornness, but the night she refused to stay and talk after what he thought was a life-changing sexual experience definitely took the cake. She'd been trying to bolt, whilst also refusing to leave without a written promise that he would keep it a secret. He'd had to stifle a laugh as he watched her reach for the closest thing she could find—a paper party cup—before she'd shoved it in his face, ignoring his joke about 'not being sure that would stand up in court.' She'd stood, arms folded in an 'I mean business' stance with a very endearing, but very serious look on her face that would have made him laugh had the circumstances not felt like tiny splinters pricking his insides. He wanted to take her back to bed and make those crease lines between her eyebrows disappear, but all she'd wanted was to leave and pretend it had never happened. And she'd found a very creative, Noa-like method of getting her own way.

So, yes, you could say stubborn was her middle name, and that would make Alex's life hard over the next few weeks.

Considering current events, maybe ignoring her when she'd returned to Freymoor hadn't been his smartest move. But when it came to her, he'd never been very good at using his head to guide him.

Nevertheless, as he sat and sipped on his steaming mug of Thai coffee, sweetness followed by heady spices overwhelming his senses, he was taken back to last night. Her sweet vanilla scent had drawn him in the second she took the corner before she almost ploughed straight through him like a woman on a mission. A mission to avoid seeing him, no doubt. She'd been doing that all day whilst she was out doing God knows what with her new friends. But then, something had changed in that moment. As she'd looked at him, a switch flicked. The way her gaze had assessed every inch of him, drinking him in, he could tell she liked what she saw.

She didn't even try to hide it and, hell, if his chest hadn't puffed out a little bit at that thought. He'd definitely banked that small bit of information for later. Her face had turned the prettiest shade of pink when she'd realised she'd been busted, and the sight had only made him want to make her blush more. And, right now, all he could do was sit and picture all the ways in which he would make that happen—his hands on her soft skin, the moans that would escape those plump lips.

*Wait, no.*

He could not be having these thoughts about his best friend's sister. She was off limits and had red tape all around her. He needed to get himself together or else this was going to be a very, very long month.

Ryan was probably right. Alex was just uptight because he hadn't gotten laid in a while. But that was easily resolved. Maybe he needed to find another body to get lost in for a little while. He was sure their hostel was teeming with women looking for a one-and-done on their travels.

There was only one small issue. When he was around Noa, he couldn't bring himself to look at another woman. She was all he saw. She took up all the space in a room, leaving none for anybody else. So, he guessed for now, all he could do was try to keep his desires under control whilst trying to keep her safe, and just hope that she didn't make it any harder for him.

Alex's afternoon was spent much like his morning, sitting in cafés, soaking up the culture, and people-watching. He knew he'd have a jam-packed itinerary once he left Bangkok, or as soon as Noa decided to stop ignoring him. So, he decided to use this time to take it easy and just enjoy being in another country whilst not having the pressures of the bar to think about at all times of the day.

Although, he must admit he'd called Bella, who was taking care of The Brew, to check up on the place twice since arriving. Turns out it wasn't falling down without him. She had, however, had some very choice words about his decision to ask Ryan to check in, despite that not strictly being true. Ryan had, clearly, taken that upon himself, and his daily drop-ins at The Brew were apparently less than welcome.

After ranting about Ryan's shenanigans, Bella had agreed to send text message check-ins every few days so Alex could shut off and attempt to be more present.

After his downtime that morning, Alex managed to see The Grand Palace Temple, which was exactly as the name described, grand. His mouth almost hit the floor when he'd arrived and saw just how vast it was. He had no words to describe it. The vibrant golden architecture towered above him and wrapped around him all at once. It felt otherworldly, like he'd been transported to another era, or a fictional world, because there is no way someone could have designed and built this. He wanted to explore every corner of it and memorise every intricate detail, all the beautifully colourful mosaics and murals throughout. He spent an hour trying to do just that.

His pulse picked up when, in the golden hour sun, each colourful piece glistened, refracting the light and almost creating its very own light display. It was magical. As a result, the colours of the tiles changed, dependant on the angle that you looked at them, taking the saying 'seeing something in a new light' more literally than ever before.

Alex read that the palace had been built in the 1700s, and he couldn't help but imagine a time when people constructed these delicate patterns by hand. He was in awe by the amount of patience and work that must have taken. And he thought he'd worked hard to get The Brew ready for reopening.

Once the sun started to set, Alex decided to head back to the hostel before it got dark. The smell of incense, a redolence of burnt sandalwood and jasmine, clung to his skin. He wished he could bottle it up to take home, along with this feeling created by the lingering memory of his day.

When he reached the street leading up to the hostel, Alex spotted Noa and a group of other travellers. They were deep in conversation outside a food vendor's market stall. He decided that this was when he was going to take a chance to reconcile and bring some civilisation back into their relationship. Because, even though they had history that he knew could never be repeated, Noa had once been a huge bright spot in his life. Having her friendship back would mean a lot. Plus, he knew that Noa would happily avoid him to avoid conflict for the rest of the trip if he let her, and that would just make things all kinds of awkward.

With that purpose in mind, he pushed forward to where she was stood. But first, he came face-to-face with Lola. Her blonde hair the colour of caramel was wild around her face in messy ringlet curls. She stood with her hands on her hips and her tongue jutted out into her cheek, like she meant business. This girl was an absolute pocket rocket. Everything about her was his usual type, but he felt no desire toward her at all. *Weird*.

'Hey there, handsome. I was wondering when you were going to show your pretty face,' she crooned, smiling sweetly and fluttering her eyelashes.

He'd play the game, maybe his dick had just gone to sleep and needed a wakeup call.

'Well, I couldn't go disappointing you now could I?' he cooed in response.

'Your girl's told us all about you. Can't say she's as impressed by your presence, but the rest of us would never turn down some eye candy in the group. Why don't you tag along?'

'My what?'

His mind couldn't focus on anything but those words. Had she just called Noa *his* girl?

'You know, the damsel in distress that you're guarding in her tower,' she quipped as her eyes flicked to Noa.

'Well, you seem to know a whole lot for someone I've barely met.'

'She seemed to have a whole lot to say about you,' she retorted, waggling her eyebrows at him.

The words gave him a strange sense of satisfaction, though he could only imagine the things she'd heard.

'Only good things, I hope?'

'I could never divulge that information,' Lola said as she grabbed his arm and pulled him toward the group. 'But you should join us for dinner, help keep the night interesting.'

As he followed or, more accurately, was dragged behind Lola, his eyes met Noa's stormy ones. Hell. She looked pissed off, and that fiery spirit looked ready to come to the surface. It made his dick almost come alive in his pants and he had to quickly think some unsexy thoughts before that fact became impossible to hide from her. So much for his sleepy manhood theory. He was clearly only affected by one woman in particular, at the moment, and that was a definite complication that he did not need.

'Hey, Trouble,' he said nodding at her.

The name slipped so easily off his tongue, and her eyes widened comically like they had the night before. Recognition clear in them at his use of her once-familiar nickname. But then, irritation followed.

'You following me?' she snapped.

'Have you always had such high opinions of yourself or did becoming a big city girl go to your head?'

He knew that he was poking the bear, but he wanted a reaction from her. Anything was better than the cold shoulder. The irony wasn't lost on him that he'd done just that to her for years. But even still, he antagonised her now, hoping she would bite, because he actually liked Noa's fiery side.

She scoffed at him, and he was again reminded of all the other beautiful sounds that mouth of hers could make. He shoved the thought to the back of his mind. He would deal with that in the shower later.

'Hey look, we should talk. You've got a lot of animosity toward me, and I think we should air it out. If you would rather carry it around and have this awkwardness between us the whole trip, then that's fine. But I, for one, would rather not ruin a perfectly good holiday with petty bickering.'

Her eyes softened for a second before the fire returned and she spat, 'Are you calling me petty?'

For a girl who hated conflict, she could certainly find anything to argue about with him.

'Of course, that's the part that you heard. Noa, I know you've always been a stubborn ass, but please, for the sake of this trip, can we just talk and call a truce?'

She looked shocked at that.

'A truce?'

It looked like she was spinning the words round in her head, trying them on for size.

'Fine,' she said, but not without an exasperated huff and an eye-roll to emphasise her displeasure.

He'd always loved this side of her. He'd let her give him hell all day long, just to see the sass and the fire she wore when she was comfortable enough to do so.

'But you are buying me one of those banana rotis for my troubles. I'll meet you on the bench so we can *talk*.'

She did air quotes with her hands as she pronounced 'talk', but he would take it as a small win.

'Yes, miss,' he winked as he joined the rest of the rowdy group in the queue. Because, as had always been the case, what Noa wanted when it came to him, Noa got.

# Chapter 17

## Noa

If Noa thought the streets had been busy during the day, the night was a whole new level.

Under the sheet of darkness that had descended, the city really did come alive. It was even more electric. There was so much to focus on, from the food stalls that seemed to have popped up out of nowhere filling the air with the scent of grilled meats, to the chatter of locals who came out in droves. The neon signs were even brighter now as they flashed in rapid succession, illuminating the night sky and busy streets.

You would think, with all that surrounded her, that Noa would have been able to find something, anything, else to focus on other than the words currently ringing in her ears.

*Yes, miss*. They bounced around in her head as she sat on a bench waiting for Alex to return with their food. They'd been surrounded by people and yet, coming from his lips in his deep, silky tone, those innocent words sounded absolutely filthy. She'd felt an unwanted fluttering low in her core as he'd said them, and Noa had to remind her traitorous body that she was closed for business, especially to him.

As Alex made his way back over to her, she had to make sure he couldn't read the thoughts in her mind, so she fixed her scowl in place.

He held up his arms in a surrendering motion, 'Hey, hey. I come in peace and bearing food. I just want to talk.'

'Okay. But only because you brought food. And, apparently, I can't get enough of that here.'

She started tucking into her delicious rotis the moment he passed them to her, the faintest moan slipping past her lips at how good they were.

'Noted,' he said, a slight smirk tipping up his lips in the corner.

He was annoyingly handsome. She didn't want to notice, but it was impossible not to. That only made her human, though. It meant absolutely nothing.

'So, why are you here?' she asked, even though she knew the answer, and knew it would do nothing but trigger her anger towards him.

Considering her latest reaction to him, maybe that was a good thing.

'I guess there's no point lying to you. It seems I was busted from the moment I got on that plane. Ryan was worried about you. I was planning a holiday to get a break in the near future anyway. He only suggested that this could be a good opportunity for us to become reacquainted after all these years. I agreed. And, well, you can guess the rest.'

'So, you and my brother decided that I couldn't look after myself, chose to go all caveman, and took away my freedom. You do realise you've taken feminism back like fifty years, right?'

'I can see you've not lost that affinity for the dramatics of yours.'

Her simmering anger was about to bubble over at his assumption to know her after all these years. Or, maybe, the indignation brewing was because he really did know her. He always had. And admitting that threatened to open a whole other can of worms that she really wasn't ready for. Whatever the cause, it had her ready to bite back, but before she could do so, he continued.

'I didn't realise my presence would feel so stifling for you, Noa. I want to make sure you're safe, yes, but that's as far as it goes. You can still do you. And if doing you means including me in anyway on your journey, then I'll take it. I don't see why we can't be friends again. Unless you really do hate me.'

'Hate is a strong word,' Noa replied. 'Dislike is more like it. I guess, after our history, I didn't expect to come home and have you ignore my very existence when it suited you one minute and then have you demand entry on an important experience to me in the next.'

'I'm not demanding anything of you Noa. I know better than that by now. I'm simply here and asking you if you'd like some company along the way. The choice is always yours.'

She hated how reasonable he was being in that moment. How was she supposed to stay mad when he did that. Maybe he had gone about this all wrong, but he was being considerate now, wasn't he?

Interrupting her thoughts, he added, 'For what it's worth, I'm sorry for ignoring you. I didn't know how to handle things with you and your brother and, turns out, I handled it wrong.'

'You don't say,' she mocked, before turning serious. 'We are both adults, Alex. What happened between us is in the past, distant history and meant nothing. I think we can both agree on that. We don't have to walk on eggshells around each other, and we certainly don't have to ignore each other.'

Alex just nodded.

He let her sit in silence as they finished their food. A pack of street dogs raced passed them, one tripping and falling over the other. Noa felt her lips turn up at the sides, thinking about her and Alex's earlier encounter and how easy it would be to bait him right now. She chanced a glance at him from the corner of her eye to see if he, too, had noticed the same thing. But his eyes were focused on her, a curious expression on his face. It caught her off guard and she thought about what he had said about a truce.

She knew she should take it. Harbouring hate and anger did nothing for anybody, and he was right about it only finding a way to ruin her trip. He was here now, and he wasn't the worst company in the world. However, she thought back to the diabolical plan Lola had cooked up to mess with him, and the idea sounded far too good not to. Alex and her brother had spent most their childhood messing with her, whether that meant chasing away boyfriends or playing boyish pranks. Maybe now it was time for payback. After all, she'd spent too long making someone else the priority, shrinking her own wants and needs for Lucas. She was done doing that. And if that meant showing Alex that she meant business, and was not to be tested, then she was here for it.

The idea also sounded like fun, and she needed some of that. That's what this trip was about after all. So, maybe Alex being here didn't have to be the end of the world, after all.

Her mind made up, she finally responded, 'I'll agree to your truce.'

He looked up at her, shock clear on his face for a minute, before a smile took over his face and he beamed like he had won the World Cup, a smile that made his amber eyes shine brightly. *Oh Alex, if only you knew what I have planned for you*, she thought. She was about to make his platonic bodyguard duties harder than he'd ever imagined. He was a man, after all, and watching him squirm might even be the highlight of her trip.

For the rest of the night, they chatted about Noa's travel plans. Alex was already aware she was leaving for Koh Tao tomorrow and, to no surprise, had already booked his ferry and hostel. Had this been the reason Ryan had shown so much interest in her trip? She was shocked at how sneaky her older brother could be when he wanted to be, and she made a mental note to make sure he got his own revenge when she arrived home. Maybe she'd set Tes on him. She could be like the Tasmanian Devil when she wanted to be, and Ryan would soon be sorry.

Since arriving, Noa had made plans with Lola to head to Krabi after Koh Tao, and then the Phi Phi Islands, before finishing off Thailand in Phuket. Noa agreed that Alex was welcome to join them if he promised to keep his overprotective tendencies on a leash. Ryan had made it perfectly clear that he was worried about 'men taking advantage' before she left, like she wasn't a grown woman and a sexual being in her own right.

So, she knew that she needed to set some boundaries seeing as he was the one to have sent Alex here and began to name her terms.

'Whatever you thought you came here to do... forget it. You want to be my friend and be included in our plans? Great. But, if you came to cover me in bubble wrap and scare off any man that looks my way, then go ahead and get back on that flight because this is my hot girl holiday or whatever. Actually, forget I called it that. It sounded way less cringe when Tes said it. It's my single girl era or whatever, and I'm going to do it right.'

She was rambling, but Alex didn't interrupt her, though she couldn't miss how his teeth ground together. She knew what she was demanding of him went against his every instinct, but she wasn't about to give him a free pass to derail her entire trip.

'Anyway,' she continued. 'I'm going to be doing what every single girl does when travelling the world...whatever I want, whenever I want. And, maybe, even *whoever* I want. I'm here to figure things out for myself. Without any intervention from you.'

Noa jutted her chin in defiance. She was sure she was coming across as a stubborn brat, but she couldn't leave any question as to how this trip was and wasn't going to go. This was her chance at absolute freedom, and he needed to either get on board or get the hell out. Simple.

'So, do you agree to my terms?'

Alex' eyes widened, flashing dark at the edges. She was sure she saw anger, or maybe jealousy, flair in them for a moment before he caught himself and returned to his look of indifference. His features were controlled and his expression even a little cold, a stark contrast to how he had looked at her during their earlier conversation.

But he just nodded, his lips pressed in a hard line, like he was trying to bite his tongue as he did. A cruel sense of satisfaction swept through her. She felt like she'd won a whole damn war. And if pushing Alex's buttons felt like this, she knew she was going to enjoy her new mission already.

# Chapter 18

## Alex

The sun beat down on them as they lay sprawled on their towels. It'd been a long ferry ride to Koh Tao, and when the rest of their newly established travel group had decided to get straight to exploring the island, Alex and Noa chose, instead, to really soak up the island lifestyle with a beach day.

Alex couldn't remember the last time he'd felt as relaxed as he did in that moment. Well, as long as he kept his eyes averted from the dangerous brunette beside him. He suspected she'd picked that bikini just to torment him and, boy, was it working. Every time he chanced a glance across at her—her sun-kissed skin dotted with freckles, her glorious tits only partially hidden under a flimsy piece of pink fabric that would be so easy to pull away—he had to repress a groan. Sweat glistened on her skin from the scorching heat and humidity, and every time her scent caught on the warm gentle breeze, his heartbeat kicked up a notch. A perfect mixture of salty and sweet from her coconut-scented suncream that drove him just as crazy as the sight of her.

So, he tried not to look. Her pink bikini strings were tied in a perfect bow, and he knew that tugging one would be like unwrapping a gift. But, instead of letting his mind linger on that dangerous thought, he closed his eyes while he lay there, avoiding the temptation and listening to the sounds of the waves dancing on the shore and the occasional flick of the pages of Noa's book. He felt a peacefulness he knew he'd always be chasing.

The whole day went on much like that. The two of them enjoying each other's quiet company, drinking fresh coconuts from the various cafés on the beach, and taking in the beauty around them. The glistening cerulean sea licked at the shore of white, powdery sand before retreating back into an endless expanse. It would be hard to tell where the sea ended and the bright, endlessly blue sky began if it wasn't for the surrounding islands in the distance, a fading hue in the background. Colourful wooden fishing boats lined the beach, swaying palm trees towering above them. The whole thing looked like a postcard.

As the day slipped into evening and the sun started to retreat below the horizon, bathing them in a warm golden glow, Alex and Noa decided to head to get some dinner. They made their way along the beach toward the nearest restaurant and took their seats. This felt a far cry from the cold shoulder he'd been afforded the past few days, and he was relieved for it.

Once they had made their orders of coconut curries and papaya salad, beers in hand, Alex saw this as his opportunity to finally get to know the woman Noa had become after all these years. The conversation came easily, and they soon slipped into old habits of bad jokes and playful ribbing. He asked her questions about her job back in London, such as where she'd lived whilst she'd been there. But, not knowing if they were that kind of friends yet, he carefully avoided the topic of her ex altogether. If she wanted to tell him about it, then she would. He'd listen and be there for her if she needed that, even if the thought of Noa with another man made him want to peel himself from his own skin and had his fists clenching at his sides.

As they watched the fire show on the beach beside them, Alex kept snatching glances in her direction. The smile that took over Noa's entire face as she watched the show was the most beautiful thing he had ever seen. He could watch her all night. He took this opportunity whilst she was distracted to really take her in.

They were close enough that he could see every freckle, like a constellation of stars across her tanned face, and just as striking. He wanted to count them. She was more beautiful than he even remembered, her eyes so blue they were piercing, reminding him of the lake back home on a sunny day when the sun reflects off it. They were endless pools of blue, and it would be easy to get lost in them.

As his eyes trailed down, he was yet again reminded of the fact that she was definitely not the young girl he remembered her to be, and quickly averted his eyes back up to her face to avoid the bulge threatening to swell in his pants. But that was a mistake, because as entrancing as her body was, her rosy cheeks, button nose that he wanted to brush with his, and her full, plump, pink lips, which were the star of the show. She was all woman. And she was breathtaking. Captivating.

In a friendly way, obviously. Because friends could notice the effortless beauty of another without it meaning anything. She could never be anything else. *Ryan's sister.* He ran those words over again and again in his mind. *God, you're screwed*, he thought.

Catching him staring, she turned to him and covered her mouth, her shoulders rising self-consciously.

'Have I got something in my teeth?'

'No,' he replied.

'Then, why are you staring at me?'

'It's hard not to,' he replied easily and without a thought, but quickly corrected himself. 'You're in my line of sight.'

He thought he saw a disappointed look on her face for a moment before she'd righted herself.

Not wanting her to shut back down again after the progress of the day, he tried to keep her talking.

'So how did you end up here?' he asked.

'At this point in my life, or in Thailand?' she chuckled. 'Because I don't think you're ready for the former. Even my counsellor isn't paid enough to hear my answer to that one.'

She was being self-deprecating, and he didn't like it.

'I'd listen to anything you wanted to tell me, so the answer to either one is fine,' he answered honestly.

He could tell he'd caught her off guard because she went quiet for a moment. He knew the alcohol they'd been drinking had made them both more forthcoming with each other, and he was enjoying this relaxed side of her that let her inhibitions and her guard slip for just a little bit.

'I made a list. A '30 before 30' list, to be exact. It may sound silly to you, but I feel like I've just woken up from a really long dream and realised my life's passing me by and there are so many more things I want to do with it.'

Alex chuckled because nothing sounded more like her.

She rolled her eyes, and he could see her walls closing around her again just a little bit.

'I knew you'd find it silly and wouldn't understand,' she mumbled.

'Who said I don't understand? I don't find it silly, Noa. It's just that, even though so much has changed, you are still the same you at heart, lists and all.'

She was a planner, a control freak as much as him and, though life didn't always fit into a list, he wouldn't tell her that. Alex knew that feeling, that sense of control, stopped her spiralling thoughts and had always brought her some peace.

He'd seen her fight to find that mental peace when they were younger and, suddenly, every instinct in him wanted to do everything to help her keep it. Even if that meant helping her tick off everything on that damn list.

Some time had passed, but Alex couldn't help asking, 'Can I see it?'

'What?'

'The list. Can I see it?'

Noa looked embarrassed for a moment, and it was adorable.

'You really want to?'

'I wouldn't ask otherwise.'

She bit her cheek, clearly mulling that over for a few moments before pulling out the notes app on her phone and handing it over. Alex skimmed the list, quickly copied it over to her messages, sent it to himself, and deleted the thread.

He was thrown back to when they were sixteen, when they'd talk for hours about her dreams for the future. This list was so unmistakably Noa, and he could almost hear the thoughts in her head when she'd written it. Because she'd voiced them to him once. And, just like then, he wanted her to have everything she desired in life, all the things that would make her smile. Because, damn, could that smile light up the whole world.

She deserved a life spent happy and fulfilled. They'd once talked about her counting the stars one day. He never would he have dreamed that they'd be sitting here today with those words written on a list. Who had her ex-boyfriend been that he hadn't done that with her? Or insisted that she grab the things she wanted for herself. The thought of him made Alex irrationally angry, and he had to quickly shut down the road his mind was travelling down.

He handed Noa's phone back over to her, nodding at her before turning his head back to the fire show. She watched him inquisitively for a second before doing the same.

As the night continued, they ventured back into more light-hearted conversation before heading back to their new hostel for the night. Noa was in a shared dorm with Lola again, and Alex walked her to the door before wishing her goodnight and heading to his own. Before getting into bed, he mulled over their conversation in his head, finally settling on something. He had a new goal for the foreseeable future: help Noa with that list.

# Chapter 19

## Noa

The Fab 4:

Dad:

Click here to see the link - Girl kidnapped in Cambodia talks about her journey since.

Just a reminder, don't talk to any strangers.

Noa:

I'm 28, not 8. I don't need the reminder

And don't worry, I have my bodyguard... REMEMBER!!!

Ryan:

I fear that was a dig aimed at me

Noa:

Great, it landed!

Noa's first day in Koh Tao had been a happy surprise. She and Alex had done a 180 when it came to their relationship, and she had actually enjoyed his company. She could see them being real friends again, and not just because they had her brother in common. She just hoped it continued. She'd always felt like he'd truly seen her when growing up and last night, despite all the time that had passed, she felt that again.

It was almost enough to make her want to reconsider her plan to torment him.

Almost.

Their current hostel was right on the beach and, as she walked down the steps towards the breakfast area she was greeted by Alex's smiling face. Teeth bared and all. Odd.

'What have you done?' she asked, sceptically eyeing him.

'What do you mean?'

'You're smiling.'

'And?'

'It's scary and suspicious,' she grumbled. 'Stop it.'

'Charming. Remind me never to catch you before coffee again.'

'Alex...'

'Noa...'

'Out with it.'

'So, about that list,' he began. 'Well, there's no time like the present right? We are ticking off number ten and we are doing it today.'

After showing Alex her '30 before 30' list, they'd moved on quite quickly. She assumed he had just forgotten about it. She'd had to bury the hurt she'd felt at his lacklustre response, his reaction feeling too similar to Lucas's often disinterested ones.

She blinked rapidly at him, now, her mouth dropping open and closing again as she tried to figure out the appropriate response.

'Sorry, come again?' was all she could come up with.

Maybe she really did need that coffee because, not only had he remembered, but this felt an awful lot like him helping her.

'I've booked us a full day diving course at Shark Bay. Come on. Chop, chop. I need you ready and right back down here in the next twenty minutes.'

'I... I...' she didn't finish the sentence, just stood there slack-jawed for a minute.

He really was helping her. And in such a thoughtful way. She'd done her research, and Shark Bay was where people went to swim with turtles and that was something she was dying to do. She'd never told him that was where she'd been longing to go, he just knew.

So, before he could change his mind, she let out an undignified squeal of excitement, turned on her heels, and hurried back where she came from to get ready for what was going to be one of the most epic days of her life. And she had Alex Fletcher to thank for it.

They sat side by side with their legs dangling over the edge of the wooden boat, bobbing up and down as it floated over gentle waves. After a long briefing and a short practice run in the shallow waters of the beach, they were now gearing up to finally take their first dive.

Noa couldn't help the nervous shaking of her leg as she thought about being so far below water, relying only on the oxygen tank that now felt heavy on her back. She focused on her breathing to quell the overwhelming urge to panic and overthink everything that could go wrong. She felt her heart beating too fast in her chest, her vision starting to blur in the corners, a telltale sign that she was about to be pulled into a panic attack. It felt like she was drowning before she had even touched the water and she just stared into the waves, trying to focus. To remember why she was here.

She had come to do things that excited her, that would push her out of her comfort zone. This would achieve both. She just had to force herself to take the plunge.

Literally.

The panic was in her head and manifesting into physical symptoms, but she could get them under control if she could just ground herself. She needed to focus on her senses. What she could hear: the gentle song of the waves, the birds in conversation above them, and the whispering of the wind past her ears. What she could smell: salt, suncream, and a warm sea breeze. And what she could see.

Peering down at the water, a stunning shade of topaz, she tried to think of the wonders that would lie below it. Their briefing had promised the possibility of starfish and turtles, colourful reefs, and tropical fish. And she knew that if she quit now, she would probably never get the opportunity again. How hard could it be?

She could do this.

As she tried to run through her senses again, focussing on what she could feel, a warm, calloused hand covered hers. She realised her breathing had rapidly picked up, her chest heaving. Lifting her chin, she saw Alex was nodding, his kind smile reassuring. Steadfast. He squeezed her hand in three steady pumps, and she had to refrain from falling into him and letting him wrap her up. She had a feeling his arms could calm a whole load of anxieties, but she could do this herself. She would.

Feeling bolstered by his presence, though, she took a long soothing breath, becoming steadier now. She realised that, without even knowing it, Alex had helped her with her grounding techniques. Although, maybe, he had known.

A memory surfaced of her sitting on her parent's sofa, clutching a pillow to her chest as a panic attack threatened to take her over. She felt underprepared for her GCSE English exam and, unable to rationalise, she had slipped into hyperventilating. As her vision started to blur, Alex rounded the corner, having clearly let himself into their house to look for Ryan. He immediately ran to her, asking what he could do. And, after she managed to choke out the grounding techniques she'd been developing with her therapist, he got to work guiding her to stock check everything around her. Using all five senses, he had talked Noa through her panic, tethering her in the present and automatically calming her.

And he'd subtly done the same right now, as she'd shown signs of the same panic all over again, giving her other things to focus on—the feel of his rough hands, the sight of his amber eyes that had flecks of white and gold in them as the sunlight reflected off them.

She realised she'd gotten lost in them when, suddenly, his lips were moving, and she wasn't sure of the words that had come out.

'Sorry, what?' she said, shaking off whatever form of hypnosis she'd just been under.

'Are you ready?' he repeated.

She nodded, and she realised she really was.

Even though so much had changed—they weren't sixteen anymore and he wasn't talking her out of a pre-exam melt down—it seemed that some things stayed the same.

So, without another word and still hand in hand, together they pushed off the boat and went tumbling into the waves below.

Noa and Alex sat in the hostel bar, surrounded by people they had met on their travels. There was Lola, Thea, and Hattie, as well as two newbies, Marcus and Tom, who had been part of their diving group and, to Noa's surprise, were also staying at their hostel. She sat there wildly scrolling through her hoard of new photos and videos from their day, unable to wipe the wide smile from her face.

Having never dived before, she'd been apprehensive at first. but, after her initial panic on the boat, the instructors had guided her through it, and Alex had been there every step of the way. She'd been in awe of the sights that surrounded her.

Pride filled her as she recognised she had embraced her fear and fought through it, only to have this as the end result.

The water had been so clear, and they'd been able to swim through schools of what looked like hundreds of varieties of fish, all an abundance of different colours. It was like swimming through a rainbow.

Reds, greens, purples, pinks. They were iridescent, scales shimmering as they undulated through the water in an almost rhythmic motion. Watching them veer left and then propel right as the water rippled and pulsed around them was hypnotic. She could have remained there, taking them in for days and never gotten bored.

The turtles were just as extraordinary. They glided through the water like they were at one with it. Majestic. There was something about them that felt so wise. Looking into their eyes, Noa felt like they held all the secrets of the sea. She never could have imagined being able to get so close. The whole thing truly was a dream come true.

She looked at the faces around her. All equally enthralled and enraptured by her story, watching every video and asking questions about every photo she showed them. She couldn't believe she had only known them five days. Time had gone by so fast, and yet she felt like she had known them so much longer. Like they were all old friends. It really was a time warp when travelling, and she loved it. Her gaze passed across the circle until it hit Alex. He was already looking at her with an expression she couldn't place.

Contemplative, maybe?

Admiration?

Giving him a shy smile, Noa looked back at her phone and tried not to think too much about the butterflies currently taking flight in her stomach. They fluttered their wings rapidly against her insides, making it hard for her not to squirm in response.

'I hate to disappoint guys, but I think I am in need of a post-adrenaline nap,' Noa interjected into the conversation as she started to gather her things.

It was probably time to put some space between her and Alex before she misinterpreted the butterflies as anything other than gratitude for the man who had supported her to face her fears.

'Girl, you are speaking my love language. No need to justify a nap to me. I think it should be a mandatory daily activity,' Lola responded.

Noa laughed at that, because this girl was so easy to be around, and she hoped this was just the start of a blooming friendship. Lola was so fun and free, and different to Noa in many ways. She had an ability to lift any mood and pull Noa from her own head. She, again, reminded her of her best friend Tes that way.

As Noa pushed away from the table, she felt the weight of a hand on her shoulder, and she turned, shocked to see it wasn't Alex this time.

Marcus pulled his arm back, having gotten her attention, and tucked his fists in his swim shorts as he rocked back and forth onto the balls of his feet. His crooked smile wasn't quite exploding fireworks in the pit of her stomach or toes curling in her sandals, but it was handsome. He was handsome. His sandy blond hair, long on the top of his head, was mussed from a day spent in salty waters. The bridge of his nose was rosy from too much sun.

He was tall and lean and, as her eyes trailed his body, she couldn't see a tattoo in sight. She didn't know why that particular bit of information caught her attention, but she noticed it anyway.

As her eyes snapped back up to his dark blue ones, she realised he had been assessing her the same way she had him and, from the glazed look in his eye, she could tell he was pleased with what he saw.

She waited for that to make her feel shy or giddy or... something. Any normal feeling that a woman should feel from an objectively attractive man looking at her with hunger in his eyes. But nothing came.

It suddenly dawned on Noa that neither of them had spoken a word since she had turned to him.

'Oh, hey,' she croaked, feeling a little awkward.

But he seemed to have enough confidence for the both of them and didn't falter when he said, 'Hey, I just wanted to say well done today. You did good.'

The unbidden praise made her feel smaller than she had done earlier, with Alex's hand in hers, encouraging her to make the jump. It didn't feel like it was coming from the same place, a place where he knew her capabilities and was proud she'd reached for them.

It felt more like surprise that she'd not cracked and run away when she'd gotten scared. The way that his lips tipped up in a slanted line and his eyes widened ever so slightly with the brief shrug of his shoulders. It felt like a man feeling the need to praise a woman for just... doing anything he could. It felt patronising. But, maybe, that was just her overthinking the whole interaction.

She was good at that, after all.

So, pushing through the irritation, she returned his smile, 'Yeah. You, too.'

'So, I... uh... I wondered whether you wanted to get a drink some time. Minus the cavalry,' he asked, gesturing to the table around them.

But, as Noa glanced around them, she realised everyone had disbursed like she'd been preparing to do before he'd stopped her.

Everyone apart from the brooding man with dark features, who still sat burning holes in the side of their heads. Or, more like Marcus's head. His expression from earlier was replaced by a dark, quiet anger, his shoulders tense and fists clenched on top of the table.

Noa remembered, then, Lola's words about making his life a little harder whilst he was here. Making him regret ever questioning her ability to do this alone and following her on her solo travels. She realised this would be a great way to push his buttons like she'd planned, and that had the giddiness she'd been waiting for suddenly pulsing through her body. She didn't know why the thought of Alex riled up excited her, but it did... more than she wanted to admit.

She didn't need to know why this encounter had gotten a rise out of him, but she could use it to her advantage.

So, turning back to smile sweetly at Marcus, she replied, 'Yes, it's a date.'

# Chapter 20

## Noa

Tes:

How's the hot girl holiday going?

Noa:

Having the best time EVER! How have I not done this until now?

Tes:

Yaaaaas!!! This is what we like to hear.

Remember everything happens for a reason and timing is key.

Anyway, where are we at in terms of the three D's of heartbreak?

Noa:

1) Why do you always have to send a billion text messages instead of just one? 2) ???? Am I supposed to know what that means?

Tes:

Denial, Distraction, and then Dicks, OBVIOUSLY! It's much like the stages of grief but applies specifically to heartbreak.

Noa:

Obviously. Tes Anderson you really are one of a kind.

Tes:

I know but thank you for noticing.

And I'll take your avoidance of the question as distraction.

But that's ok because dicks are just around the corner, and we all know the best way to get over somebody...

After sending off a bunch of photos to Tes of her diving trip yesterday, Noa tucked her phone into the pocket of her jean shorts before focussing again on the trail they were walking. She'd talked Alex into taking a break, as her heart felt like it was going to crawl up her throat from the heavy exertion she wasn't used to.

Her breaths were laboured as she pushed forward up the rocky terrain. Sweat coated her upper lip, and she was reminded of why she had made it her mission to avoid all forms of cardio for most of her life. Her kind-of workout involved pushing herself with weight training. Cardio was her version of hell, and she'd made that clear as she groaned and grumbled for the last twenty minutes of their trek.

Blisters burned the bottom of her feet from the trainers that she had not had the foresight to break in before their trip, and the weight of her backpack pressed heavily on her back. The straps chafed her already-burnt shoulders. She cursed herself for not packing light like Alex had suggested, but she wouldn't tell him that.

She tried to focus again on the events of yesterday as a distraction and a huge, jaw-aching smile split across her face at the memory. She felt like there was nothing in the world that could top it.

Her and Alex were making their way up to the top of John-Suwan Viewpoint. Lola and the other girls had recommended it. They'd made the trek whilst she was diving yesterday and their photos from the top looked breathtaking. But they'd missed the part about the slow torture they'd face to get there in their description.

As they walked, Noa took the time to reflect on her trip so far. She felt like something had changed inside her in such a short space of time. She was having the most incredible time and had met some amazing people. She felt nothing but grateful for the experience, so far. And she was coming to realise that, sometimes due to her incessant planning, maybe she was missing out on some of the best bits, some of the unexpected and messy bits that came from the grey areas in life. Somehow, from her breakup with Lucas, something that she had never planned for and felt like the end of the world only a month ago, had led to the adventure of a lifetime. And she couldn't bring herself to be sad about that right now.

Despite feeling like guilt should be tearing apart her chest at this stage, it just wasn't. It merely felt like a quiet murmur in the back of her mind. It was fleeting, and didn't feel like it would break her like it had a few weeks ago. Instead, she felt free. Lucas had been right to make the call when he did, and distance had given her that clarity. She decided that, when she got home, she would try and take this lesson with her, to live in the now and realise that the present was where the beauty really lay. No matter what the future brought her, whether it fit her master plan or followed societal expectations or not, she suddenly knew she would be okay.

Distracted, deep in thought, and losing her footing on the steep rocky trail, Noa stumbled backward until a firm hand caught her and grabbed her ass to steady her. She had almost forgotten he was there. He had been so quiet. It was like he knew she needed this time to think. She had been so wrong about what this trip would be like with him on it, and she almost felt bad for that. Almost.

'Easy, tiger,' he smirked.

She looked down at where his hand still rested on her Lycra-covered ass, then back up at him.

'I could say the same to you.'

He laughed and removed his hand, lifting it up in fake surrender.

'Hey, I needed something to grab onto. I couldn't exactly miss that it was there. I can't be blamed.'

She mocked offence and put her hands on her hips to really sell it.

'Are you saying I have a fat ass?' she whisper-shouted.

'I'm saying... you have a great ass.'

Suddenly, it felt like there was no air around them, which was surprising considering they were in the outdoors. Noa couldn't believe he would be so brazen like that, and she didn't know what to say in response or where to look. So, instead, she swung herself back around, carried on walking up the trail, and threw a 'stop looking at my ass' in his direction.

But, adding a little bit more of a sway to her strides, she decided she might not be all that mad even if he was.

After another fifteen minutes of walking and no more near misses, Noa stopped, looking around her inquisitively.

'The girls never said anything about it taking this long. We don't even look anywhere near the top,' she exclaimed, squinting to try and see through the endless green shrubbery that surrounded them.

'No, we lost the trail about twenty minutes ago, but I figured why not just see where we end up,' Alex shrugged.

'What!' Noa squawked, not even trying to hide her horror.

He looked unfazed, like this wasn't the part in a Netflix documentary where the tourists got lost on their hike and were never seen again, presumed to have been eaten by bears.

Shit, do they have bears in Thailand? Why hadn't she looked into that sooner?

Shit, shit, shit.

'Noa, breathe,' he responded.

His voice held a command, like he was trying to break through her panic.

'We are fine. This is one of those adventures you were looking for right? I have been walking mountains far scarier than this at home for many years. Trust me, okay?'

Did she even have to question him?

Looking at his face, overgrown stubble coating his jaw, warm eyes showing no signs that she shouldn't trust him, she knew that she could.

Her lip wobbled with uncertainty, but then she let his presence calm her like it had yesterday. And like it had many times before when they were younger.

Alex had been the one who patiently helped teach her to drive, a skill that hadn't come easily to her and, when her brother had grown frustrated and made her feel more worked up than relaxed, Alex had stepped in.

This was the same. With him she would be okay. She would be safe.

And, maybe, this could be another example of the beauty that can be found in the messy moments in life. Sending out a silent prayer that would be the case, she strode forward, ready to step into the unknown.

Once they got to the viewpoint, an entirely different one than originally planned, Noa's shoulders sagged in relief.

Noa one, bears zero.

She let the fact they had made it to the top safe and sound sink in, then looked up to really take it in.

Yet again, Noa felt like all the air had left her lungs. It was utterly breathtaking. The almost snow-white sand bar a striking contrast to the turquoise ocean rippling around it. Vibrant green plants and shrubs blanketed the rocky mound across the water, and the people below looked small and insignificant compared to the endless beauty that surrounded them. A humid breeze whipped at their bare shoulders, whispering in their ears and through their hair, carrying the smell of salty skin and sun cream. Noa let it fill her lungs. She wanted to bask in the moment and take it in with every sense possible so she would never forget it.

'Have you ever seen anything so beautiful?' she thought out loud.

'No,' was his only response.

She stood in silence for a long while, soaking it all in.

'It's... it's just so breathtaking,' she sighed, and Alex agreed.

But when she looked over her shoulder at him, he was no longer looking at the view, but right at her.

# Chapter 21

## Alex

Krabi Old Town was somewhere Alex could lose himself in for days, given the opportunity.

It was so vastly different from Freymoor, the dusty streets lined with busy market stalls, the blues, pinks and greens of the shop fronts making it feel like they'd stepped into a rainbow, the sun painting the bricks in a warm glow that only enhanced that feeling. Yet, being there made his mind still in a similar way that it did when he was home. Maybe it was the change in pace from the rest of their trip. Being in a small market town again, despite its differences, felt familiar. Like he knew the locals who scurried through the streets, stopping to talk to their neighbours, and could understand the collective belonging they all felt for a place like this.

It was special. Just like Freymoor was special.

Noa's hair fanned over her shoulders and down her back, wisps getting caught in the gentle breeze. Her waves mimicked the sway of her hips, snaking from side to side as she walked. She smiled brightly at the vendors who occupied the street, radiating sunshine to everyone she passed.

She was an image worthy of a postcard in itself, but with the town as her backdrop. He seriously debated pulling his phone out and capturing the moment.

It felt like they'd made progress in Koh Tao, and Alex was relieved that Noa hadn't tried to fight him when he not-so-subtly started to help her work through some of the activities on her list.

They'd remained at the viewpoint until the sun started to set, and the whole experience had felt more intimate than it should have. He'd been entranced by her and the way her face illuminated at the view, her nose wrinkling in concentration as she took it in, drawing her freckles together until they almost became one. She'd come alive, and he'd noticed that her eyes had regained a sparkle in them that he hadn't seen since she'd come home. The same sparkle he saw now directed at everyone who came into her orbit. A warm glow. An aura she just seemed to wrap people in without even knowing it.

He loved seeing her like that and wasn't sure he would ever tire of seeing this version of her. Friends like to see their friends happy, right? That was the reason he couldn't tear his eyes away from her like she was the best view in Thailand. Because he was nothing if not a good pal, and he wanted to make sure she was having a good time.

After their hike, he'd almost managed to get the words she'd directed at Marcus days earlier out of his head… almost.

'It's a date.'

*It's a fucking date!*

And he could have sworn she'd narrowed her eyes directly at him as she said it, as if in some sort of challenge.

*Fuck.*

Then, when he went back to their hostel that night, he'd had to try to tamper down the rage he felt as Marcus boasted to the guys that he had 'bagged himself a date with the hot brunette from diving'.

Alex wanted to punch him in his stupid, smug face. The way he'd announced it like he'd won her, accepting the pats on his back he was awarded by his friends as they talked on and on about how 'hot' she was. Like that was all he saw. Because, of course, he did. He hadn't bothered to look any deeper, but Noa's beauty was impossible for anyone to miss. It stole the breath from his lungs most days. But she was so much more than her physical beauty. And she deserved to date a guy who saw that.

Not Marcus, the douche.

The thought had his fingernails biting half-moons into the inside of his palms as he squeezed his fists painfully tight. Uncurling them, he wriggled his fingers in an attempt to disperse the tension and, with it, the thoughts of Noa and her 'date'.

He wanted to be in the present, taking in the wonders around him. They were now well into their second day in Krabi, and this was definitely his favourite destination so far. Yesterday, they'd gone with the rest of Noa's new friends on a walk through a monkey trail, and then to an elephant sanctuary, which Lola had stated was 'a rite of passage when in

Thailand'. He was starting to realise that he didn't entirely hate the company of the rest of the group either, but he wouldn't tell them that.

Prior to their visit to the sanctuary, Noa had been keen to research the hell out of the most ethical place to go. They had ended up spending an entire afternoon feeding rescue elephants, listening to the guides talk in depth about their background, and then trekking through what was basically a safari by foot. They'd been so close to so many beautiful giants as they roamed freely through knots of waist-high grass, finding shade underneath towering, tangled trees. It was an experience he would never forget.

In fact, he wouldn't forget a single moment of his travels so far. It'd become abundantly clear to him that he'd spent too long going nowhere but Freymoor. Moreover, whilst remaining in Freymoor for most of his life had been a choice—it was his home, and he loved it—he'd decided that it wouldn't kill him to get out and see the world some more. He'd spent so long trying to prove to everyone, himself included, that he wasn't the flighty bastard his dad was, he realised, maybe, he'd taken it too far. He never wanted people to think that the apple didn't fall far from the tree where his dad was concerned, but that shouldn't come at the expense of him living his life. Because of that, he wasn't going to waste a moment of his trip.

The group that they'd clearly inherited wandered through the old town, looking at the picturesque buildings of a multitude of different colours. It really did make the dry stone and red bricks at home seem so lacklustre in comparison. Krabi Old Town was vibrant and full of life. Ambling through the streets, Alex's eyes caught on a local gift shop, and an idea clicked into place, a vision suddenly playing out in his mind.

'You go ahead,' he said, 'I'll catch up.'

Noa considered him for a moment, but shrugged it off, carrying on down the bustling street, deep in conversation with Lola and Marcus. He paused briefly, debating whether to leave her alone.

The thought of leaving Marcus to weasel his way any further into Noa's life irked him, but suffocating Noa with his own presence wasn't the answer either. It was a surefire way to push her further into Marcus's scrawny arms and drive a wedge back between them.

But that didn't stop him from wanting to glue himself to her side and never leave. Like hell was Marcus going to be the guy she'd have her 'holiday rebound' with. Even though she'd made it perfectly clear that Alex was not to interfere, he would have to keep a closer eye on them. It's what Ryan would want, after all.

Lola pushed at Noa's arm, a deep laugh erupting from her at something Noa had said. A rosy blush crept across Noa's cheeks in response, an adorably bashful look on her face.

So, slipping away from them, Alex decided that, for now, Lola was as good of a buffer as he was going to get.

After finishing up in the shop, Alex caught up with the group in what appeared to be a small family-run café.

A few more additions had joined, some he recognised as guys from their hostel last night, and others he didn't think he'd seen before. Lola and Thea were curled into each other, lost in their own conversation, but it wasn't them he was looking for.

His eyes found her immediately. She sat at the table, her white linen dress riding high on her thigh, highlighting her tanned skin that glowed like it had been kissed by the sun. Her rosy cheeks and freckles were on full display as she pushed a stray piece of hair behind her ear. She was giggling, and it made him smile until he looked to see what exactly she was giggling at.

Marcus sat too close to her. His messy, blond curls—that Alex really didn't think gave the 'surfer dude' look he was going for—flying all over the place as he shook his head in some animated impression. Noa's bare shoulder shook as she laughed some more at whatever he had said and she reached out, her arm wrapping around his bicep and squeezing in response. Alex couldn't help the irrational anger wanting to bubble up inside of him. He stood there for a second, trying to count to ten and calm himself, but when Marcus turned to wink at the men behind him before his hand fell to Noa's knee, his legs were moving without his permission. *Not in my lifetime, fucker.*

Reaching their table, he loomed over them, shooting a glare in Marcus's direction, hoping it was enough for him to get the message. This guy was definitely not worthy of having his hands on Noa.

Hell, *he* wasn't worthy of having his hands on her.

Didn't stop him thinking about it, though—her soft skin under his, watching that blush creep from her cheeks across her entire body. He thought about it regularly, actually. Usually at night with his hand gripping his cock in the shower. It was the only way to keep from actually reaching out and tugging her to him. Yes, he knew he'd be dancing with Lucifer in the fiery flames of Hell, but that was a battle for another time. Right now, he had to find a way to remove the dipshit in front of him from his and Noa's vicinity and fast, before the red haze threatening his vision won out.

He couldn't directly tell Noa that the guy was a dick. She'd only square her shoulders, find a creative way of accusing him of being overprotective, and then stubbornly be even more drawn to the guy than before. Exactly like she had when he and Ryan had tried to convince her against dating Freddie Riley in college.

Luckily, it only took a minute before Marcus must have sensed the steam almost billowing from Alex's ears, and he quickly lifted his hand from Noa like she was a hot poker. That caused Noa's head to whip between them as if she was trying to decipher a code. Alex cleared his throat before he looked at her.

'Want to take a walk?' he asked.

She didn't hesitate and started gathering her things.

'Sure, anywhere in particular?'

'No, I've just got something I want to give you.'

'Ooooooh. So mysterious,' she teased before saying her goodbyes to everyone.

As they began to walk away, Alex instantly felt more relaxed. He was trying not to read too much into his reaction just now, but it couldn't mean anything good, that's for sure. Ignoring the fact that his feelings for Noa Drake probably stretched beyond the boundaries of friendship was getting harder and harder.

As they made their way back through the town, down the busy streets, Noa incessantly tried to guess what he had to give her. Impatient little thing. He just watched her and smiled at her animated babbling, because seeing her relaxed and happy, with her guard down, might just be his new favourite thing.

Once they reached the beach, they both settled on the sand. Alex pulled the clothbound notebook out of his rucksack and handed it to her, suddenly realising that, maybe, this was too much. Maybe, she had her own process, and she wouldn't like it. Or, maybe, she would just think it was childish, stupid, or cringey. Any of those words likely fit. It wasn't as if he knew anything about how to write a book. She just looked up at him with wide, questioning eyes as she took it from his grip.

'I thought you could use this to write. Number twelve on your list, right?'

She swallowed hard, his eyes tracking the movement of her throat. He wished he could trace the trail it took with his hips and see how she would react, to see if her pulse would race as he reached her pulse point, and then...

'How... how do you remember all of this?' Noa stuttered, breaking through his thoughts and bringing him out of his daydream.

'Oh, Trouble. I could tell you, but then I would have to kill you,' he joked, trying not to let his current desire bleed into his voice.

But the hoarse words betrayed him. She didn't seem to notice, though, and just rolled her pretty blue eyes at him.

'*Now* who's being the dramatic one?'

'Do you like it? If it's not what you want to use for writing, then that's okay. It was just an idea. I saw it and I thought of you.'

'You thought of me?'

'I think of you, Noa.'

A sudden tension surrounded them. Unspoken words that neither of them were willing to spill. Noa licked her juicy bottom lip and bit into it. She had no idea what that did to him. After a few moments of them locking eyes and just taking each other in, Noa finally broke the silence. He was glad she did, because he could've sworn he was about to kiss her otherwise.

'This is so thoughtful, Alex. You are thoughtful. Thank you for this and everything else. I really mean it.'

'Careful, Trouble. I'll start to think you actually like me.'

'Don't push it,' she teased, trying to look serious.

He loved this side of them. The easy banter that they always had.

'You could start writing now, whilst you're travelling. I can't think of a time when you'll be more inspired.'

She nodded at him. Her eyes looked glassy.

'I will,' she whispered, like she didn't want to let anyone else in on this moment between them.

The rest of the day passed, as did the next and the one after that. Every day Alex could find Noa, at one point or another, with her head down in her book, scribbling away. She would have her tongue sticking out, deep in concentration, and it was adorable.

Soon enough, another week had passed, and their Thai adventure came to an end. And, this time, as they boarded their flight from Phuket to Ho Chi Minh City, he did not feel like the girl next to him hated him. And nothing had ever felt so good.

# Chapter 22

## Noa

Four white walls with four sets of bunk beds pushing against them welcomed her and Alex to their hostel. Noa closed the door as they entered and turned to Alex where he stood completely still, just taking it in. Bags were strewn all over the place and shoes littered the floor, a hazard Noa had come to predict when it came to late night toilet trips. A travel-sized washing line was tied between two bunks, someone's once white washing hanging from it. Lola and the others had all stopped by the expedition stand when they'd arrived, not wanting to miss it before they closed, but Noa wished she wasn't the only one bearing witness to this.

Alex was almost catatonic next to her, and she rubbed his back, trying to stifle the laugh that wanted to break free from her chest. This had to have been the best idea she'd had yet. As an almost-distressed whimper slipped free from Alex's lips, Noa had to dip her head and bite her lip so she didn't give her satisfaction away.

When they had arrived at the hostel in Ho Chi Minh, Alex agreed to stay in a shared dorm for the first time during their stay, and she could tell the thought pained him. Noa knew that he liked his own space, but he was adamant on proving a point.

'You know, you really don't have to do this. You can stay in the comfort of your posh little single if you want,' she teased.

He shook his head, either at her or, maybe, trying to shake off the image in front of him. She couldn't be sure. It wasn't that he was a snob. The opposite, actually. But Alex had always been a little bit of a clean freak. When they were younger, he'd follow her and Ryan into their home and, as they flung off their shoes in all directions, he'd pick them up to line them up along the hallway.

Dorms, she had discovered so far, were loud and chaotic and were only as clean as their messiest occupant.

They sounded like Alex's worst nightmare.

So, in an effort to bait him, Noa and Marcus had spent their plane journey taking much delight in ribbing him about being a travel snob. And the second he discovered she would be in a mixed gender dorm, Marcus included, Alex had been quick to want to prove them wrong. Despite Alex thinking he behaved with stealth, Noa knew that he didn't like Marcus. Where testosterone was involved, men were just so obvious sometimes, and Alex was no exception. The only thing she could assume was that it was fuelled by Marcus's obvious attraction to her, and the idea that this bothered Alex sent a thrill through her body. He probably got similar vibes from the guy that she did and wanted to protect her, but either way, she could definitely use it to her advantage. And she had.

It was clear that Marcus was the kind of fuckboy that liked to set himself a challenge and then persist until he'd won the trophy. But it was nice to be desired, even if it was only for one thing. And it was nice to flirt, even if she knew she wouldn't take it any further.

Marcus was harmless and fun, but Noa wasn't naive enough to think that a night with him would solve any of her problems and would likely only lead to his entire group of friends hearing about it.

However, every time she batted her eyelashes in flirtation with him, she'd watch Alex's nostrils flair, and his jaw become locked with tension.

So, she'd made sure to emphasise the fact that her and Marcus would be sharing a dorm. She took too much pleasure from provoking Alex, and it had led to their current stand-off. He refused to back down to the challenge, which was why they currently stood on the threshold of an eight-bed mixed dorm room.

To Noa's delight, Alex gaped at the dingy room in front of them. Barely a few inches of floor space separated the opposite bunks, and the slither of light that was creeping in from the tiny window in the corner did nothing but highlight how basic it all was. For her, this was no different to any of her previous nights on her travels, but Alex looked like he was in physical pain.

Noa unsuccessfully tried to hold back a snicker as she watched him try and fail to wipe the horrified look off his face. Alex could be just as stubborn as she was, and she knew he wouldn't back out now he'd said he could do it. This would be so much fun.

'What? No. I'm fine. More than fine, actually. It's great,' he coughed and muttered something undistinguishable under his breath.

Noa just smiled sweetly at him. She turned before he could notice just how much she was enjoying this and started to lift her very heavy rucksack onto the top bunk, feigning innocence that her master plan to make his life a little more difficult was going perfectly.

Before she could lift her bag above her head, large and sturdy tattooed arms came around either side of her, boxing her in against the bunks. Alex's chest was pressed against her back, and she could smell his musky and rich cologne. He smelt like tobacco and spices, and breathing him in at this proximity almost made her go faint. *What on earth is happening?*

Maybe it had nothing to do with the giant hunk of a man pressed against her but was, instead, the early morning and lack of sleep that was currently making her weak at the knees. Yes, that must be it. She needed food and sleep. Nothing else. Definitely not his hands on her. Food and sleep. Her body's reaction could not be trusted until then.

Oblivious to her racing thoughts, Alex placed his hands on top of hers and took the bag from her grip, lifting it with ease onto her bed. His hands were large, with bulging veins snaking across them and up his muscular forearms. She was starting to rethink the whole not-wanting-them-on-her thing. It was clear that he could likely inflict all kinds of pain and pleasure with those things, and even just the thought alone made the blood coursing through her veins feel like it had hit the boiling point. Her entire body felt molten hot, and Noa prayed that Alex couldn't feel it emanating off her. She watched out of her periphery as his muscles flexed and rippled against the strain of his white T-shirt and, suddenly, all the heat pooled and settled in her core. She was quite sure it was visible on her cheeks, making her want to hide from his gaze that was no longer on the bag but fixed on her.

Aiming for anger rather than lust, she turned around to chastise him for the fact that she could, in fact, do it herself. But that was an error on her part and the words quickly died on her tongue as she scrutinised him. He was so close and devastatingly gorgeous. She could feel his breath fan across her face, but he didn't pull away. Not at first. He kept his eyes on hers, their chests touching. Was he holding his breath? But then, his demeanour changed. As if she had imagined the whole thing, a coldness took over his features and he rushed away from her like he would catch fire just from being in her vicinity.

She ignored the sting that she felt from that. They were friends, nothing more. He was her brother's best friend. She needed to remember that she had not invited him here, and she needed to make sure she reminded him of that, too. They'd clearly forgotten and had gotten way too close lately. She would have to be more careful not to get sucked into romanticising things between them again. That was a road that could lead nowhere good.

The two of them busied themselves in silence for the next hour, brushing past each other in the small confines of the room as they unpacked and got themselves ready for the rest of the day.

After both of them engaged in separate activities for the day, they had made their way back to the dorm. Noa tossed and turned in her bed, only feet from where Alex lay, and she couldn't stop playing those moments from earlier in her head over and over.

# Chapter 23

## Alex

After another near miss yesterday, where it had taken everything in Alex not to kiss Noa, he had come to the conclusion that he was well and truly fucked. Well, he'd known that before, but he had clearly been in denial. The way he'd wanted to devour her last night was completely inappropriate. Nothing about how he'd imagined tearing off her clothes when he was in bed last night was friendly, and it meant that it was time for him to put some distance between them.

They'd both spent the entire day doing their own thing after barely speaking at breakfast and he could tell there was tension there. Then, she'd come out of their shared shower in nothing but a towel, looking like a goddamn goddess with her damp hair clinging to her tanned shoulders, and he thought he would have a heart attack. He'd had to force himself to stop staring after he'd let his eyes follow the route a droplet of water took from her collar bone, down the middle of her full breasts. He'd felt an irrational level of jealousy towards said water droplet in that moment.

She'd eyed him sceptically for a second before carrying on applying her make up for their night out that evening. He'd thought he could be friends with her, but now he knew that was a naive concept and that he needed to put space there sooner rather than later. She needed to see him again as the playboy he had always been, the version of him that he'd seemed to have forgotten about since they'd been away, and so had she. Maybe a good fuck was all he needed to rid himself of these intrusive thoughts when it came to her. And a night out felt like the perfect time to make that happen.

Alex waited in the bar with Marcus and Tom, playing pool and waiting for the girls to finish getting ready. He liked this hostel more than most of the ones they had stayed in so far. The bar had a very outside-inside feel to it. Plants grew from pots scattered across the stone floor and hung from every rafter, or any place they could gain purchase. Cool fairy lights and colourful Vietnamese lanterns looked like they were raining from the ceiling, and it made him want to do something similar with The Brew back home. The constant flashing lights and noise of the city of Ho Chi Minh felt relentless, and it was nice to be somewhere that quietened the soul for a while. Even if they were about to venture out into the chaos again later.

Alex sat on a bar stool, a pool cue in one hand and a beer in the other, as he found himself zoning in and out of the game currently underway. Since they'd met, Alex had been perpetually irritated by Marcus. So, blocking the guy out as much as possible seemed like the safest thing to do.

His and Noa's 'date' thankfully never came to fruition, but that didn't mean Marcus didn't give her eyes that said he was imagining her with her clothes off every time she walked past. The last time he'd done that was when they'd left the dorm tonight, and Alex had practically growled in response.

But he must be either completely stupid and oblivious or have some kind of death wish, because the wolfish smirk he'd given Alex in return told him that he was completely unfazed.

Alex only tolerated him now because, for whatever reason, Noa did. And he'd given his best friend a promise that he'd look out for her. So, if that meant biting his tongue and waiting with a floppy haired douche-for-brains whilst she got ready for their night, then so be it.

Seriously, Ryan owed him.

A blonde little thing had been eyeing him from the bar since he'd arrived, and he watched her as he took long pulls on his beer. Deciding to really move forward with his plan to put space between him and Noa, he tipped the neck of his bottle in her direction as his eyes made contact with hers, a subtle gesture to let her know he was interested. She shuffled on her seat, a little bit flustered that she'd been caught, and her tongue darted out to wet her lips. His gazed followed it, but his body didn't react the way he'd expected it to. He didn't have the urge to bite along the path her tongue had just travelled. And, as he watched her hand reach up to play with straight blonde locks, he didn't want to wrap them round his fists and tug.

Not the way he had when he stared at rich brunette waves. He closed his eyes in frustration and a pattern of soft freckles danced across the back of his eyelids, but when he opened them, the blonde's face in front of him was clear.

She gave him a flirtatious smile as she sipped her drink, puckering her lips a little more than necessary.

A tease.

What was wrong with him? He'd always loved this game. Loved the part where he waited for them to finally put their pride aside and make the first move. He'd give them eyes, making sure they knew, from just one look, the promise he was making if they came and took exactly what they wanted. But tonight, the thrill wasn't quite the same.

He needed to move past it, though. But, as he began to imagine all the ways that he could make this woman scream his name tonight, a loud whistle came from beside him where Marcus leant against the pool table.

'Pheeeeew, that girl is fire,' he hollered.

Alex found himself turning his head in the direction Marcus was looking to see who had caught his attention. His grip immediately tightened around the pool cue he was holding, enough that he felt it crack under his white knuckles, and he thought he might break it.

Coming down the stairs were the girls. Noa was front and centre, warm brown curls he wanted to run his hands through cascading over her shoulders, framing her beautiful, freckled face. She wore a little red two-piece that hugged her curves and matched the colour of her painted lips. He wanted to know the name of her lipstick. For her to paint him with it. To paint his lips and body with it so everyone knew who she belonged to, specifically the bastard standing next to him.

He felt an overwhelming and feral need to claim her. That's all he'd ever wanted, but she was off limits to him and nothing had changed. Her eyes homed in on his, seeking him out in the crowd, and the fire in them made his mouth go dry and left him breathless. This woman could bring him to his knees. She could chew him up and spit him out again and he'd ask for more. She'd done it once before and he'd hurt so much that he'd locked his heart away ever since. He couldn't go there again. Losing Noa Drake once was hard, but to lose her twice might be something he simply would not survive.

For his own self-preservation, his pining needed to stop. Downing the remains of his beer, he slammed it down on the table and, without even thinking what he was doing, he stormed toward the blonde at the bar.

# Chapter 24

## Noa

He had looked right at her with a fervent expression that sent tingles through her entire body. He had looked right at her like a man starved and he wanted to devour her. And, in that moment, she might just have let him. The way his amber eyes, which looked more like swirls of molten lava, seared her skin made her feel like she was naked. She felt hot and bothered, but it made her come alive all at the same time, and she knew the choice of dress she had picked in an attempt to drive him just a little crazy had done the trick.

She didn't know why she was playing with fire when there were so many reasons it was a bad idea, but she couldn't deny she wanted him. But, true to that hot-and-cold game he'd been playing with her lately, he'd shot straight across the bar. But not to her. To a gorgeous blonde girl who was all long legs and perky boobs. His exact type and her very opposite. And he'd remained there all night.

For a while she'd sat staring, like it would cause a trap door to open in the floor and swallow them both up. But when Lola pointed out that she was being as discreet as a birthday flashmob, she'd decided to change her tactic.

*Two can play at that game*, she thought. In fact, this had played right into her hands, and she couldn't think of a better way to execute her 'mess with Alex' master plan than to give him something to truly go caveman over. It was time to see how far he would really go.

They made their way from bar to bar down the famous Beer Street. As Alex continued to flirt with the blonde bombshell, Noa decided to up her flirting game herself and thought Marcus was just the man for the job. He'd been giving Noa heart eyes since they'd met in Koh Tao, and she'd just brushed him off until now. But, maybe, that was a mistake. Yes, perhaps he had been a bit too clingy and forward, but she wasn't trying to marry the guy.

He was nice enough, after all. She'd enjoyed hanging out with him and he wasn't awful to look at. In fact, maybe he was great rebound material. Not to mention he seemed to infuriate Alex without even trying. It was a win-win. So, flirting her ass off is exactly what she did.

The drinks were flowing a little too easily, and Noa was feeling good. They were in a bar called 'The Good Time Bar.' And that it definitely was. Music vibrated off the walls as women danced on tables all around her and Noa got the sudden urge to be reckless and join them. Stumbling up onto the table where they were sitting, Noa started to sway her hips, enjoying the music and the buzz of the alcohol that was flowing through her veins. She felt sexy as hell with everyone watching her. The group cheered and that made Alex's gaze lift to her from the corner where he stood with his hand on Blondie's waist to see what was going on. He continued to intensely stare in her direction, and it felt like there was a warning in his eyes. His jaw ticked and that only spurred her on more. Screw him, she thought.

Seductively waving her finger toward Marcus, Noa beckoned him over and grabbed his T-shirt, helping him onto the table. His hand made it to her hips as they moved together and she ignored the fact that the touch felt all wrong, trying her best to melt into it. She continued to dance with the dedication of an exotic dancer, but before she knew what was happening, her world turned upside down or, at least, her view did. She was hauled over a set of strong shoulders, the scent of tobacco and spices invading her senses, and she realised they were moving toward the exit.

*Oh, hell no.*

She pounded her fists against what felt like a brick wall and kicked her feet in protest, but Alex didn't falter. He just carried her out of the bar like it was nothing. She was so angry but, still, the thought of his hands on her in any capacity, even now, caused her body to betray her and she could feel a pulsing between her legs.

*Now is not the time to get turned on! Stand down!* She mentally chastised.

Choosing to ignore it, she continued to fight against his hold, shouting at him without a care for the scene they were causing.

'Put me down, you brute,' she shouted. 'I'm not finished.'

'I think you are,' he growled.

'Oh, here is the bodyguard I've been waiting to see. I knew you couldn't help yourself. Who do you think you are?'

'The only thing standing between you and that prick having his hands in places they don't belong.'

She had stopped fighting. It was no use. She whipped her head in is direction, scoffing.

'And who said I wanted you to stand between us? Maybe that's exactly what I wanted... his hands, amongst other things, touching me.'

She could see his jaw clench, his teeth grinding together.

Alex let out a humourless laugh and his words dripped in venom, 'Oh baby, we both know it's not his hands you want on you tonight. I did you a favour, and you know it.'

*Baby*. Was she hallucinating? She shook it off because the word had sounded far too sexy coming out of his mouth, and she was in far too much of a compromising position right now. But also, who else's hands did he mean? His?

'You want to go running around, dancing on tables and shaking that ass for men that don't deserve to see it, then you better be willing to take responsibility when they all end up eating their teeth if they touch you.'

She felt the briefest flutter in her stomach, but then it was her turn to let out a maniacal laugh as the lust-induced fog cleared and her anger returned.

He chose that moment to set her right onto her feet and started to pull her through the streets in the direction of their hostel. But she pulled back and set her hands on her hips, glaring at him.

'Are you for fucking real right now? Again, who do you think you are? You are such a hypocrite! You spend the entire night eye-fucking and flirting with some horny blonde and then have the audacity to dictate who I can and cannot have a good time with. I'm surprised you could tear your eyes away from her cleavage long enough to notice. Fuck you, Alex!' She spat out the words and it only made him smirk, his lips lifting up in the corners.

Was he enjoying this?

Quicker than she could process, she was being pushed down a quiet street, her back against a wall and his body pressed to hers. The bricks were cold against her flushed skin as he caged her in.

# Chapter 25

## Alex

Noa was so damn sexy when she was angry. She was sexy all the time, but angry Noa, she was another level. It almost made Alex want to piss her off more often.

He couldn't stop himself when she'd shouted at him like she wanted to rip his balls from his body. This feisty brunette would be the death of him. And the shocked look on her face when he'd pressed her against the wall had been priceless. But he hadn't thought much further than that, and now they were so close and completely alone. All he wanted to do was crash his lips to hers and show her just how crazy she had made him all night.

'Jealous, Trouble?' he taunted, knowing she'd bite.

She pushed against his chest, but the move lacked all conviction.

'Sorry to disappoint, but I don't do the caveman type. And I *definitely don't* do the fuckboy type,' she retorted, but her hands fisted in his T-shirt as she said it, and his eyes tracked the motion.

Her pupils were blown, her blue eyes now almost black, desire swimming in them. The look she gave him set him on fire. He itched to touch her. But he wouldn't. Not until she asked. It felt like they'd been dancing around their feelings for each other recently, and the look on her face now made him sure this thing did not just go one way. But it was a dance he would happily continue until he knew she was sure.

Because, once he had her in his arms, felt the touch of her lips and been buried inside her, he knew there would be no going back. He would not repeat his previous mistake—have her there with him one minute only for her to bolt the next. Even though everything in him ached for her, she was worth the wait. Just as he'd expected, he could see the turmoil behind her eyes, her impulse to overthink everything kicking in and suddenly she pulled back, putting space between them that felt like a giant, gaping hole.

But he just grabbed her hand and led them back to the hostel in silence. He would allow her the space she needed to process the feelings she had accidentally made clear she had for him. But after tonight, he was not holding back and, once she realised that he could give her everything she wanted, Noa Drake would be his.

# Chapter 26

## Noa

Ho Chi Minh City had turned out to be a flying visit. Even for Vietnam, the city was busy in a way that just felt exhausting, and none of them had felt very connected with the place or inclined to stay. That was the perks of going with the flow Noa realised, complete freedom. They'd had no restrictions on their time and could jump onto the next available flight to Da Nang, where they had now been for the past few days.

After the events of Ho Chi Minh City, Noa had been on edge around Alex. She didn't know how to act. She knew he and everyone around them had noticed it, but they had, luckily, given her space to figure it out. She considered whether to acknowledge what had happened, but her head was honestly swimming with so many thoughts that she didn't know what she would say or do if she did.

She had been jealous the night he flirted with the blonde in the bar, and she had accidentally let the mask fall. He saw the jealousy and called her out on it. She couldn't take it back now. But did she like Alex Fletcher like that? It all felt so messy and, despite how busy they'd been as they travelled through Da Nang and explored the huge city with all their new friends, she just couldn't keep her mind from wandering to him. She needed to make sense of it.

She'd once thought she had feelings for him before. However, that was back when she was twenty, and it all ended in a one-night stand followed by a very quick pros and cons list that resulted in her decision to make a pact to put the night behind them. They swore that they would never think about it again. But now, that's all she could think about and, unlike back then, telling herself that this would only hurt Ryan and Alex in the long run was not enough to deter her from her thoughts of pouncing on the man.

What didn't help is that, as if he knew something had shifted in her, Alex had been so kind and attentive over the past few days, and they had started getting a lot closer. That, accompanied by the fact that they were both in Hoi An Old Town, in a longboat, sailing down the river as part of the lantern festival, was causing all kinds of crazy butterflies to set flight in her stomach.

They sat side by side in the wooden boat, an older Vietnamese woman rowing behind them. The whole scene surrounding them was lit by so many different colours of lanterns. They glowed in the dark night, and the gentle sway of the boat, along with the soft lapping of the water against the wood, made a sudden rush of emotions wash over her. She had once dreamed of being here and sitting here now, with him, it felt so intimate. Romantic almost. She felt so comfortable in his presence. Neither of them felt the need to fill the comfortable silence with words as they sat and just enjoyed the perfect moment.

Noa came to realise that, somewhere along the line and without even knowing it, she had stopped trying to mess with Alex. She'd lost sight of that. It no longer seemed important as she focussed on the pull that still existed between them instead. She'd also lost sight of her need to put herself back together after her breakup, because she was never truly broken. She never gave Lucas all her pieces in the first place, and that had made getting over him easier than she'd ever imagined. And, here and now, she felt more whole than she'd ever felt.

She watched Alex from where he sat beside her. Thick stubble framed the quiet smile on his face. His hair was a perfect mess from the evening breeze. He was completely relaxed and entranced by the display around them, and Noa was entranced by him. She felt her chest squeeze.

Because it wasn't the light display dancing across the water that had her unable to look away. Or the colourful buildings blanketed in ripe green leaves and pink-petaled flowers. It was him.

A lump formed in her throat as another realisation dawned on her: she had deep, messy feelings for her brother's best friend. And, she thought, maybe she always had.

Ryan:

I want you to know I come in peace. My white flag is in the air, and I know I was in the wrong. I am requesting forgiveness and a truce to be formally acknowledged in the family group chat. Let me know your terms...

Noa:

Oh dear, did Mum ground you again?

Ryan:

I am not a child!

But as good as. She cancelled family dinner this week after promising my favourite. So, let's just say I have been fairly punished and lesson learnt.

Noa:

Ohhhh messing with you and your lasagna, she brought out the big guns.

Ryan:

So... we even?

Noa:

Nice try, but not even close!

Ryan:

Jeeeez, I had no idea Alex's company was that hard to tolerate.

Noa:

If you think Alex is the only issue here, then we have bigger problems. Ryan, you interfered with something I specifically told you I wanted to do on my own. How do you think that makes me feel?

Ryan:

If I tell you some self-improvement will be done, will you forgive me?

Noa:

I'll consider it.

Ryan:

[Sent Image]

Does this cute picture of me and Tinks help? I really think this animosity is getting to her.

Noa:

Maybe a little. Now don't push it.

After her realisation about her unplanned and wholly unwanted feelings toward Alex, they spent two days in Hoi An taking part in numerous group activities, such as food tours and lantern-making, so Noa was able to continue ignoring them for the time being. Putting them in a box and not dealing with them until later felt like the most sensible solution she had right now. The only solution.

Noa used any alone time that she had as an opportunity to bury her nose in her writing, and it was paying off. Turns out, a messy life makes for great inspiration. Who knew?

Today's activity included Vietnamese cooking classes followed by a coconut boat trip down the river.

Whilst they were in the shuttle that had picked them up at the hostel, the heavens opened and water droplets attacked the bus from all directions. The grey sky proved there would be no let-up anytime soon, and Noa felt deflated that Mother Nature was plotting against her to try and ruin their day.

Her raincoat clung to her skin as they ran to take shelter in the bamboo hut that their class would be held in. The temperature was significantly lower in Vietnam than it had been in Thailand and, even though it had been comfortable so far, her wet skin cooled her to the bone, causing her to shiver. She suddenly wasn't looking forward to the next four hours.

Despite them being warned at their hostel that there was the potential for a monsoon this week, Lola had insisted they still book the trip, adamant that they shouldn't let something as unpredictable as weather make them waste their trip. But, right now, as her matted hair stuck to her forehead and water droplets trailed down her face, she wished she hadn't listened.

A sudden, welcome warmth crept up her back. She wanted to lean into it, her eyes momentarily fluttering closed. But when that same heat brushed across her neck and made it to the shell of her ear, that shiver was back. The earthy scent of the coconut forest was replaced by notes of tobacco and vanilla, and Noa's eyes flew open again.

'We can go back, you know. I know this isn't what you planned,' a husky voice whispered in her ear.

His fingers came up to pull her jacket over her shoulder, where it had fallen down, and the brush of them against her arm sent a spark of electricity through her. Her body was a traitor. She couldn't stop it from reacting to him.

She jumped forward then, like he had burned her, and, had she been watching from the outside, she would have found the whole scene overdramatic and comical.

Alex's eyes widened, but then his expression softened like he understood her need to put space there, to find a way to dampen this attraction between them.

Like he understood her fears.

And he did.

Because, surely, he had the same ones that she did.

She was suddenly thrown into a memory from twelve years ago. She'd known her and Alex had a special connection growing up, but she had always been Ryan's little sister, a little too young for him, and anything beyond friends had felt out of reach. He and Ryan loved tormenting her, scaring off any boys who looked her way. And she had thought that was all it could be.

Until, when she turned sixteen, that two-year age gap suddenly didn't seem like a barrier. And neither had Ryan, until the night she had spiralled into a panic attack on the living room sofa and Alex had been there to comfort her. It was the most intimate moment she had ever experienced with anyone, letting him see her in such a vulnerable state. But she hadn't felt any fear letting him see her that way.

She'd been so lost in that moment with him. He was all she saw, and it was on the tip of her tongue to ask if he'd ever seen her as more.

They sat close enough to share a whisper between them when Ryan had walked in. He turned on his heel, claiming to have forgotten something in his room, and Alex had followed him. To this day, Noa didn't know if either of them knew that she, too, had followed and overheard the conversation that came next.

Ryan had asked Alex what he'd walked in on, and then warned him not to cross the line and make their friendship 'weird'. Her heart had sunk. And she'd never forgotten it since. It had been on repeat in her mind the night they had indeed 'crossed the line' and why she'd panicked and withdrawn.

'Noa?'

Alex's voice cut through her thoughts, and he looked concerned. His brow was furrowed and his eyes flicked across her face as if assessing what he could see on it. How long had she stood lost in that memory? It had, however, acted like a bucket of cold water over her head, a reminder of why she needed to ignore the desire she felt whenever he was around.

Looking around, she saw Thea and Lola were getting their life vests ready to jump into their boat.

'Guys, wait up,' Noa called, ignoring Alex's concern completely and tugging to fasten a life vest over her shoulders as fast as possible. The pre-cooking class outing suddenly felt like a wonderful idea if it got her off this dock.

Now the rain felt like the least of her worries, and she jumped into the coconut boat like it was her route to safety. Lola and Thea jumped in beside her and the boat rocked back and forth in a see-saw motion with the movement, until their weight balanced, and they were ready to set out onto the river.

Noa stared ahead as a man paddled them through the grey-green water that snaked a path through the densely packed forest. Tall fans of vibrant green leaves curled outwards over the river like umbrellas, but it wasn't quite enough to shade them from the rain that lashed down, bouncing off the water. The grey sky mirrored her own sombre mood and Noa turned to the girls, who were staring at her with questioning gazes.

'Don't,' Noa warned, hoping it would deter them from probing her to talk.

Instead, Lola and Thea shared a look that made her think she was about to be part of some kind of intervention.

'Why do I get the feeling I'm not going to like whatever you're about to say?' she groaned.

Thea nodded at Lola, and it made Noa laugh. They had all very much settled into their roles within the group and Lola, the most outgoing one of them, had somehow become a kind of spokesperson. But, if they needed Lola's tendency to not beat around the bush here, Noa worried about where this conversation was about to go. She shifted in her seat with anticipation.

'Well, I'd like to remind you that we are your friends, and we say this because we care,' Lola began.

Noa felt her heart pinch at that, because she knew it was true.

'We only speak the truth, and we have absolutely no control over how you react to that truth,' Lola reasoned in a manner that made her look like she was delivering some kind of presentation.

Noa almost burst out laughing at her serious expression but, somehow, managed to keep a straight face.

'Yeah, we wouldn't be very good friends if we didn't point out the glaringly obvious truth that you seem to be ignoring. Whether you like it or not,' Thea shrugged.

'Okay…' Noa said apprehensively. 'And the truth is?'

'Well, that man is hot as balls, could have any single woman in all of Southeast Asia, but he only has eyes for you. And you just ran away from him like he was a serial killer,' Lola said matter-of-factly.

'Eyes that he likes to fuck you with on a regular basis, no matter who's watching,' Thea added, wagging her brows. 'And, before you try to play dumb, the man we are referring to is Alex.'

'And if you really do think that the two of you are 'just friends', then, yes, it is time that we stage an intervention. So, what's going on?' Lola asked.

These girls. Noa felt so much love for them in such a small time, and these moments of girl talk with them would be some of the fondest memories of her whole trip. Even if they were currently being assaulted by rain from all angles as a tour guide spun their boat in circles. She knew she'd made friends for life and, staring at their serious faces now, she didn't know whether to roll her eyes, wrap them all in a hug, or burst out laughing.

Gripping the side of the boat, she went with the eye roll and decided to brush them off.

'You guys have lost your minds. If you knew his reputation back home, then you would know that Alex sees any hole as a goal. I am nothing special. In fact, if I wasn't Ryan's sister, I doubt he would even notice me at all,' she said, her own words stinging and tasting bitter as they left her mouth.

'Oh, girl. He would notice you,' Lola responded. 'And whether that was true or not before, I've not seen him take one girl home since you both arrived, but I have seen the way he looks at you. And it's not like a guy who sees you as any other single woman for pursuing. But I think you know that, too... so truthfully, what is actually holding you back?'

Noa sighed. They were so perceptive, and she did need someone to talk to about her feelings. Knowing she could trust them, she decided to finally admit the truth.

She told them about Ryan—the conversation she had overheard between him and Alex, and the offhanded comments he had made that felt like a warning over the years since. She told them a CliffsNotes version of why she felt protective over Ryan's and Alex's friendship, and why she didn't want to come between them. When she was done, she felt lighter. Unburdened.

'You know that's not your responsibility, though, right?' Lola pressed, looking Noa straight in the eyes for emphasis. 'You do not own their feelings, Noa. They are both big boys and their feelings and reactions are their own. You can't go about your life censoring yourself and denying yourself something that will make you happy just so you don't upset other people.'

'Do you really think that the feelings between you and Alex are wrong?' Thea asked, and Noa had to think about that for a minute before she shook her head. 'And have you ever stopped to think that, maybe, if your brother's relationship with his best friend couldn't survive this, then it is not as strong as you think?'

The truth was, Noa had never looked at it like that. And she knew that what the girls were saying was right. It was not her relationship to protect. And a realisation like that felt heavy.

As if trying to lighten the mood and rescue Noa from her own spiralling thoughts, Lola winked at her, nudging her with her shoulder before saying, 'I say you climb that man like a tree the next opportunity you get. Before someone else does.'

The thought of anyone else 'climbing Alex like a tree' more than rattled her.

She considered them, trying not to think about Alex with another woman as the conversation changed. But, as they pulled back up to the hut on the riverbank, and Alex came back into view exactly where she'd left him, she had one thing on her mind. Him.

# Chapter 27

## Alex

'Noaaaa,' Alex warned, dragging out her name for emphasis. 'I am not playing around right now. You are not getting on a moped on your own. I've been a reasonable man, but even I have my limits. I am putting my foot down. Over my dead body…'

Before he could even finish, he was forced to jump out of the road and press his back to the café wall. The five bikes that had threatened to either knock him on his ass or flatten him like a pancake just carried on their journey like nothing out of the ordinary had happened. Meanwhile, he tried to calm his racing pulse as Noa smirked into her fist, probably at the irony of it. Or because the little troublemaker enjoyed seeing him all flustered.

Hanoi was like a whole other planet. In his entire life, Alex had never been anywhere quite like it. He'd never been a city boy, preferring the small-town life, but he'd always thought London was busy. This place was next level and never stopped. The noise was constant, car and scooter horns being the main source. He wasn't even sure where all the people came from. He'd never been to a place so hectic.

Since the moment they arrived, he'd been on high alert, constantly needing to have a hand on Noa, scared that one of them was about to be taken out by the insane number of vehicles that flew through the streets with no particular rules of the road whatsoever.

Noa, however, had taken to it like a natural. He was surprised but, then again, she and Lola had been practically joined at the hip, so maybe she was rubbing off on her. Noa would walk out into the road like a local, shoulders held high, demanding that people stop for her. His stomach almost bottomed out every single time, and Alex couldn't wait to get her out of there safely and in one piece.

Today was their last day in Vietnam, and the reckless girl in front of him wanted to rent a moped as a means to travel around the city and see the sights. She must have bumped her head if she thought he was about to allow that. She'd tried saying that she'd added it to her '30 before 30' list to justify the act of lunacy, but there was absolutely no way in hell he was allowing it. If she wanted to go on a moped, he would take her so that he could keep her safe. All she needed to do was ask.

'No,' he stated, after he'd righted himself from his near miss with the other side.

His voice was firm and steady, leaving no room for her to question him. But that stubborn streak reared its head, meaning she would try anyway.

'I'm sorry? When was it that you think that I asked for your permission?' she argued with a serious face that would be so cute if she wasn't currently trying to put herself in danger.

'Noa,' he warned.

'Alex.'

She was absent-mindedly testing the stability of the moped as she sat on it, like he wasn't standing there warning her otherwise. Testing his patience, too.

He was already irritated by the humidity that hung in the air and the inconvenience it caused. The monsoon they'd been caught in during their time in Hoi An had drenched their clothes, and drying anything here felt like trying to start a fire with ice. His jean shorts now felt rough on his skin and his T-shirt clung to him in an uncomfortable way that had his fuse already pulled short.

So, Noa trying to take risks today? Not happening.

The excitement on her face was adorable, but he ignored how her smile made his stomach flip, putting her safety at the forefront of his mind. He loved seeing the carefree, spontaneous Noa, but this was just reckless.

'Those things are a death-trap, and don't even get me started on the roads,' he stated, waving in the direction of the chaotic side streets outside the café entrance that they were currently blocking.

They happened to rent out mopeds at this particular café and, God, was he wishing now that they had stopped somewhere else for breakfast. In the space of five minutes, he'd ordered and been to the toilet only to come out to find her straddling this death-on-wheels outside.

'Honestly, you call me the dramatic one, but you are being such a baby about this,' she pouted.

The action sent a warning bolt of electricity through his body. No, he couldn't think about what it would be like to pull that plump lip in between his teeth. Now was not the time. He quickly rid himself of his inappropriate thoughts to deal with the current task at hand.

'I don't care what you want to call me. As I said, over my dead body are you getting on one of those things on your own. I will not be peeling you off the road, Noa. I don't plan on having to call your brother to tell him I failed to do the one thing I promised him I would. Be smarter.'

Questioning her intelligence seemed to rattle her for a second, but then he saw the mischievous glint in her eyes return and he knew he wasn't going to like whatever was coming. It was almost as if she liked torturing him and seeing how far she could push him, like she was trying to make it as hard as possible to keep her safe. It was infuriating. And the grin on her face said she knew it. He wanted to bend her over his knee and smack that perfect ass of hers, punish her for arguing with him and driving him crazy like this. He wanted to show her who was really the boss. He wanted to, but he wouldn't.

'Fine,' she said, shrugging her shoulders casually.

Fine? She couldn't be giving in that easily, could she? He felt uneasy at her calm tone now, like he was walking into a trap, but he just couldn't see it yet.

'Fine?'

'Yes, fine. I'm not *unreasonable*.'

He sighed, relief flooding him for a moment but, before he knew what was happening, Noa was waving someone in their direction from over his shoulder. As Marcus appeared, she whispered in his ear, then he hopped on the back of the moped, wrapping his arms around her tightly. Alex stepped forward, his fists balled at his sides, ready to rip him from the moped.

But then, Noa looked at him with defiance in those eyes and said, 'Like you said, I shouldn't go on my own. So, I won't.'

And, with that, she sped off into the busy streets, with Marcus grinning like all his Christmases had come at once. He looked like the cat that got the cream and, as they drove away, the bastard shot Alex a wink over his shoulder. A fucking wink that had the hairs rising on his arms as he pictured all the ways he wanted to make him regret it.

Watching Noa leave, her hair dancing in the wind behind her, Alex felt a familiar sting in his chest. He stood there, alone, watching her disappear into the crowded street, leaving him behind like she always was.

He was unable to control the rage and fear overpowering him and, unlike Marcus, Noa didn't look back.

Shoulders slumped and feeling heavy, Alex walked through the hostel, praying to make it back to his room without having to socialise with anyone. He wasn't company worth keeping in that moment, and he needed to go and pull himself together. He needed to figure out his next move, because it was becoming more and more clear that, with Noa, he was only seeing what he wanted to see.

That, maybe, he'd imagined the chemistry that seemed to pulse like a constant undercurrent between them. That, in all of this, he'd been the hopeless one, pining for the girl who would never see him as more. And nothing had ever changed.

Coming here had been a mistake. Once Noa and Marcus left, Alex spent hours aimlessly wandering the streets, thinking about nothing else. After all, she'd said it before. She was a grown woman that didn't need his protection, so what had he hoped to achieve? Time and time again her actions had made her disinterest clear. Maybe it was finally time to listen.

But why did that feel so wrong?

As he walked past the pool tables that took up the social area of the hostel lobby, familiar voices carried in his direction with a familiar name on their lips.

'He's finally gone and done it, you know. Noa was clearly gagging for it when he got on the back of that bike. It looks like his plan's coming together,' came from a guy Alex had seen hanging around Marcus, but he hadn't learnt his name.

Slowing his pace, he kept his eyes low, not wanting to give his presence away. He knew they were talking about Noa, and the direction the conversation was heading made his skin hot, but he needed to hear more.

'Oh, come on, there's still time to fuck it up yet,' was someone's retort.

'It's a watertight plan. Marcus said once they come back, he'll take her out for some drinks. She loosened up after some rum last time, remember?' the first dickhead sniggered.

'Remember? It's all he's droned on about. That and how quickly he'd be able to get her on her knees.'

'Yeah, I think he's hoping his charm will have worn her down enough that, after a few cocktails, tonight will be his lucky night.'

The asshole's casual tone had Alex balling his fists and wanting to teach him a lesson, but he also wanted to listen to anything that could help him keep Noa safe. So, instead, he just bit the inside of his cheek to stop himself from erupting and quietly listened to their conversation.

'That's fucked. But also, I don't buy it. She couldn't be less interested. He just needs to give it up... It's not like there isn't plenty more actually available women around here.'

'And less dangerous ones at that. If Alex finds out, Marcus may as well get a flight back home. I wouldn't like to be on the receiving end of that when it blows up.'

And wasn't that the truth.

Having heard enough, Alex stormed out of the lobby toward his room.

Once he got inside, he didn't even bother to close the door before he began pacing.

*Fuck.*

Should he go looking for her? The dipshits downstairs seemed to think they'd be coming back, but was that a risk he was willing to take? The thought of anyone taking advantage of a woman like that, let alone Noa, made him feel sick. He had to muster all the strength in him to fight the nausea that threatened to fold him over.

If Marcus so much as laid a finger on her...

Just then, Alex's thoughts were interrupted by the sound of conversation outside his door. It was still ajar, and the sweet sound of Noa's voice felt like an instant balm for his anxiety.

Christ, was this what she dealt with every day?

He didn't know how she did it. The past twenty minutes were confirmation that she was the strongest person he knew.

The calm didn't last long, though, as her voice was followed by one that had his jaw crunching with the strength of his gritted teeth. Marcus's flirtatious tone grew closer as the next words spilled from his mouth.

'I just thought, why end it here? Maybe we could go for—'

And just like that, Alex knew he couldn't hold back.

# Chapter 28

## Noa

Arriving back at the hostel after a full day of sightseeing, and feeling proud of the rise that she managed to get out of Alex earlier that morning, Noa sauntered toward her room. It had been a busy day and they'd made no plans for the evening, so she had decided that a date with her Kindle and her bed to recharge was exactly what she needed. They had an early flight to the Philippines the next day, and she didn't want to be exhausted when they arrived.

'Noa, wait up,' Marcus called, jogging down the corridor behind her.

The two of them had spent the whole day together and, despite enjoying his company, there was no deep connection there. No spark or heat. No desire. All the day had done was reinforce how much she felt those things for a man that she couldn't help but feel like she shouldn't. As Marcus moved toward her now, she felt unease spread inside her as she also wasn't sure that he shared her feelings. Or lack thereof, as it was.

'Hey. Are you okay?' she asked.

'Yes, I'm more than okay. That was one hell of a first date,' he beamed, and she just continued to stare at him.

*First date? Shit.* Had she blurred the lines and lead him on, or was he trying his luck? It was hard to tell when it came to Marcus, so she just waited for him to continue.

'I usually get what I want and, I have to say, you drive a hard bargain, Noa. You're quite good at giving a guy the run-around. But the wait was worth it.'

Was he for real?

She gaped at him, not hiding her shock. This year was set on trying to swear her off men, she was sure of it.

'Marcus...'

He didn't let her finish, just leaned in close enough that she had to back into the wall.

'I just thought, why end it here? Maybe we could go for—'

Quicker than she could process, he was cut off by a fist that came flying in his direction. A cracking sound filled the air and Noa gasped. Alex charged at Marcus, pinning him against the wall. Noa's heart beat more rapidly.

In fact, it felt like it may break free from her chest any moment.

'Jesus fuck—' Marcus cursed as he wiped at his nose and tried to shake himself free of Alex's grip.

'Be very careful with those next words,' Alex snarled.

Noa hadn't seen this side of him in a long time. Not since they were younger. Not since he'd been abandoned by his dad and been that lonely boy across the street. The realisation hit her with the force of a brick. She'd left him. He'd asked her to stay, not to go on the moped on her own, and she'd chosen to ignore him. Not only that, but she'd chosen to take Marcus over him. She was such an idiot and, now knowing that all she had done was feed into Alex's deeply embedded fears, she wished she could take it all back. Even if Alex had never expressly said it, Noa knew him well enough to know that he'd been left with abandonment issues after his dad left. She had been so careless with his feelings. His face told her that as he turned to her, and she could see the hurt in his eyes.

'I warned you, Noa,' he growled.

She felt like her eyes had doubled in size, and she just gulped down the lump that had formed in her throat. She couldn't find an appropriate response before he continued.

'I told you. I told you if you let another one of these men touch what they don't deserve, then I wouldn't be responsible for what came next.'

There was so much anger in his tone, but she could still see the hurt and even fear, if she wasn't mistaken.

'You're fucking crazy,' came from Marcus, whose eyes were wide as he glowered at Alex.

Noa paid him no attention, focussing only on Alex. He really did care for her. Behind the tough guy act and angry bravado, he cared. But this didn't feel like the way a friend cared for another friend, or like protection for the sake of her brother. This felt deeper. Real. More.

It was that thought that made her move toward him, slowly, as if he was a bomb that she didn't want to go off. She placed her hands on his, pulling, and slowly removing them from where they still held Marcus against the wall, who just stood there, dazed and a little exasperated, his head whipping between them both.

As Alex's hands fell away, Marcus mumbled something that sounded like, 'I am not getting involved in this shit,' and scurried off.

Alex loomed over her, chest heaving and nose flaring. He looked feral. He was so angry, but she wasn't scared of him. She did need to defuse the situation, however.

'I'm sorry,' she whispered, trying to pour all her remorse into those words, and grabbing his hands in the hope he would feel it.

They were big compared to hers and she could feel the callouses there from all the days he'd spent putting work in at the bar.

He grabbed the back of her head, pulling her forehead against his so that they were staring right into each other's eyes, and whispered back, 'You are so goddamn reckless sometimes, Noa.'

She didn't know what to say, so she just stayed there, letting him know that she was with him and that she was safe. What had started off as a fun game to mess with Alex had turned into so much more, and she knew her growing feelings were going to catch up with her soon. She felt them in every cell in her body now, every fibre of her being came alive for this man.

'You drive me crazy. Do you know that?'

Alex's eyes softened, the anger dissipating, like all he'd needed was to touch her and have her close. She knew she'd been reckless, and nothing was probably more so than what she was about to say.

'Show me,' she breathed.

'Show you what, Trouble?'

The pet name that had always gotten under her skin felt more like an endearment now, and it sounded sexy as hell coming from his lips.

'How crazy I make you.'

She was breathy, and her heartbeat thrummed in her ears. Everything else around them fell away and Noa forgot where they were, forgot they were in public. But then, Alex was reaching behind him to the closest door which, conveniently, must have been his own. That's how he'd got to her and Marcus so quickly, she realised.

Then she was pulled inside, the door being closed behind her, and she was swallowed by darkness.

# Chapter 29

## Alex

It took Alex a moment for his eyes to readjust to the darkness of his room, only the light bleeding in from the street lights outside providing any ability to see.

'Say that again,' he demanded.

'Show me.'

Her voice was shaky, and he knew she was trembling, proof that he affected her just as much as she did him.

'You don't know what you are asking for, Noa.'

He knew that she had talked about a rebound in the past, but if she thought any of this was a one-and-done situation, then she was mistaken. It was taking everything in Alex to hold back right now to make sure she knew that.

If she thought he was a good choice because of all his one-night stands in the past, he needed her to know that applied to everyone but her. He had never felt this way around any other woman, felt so undone. Because she'd always felt like more. Her eyes had always been the only ones that had made him feel truly seen. Her lips had always been the only ones he craved. She'd always been the only one he'd been able to share his fears with, who'd seen through his anger and challenged it, challenged him. Understood.

So, now, he wanted all of her. Not just one night. It wasn't enough then, and it wouldn't be enough now.

She looked down, like she was suddenly self-conscious. His hesitance had made her question whether or not he wanted her, and that he couldn't have. Placing his forefinger and thumb against her chin, he lifted it so that she was gazing up at him.

'You don't want this, Noa. You never did. Not back then anyway, and I will not be your rebound guy. I will not have you only to watch you walk out on me again.'

'I want this. I *need* this,' she whispered. 'I don't know what I'm doing, Alex. All I know is that *this* feels right. I overthink and analyse every aspect of my life, and I don't want to do that now. Not with this. Not with you. Please don't ask me to.'

She was looking at him with pleading eyes.

The tension crackled between them like static electricity. The room felt smaller than it did minutes ago, and something inside him snapped. The last thread of control he had over his untameable desire for her, it seemed.

'Fuck it,' he rasped, and in the next breath, he was on her.

His lips crashed to hers and she opened up for him like her lips had been made for him. He licked a trail across them before she gasped, and he took the opportunity to nip at her full bottom lip before he kissed her again to sooth the sting she likely felt.

Nothing had felt like this since that night. No one's lips felt like home the way hers did.

Grabbing her under her thighs he lifted her into his arms easily and pressed her back to the wall. Her breath caught in her throat, and he knew she could feel how hard he was right now. He smiled into her neck as he planted little kisses there. Her skin was hot, and he loved knowing that he had done this to her. She should know what she did to him, too.

'That's all on you baby,' he rasped, as he pushed his hips into her, grinding himself against her centre.

A gasp escaped her lips, followed by a whimper, and it sounded like heaven. She grabbed his hair, pulling his mouth back up to hers. This greedy girl, asking for exactly what she wanted.

They were fully clothed, and yet this already felt so much more fervent and wilder than their first time. Back then, they'd been quiet, gentle, maybe a little unsure of themselves. But this version of Noa was letting him know what she liked, and that elicited a feral need in him to give it to her.

And he *would* give it to her. He would give it to her every single time. They kissed, and there was nothing gentle about it. It was hard and passionate, and as his tongue slipped into her mouth, exploring her, he knew he would never get enough of this. He kissed her until they were both breathless and panting, then he pulled away and rested his head against hers.

'You make me so greedy for you, Noa. I want everything that's happened here, but I want to be patient with you. I won't rush this,' he managed to get out, even though all he wanted to do was rip her clothes off and explore every inch of her incredible body.

He'd rushed before. This time, he wanted to worship her like she deserved, to make it impossible for her to ever leave again, to unravel her the way she had unravelled him. He wanted to see her come undone for him over and over. He'd thought of nothing else since she had walked back into his life.

But it was the thought that she had left before, and could easily leave again, that kept him from going any further. He wanted to be patient with this, to make sure she wanted this the same way he did. After all, when it came to him, people didn't tend to stick around. For all he knew, this could just be a holiday fling for her. A rebound. But, on the off-chance that she did want more, he'd wait until she realised it and he was certain he wouldn't be left in the dust again. He wouldn't survive the loss of her again.

She just nodded, but he could see the disappointment in her eyes. He didn't want that. He wanted her to know that she could have all of him when the time was right.

'It will be worth the wait,' he said before grinding into her one last time, then, begrudgingly, putting her down. She swayed a little before she got her balance and looked at him again with glazed eyes and a wide smile.

'It'll be worth the wait,' she agreed.

# Chapter 30

## Noa

Noa stood on the jetty in Coron, waiting to board the boat that would take them on a four-day expedition to El Nido. It was the part of her travels she had most looked forward to, having heard so many amazing reviews online. She'd be island-hopping each day and camping in tents and huts each night. It sounded like an experience so stripped back from reality, and she was so excited.

But the fluttering in her stomach as she watched people busy loading colourful wooden boats with all their gear, were not caused by her anticipation for the trip.

No. They were a result of her thoughts constantly wandering to her and Alex's kiss days earlier. Though 'kiss' felt like too tame a description for what they had shared.

Her phone buzzed in her hand, and she pulled her eyes from the turquoise waters to see the family group chat.

The Fab 4:

---

Mum:

I need numbers for Christmas dinner. Noa, are you going to be back by then?

Ryan:

Mum it's April!

Mum:

We are in all new territory here. How am I supposed to know how long this quarter-life crisis will last?

Ryan:

It's all so Eat Pray Love of her.

Dad:

She can't be expected to be gone that long or she'd be asking for a loan from the bank of dad.

Noa:

You guys know I'm in this group right? I could just leave if that's easier for you to speculate about me.

Ryan:

Don't worry, we have our 'favourite child' group specifically for that.

Mum:

You named it that.

Ryan:

You didn't deny it.

Mum:

Give me strength

Noa:

Ry, it never ceases to amaze me how you have space for a single other thought in your brain with an ego that size.

I'll send across my flight details. We decided to prolong the trip, so we have a couple of weeks left in the Philippines and then we are heading home.

Ryan:

Did everyone here witness that? She definitely just called them 'we' and that was definitely a sad face. I am glad to see you guys are finally getting along!

Getting along was definitely one way to put it. Noa had replayed that night in Hanoi in her mind over and over the last several days, to the point where she was sure her thoughts were obvious for everyone around her to see. She didn't think that she had the ability to hide them at this point.

The way his calloused hands had grabbed her, his firm grip making it feel like he owned every inch of her body. His warm, soft lips on hers, commanding she open up for him and kiss him with everything she had. And, boy, had she. She had melted into him, met his lips with abandon. It was exhilarating, a high she wanted to keep chasing with him.

But, in the several days since, she had felt a crash landing back to planet earth after her brother had sent her several texts to check in. She thought he'd likely sent them to Alex, too, because the guilty look he kept giving her had her questioning everything.

She wanted him. And he wanted her. That was all clear as day now. But was it enough to get past the huge roadblock that had always stood in their way? Was it enough to risk Alex's friendship with Ryan? She knew she couldn't be the one to answer that. She had tried to do what was right the first time, when she had considered her feelings for him a long time ago. She had taken the decision out of Alex's hands and made it for him. She had tried to forget him and walk away. But she wouldn't do that this time. She couldn't. Maybe she was a stronger woman back then but, when she came home this time, she told herself she would be selfish and go after the things she wanted in life. That's what her entire list was about at the end of the day. And the selfish part of her wanted him.

Then, there was the other part of her that couldn't help but consider the fact that she hadn't long broken up with Lucas. Only two months had gone by. She should be sad, shouldn't she? She should be sniffling into tissues and vowing to never go near another man again. And yet, Alex didn't just feel like another man. She felt safe around him, like it had always been her and him, but they had both just been too scared to see it. She didn't know what that said about her relationship with Lucas, but she had always tried to believe that everything happens for a reason. And lately, every time she thought of Lucas, she didn't feel sad. Just grateful for the good times that they had shared and the lessons she had learnt from both their relationship and the breakup. So, she refused to let her brain overthink this, to talk her out of it again. She would not let fear dictate her life anymore. Life had given her and Alex a second chance, and she was determined not to waste it.

Deciding to put her busy thoughts to good use, Noa had been writing a lot over the past week. She'd found it a cathartic outlet to help her make sense of things. She used her own experiences to shape her characters and her storyline in a roundabout way, and she was enjoying the process. Alex had been right, travelling the world really did spark artistic inspiration in her. She just couldn't help the words from flowing.

She kept the book he'd bought her close by at all times, because she didn't know when an idea was going to hit and she'd have to quickly scribble it down. She still couldn't get over how thoughtful he had been to get it for her. These small, meaningful gestures, like acts of service when she thought about it, were such a contradiction to the tall, dark, and broody-looking man that sat in front of her. He was an enigma in many ways. A riddle she wanted desperately to work out.

She felt like Alex liked to watch her write, because he seemed to do so at any opportunity he got, barely taking his eyes off her. The butterflies that knowledge set off in her stomach were equally as distracting as they were pleasurable. He'd been making her feel all kinds of ways lately, and it was getting harder and harder not to just pounce on the man any time he was near.

And that's what she was doing now. Writing. Or, something like that. As they sat on the open-top boat that was sailing them from Coron to El Nido, she kept finding herself trying to write anything she could to feel his eyes on her.

Staring down at her page, it was clear to see that all she'd really been doing was daydreaming about a certain handsome bartender as a list of his best physical attributes stared back at her.

-Rock hard, lickable abs
-Firm, bitable ass
-Plush, kissable lips

Eyeing the page, Noa worried that cannibalism had made it into her list of kinks and that, maybe, she really had been reading too many dark romance books. Was that all she wanted to do, explore him with her mouth? Maybe.

She felt her cheeks heat and, as if he could read her thoughts, Alex's lips tugged up into a grin as he continued to assess her from across the small boat. Something had definitely changed. He was much more obvious about it. Lola had teased her about his ogling, but Noa revelled in it.

Keeping her eyes on him, she decided she would do the same. He had no business being that sexy. Her pulse raced and her palms were sweaty as she squeezed her thighs together. The sight of him elicited a full body response she wasn't sure anyone had ever made her feel before. not even Lucas. The thought was depressing, but also exhilarating all at the same time.

His skin had a bronze glow now, after so much time spent in the sun. His eyes shone brightly, like pools of deep honey, as the light hit them, and his sharp jaw line was peppered in a dusting of light stubble. She had to make a conscious effort to not let her eyes stray south to his naked torso, as she had a funny feeling she might not be able to stop herself from drooling if she did.

With the confidence that having his amber eyes raking over her gave her, Noa closed her book and pushed herself up as the boat came to a stop at their second-to-last island for the day. Making sure to add a little extra sway to her hips and push her chest out just enough, she made her way over to him.

'Take a picture, Fletcher, it'll last longer,' she teased and pouted her lips.

His gaze focussed on them like she'd planned, and she pulled her bottom lip into her mouth, wishing he would replace her lips with his and do the same. Wishing he would do a lot more than that, but it would be a start. Just the thought left a needy, throbbing ache between her legs.

'Oh, Trouble,' he said rising to his feet and resting his lips close enough so only she could hear.

As he spoke, she felt his breath on her neck, spreading goose bumps across her skin.

'Last longer? You have no idea what I remember when it comes to you, picture or not. Your perfect body under mine is engraved in my mind's eye forever.'

She felt all the breath leave her lungs. When she first arrived home, she'd thought he'd forgotten her and that night, that he'd replaced thoughts of her with the many women that followed after.

But he'd kept proving otherwise, and as he looked at her dead in the eyes now, he almost knocked her off her feet when he said, 'It's only ever been you.'

She could swear her heart threatened to stop. She felt hot all over, and it had nothing to do with the sun shining above them. She wanted to ask him so much more. She wanted to wrap herself in him, and for them to get lost in each other. But she was pulled from her momentary daydream when she realised that they were, in fact, on a boat full of people. She tried her best to look back at him and talk through the lump in her throat.

'Care for a swim to cool down?'

'Be careful what you wish for,' he responded with a wicked grin before picking her up bridal style and launching them both from the side of the boat.

Kicking up and reaching the surface, she reached out for him instinctively. Within moments he grabbed hold of her and pulled her close enough for her to wrap her legs around him, in a way that felt awfully similar to the other night. He'd clearly been tossed a float, and he lounged back on it with a smirk whilst she clung to him. His muscles flexed under her palms, and the feel of it had her legs tightening around his hips, pulling him closer to her core.

Alex chuckled like he saw right through her.

'You're dead,' she threatened, in an attempt at a serious tone, before she put all her effort into splashing him with the salty water.

Her efforts were soon cut off as he easily wrapped her in his arms, nipping playfully at her ear in an attempt to stop her water assault. She shoved her hips back, trying to get free, but the move only resulted in her grinding into his crotch. Noa could feel him growing harder against her. The feeling was intoxicating, sending tiny sparks of electricity through her entire body.

'Careful, Trouble,' he growled into her ear again.

The raspy sound of his voice caused the bundle of nerves between her legs to throb. No one had ever had this effect on her just by their voice, and her sudden need to see what else he could do made her dizzy.

'A man's restraint only goes so far... I would hate for it to break with an audience just over there.'

Alex's roaming hands gave her ass and thighs a firm squeeze under the water, and she ached for more, audience be damned. But, before she could voice her needy thoughts, the tour guide called their stop to an end, and they were shepherded back to the boat.

Noa wanted to curse and scream at their guide like a stroppy teenager. Alex just smiled a devilish grin at her while she sat there dazed and feeling like a horny teenager all over again.

The four days and three nights on the exhibition to El Nido had truly been a once-in-a-lifetime experience. They'd met so many new people, and Noa couldn't remember the last time she had felt as free as she had here. Any real world problems just seemed to fade away when they were sailing through the ocean with no real itinerary, merely a final destination in mind. Not having a plan had never felt so good. Despite the growing tension and desire between her and Alex, they had both managed to keep it on a leash long enough to focus solely on this experience and nothing else.

After her diving lessons in Koh Tao, Noa felt much more comfortable underwater, allowing her to make the most of every single swim stop on their journey. Every island they stopped at on their way was so different. She snorkelled around every single one, exploring anything from the huge coral reefs, which were home to an abundance of marine life, to old shipwrecks, which blew her mind.

The water was like nothing she had ever seen, an endless expanse of a kaleidoscope of blues, only highlighted by the sun beaming down on it. The peacefulness of every secluded island they stopped at brought with them a stillness that one could only dream of experiencing. Or so Noa thought. It truly was like experiencing a slice of paradise, and 'grateful' did not even begin to describe how Noa felt about her time there.

They played games, cooked barbecues, dived off rocks, explored sand banks, and drank out of enough coconuts for a lifetime. Each night, they either pitched up tents or stayed in quaint little wooden huts, and it was like something out of a fever dream. If heaven was a place on earth, this would be it. A tropical nirvana.

From the white, sandy cove where they had docked for the evening, Noa watched their boat bob up and down, guided by the rhythm of the waves. Her breathing seemed to have slowed to mirror the same rhythm, and she felt at peace. Colourful birds, that Noa assumed were parrots, flew overhead toward the various rock formations covered in non-deciduous plant life, that jutted out of the water.

Laid back, sprawled in a hammock between two palm trees, Noa closed her eyes and enjoyed the shade they provided. The day was creeping into evening, and everyone was getting ready for their group dinner of local Filipino dishes. So, Noa was enjoying the quiet this time allowed. She could hear nothing but the lapping of waves against the shoreline and the constant singing of cicadas from within the shrubs. The gentle swaying of the hammock had nearly lulled her to sleep when she felt water drip onto her chest.

*Is it raining?* Opening one eye to look up, she was blessed with the sight of a shirtless man towering above her. Not only that, but a shirtless man currently sporting a wet-hair look that was pushed back out of his face. His broad chest was covered in water droplets that she wanted to trace with her finger as they trickled down, down, down. Her eyes stopped in a place they probably shouldn't before she quickly lifted them back to his. Alex smirked at her, and she knew she had been caught with her hand in the cookie jar.

'Evening swim?' she asked like it wasn't the most stupid question in the world.

That much was obvious, but she was clutching at straws to try to distract from gawking. She was flustered and couldn't think of any other words, but he allowed it and, luckily, didn't tease her about it. She didn't think her brain could think of one witty comeback right now.

Choosing to ignore her question, he asked her one of his own, and it was something Noa was not expecting.

Nodding his head over to the opening in the cabins where the rest of the group seemed to be huddled around the barbeque, Alex started, 'Looks like dinner will be ready soon, but I was hoping, maybe, you'd like to join me to watch the sunset on the beach this evening. It's not quite a viewpoint like on your list, but the view is incredible. And we could lie and watch the stars for a bit afterwards. There's no light pollution out here. I don't think you'll find a better stargazing spot, even if you tried.'

He paused as if expecting her to protest before he continued, 'Two things ticked off your list for the price of one.'

Noa smiled up at him.

'Wow, I don't think I've ever heard you speak so many words at once,' she joked, because if she didn't make light of the situation, she might throw herself into his arms for how thoughtful he was being.

This man had supported her at every turn, and she hadn't realised how much she had needed that. She had always wanted to be her own person, to be able to stand on her own two feet and not need anyone to hold her up. But he never made her feel like that. It was like he just wanted to be there beside her whilst she worked on her goals, and to be there for her to lean on if she asked.

He rolled his eyes at her teasing and kicked the sand, 'Do you know what? Forget it. Maybe Lola's free. She's better company than you anyway.'

Noa gasped in mock offence and let her hand hit her chest.

'You will never get better company than me, Alex Fletcher, and it'd benefit you not to forget that.'

'Don't I know it,' he replied.

The look on his face was so sincere she knew he really meant it. This man valued her and enjoyed spending time with her for exactly who she was.

'Well, okay then,' she said. 'But I am starving. So, let's go fill our bellies, because even my sunshiny personality has its limits when I'm hangry. But, after that, I am sure I can move some things around so I can spend the evening with you, seeing as you asked so nicely and all.

She winked at him as she moved from the hammock so that that they could do exactly that.

# Chapter 31

## Noa

Since shortly after finishing dinner, Noa had felt off. Her stomach seemed to be protesting about something, and the churning she felt there had bile rising up her throat on numerous occasions. Was she getting sick? Regardless, she refused to let it ruin this time with Alex. Was it stupid that it almost felt like they were on a date? After all the time they had spent together whilst on their trip, this one night shouldn't have felt any different.

But it did.

They sat shoulder to shoulder on the chalky sand. The cove they occupied felt sheltered, adding to the intimacy, with the rocks jutting out of the island around them and continuing into the water, the waves licking at the base of them.

If only she could get her increasing nausea to settle, then the night would be perfect. She shoved it down, choosing to ignore the sweat starting to gather at the nape of her neck.

They watched the most incredible sunset. A mirage of colours illuminated the sky like a wildfire rising from the still serenity of the dark sea. Watching it brought a calmness over both of them. They simply sat there, in each other's company, letting the sun make its final retreat for the day.

Once night descended, they laid back on the soft sand that warmed their backs and were easily swept into deep conversation. Alex asked her questions about her life since she'd left town and her dreams for the future, listening attentively like everything she said was the most interesting thing in the world. She never once felt like she was too much, too boring, too emotional, or any of the other things she had felt when talking to men in the past. He made her feel seen and important.

'You always used to talk about being an author one day. I see you scribbling your ideas in that book now, and your face lights up. Do you think you could make a go at the writing thing?' Alex asked.

And, compared to when she'd had conversations with Lucas about changing her career, Alex actually sounded supportive of the concept. She felt like she could get excited about it with him, and he would get excited back.

She'd been questioning whether it was too late to change career paths for a while, whether she was being naive to think she could make a living from her writing.

The anxiety around that, and the voice in her head telling her she couldn't, had won out until now. The voice of Lucas as he said, 'Do you even know how many books an author has to write to breakeven?' only reinforced it.

His question had been an insult in so many ways. One, because she had made a career out of helping authors reach their goals, so the fact he doubted she knew what she was doing irritated her to no end. But the fact he clearly didn't think she could do it had only fuelled her imposter syndrome.

'I'd love to. I really would. It just seems so scary. I wonder if it's too late,' Noa now admitted to Alex.

'It's never too late, Noa. Maybe now's the perfect time. Maybe all the work you've put into editing has only led you here, given you the tools to finally make your own dreams come true. But you'll never know unless you try. You can forge a new path whenever you choose to. But you *do* have to choose it. Nothing comes to you unless you grab it.'

His words meant more than he would ever know. She mulled them over for a while, really letting them sink in.

Was she really her greatest barrier? Could it be as easy as just taking that first step toward the life she wanted?

Noa barely noticed the passing of time as they continued to lie there, talking about everything and nothing. It was the perfect night, just the two of them under the blanket of stars that lit up the night sky.

The scene felt familiar, in a way, and Alex must have thought so, too, because it didn't take long for him to see straight through her and say, 'I didn't expect this to still be on your list, but I am glad to be back here.'

'I don't know what you mean,' Noa answered, raising her hand to her chest in an attempt to feign innocence.

'You mean you didn't decide you wanted to count the stars because a twenty-one-year-old version of me told you that you couldn't? Because your stubbornness refused to let that go. Because I know you Noa, and that would be a lie!'

Noa thought back to that night. It hadn't been long before her twentieth birthday party. She'd walked home from her bar job, where she'd been saving money for university. She spotted Alex on the swings of Freymoor's play park, kicking at the ground as he swung back and forth. She'd felt a need to make sure he was okay, something instinctual telling her he needed a friend.

They sat in comfortable silence at first, cloaked in the darkness of the night sky if it wasn't for the light from the winking of the stars breaking through.

Noa had broken the silence first.

*'A leftover Starburst for your thoughts,' she said, pulling a green, misshapen sweet from the depth of her pocket.*

*Alex grimaced.*

*'Is that all they're worth?' he joked. 'That's the worst flavour. I should be offended.'*

*Noa smiled at him sweetly, batting her eyelashes overdramatically in a way she did when she wanted something. He rolled his eyes at her, but the expression was filled with amusement.*

*'Okay, well, what about sharing them with a friend who cares for free?'*

*She could have sworn his shoulders sagged a little at her use of the word 'friend', but before she could give it much thought, he was speaking.*

*'I just. I... I feel bad all the time. My mum's exhausted. She came home tonight and could barely stand up straight. She's never at home. Always working, always making up for him.'*

*Noa didn't have to ask who the 'him' was that Alex was referring to, and she felt the need to reach out to him, to comfort him somehow, hating the scars his dad had left on his heart. She was glad this was never something he had hidden from her, because the weight must have been so heavy to carry alone.*

*'She's emotionally and financially trying to be two parents at once. I'm trying to work and save to start a business, to make a future for myself, but I feel like such a selfish prick when I see her burnt out like she has been my entire life. Because we were never even worth that to him. A few lousy pounds every month to the spawn you fathered would simply be too much to ask.'*

*She sensed his anger. But also, the hurt. He had insinuated many times that he thought his dad leaving was a reflection on him, and she hated that the most.*

*'Your mum loves you, Alex. She probably didn't see her life turning out exactly like this, but I know, given the opportunity to do it all again, even if she had the opportunity to have all the freedom and money in the world, she would choose this. Choose you every single time.'*

*Alex didn't respond. He just sat there looking younger than she had seen him in a while. So, she continued, needing him to really hear her.*

*'You are a person worth knowing, Alex. And I only feel sorry for him that he doesn't get to. I hope he regrets that until his dying day, because his shortcomings are his to bear and his alone. None of it is on you.'*

*She reached out for his hand then. And, although his eyes remained on the ground, he nodded and his lips turned up at the sides into a half-smile. She loved being the reason he smiled.*

*He lifted his eyes to the sky, continuing to slowly swing back and forth.*

*'I bet you can't count the stars,' he challenged, clearly trying to lighten the mood.*

*Noa saw it for what it was, a distraction. She took his cue, if for no other reason than he knew she couldn't back down from a challenge.*

*Gazing at the twinkling lights in the sky proved harder than she thought, though. They lulled her into a relaxed state, her concentration waning, and she constantly lost track of where she was. The more she tried to focus, the more stars seemed to appear.*

*He chuckled next to her, like he thought he'd won. Her eyes cut to him, and she narrowed them.*

*'You know, you've caught me on a bad day. I'm tired. But I promise you this Alex Fletcher, I will count all those stars one day.'*

From the beach, Alex watched her, and she thought maybe he had been lost in the memory, too.

'I thought you'd have counted them ten times over by now. You're never usually one to drag your feet when it comes to a challenge,' he joked.

But, for some reason, the joke made something inside her feel like it was sinking. It was a reminder of how much she had lost herself.

A light from a boat caught her attention in the distance as it rocked in time with the waves. That was what her twenties had felt like, she thought, being lost at sea with no idea which direction to take. She wasn't where she had pictured herself being when she was a young girl. But then, did she want that? Or did she want to forge a whole new path and set off in a different direction with a destination she had never planned for? Or would continuing on the same route she had been be the safest bet?

She, honestly, felt like she could imagine ten different versions of her life for herself, and she was running out of time to do them all. And the prospect of picking one felt overwhelming.

This had always been her problem, her inability to go with the flow and let life work itself out. It was something she longed to be able to do.

'There are a lot of things I thought I'd have done, that I said I would do, but have been forgotten, somehow,' Noa whispered, not knowing if she was only talking to herself.

But Alex heard, and his eyes softened. But not in pity. Understanding.

'Whatever you want to do, Noa, you can make it happen. But just know, you don't need all the answers right now. Maybe just being here and enjoying the moment can be enough?'

She nodded, because for some reason, she felt like if this was all she had, moments in time like this with him, then it really would be enough.

When Noa wrote that list almost three months ago, she could never have envisaged this in a thousand years and yet, Alex had. He had remembered what she had written and made it happen.

And the fact that it felt like a déjà vu moment made it even more significant.

The longer they lay there, the closer their bodies seemed to move toward each other without their permission, like there was a gravitational pull between them, until they were practically cuddled into each other on the beach.

'Alex.'

'Yes, Trouble?'

There was something she'd been dying to ask him, but every time she'd tried, the words got caught in her throat and she'd been too embarrassed to speak them aloud.

'Why have you never been in a relationship? I mean, not that there's anything wrong with that. I promise, I'm not judging. I'm just curious is all. I know there have been a lot of women and...'

'You been keeping tabs on me?' Alex smirked towards the sky, like he had been loving every second of her ramblings and he was not going to put her out of her misery just yet.

'Well, when you and my brother practically live in each other's pockets, it's not exactly hard,' she quipped. 'In fact, it's impossible not to.'

He turned his head from the stars to look at Noa then, 'You really want to know?'

'I wouldn't have asked if I didn't,' she whispered, because the moment felt too intimate to be shared.

'Well, as you so politely put it, there have been a lot of women, but there has only ever been one who felt worth working on my insecurities for. It feels embarrassing to admit at age thirty, but when your dad leaves like that, like it's the easiest thing in the world and you mean nothing, you believe it for a while. Like, if the one person who is meant to love and support you endlessly can cast you aside without a second thought, then what does that say about you? And then you start to think that, if he can, then everyone else can, too. So, keeping everyone at arm's length, lashing out in anger and making yourself harder to love, just seems like the easiest choice.'

Those words wrapped claws around her heart and squeezed.

'But there was one girl who was worth making the hard choice for?'

Alex nodded, his eyes locked on Noa's.

'But then, she left, too.'

An emotion passed across his face. She couldn't place it before he blinked it away.

'I decided that feelings and relationships didn't have a place in my life after that.'

*She left.*

Her heart dropped, and she felt all the blood drain from her face. She didn't want it to be true. She didn't want to say it, but she had to.

'Who was she, Alex?'

'You, Trouble. The only girl who has ever made it past the barriers of my cold, dead heart is you.'

Time stopped for a moment. The world spun around her and her ears rang. She didn't know if she really was becoming sick, or if it was the magnitude of the words he had spoken that threatened to sweep her feet from under her.

She had heard him use that nickname for her throughout every stage in her life and thought nothing of it. It had irritated her for the longest time. Then, recently, it had turned into an endearment that warmed her heart, had started to wrap itself around her like a comfort blanket. But, right now, it weighed on her, so much more significance in that one word. Like, all this time, it hid a thousand meanings that she had ignored, until now when it glared at her in her face.

Noa felt a tear fall from her eyes and trail down her cheek and Alex reached out with his thumb to catch it. But, in that same moment, as if the world couldn't just let them have this, her stomach started to churn in a way it hadn't before, and she felt the heat rising up her throat like she was going to be sick.

*No*, she thought, *not now*.

She needed to say something. There was so much she needed to say. She needed to hug him, and hold him, and make sure he knew what he was worth to her, make him understand that not everyone set out to leave him. But when she opened her mouth and the bile rose, threatening to bring with it her entire stomach contents, all she could do was rise from the sand and run to the nearest toilet.

Abandoning him, yet again.

# Chapter 32

## Alex

Alex spent the last hour pacing up and down the beach trying to fight the intrusive thoughts trying to come to the surface. Had she really just left like that? He'd thought they were having a moment. The entire night had felt so perfect. They'd talked for hours. She'd opened up to him in ways she never had before, and it made him want to do the same, to be vulnerable and put it all on the line, too. But now, all he felt was overwhelming regret and unfiltered rage.

How had he so badly misread the situation? Why did he think this time would be any different? Why did he think she was any different?

The questions bounced around Alex's head on repeat, and there was so many of them that he couldn't sit still. He scoffed to himself and kicked the sand like it had personally offended him. There were no sounds on the beach but the rhythmic crashing of waves, the distant cries of birds, and the faint staccato chirping of cicadas. Where the quiet had felt soothing earlier, it now felt deafening, allowing his thoughts to run wild. He tried to tell himself that, maybe, it was too much too soon. Maybe she had gotten overwhelmed, maybe he'd scared her. She'd only just come out of a long relationship. God, what was he thinking? He should have just kept his mouth shut.

As his thoughts started to spiral, he realised that maybe hers were doing the same. Noa Drake was many things—beautiful, smart, stubborn, and a serial overthinker. He knew well what being in your own head was like, and it could eat you alive at times if you allowed it to. He didn't ever want to be the reason she was struggling like that, so he turned and started to march quickly toward their cabins in the hopes that they could talk it out together.

But when Alex arrived at Noa's cabin, she was nowhere to be seen. Turning and glancing around, he spotted the dim lights coming from the shared bathroom a few huts down, but no noises were coming from inside. He waited on Noa's porch steps for ten minutes, but when she didn't arrive back, he felt like invisible creepy crawlies had started to embed themselves under his skin. Something didn't feel right.

He stood, dusting himself off, and then headed in the direction of the bathroom. Knocking, there was no reply, so he gently eased the door open and almost fell back at the sight before him.

Noa was slouched between the wall and the toilet, a deathly grey colour to her usually rosy cheeks. Her eyes were closed, and for a minute, he wondered whether she was even conscious until a garbled groan escaped her lips and the fear gripping his chest loosened. God, he'd been so busy thinking the worst and she was in here, sick and alone. She was shivering despite the humidity on the island. He pressed his palm to her clammy forehead.

'Shit, Noa, you're burning up.'

Her eyes fluttered open, but only for a brief second before she spoke. Her voice was so small it was barely audible.

'I think I ate something and I...'

Before she could finish her sentence, she was back over the toilet bowl, emptying her stomach, letting out small whimpers as she went. Noa had practically inhaled a vegetable stew at dinner and, trying to run through the evening in his head, he hadn't seen anyone else so much as touch it.

*Damn it.*

Between every retch came soft sobs that threatened to rip his chest clean open. He'd never seen her this vulnerable, and the thought of her being sick made a knot form in his stomach. He frantically wracked his brain for what his mum used to do for him when he was sick, then dropped to his knees beside her, gently rubbing circles into her back with one hand and holding the hair from her face with the other.

Once she'd finished, her entire body went limp as she slid back onto the toilet floor. Finding a wash-cloth in her mess of toiletries he dampened it with cold water, running it across the fevered skin of her arms, neck, and face.

'Please, Alex. I don't want you here. I'm gross. I don't want you to see me like this.'

Her voice was hoarse and weak.

Alex sighed and slowly rose from where he was crouched next to her. He left the room for a few moments, jogging back to his hut. When he returned to her side, her face morphed into a shocked expression. He knew he should be offended, but he realised, maybe, she just wasn't used to someone looking after her the way she should be, and the thought enraged him. He quickly tried to squash that thought and focus on nothing but the sick girl in front of him.

Looking down at her, he made sure to soften his tone before he spoke, 'You thought you could get rid of me that easily, Trouble? Not a chance.'

He passed her the bottle of water he'd gone to retrieve and with shaky limbs, she reached out to him, accepting the water. Every protective instinct in him was on high alert in that moment, and he was trying to keep his own anxieties at bay and just focus on making sure she was okay. She remained slumped there, making no attempt to drink the water her body so desperately needed.

'Drink.'

His commanding tone left no room for argument and, in her current state, all traces of Noa's feisty and usually stubborn personality were nowhere to be seen.

She took small, slow sips. Alex's shoulders fell a little as he let out a breath he didn't know he was holding.

'Good girl,' he coaxed. 'Keep going.'

He used his hand to smooth down her hair, encouraging her to let him take care of her in that moment.

She looked up at him like she wanted to argue, and he didn't know whether it was her lack of energy or that she'd seen in his eyes how much he needed this, but all protests died on her tongue and she continued to drink. He needed to take care of her, and the relief he felt that she wasn't fighting him on it immediately washed over him.

They sat like that for a while, the two of them on the bathroom floor side by side, the room barely big enough for them both. Noa's eyelids began to flutter open and shut, like the effort to stay awake was too much. Taking her tiny, clammy hand in his, Alex started rubbing soft soothing circles on her wrist.

After a while, her breaths became shallow and her head lolled onto his shoulder. His heart twisted. She looked so peaceful, but her face was still pale and her wispy hair clung to her sweat-coated skin. There was a furrow to her brows that he wanted to press his thumb between until he smoothed out the creases.

Slowly and careful not to wake her, Alex lifted her to his chest with one hand behind her back and the other under her knees. She was so soft, warm, and pliable like this. Even sick, he couldn't help but notice how well she fit there in his arms. He carried her the few short steps to her room and placed her down on the bed, stroking the top of her head and watching her sleep like a creeper. He couldn't bring himself to care, though. The need for her to be okay was overwhelming.

Soft snores escaped her lips, and he just smiled down at her, continuing the massage through her sweat-soaked hair. Soon, though, she started to stir.

'Shhhh, baby. Go back to sleep. You're okay. I've got you.'

And he meant every word.

Unable to fit beside Noa in the single bed, and fear gripping him at the thought of leaving her alone, Alex slowly lifted her head, resting it back on his lap as he used the wall to lean against. Muttering something indecipherable in her slumberous state, she nuzzled into him like, even sick, she too, couldn't get close enough. Resting his hand on her chest so he could feel the steady rise and fall for reassurance, he remained right there. Late into the night, sleep finally took him.

# Chapter 33

## Noa

Waking up, Noa's head felt heavy, but at least the roaring pain in her gut and the non-stop vomiting she had dealt with yesterday had finally ceased. She'd heard about people getting ill when travelling on her routes, but she had come to think she had outrun it. Clearly, she'd been wrong.

With a groan that sounded more bear than human, Noa flung her legs over the side of the small bed and put her head in her hands. Her body felt like lead, and she knew the pounding in her head had to be from dehydration.

Images of last night flooded her mind—her on the cold toilet floor, vomiting for what felt like hours, strong arms wrapped around her, hands comforting her and massaging her hair. Had she dreamt it? She imagined she'd feel a lot worse today if it hadn't been for Alex coaxing water down her throat. But she had never seen that side of him before, and that had her questioning whether she should be adding 'hallucinating hot men playing nurse' to her list of symptoms. Just when she started to rise to her feet, gently swaying as the gravity of how weak she really felt kicked in, the light that had been streaming in from her doorway was suddenly blocked. She looked up to see who it was.

Bright amber eyes met hers, and she could see concern swimming in them. Her heart pinched at what that meant—to have Alex, the no-strings-attached bad boy, genuinely care about her and worry about her well-being. She remembered his confession about his feelings for her last night before she had run away. It was almost too much, and she had to swallow down the lump that was building in her throat.

'How you feeling?' he asked.

'Like I've been hit by a herd of angry wildebeests four or five times before falling down six flights of stairs as I made my escape,' she croaked.

Alex raised one eyebrow at her.

'That's awfully specific. Wildebeests, though? How many of those do you see round here?'

She let out a loud exasperated groan.

'Wow. That bad, huh? Can't even think of a way to curse at me for being a know-it-all?'

He said it like he was trying to use humour to make her feel better, but there were no traces of humour in his eyes as he scanned her like he was checking for any signs that she wasn't okay.

'I'm through the worst of it, I think. I don't think it's a parasite, because I would probably still have my head in the toilet now, but the thought of eating anymore boat food for a while might send me running straight back there.'

She covered her mouth with her hand, just in case she had willed it into existence. But her stomach remained settled, so she lowered her arm and walked toward him.

'You stayed with me last night?'

She didn't know why her voice lowered as she said that but, for whatever reason, it did. She stopped in front of him, their toes almost touching. After feeling his lips on hers in Hanoi and having his arms wrapped around her last night, the need to be close to him made her feel dizzy. She didn't know when this attraction to him had started, but it was undeniable now.

'I needed to know you were okay.'

His voice was hushed. He reached his fingers out, the backs of them brushing against hers and sending tingles up her arms.

'Well, I am. Thanks to you. So, thank you.'

Without even thinking about it, she stepped forward, wrapping her arms around him, or as far around him as she could reach with his massive form, and rested the side of her head on his chest. She felt the rapid beating of his heart and smelt his spicy body wash. He was clearly fresh from the shower, which reminded her of how gross she must be.

Going to step back, she was stopped when he wrapped his strong arms around her, barricading her in. She nestled into him, no longer caring about anything else but this moment, and wondering whether there was ever a time she felt this safe. She couldn't help but think that, even thousands of miles away, in his arms she felt at home.

They had arrived in El Nido just over an hour ago and, immediately after they got to their hostel, Alex had accepted no push-back about her staying in a single room instead of a dorm tonight. She had tried to protest for all of a few minutes, but after the night she'd experienced, the thought of her own room, air conditioning that actually worked, and her own shower was enough to make her bite her tongue and allow him to book it for her.

She wouldn't admit it, but she actually liked him taking care of her. He'd also gone to the liberty of making sure she was in the room right next door to him and, when Lola had invited them both out this evening, he had been quick to decline for the both of them. Noa chuckled. He really was taking this whole overprotective thing to the next level after seeing her sick last night and, though a short time ago that would have had her blood boiling with rage, it now had butterflies taking flight in her stomach. Because he cared. He had shown it in so many small ways in the last few weeks—the willingness to help her tick off her '30 before 30' list, buying her a writing journal to help her chase a dream of hers, constantly encouraging her with her writing, taking care of her. There was also the fact that, wherever she was, his eyes didn't seem to be anywhere else for too long. And his insistence that they not rush into anything and take it slow.

She wanted to kick, scream, and protest, but it had also felt special and different to the one-night hook-ups he usually had. She knew him, so she also knew that deep down, some part of that was due to self-preservation.

But she was done taking it slow with this man.

Maybe all he needed to truly take his guard down was for her to make the first move. The way her heart pounded in her chest when she looked at him, the way he made her feel like the most beautiful girl in any room, and the way he built her up and made her feel strong in her own skin. She knew all of this meant he was not just a rebound guy, no matter what he thought. And she needed to make sure he knew it, too.

Once they had settled into their rooms, Alex demanded they go and get some food so she could fill her belly after bringing up everything in it last night. Lola tagged along and, as always, kept the conversation going. However, it was more of a one-way conversation, even if she didn't seem to notice.

Noa couldn't tell if it was last night's sickness or the permanent butterflies that had found a home inside her that meant she couldn't eat much. She slowly picked at some dry noodles as Alex stared at her. At first, it was assessing, questioning if she was okay. But then, as if he had seen the heat in her gaze, his own had quickly changed.

Despite the thrall of tourists passing by the restaurant and Lola's continued monologue, it felt like they were the only two people there. He was a panty-melting kind of handsome, sitting there in his linen shirt rolled up at the sleeves, his inked arms on display. He wore a simple gold chain around his neck that Noa wanted to use to pull him in and anchor him to her.

Somehow, dinner managed to go by without either of them throwing themselves at each other and causing a display of public indecency. They walked back with Lola to the hostel before Lola asked Noa if she could borrow her white sundress.

The two of them disappeared into Noa's room and left Alex to head to his.

'You two are so banging,' Lola squealed as the door closed.

'Shhhhhh!' Noa put her hand over Lola's mouth before she could add to her embarrassment anymore. 'We are not!'

Lola stood there with her hands on her hips, brushing Noa's arm away from her, with a 'don't bullshit me' expression on her face.

'Not yet, anyway.'

There was another squeal, and then Lola was jumping around like this news directly affected her in some life-altering way.

'I knew it! I just knew it! God, you are such a dark horse, Noa Drake. The others believed you when you spewed all that bullshit about never wanting him, but I just knew you were lying.'

Noa went to protest but was cut off by Lola's hand being held in the air.

'Listen, I am not judging. I think you were lying to yourself as well. But all I'm saying is, after watching the tension between you grow enough to almost cut off the oxygen supply in the room for the rest of us, I, for one, wholly support this. For public safety. You get it, girl.'

Noa laughed, 'I mean I wouldn't have been as dramatic about it but, yeah, things have definitely escalated over the last few weeks, and maybe I didn't want to admit it because of my brother, or because I should be pining over my ex, or because his reputation scared me. But none of that even matters anymore.'

'Reputation or not, that man has never had eyes for anyone other than you. Even when he was pretending to. And

I know this because, when we first met, I even put on my best flirtations for him...' Lola held up her hands in surrender before continuing. 'To test the theory, of course. But he was oblivious. Too busy making googly eyes at you.'

A blush crept across Noa's cheeks at Lola's observation.

Completely unheeding to the reaction, Lola continued, 'Plus, pining is overrated.' She shrugged her shoulders excitedly. 'I much prefer the rebound option. It's true that the best way to get over someone is to—'

Noa sighed and cut Lola off mid-speech.

'That's just it, though. I don't think any of this has anything to do with a rebound. If it did, I could get that from one of the other men here, but he's different. And, whether it's wrong or not, I guess I'm done fighting it.'

'Hey, nothing that feels this right can be wrong. There is no timeline for any of this, and if you spend too long caught up on what you think you should be doing then you'll miss all the good parts that are happening along the way, right in front of you. Stop letting how society says you should feel or behave dictate your decisions. And that goes for your brother, too. If he loves you, and Alex will truly make you happy, then he will get over it. And if he goes all pistons at dawn, like that scene in *Bridgerton* when Anthony demands he and Simon duel, please just make sure you take a video so that I don't miss it. A girl's got needs.'

Lola was laughing and, though Noa pushed her shoulder, she couldn't help but join her in her fit of giggles. 'Ewww! Gross,' Noa complained through her laughter.

This girl could rival Tes when it came to her grand speeches. Wiping her eyes, Noa hopped up from the bed and strutted over to the wardrobe with much more of a pep in her step now.

'Anyway, what dress will it be?'

Lola scoffed, 'Bitch, I appreciate the compliment, but if you think my ass was ever going to fit in any of your clothes, you should have gone to Specsavers, because that just ain't happening.'

'But I thought...'

'I just wanted to hear all the spicy gossip and didn't think you'd appreciate me demanding you spill the beans in front of Mr McHotty.'

'That nickname's sticking then?'

'Like glue. I'll write it on your wedding present.'

'Right, that's enough. Get out. I have better things to do,' Noa said, pushing her friend toward the door.

Luckily, Lola didn't protest but, winking at her from the half-open door as she left, she managed to quip back, 'Damn right, you do.'

Noa knew that Lola was sure to become a permanent feature in her life going forward, and that she wouldn't be able to get rid of her. But she knew in that moment, with a warmth blooming in her chest, that she would never want to.

Finding those easy female friendships was always a blessing, and one of the great joys of her life. Because they would always be each other's army, there to weather any war. The ones to bolster confidence and provide a shoulder to cry on without question or expectation of more. Whether they are the easy friendships that come and go within the space of five minutes in the girl's toilet stalls, or the ones to last a lifetime, Noa wouldn't trade a single one.

She wasn't sure she would have survived in her life without the women who had built her up, who'd been a safe place to land if she needed it. They had shown her the magic of platonic love, whether that be in endless group chats or dorm rooms, bus queues or bar stools, she knew she was part of a community that simply couldn't be replaced.

# Chapter 34

## Noa

Noa had a new plan. After an 'everything shower', and feeling more like herself than she had twenty-four hours earlier, she was determined to go through with it. Tonight, she would know what it was like to be with Alex Fletcher. Truly be with him. Not some quick drunken shuffle in the sheets when neither of them knew what they were doing. Tonight, she wanted to give it all up for him. The thought had static electricity thrumming through her veins with anticipation.

In the shower, she couldn't think of anything else. The visual of what it would be like to have her hands tangled in his dark hair as he looked up at her with molten eyes from where he was buried between her legs meant she had spent the whole time fighting the urge to get herself off before he even arrived. God, she really did feel like a horny teenager when it came to him.

So, after sending off a text asking him to come over, she sat on her bed, a thrumming between her legs, and she felt nervous for the first time since deciding what she wanted and setting out to get it.

There was a rapping at the door, and she stood, quickly shuffling over to it.

'Hey, come in,' she said.

'Is something wrong?' Alex scanned her, again looking for any sign of injuries.

He tended to do that a lot, but just the feeling of having his eyes tracing over her set her body alight. The air in the room felt non-existent, and suddenly, all the confidence and bravado she had earlier slipped away as she took in his six-foot-two, towering form in the doorway. Her mouth was like sandpaper, throat tight as she struggled to choke out any words.

'No. I… I… well… I…'

She shook her head and looked down at the floor. She needed to get it together. Why was it so hard to ask for what she wanted?

Maybe, because all we are taught as women is that we shouldn't go after it, that our needs are less important or silly.

Or maybe, because the last time she had asked for what she wanted in the bedroom, she had been shut down immediately by her ex who liked to 'keep things simple'. It was clear now that his ice cream flavour of choice was vanilla, and hers was raspberry ripple. Both very yummy and admirable flavours, but you can't switch out one for the other. The memory still made her feel vulnerable when she thought about putting herself out there and talking about sex.

Suddenly, like he could sense her spiralling inside her own head, Alex's hands brushed against the skin at her collar bone, then her chin was locked between his fingers and being lifted to look at him.

'Use your words, Trouble. Tell me what you want.'

That name that she once hated she now didn't want him to call her anything else.

'I want you. Like, really want you.'

He made no move to take what she was willing to give, but his eyes darkened. That wasn't just a saying she read in one of her books anymore, she actually saw it. The blacks bleeding into those amber irises, until all that was left was unmistakable, raw desire. It was clear that no one had ever looked at her that way until right now, because, before that, Noa had just thought they were pretty words on pages. No.

Sizzling heat smouldered between them. So much lust and need. She couldn't move, couldn't breathe. Not three months ago, Noa thought Alex was a walking red flag, but right now all she could see was fifty shades of green. She wanted him more than she had wanted anyone, and she had just laid that bare for him.

'It's been a long day, Noa. I'm going to need you to be a little bit clearer.'

The challenge in his words that would have usually made her feel shy and retreat, just made her bold. She had never been so sure of anything, and if he needed her to prove that, then she wouldn't waste another second.

Before she could second guess herself, she fisted her hands in his shirt, pulling him toward her. She kissed him tentatively, at first, but he returned it in spades. He grabbed the flesh of her hips, sending jolts of pleasure to her core and he spun them, pushing her against the door. With one hand travelling up her body to cup her cheek and the other resting on the wall next to her head on the wall, he boxed her in, pulling away for a second before he dove straight back in, his lips crashing against hers.

The kiss turned desperate, like they were running out of time for something, but she wasn't sure what. A delicious heat coiled between her legs and pooled there. She had never felt this turned on in her life, and all he had done was kiss her. His mouth slowly let-up from her lips, travelling toward her ear, then her pulse point, nibbling as he went. His breath was hot against her skin, yet it left goose bumps in its wake. She let out a moan, and it seemed to spur him on to continue his assault on her senses. Their bodies were pressed together against the wall, but she pulled his shirt, still wanting him closer. He smelt musky, like tobacco and spices and sex. It was her new favourite scent, and she wished she could bottle it up.

His smell alone was almost enough to make her come undone, and she moaned again. She was aware that she was a panting mess, and she was sure that, if he wasn't holding her up, she would be a puddle on the floor. But she didn't care.

'God, I could listen to that sound every second of every day and it wouldn't be enough,' he growled close to her ear.

More goose bumps scattered across her skin like gooseflesh.

Without warning, he let go of her, stepping back and looking her up and down with a hunger she had never seen before. The way he looked at her with lust-filled eyes made her feel vulnerable and powerful all at the same time. She hated the space between them but, with his eyes roaming up and down her unapologetically, she was glued to the spot, unable to move. Despite the way he looked at her now, she could still see a part of him holding back and she didn't want him to. She knew what it was like to overthink things. She had done enough of that for the both of them, but she had decided enough was enough. She needed to get him out of his head. Taking a deep breath, she reached behind her, slowly unzipping her dress and letting it fall to her feet.

'Jesus,' he breathed, his fists flexing at his sides like he was dying to touch her but needed permission.

He looked her up and down as if committing every inch to memory. She just stood there, letting him take her in for a long minute, before she spoke the words she hoped would pull him from his daze.

'What are you waiting for?'

# Chapter 35

## Alex

'What are you waiting for?'

*What was he waiting for?* His brain seemed to be short-circuiting. He couldn't think straight. He'd thought of nothing else but this. But, looking at her now, she was perfect. Even more beautiful than he ever remembered. He couldn't believe he had gone so long without having her in his life. He should never have allowed that. He couldn't think of a single thing worth giving this woman up for in that moment. It all melted away and there was only her.

But there was still that niggling fear. The relationship they'd developed since she came home had brought him back to life. It was everything good about his day, and he didn't want to do anything to ruin that. She'd run away scared last time, and the thought of that happening again terrified him. Once they did this, there would be no going back to before. He knew he'd stood silent for too long. He needed to move. Shifting his gaze to look into her eyes, the fire in them left him breathless and, like a flick of a switch, the decision was made. If being with her like this ripped his heart out in a way that was irreparable, it was worth it. Because she would always be worth it. Besides, what use was his heart if it wasn't for loving her anyway?

He wasn't gentle as he wrapped his hand around the back of her neck and pulled her closer, the need for her taking over. He kissed her again possessively, letting his hands roam across her body. First, across her collarbone, then gently dusting down her arms to the tips of her fingers, where he grabbed her hand and brought it to cup his erection. He felt himself grow rock hard under her touch. It was almost painful.

'Do you see what you do to me?'

Her eyes were hooded with desire, those icy blues had turned to cobalt and her tongue darted out to wet her lips.

Damn, this woman.

'Are you wetting your lips for me, baby?' he rasped in a half-groan.

Her mouth dropped open in shock, and he let out a raspy chuckle, bringing his hand up to her chin to close it.

'Don't do that again unless you want me to fill that pretty mouth of yours, okay?'

She nodded at him, but her legs rubbed together like she was searching for friction. He knew the thought had turned her on.

Good to know, he thought.

Physically, there had been a lot of women before Noa, but none of them made him feel this out of his mind with need. And he wanted to make sure she knew it.

Dropping his head, he trailed reverent kisses along her collarbones where his hands had been, then moved south, blowing his hot breath over her lace bralette where he knew her nipples would be. To his delight, they responded by pebbling into hard nubs. He reached out, pulling the lacy material down before sucking her into his mouth. She let out a mewl of pleasure and her nipples hardened more under his attention.

Moving to the next breast, he used his teeth to tug, then left soothing kisses and swirled his tongue around the sensitive peak. She arched her back into him and whimpered. It was enough to make him come undone right there.

Thinking less-sexy thoughts to make sure that he didn't blow his load before he'd seen her come, he continued to devour her breasts until a 'please' escaped her lips. He looked up at her, smiling against her flesh.

'Tell me what you want, baby. Tell me what you need.'

'I… I… I'm already close, but it's not enough.'

'Greedy girl,' he tutted, dragging his teeth over her nipples one more time. 'Patience. We haven't even started yet. We have all night. But, by the time we're done here, you'll have come all over my fingers, tongue, and cock. Then you can tell me if it's enough.'

Another needy groan escaped her lips, and she fisted his hair. The sting of having her hands there, holding him in place felt like a claiming, and it just turned him on even more. He lifted her effortlessly and tossed her onto the bed, earning a surprised shriek from her. Every sound she made delighted him, and he wanted to hear them all, earn them all.

'Now, I just need to know where you want me to start first?'

Noa grabbed Alex's hand, moving it so he cupped her, and she bucked her hips, grinding into him.

'I knew you'd be soaked for me.'

'God, Alex, please. Touch me or I'm going to explode.'

With that, Alex thrust two fingers inside of her and she gasped as she immediately tightened around him. He gently crooked his fingers in a 'come here' motion, to brush against the spot he knew would have her writhing around the bed, and he wasn't wrong. He used his other hand to hold against her abdomen to stop her squirming from his touch.

'Oh my god, yes. No, it's too much,' she whined.

'Look at me,' Alex demanded, and she obeyed.

'Good girl,' he praised, her walls tightening around his fingers again. Interesting.

'It's never too much. You can take it. Let go and relax,' he said.

She relaxed into him, and her body started to quiver. She carried on bucking against his hand, taking exactly what she needed.

'Come for me, baby. Then you can have my cock.'

As if she had been waiting for permission, Noa's entire body went rigid, her eyes rolled into the back of her head and her walls clamped around him like a vice. She called out his name, loud enough that he knew other guests could hear her, but the possessive part of him wanted them to.

'That's it, baby,' he cooed. 'You look so beautiful when you come undone for me.'

Noa's body went limp, and her breathing slowed as she came down from the post-orgasm high. Covering her eyes, she giggled, and it was like music to his ears.

'Well, that was... Mind-blowing,' she spoke into the pillow.

'Don't feel like you need to stop telling me that any time soon,' he laughed as she pushed at his shoulder.

Rolling onto his back, Alex pulled her with him so she straddled him, her legs either side of his waist and long chestnut waves cascading over her swollen breasts.

'You have no idea how perfect my view is right now.'

'You do know I'm a sure thing, right? Flattery is not necessary but always accepted.'

He squeezed her waist where she was ticklish. She tried to squirm out of his grip, but the movement only caused her bare core to rub against his erection and the friction was almost enough to make him come.

'Stop teasing me,' he commanded. 'I wasn't joking about all the ways you're going to come tonight, but I want to see you take it. Sit yourself on my cock, baby. Use me. Make yourself come... again.'

He saw the hesitancy in her eyes as she stared down at his crotch, then back at him.

'I thought this was a good idea before, b...but now I don't remember how that ever fit.'

'Your perfect body was made for me, Noa. Not only is it going to fit, but you are going to ride my cock like the goddess you are.'

He stroked down her back and pulled her down to kiss her gently.

'Hey, look at me,' he said, and she obeyed, their gazes fixing on each other.

Hers was filled with so much lust. He knew she wanted him, but he wanted her to let go and not hold back anymore.

'Relax, don't overthink this. You just do what makes you feel good, okay?'

With what looked like bolstered confidence, she moved quickly, lifting herself up and sliding herself down on him so that an inch of his throbbing cock was nestled inside of her heat. She hissed out and he reached down, making small circles on her sensitive clit until he felt her relax around him until she gently moved down his shaft.

'Breathe, baby,' he whispered into her ear. 'Let me in.'

She let out a long exhale and he continued to massage her just above where they met. As she bucked forward, he thrust the rest of the way in. She met his thrust with her own and they slowly found their rhythm.

'You feel so fucking good, Noa. This pussy is heaven. I never want to be anywhere else.'

She seemed to revel in his words as she continued to chase her high. He couldn't take his eyes off her as she ground against him, her breasts bouncing with the motion.

Her head fell back, mouth dropping open in pleasure, and she came with his name on her lips, taking him right along with her. She pulsated around him, milking him dry. He continued to move her hips, prolonging her orgasm until they were both spent. She collapsed on top of him on the bed.

They remained like that for a while before she rolled onto her back next to him. He opened his arm for her to move in close, her head on his chest and leg bent over his stomach. Their breathing slowed until their chests rose and fell in sync.

'Don't think I've forgotten that third orgasm,' Alex said, swatting Noa's ass. 'I'll let you get your energy back because you did so good, but then I want a taste.'

She let out a content sigh, and they both fell into a comfortable silence. And all Alex could think was that he hoped it would be enough to make sure she stuck around this time.

In an attempt to ensure that any thoughts of running away were the furthest thing from her mind, he made good on his promise and spent the rest of the night with his head buried in the warmth between her legs. And he knew it would never be enough.

# Chapter 36

## Noa

Waking up in Alex's arms had Noa feeling so many mixed emotions, and she didn't know which to focus on first. Her brain could be likened to a tumble dryer right now, going around and around at an unrelenting speed. The anxious part of her brain wanted her to analyse everything that happened last night, what it meant and what happened next. But since coming on this trip, Noa was trying to live in the here and now. It just proved harder in some moments than others, but she was only human, and she couldn't expect an entire personality transplant.

She lay rigid next to him, wanting to toss and turn, or grab a pen and write down everything she was feeling so that she could make sense of it. But she also didn't want to wake him up. When a firm grip tightened around her waist and pulled her into his warmth, she settled into him and her mind instantly quietened to nothing but white noise. In the now, she felt satiated and content, and that should be enough.

'I can practically hear you overthinking,' Alex said, placing a kiss on the top of her head.

There go them damn butterflies again. She was going to have to start charging them rent at this rate.

'Another orgasm for your thoughts?' he said, pinching her sides as she squirmed away and giggled into his chest.

'No one can ever say you aren't selfless, Alex Fletcher. Who knew?'

'Stick around, and you'll see how selfless I can really be,' he joked, but she could tell that the statement ran a lot deeper than he made out, and it was not really a joke at all.

'Hmmmm, I'll consider it. But what do I get if I do?'

She moved her hands under the sheets to cup him. His jaw tightened as a rumble escaped from low in his throat.

'Well, I'm glad you asked. Aside from having your own walking, talking sex doll, I believe my skills extend far beyond the bedroom.'

'Oh yeah?' Noa teased.

'Yeah. In fact, I had an idea I was coming over here to discuss with you last night before you distracted me. Get up. We have plans today,' he said, rolling out from under her grasp and standing from the bed.

She groaned at the thought of leaving. She wanted to stay wrapped up in each other all day long. Sightseeing seemed overrated, all of a sudden. As she stared up at his naked form, her mouth watering at the thought of having him inside her again, his skilled hands working their magic, she decided that this was the only sight she needed to see.

As if her impure preoccupations were being displayed for him to see, Alex gave her a devilish smile as he headed toward the shower.

'Don't worry, Trouble. Now I know how greedy for me you are. I'm not a complete monster. So, if you get your fine ass in here in the next five seconds, I'll make sure you have one for the road.'

With a wink, he disappeared into the bathroom, and she was soon flying from the bed and rushing in after him, because he didn't have to tell her twice. She was an addict who would do anything for her next fix. And Alex was her new addiction.

Noa eyes rolled in the back of her head as Alex pulled up outside the hostel on a moped that he had hired.

'You're kidding, right?'

'What is there to joke about? Come on, Trouble. Hop on.'

She loved her nickname on his lips, especially remembering how he had groaned it in her ear last night. But she still, stubbornly, remained in the spot where she stood. She couldn't believe the hypocrisy of this man. Not even a week ago he had lost his mind over her getting on a moped, and now, here he was demanding she get on his. Well, she wouldn't make it that easy.

'Have you suffered memory loss or something? Were you not the same guy who demanded I not get on a moped last week because they are, and I quote, "a death trap"?' she said.

'Oh, so you *were* listening to me but just chose to be a brat and ignore me. Good to know,' he replied with a pointed look.

'I was not being a brat. You were being an overprotective ass and I'm a feminist who does not believe in letting a man tell her what to do so...'

'Not what it looked like to me last night,' he interrupted with a knowing smirk.

'Alex,' she whisper-shouted, desperately looking around like someone could have overheard what he had just said.

Chuckling, he tapped the seat behind him again and held out a helmet for her.

'This time I'm driving, so I can keep you safe. It's different.'

'Like I said, caveman,' she rolled her eyes, but walked toward him and accepted the helmet.

'For you, always. Get used to it.'

She hated how much that simple statement made her stomach flip, warming her from the inside out. Feminist, her ass.

He leant into her, fastening her helmet tight under her chin and shaking it to make sure it fit.

'There. You're not going anywhere now,' he whispered.

Noa wasn't even sure it was meant for her ears, so she slipped on the back of the moped, wrapping her arms around him as they peeled away from the hostel and down the dirt track road.

They pulled up at the side of the road, a clearing to their left that obviously led to a walking trail. She glanced around, searching for any clues as to where they were, but came up short. There was nothing but green for miles and, if she squinted, she could make out a narrow clearing with what could potentially pass as a dirt path. There were no smells that suggested they were close to civilisation, only the earthy scents of damp leaves and mud.

‘So, hey, is this the part where, now that you have had your way with me, you take me into the woods and kill me?’

‘I don’t know what crazy shit you’ve been reading or publishing recently, but necrophilia is not my kink.’

Noa’s face grimaced at his choice of words, but she cleared the thought from her mind as she followed him down the trail.

‘So where are we then?’

‘You ask a lot of questions, Noa,’ Alex chuckled, and she let out a deflated sigh, her shoulders dropping.

‘I know. Sorry. It’s a control thing. I...’

‘Hey, it’s not a bad thing. I love how your mind works, how inquisitive you are. I know it’s a hard place to be sometimes, but don’t ever be sorry for the things that make it easier, okay?’

She nodded, but didn’t reply. She didn’t think she could. She was sure her throat had almost fully closed up. In those few sentences, he had completely unravelled and obliterated one of her biggest insecurities, and it left her feeling naked.

She had always felt like too much for people, especially when it came to her anxiety and the way it sometimes made her behave, always seeking to predict and control the world around her and spiralling in a way most others didn’t when she couldn’t. She frequently found herself apologising for it, scared that people would just get tired of her if she didn’t.

Alex had just made her feel seen and validated in a way that she never had before. Lucas had made her feel like she had to shrink that side of her and would often tell her to 'lighten up', or tell her she was 'relentless', like she exhausted him. A sense of being in exactly the right place, with exactly the right person, washed over her. A feeling she'd been searching for and had experienced several times over the last few days. Complete contentment.

Alex cut through her thoughts as she just stood there like a statue staring at him, blinking rapidly to clear her eyes of the tears that were building behind them.

'There are times where I will demand you give up control, Noa, and make it real good for you when you do. But only in situations where you feel comfortable. Do you trust me?'

'Yes,' she rasped, because that was something she knew to be true with her whole heart.

'Then do you want to know where we are going right now?'

She decided to embrace that trust she had in him and hand him all the control. To not think and just enjoy the moment, strolling into the unknown with him. It, somehow, felt less daunting by his side. Because Alex was steadfast. Alex was her safe space, and with him, she felt brave and bold.

They walked in a companionable silence for a while, taking in the sights around them.

The trees towered above them and Noa got that feeling she got when staring at the rolling hills in Freymoor, that feeling of being small and insignificant. These trees had been here for hundreds of years, and would likely be here a hundred more. In the grand scheme of the world, her problems wouldn't matter.

As she passed them, she reached out to feel the leaves of an evergreen shrub, letting it make her feel connected to the earth. The leaves looked so much more vibrant than any at home, and droplets of moisture coated them. She was curious what they were called.

The sound of their heavy footfalls on the ground, as well as the rustling trees and birds above them was interrupted when Alex spoke.

'So, I realised something when I picked you up this morning. God, last night was so perfect, and we both got so caught up in the moment that I didn't even think or to ask, and I'm so sorry about that. That's on me as much as you but...'

It was his turn to ramble and spiral for a change and it was cute, but sensing where he was going with this, and wanting to put him out of his misery, Noa cut him off.

'I'm on the pill,' she said, hearing a whooshing sound as he seemed to exhale the entire contents of his lungs.

'I'm clean,' he said. 'But I'll get tested again if you want.'

'Me, too. And that's okay. I meant it when I said I trust you. If you say you're clean, then I believe you.'

And that seemed to be the matter settled. They continued for a few more minutes until the sound of running water filled her ears. Then the huge pool of water came into view. A clear blue waterfall tumbled over a tall rock face and plunged into the glistening pool below. Noa blinked several times, wondering if she was imagining things. Then she turned to look at Alex, who just stood staring at her with a dazzling smile on his handsome face.

# Chapter 37

## Alex

'Alex.'

'Noa.'

'Why have you brought me here?' she whispered, like there was anyone around for miles who might actually hear them. He shrugged casually.

'We've been travelling Southeast Asia for the past two months now, and we still haven't been to a waterfall. This seems like as good a place as any.'

She had that shy look on her face that he thought was the most adorable thing in the world.

'That's the only reason?'

'What other reason could there possibly be?'

'I... Oh nothing. Never mind,' she shrugged off whatever she'd wanted to say, nerves clearly getting the better of her.

'It could also have something do with that list of yours.'

She looked up at him then, with wide, hopeful eyes. It was one of those moments where she looked at him like he hung the moon. He tried not to read too much into that, especially since helping her to achieve her goals was simply the bare minimum. It gutted him that the look in her eyes made it clear she hadn't had that before.

'Seemed to me like you still had some things that you needed to tick off. Number six, if I remember rightly.'

'Swim naked in a waterfall.'

'I'm just here for the show. Completely selfish really,' Alex said, trying to sound nonchalant as he leaned against a nearby tree.

His eyes didn't stray from her for a moment. Because what a view it was. He knew their trip was coming to an end, and he didn't want to think about what that meant for them once reality kicked back in. So, he just wanted to enjoy these moments with her.

He pushed out the voice in his head that worried he was just a fun adventure for Noa like the rest of this trip, a brief lifting of inhibitions that would snap back into place when the holiday was over.

He didn't ever want to have to watch her walk away again but, unlike when they were younger, he wouldn't let her go without a fight.

She beamed at him and all his worries dissipated. That's what she was for him, a brightness that permeated all the darkness. A lighthouse in the storm. She made him believe in the good and effortlessly quietened his demons with nothing more than a smile.

'I will if you will,' she teased, nodding toward the water.

'Oh. Trouble, I thought you'd never ask.'

He kicked off the tree and, with predatory steps, stalked toward her, tugging his T-shirt over his head as he went and letting it fall to the grassy floor. Noa tracked the movements his arms took as he undressed himself the rest of the way until he stood in front of her wearing nothing but a wolfish grin.

'Your turn.'

She looked at him, then got to work on the button of her denim shorts. He watched her shaky fingers move as she undressed herself and he didn't know whether it was anticipation or nerves. He never wanted her to be nervous around him.

As she stood there, finally bared to him, he let his gaze sweep over every part of her.

'You are incredible, Noa. You have the hottest body I have ever seen.'

She dropped her eyes as if she didn't believe him and didn't want to see the lie in his eyes, but she wouldn't find it. So, he pinched her chin between his thumb and forefinger and lifted it until their eyes met.

'You believe me, don't you? Do you know how many times I have dreamed of being able to see you like this? To touch you like this?' he asked, letting his hands graze down the side of her body, across her ribs, and to the back of her thighs.

He lifted her and her legs reacted instinctively by wrapping around him so her bare pussy was pressed against his abdomen.

'The you I pictured in my imagination had nothing on the real thing. It must have been self-preservation that made me block out those memories of you like this. Because there is no way I'd have been able to keep my hands off you all these years otherwise.'

Reaching behind his head, she pulled him into her, their lips meeting in a frenzy of open-mouthed kisses before his tongue slipped inside, savouring the taste of her. The lingering taste of this morning's coconut coffee. This taste was undeniably her. His little coffee fiend, despite all her best intentions to cut back. He hoped she never did, because she was delicious.

Breathlessly pulling away, he said, 'Let's go for that swim, shall we?'

Noa's mouth parted as she let out a needy groan like a child not getting their own way, and the sound travelled straight to his cock, which now stood to attention.

Knowing exactly what she was doing, she ground against him as he carried her across the grass and through the shallows of the water.

Nipping at her ear, Alex picked up his pace before dropping them both down with a splash, dousing them in the cool water. It did little to douse the fire burning inside of him, though. The same fire he could see reflected in her eyes. Her skin was so hot beneath his fingers. And he thought she barely registered the cold water, other than to let out a small gasp, before continuing her movements. God, he could get used to that sound.

'We need to teach you some patience, don't we, Trouble?' he managed, despite the desperation coursing through his own body.

'Patience is overrated,' she breathlessly retorted.

'Oh, I think I can prove to you otherwise.'

'Well, I guess if you must. For research purposes,' she quipped before he pulled her lip between his teeth, hard enough to sting.

He loved this bratty side of her. In fact, he loved every side of her.

Lifting her onto the rock at the side of the water, he pulled her to the edge. She looked like a fucking queen on her throne. The water dripping from her every naked curve made him want to lick every droplet from every inch of her.

'Feet flat on the rock, Noa. I want to see what you look like spread out and waiting for me.'

She did as she was told, and his chest rumbled in response. He watched her intently, licking his lips as he took in the magnificent curves of her body. The swell of her breasts called to him, the hardened peaks begging to be touched. He reached out to do just that. As his fingers grazed her sensitive nipples, tugging slightly, she arched her back, pressing them further into his hands.

'Look at you, practically begging to be touched.'

She only moaned in response, and the sound spurred him on.

His eyes dropped to the space between her legs. She was spread wide for him, just like he had demanded. The sight had him wanting to burry himself deep inside her, but right now was about the long game.

Dropping to his knees in the water, he let his lips fall to her inner thighs, just above her knees, starting their trail towards the spot that he knew she really wanted him. She writhed below him as he continued licking and nipping up toward her pussy and, as she bucked against him, he held her thighs down against the rock below her.

'Lesson number one, you do as I say and you will be rewarded. I can make you feel so good, Noa, but you have to trust me. Can you trust me enough to let go and be present with me?'

She whimpered in response. That satisfied him.

He blew against her clit, hovering there for a few moments to test how sensitive she was and, again, she tried to buck against him, failing when his hands pinned her in place. She let out a loud mewl. He loved how responsive she was to him, and it was going to make what he was about to do all the more enjoyable.

'That's it, baby. Let me hear how much you want me.'

'God, I want you. So bad. Stop teasing me.'

'Lesson number two,' he answered, slowly licking her from back to front, savouring his first taste of her before he would dive in.

She was exquisite.

'Teasing is all part of the fun. I'm going to show you just how fun it can be. So, sit back and get comfortable, baby. This won't be quick, but if you can show me how patient you can be, I will make you feel better than anyone has before.'

She whined in protest. And if he hadn't been trying to learn her—paying attention to every way that her body reacted—he would've missed it when she whispered, 'You already have.'

That only made him more determined to wring every ounce of pleasure from her, making sure that the statement would always be true.

She was at his mercy, spread out before him, and the thought had him more turned on than he'd ever been before.

# Chapter 38

## Noa

It was true that there was a fine line between pain and pleasure, and what Alex was doing right now felt like the most enjoyable form of torture. Her legs quivered again and again as he continued to lap at her, bringing her so close to her release and then pulling away.

'Alex, I can't take it anymore.'

He looked up at her from between her legs, like she had pictured so many times, his stubble coated in her desire with a sinful grin on his face. 'You're doing so good, baby. This is all for you, I promise.'

But before she could respond and demand he let her come right the hell now, he pulled her clit back into his mouth, sucking and biting and kissing the ache he left there. She couldn't form words as he continued to torment her. She needed to come so badly it was painful. How many times had she been close and he'd denied her? Six? Seven times? It could be more, but she had lost count. She was so lost in the pleasure of it all. There was a burning sensation coiling deep in her stomach and she knew she was close again.

'Should I let you come, Noa?'

'Yes,' she moaned. 'Please.'

'God, you sound so good begging for me.'

Her head dropped back and she arched her spine, trying to close her legs for some release from the sweet torture he was inflicting, but he held her in place. She was caught in a purgatory of desire, waiting for the pleasure that would follow next.

'Would you get on your knees and beg for me if I didn't give you what you wanted?' he crooned.

'I would do anything. God, Alex. Please.'

In response, he added a finger inside her, then a second, crooking them to stroke a spot deep inside her again and again. She couldn't compare what this felt like to anything she had felt before. It felt transcendent. Ethereal.

The sensation alone with the flicking of his tongue against her clit had her on the brink of orgasm in seconds. It was clear that he loved the control he had over her body in this moment, but she needed this and the look in his eyes as she glanced down at him said he knew it. He spoke against her sensitive core, slowing the pace of his fingers again.

'On the count of three, Noa, not before and not after. You're going to come for me, and you're going to scream my name when you do. Let everyone know who this pussy belongs to.'

He gave one quick flick with his tongue and then continued, 'Can you do that, gorgeous?'

She nodded.

'Say the words, Trouble.'

'Y... Y... Yes,' she stumbled out her words, but she knew it was the truth.

He played her body like the strings of a guitar, and she knew she would come undone like putty in his hands the moment he allowed it.

'That's my girl.'

That one simple sentence had a warmth spreading through her chest and that, with the sensations she felt between her legs, were almost too much.

Right then, his mouth returned to her, and his fingers increased their pace inside of her, fucking her like she had never been fucked. He was unrelenting. His tongue made circular motions on her clit before he sucked her into his mouth. Hard.

'One...'

Lick.

'Two...'

Thrust.

Seconds that felt like hours passed before he finally growled out the word, 'Three.'

She shattered around him, seeing stars as her entire body convulsed and she came like she never had before. It was so intense she thought it might kill her. He coaxed her through it, continuing to lap at her and fuck her with his fingers. Her legs tightened around his head as the final tingling of her orgasms—because there was no way that had only been one—made their way through her body. Then, she relaxed. She was panting and her legs were shaking, but she had never felt pleasure like it. She looked at him as he licked her off his lips and sucked his fingers into his mouth.

How could he make something like that seem so sexy. Even the thought would have repulsed her before now. She should be embarrassed, but she was enthralled by him.

'You taste incredible,' he rasped. 'Taste yourself on me, Noa,' he demanded and, like she always did, she obeyed him, kissing him passionately.

She tasted her tangy release on his lips and the whole thing felt so dirty and erotic that she grew wet all over again. There was definitely nothing vanilla about what they had just done, and she hadn't even had to ask him for it. He just knew what she needed, and he had needed it just as much.

'Do you know what that tastes like?' he asked.

She shook her head, still struggling to form words.

'Mine, Noa. Tell me this pussy is mine.'

Because she had a feeling she would never get enough of this, that he really had ruined her for all men to come, she replied, 'Yours.'

And it scared her how much she meant it.

Once Alex finally came up for air from between Noa's legs, he demanded no less than three more orgasms from her on his cock. And, like his 'good girl', as he liked to put it, she obliged. *Praise kink well and truly unlocked.*

Noa felt like she had been transported out of her body as she tumbled over the edge for the third time, legs wrapped around his back, nails digging into his shoulders enough to leave little purple crescent moon shapes. He had pounded into her at an unrelenting pace, truly fucking her senseless as he stood under the waterfall. The water cascading around them beating against their shoulders had just added another layer of sensation to her sensitive skin.

As she'd watched him let go, coming inside of her with sloppy, desperate movements, the whole picture seemed like a scene from a movie—the crystal-clear water, looming rocks towering around them, the thick green shrubbery barricading them from the outside world like they were in their own secret haven. She felt like no moment in her life would ever top this, and she wanted to imprint every detail in her mind so that she would never forget it. Fat chance of that happening anyway.

After they finished, Alex kept to his word, and they swam in lazy circles, passing under the waterfall and basking in the afternoon sun, until he decided they should get going before it got dark.

It was sensible, but she didn't want the day to end. Hell, she didn't want the trip to end. Would returning to reality burst their perfect little bubble? Would he even want to carry on whatever this was when they got home? Was she enough for Alex to face the wrath of her brother, which she knew was inevitable when he found out? Or, would they bury the fact that this had ever happened like they had the last time? The thought of that made her feel sick. She knew she should ask him, that they should talk it out like adults, but she was scared for the answer.

Besides, living in the moment meant not stressing about every little detail of the future. So, as they drove back to the hostel, the wind in her hair, her cheek to his back, Noa took deep, calming breaths and decided she would enjoy him for as long as she had him.

# Chapter 39

## Noa

Four days later, Noa and Alex stood on the kerb-side outside their hostel as they prepared to leave El Nido. The minibus that was collecting them for the airport spat and spluttered beside them as plumes of black smoke rose from the exhaust. After months of adjusting to Southeast Asian public transport, Noa ignored the small unease that the dilapidated motor created. But Alex's stiff posture and assessing glare in the driver's direction as he loaded their bags, told her that he still hadn't quite accepted the differences here.

Noa hugged goodbye to Lola and Thea. She couldn't believe how lucky she was to have met so many amazing people on this trip. Some, like Hattie, Marcus, Carly, and Bridget, had come and gone along the way. But these two were different. To have met them both on day one, to have connected as they did and have been able to spend her entire trip together, felt like they shared something so special. Something that not many people would understand. That linked them, and Noa knew they'd be friends even after they returned home.

Noa couldn't help the few stray tears that tumbled down her cheeks as she prepared to get on the minibus. Lola gripped her tightly, then pulled away to look deep into her eyes.

With a very serious look on her face, she said, 'You know, you're crying now, but you can't get rid of me that easily. I'm going to be in Freymoor all the damn time and, soon enough, you're going to be crying because you're so sick of me. Plus, you've got to keep me up-to-date on the whole Ryan showdown.'

They both laughed. This girl really was so much like Tes. She had a warmth about her, a lightness that seemed to make any heaviness slip away when they were around. She could use more of that in her life, and she was so grateful that they had met. She couldn't wait to welcome her to her hometown and introduce her to her best friend. She had a feeling that they would either get on like a house on fire, or be so similar that their fiery personalities would clash. Either way, knowing that they were both part of her life now made going home seem less of a struggle.

As well as the friendships she had made, Noa knew she would take so much away from this trip.

Thanks to Alex, she was well on her way to ticking off her '30 before 30' list. But not only that. Along the way, the list had become less important to her. She realised it was all the little moments throughout their journey that she would likely remember forever.

Before leaving Freymoor, she had felt a sense of failure, a sense of feeling behind in life based on some kind of schedule she had set for herself. At the time, she didn't know if those expectations had been based on her own dreams, or based on what everyone was doing around her. Now, she was sure. She had let the people around her dictate how worthy she felt for far too long. Anyone from strangers on the internet to her ex-boyfriend had helped her create this unrealistic standard and timeline for herself.

But who said life ends at thirty, or where she should be by then? Who really cared, as long as she was living her life and happy, how she was living it? She'd let the ticking of time scare her for too long, and it was an anxiety she had shifted whilst being away.

She realised as she'd watched her new friends that everyone was on a different path, and there was beauty in that. Beauty in the messy and unpredictable parts of life.

She would never forget the lessons they had all taught her. She was going to take risks, and reach for her own goals, moving forward—something she had stopped doing somewhere along the line as she prioritised other people and their expectations. And, whether she achieved them or got knocked down and had to fight to get back up, this trip had taught her that she always would. But there were also people she wanted to have around to help her. Being strong and independent did not mean being alone, but knowing when to ask for help and learning to lean on the people who care.

The man beside her felt like one of those people. So, as she and Alex jumped in their cab and drove away, waving out of the back window, she let out a content sigh, ready for whatever adventure life had in store for her next. Because you couldn't predict it or control it anyway, so she could only look forward to the ride.

As if sensing her deep in thought and not wanting to disturb, Alex placed a firm hand on her thigh, squeezing gently. In that moment, it really did feel like he was along for it, too. She couldn't help that spark of hope that flared inside of her, that maybe, like the lessons she had learnt along the way, he would also be a permanent memento she would take home.

But was hope a fickle thing?

Refusing to let that thought take flight, or give her mind permission to overthink, Noa watched the moving picture that passed by her window, knowing that only time would tell.

# Chapter 40

## Alex

Holding a mug of steaming hot coffee in his hand, Alex leant against the windowsill in his living room, watching people go about their day on the street below. They meandered through Main Street, dipping in and out of the small independent shops, in what seemed like slow motion after the busy streets of El Nido. There was no rush. No blaring of horns or raised voices. And he was reminded of why he loved home. The peace and tranquillity of a sleepy town, nestled in the mountains.

What he did not love, however, was the space that Noa had put between them when they first arrived home a month ago. Even though he'd done his best to bridge that gap over the last four weeks, and he knew they were moving in the right direction, he still couldn't ignore what had felt like her initial instinct to run. Maybe that was his own fear, skewing reality and letting the past bleed into their future, but it played heavy on his mind.

The only thing he knew, though, was, unlike when he was twenty-one, he knew she had real feelings for him now. And, if she tried to leave him this time, he wouldn't just watch her walk away again. He would put up the fight of his life. So, for the past few weeks, he'd been playing the long game.

Things felt a little tense and awkward when they first arrived home, like neither of them knew how they should behave. The feeling gnawed at him, and he ached to be close to her, but he fought to be patient, to give her some time to catch up with her friends and family.

Eventually, after a week of being home, he pressed Noa to come to his for dinner. He wouldn't allow her any more time to overthink, and he certainly wouldn't allow her to put any more space between them after the progress they'd made toward the end of their travels.

The feel of her lips was imprinted on his mind forever now. He still felt the ghost of them there, and he had no desire to go another eight years before he got to feel them again. *Been there, done that, bought the ill-fitted and scratchy T-shirt!*

He tried to cook her new favourite dish, Pad Thai, which, in reality, had been nothing like what they had eaten on their travels.

But Noa politely ate it and complemented him on his cooking the entire time. He had planned on talking to her after dinner about what was going on between them, but when she licked her lips clean after finishing, he lost any train of thought and, instead, fucked her on his small dining room table. Then, against his living room wall, and again in his bed, until they had crashed there and woken up wrapped around each other the next morning. All awkwardness and tension had dissipated, and they were just them again.

That thought had him smiling as he took slow sips of his coffee. The filter coffee he'd grabbed from the machine downstairs at The Brew didn't taste anywhere near as nice as the sweet coconut coffees they'd been drinking in Vietnam, and Alex wondered if he'd be able to source that somehow.

The movement of the trees swaying outside his window pulled his attention back to the present. The leaves had started to turn dry in the summer heat, shrivelling in on themselves. When he first came home, he remembered thinking they were mocking the state of his and Noa's relationship. But now, they reminded him of the passing of time and the changing of seasons, which he noticed so much less in the places they had travelled compared to here.

He'd always loved the changing of the seasons and, actually, found himself looking forward to when it would soon be autumn. The thought made him smile. That had always been Noa's favourite season. He'd caught himself smiling a lot lately, usually triggered by thoughts of her. But, unlike before they left, these thoughts were welcome. As everything in Freymoor reminded him of her, he guessed his jaw would soon start to ache.

He hoped they'd get to do some of her favourite autumn traditions, like pumpkin-picking at Mr Morley's farm, followed by carving them in front of a scary movie. Growing up, she used to insist that she, Tes, Ryan, and he take part in the activity. This year, he craved it.

But, despite nights spent together having become a regular thing, they still hadn't talked about what it meant, and had continuously danced around the subject of Ryan. So, pumpkin-picking was probably out of the question.

Instead of addressing how to come clean to Ryan, their new routine involved Noa coming to open mic night at the bar every Friday, with Tes, as an excuse to see him in public. More than a few times, he'd been unable to control himself as he watched her swaying her hips on the dance floor and had taken her to his office to bury himself in her and show her, no matter how many men's attention she drew out there, it was him she belonged to. If she had called him a 'caveman' before, then the possessiveness he felt toward her now was a whole other level, and he had to constantly reign himself in.

Any time Ryan had been around, though, they, somehow, managed to behave normal. Maybe? He wasn't sure how they'd pulled it off, seeing as he couldn't remember what their normal was now. But Ryan hadn't mentioned any suspicions, so Alex took that as a good sign.

He didn't know if it was wishful thinking on his part, but he'd started to wonder if, maybe, this was okay. Maybe, if they continued as they were doing, everything else would just fall into place before they knew it, and he would be left feeling like an idiot for ever worrying about it in the first place. Noa had been trying really hard to live in the here-and-now, and he didn't want to be the one to ruin it. He'd seen the change in her and was proud of how far she'd come.

All he'd ever wanted to do was build her up and support her, never adding to the anxiety she carried around on a daily basis. He knew now that they were meant to be together. Everything would be okay if they faced it together, but he needed to let her come to that conclusion in her own time. So, he would love her in secret for as long as he had to. And, despite needing to fight his instincts to make sure everyone knew that she was his and he was hers, he wouldn't rush her.

Because he did. Love her that is.

A few more weeks passed by just like that, the two of them sneaking to find any amount of time together. Evenings spent, when he wasn't at the bar, on his couch watching movies under a blanket, him cooking her meals whilst she wrote at his table. Stolen glances over his bar whilst their friends were around. And the moments of passion, where they got lost in each other's bodies, fucking like it was both the first and last time they would ever have each other like that.

Alex continued to run through all the scenarios where this could go wrong in his head, all the ways he could be hurt if she left. Whether he was good enough for her. But she never made him feel that way, and it made him realise that, maybe, he had internalised his father's abandonment when he was a child. Maybe Alex had lived with the idea that his dad had left because he hadn't been good enough to make him stay. But Noa had made him see that was just a negative thought pattern, because under her attention, he knew he was good enough.

Noa was not his dad. She was not a selfish person who would be careless with his heart. She was beautiful and kind, thoughtful when it came to the people around her. She protected those she loved, even gave parts of herself she shouldn't just to make them happy, and he knew in his heart that she would never intentionally hurt him. More importantly, she'd seen all of him—the good, the bad, and the ugly—and she wanted him anyway. She had been showing him that every day, and he believed her.

But that didn't stop the evil voice that liked to slip into his head from time to time, ever since he was a kid, from rearing its ugly head and reminding him of his biggest fears and insecurities. Some days, he thought, if he became the man she deserved, worked his ass off to be everything she needed, gave her everything she could ever want, that it would be enough to make her stay. But he knew love and relationships didn't work like that and, at some point, he would have to take the leap of faith, put all his trust in her, consequences be damned. Even so, if anyone was worth working through his messed-up thoughts for, then it was her. She'd always been worth the risk.

Kicking off the wall, Alex strode away from the window. Despite having spent most of the morning watching the world and being lost to his thoughts, he was intent that he, too wanted to live in the moment. And he wanted to do it with Noa.

They lay in his king-sized bed, not an inch between them. Noa curled into him under the covers and Alex watched her as she scrolled manically through her phone, sighing defeatedly every so often. He'd been busy at the bar the last few days with stock take, so this was the first bit of quality time they'd managed to squeeze in for nearly three days. It was irrational how much he'd missed her in such a small period of time, but nothing he did could free her from his mind. He'd ached to have her in his arms with every day that passed.

Nuzzling into her neck now, breathing in her vanilla scent, Alex pulled her even closer. It would never be close enough.

He kissed the top of her exposed shoulder where her T-shirt had slipped down, and then the crook of her neck.

He pulled back before asking, 'What's wrong? You sound like your phone has personally offended you in some way.'

'It's just another rejection letter,' Noa sighed.

*Rejection letters?* His heart dropped into his stomach with what this could mean, but he tried to hide it.

'What letters? What do you mean?'

Noa turned around so their backs were no longer touching so she could look at him.

'So, I've been so busy I've not had chance to tell you, but I've been applying for jobs. I've decided what I want to do with my future, but I'm just struggling to find a way to make it work...'

She paused, looking at him for any signs that he was somehow bored of her story. He just nodded, silently encouraging her to continue.

'Well, when I first started struggling with anxiety, books were my escapism. They helped me in a way that I can't even explain. It's silly really, but...'

'Don't do that,' Alex said. 'Don't say that anything you enjoy or find comfort in is silly. It's not.'

She nodded and continued, 'Well, I always thought that one day I would write my own book, as you know. The idea of helping someone the way books helped me would just be the most amazing thing. I love creative writing, but somewhere along the line, becoming an adult meant making the hard decisions necessary to make sure I could support myself and pay the bills. That's when I went into publishing. I still got to work with authors and readers, and it has made me so happy, for the most part.'

There was a slight pause.

'But...'

'I guess this whole thing has just reminded me that we are never too old to chase our dreams, you know, no matter what they are or how unrealistic they feel. You helped me realise that. Our time away was healing for me in so many ways, and one thing I realised is that my life only has to make me happy, no one else. My passion, and my happy place, is writing, and I think I owe it to myself to really explore that.'

His chest swelled with pride at her words. The look of determination he saw painted across her beautiful face might have been the sexiest thing he'd ever seen. If he hadn't been dying to hear her every thought, he would have crawled between her legs right then. But he did need to hear what she thought about in that incredible mind of hers, more than he needed his last breath. So, he just reached out, tucking a piece of hair behind her ear as she continued her speech. She looked wild and unruly as she spoke, and it was just the way he liked her—hair mussed from having his hands running through it, his shirt on her back that sat just above her knee. The only thought that the sight elicited was *mine*.

'I know writing makes me happy, and that I could write something that really matters to people. I've been helping people publish their books for years, it-it feels like it's my turn. I started writing in the book you bought me whilst we were away. You were right, I was inspired. I have a good portion of a book already, but I still need a lot more time to finish it and get it where I want it to be. It's, honestly, just like I had so much that I didn't know I needed to say, but once I started, I couldn't stop.'

'So, what's the problem?' Alex asked, feeling like there was something she wasn't saying.

'Well, I've been looking for jobs in publishing. I need something part-time to allow me the time I need to write when

I'm not working and, because we live in the middle of bumfuck nowhere, I'll probably need to have at least one day a week working remotely from home so I don't have to drive into the city every day. Apparently those two requirements make me a little unappealing to employers, because that's the second rejection letter I have had from a publishing house this week.'

She looked deflated now, her usually sparkling eyes were dull, like the light she had recently gained was threatening to be put out. He couldn't allow that. Even if fear rolled in his gut; fear of this being the beginning of the end. The very thing he'd tried to protect his heart from all along—Noa leaving. But, even amongst all that fear, he still wanted her to have everything she ever dreamed of, so the sad expression she wore as her confidence waned wrecked him even more.

'Maybe it was more unrealistic than I thought, after all. I guess, at least, I tried right? It's more than I've done so far, so I can feel good about that.'

'You're not giving up, are you?'

'No. I will write the book. It just looks like it'll end up taking a few years instead of a few months as I'm probably going to have to look into full-time posts and focus on writing as more of a side hobby for the time being. It's okay, though. I'm not in as much of a rush to have my whole life wrapped up in a neat bow these days. It's just frustrating, because I was excited to be finally making a decision that would have brought me so much happiness and, if I'm working in the city, I'll probably have to consider moving closer to there.'

His eyes almost doubled in size. And there it was, the other shoe dropping. He needed to find the words before she heard the sound of his breaking heart.

He'd just got her back. God, this was it, wasn't it? Everything he'd been afraid of. This was when she left him.

Could he even be mad at her if it was what she wanted? If it was a good career move that would make her happy? Noa's happiness had quickly become one of the most important things to him, and he would move heaven and earth to keep a smile on her face.

'Is that what you want?' he, somehow, managed to croak out.

'No. You've seen my list. I always dreamed of coming back home and being closer to family. It's one of the things that helped me move on from my relationship so quickly. I knew it could never last because he kept me from here, and moving back felt like a dream. I've loved being close to my family, and Tes and... having you close by hasn't sucked.'

Alex squeezed her hips playfully and she giggled, wiggling out of his grasp.

*Well, screw it, then.*

She didn't want to leave, and he wouldn't let her. This was his moment to either shy away and accept that everyone always leaves eventually as inevitable fact, like he usually did, or fight for her to stay. It wasn't even up for debate; fighting was his only option.

Putting his hand against her cheek, he whispered, 'Don't go then. Just... stay.'

'But how?'

She looked up at him, wide-eyed and beautiful, like he had all the answers. He only had one.

'Work for me. The bar is becoming increasingly busy, and I've needed more staff recently. Work for me, and you will have the flexibility to write whenever. Want weekends off? Done. You want to work evenings only so your days can be filled putting that brilliant little mind to work writing? Done. We can make it work however you need it to, Noa. Just don't go.'

Her mouth fell open in shock before she righted herself.

'Careful, Alex. You're starting to sound a little like you'd miss me.'

He kissed her then, really kissed her. Hoping he could pour all his emotions into one searing kiss, and she would know just how true that was.

'Oh, Trouble. I just went three days without having my hands on you and turned into a lost puppy. We are way past just missing you, don't you think?'

She scoffed, as if to mock him, before saying, 'God, I knew you were obsessed with me.'

He swatted at her ass and nipped her ear, 'I'll punish that bratty little mouth of yours later. But, seriously, what do you say?'

'I... I... Are you sure? You might get sick of me. And... well, you know, how well I take being bossed about... by you, of all people.'

She held her hand out as if to stop him from his next retort. It was probably just as well.

'Don't even say it.'

'I know you, Noa. And I want every stubborn part of you to stay here and work for me. I want you to fight me and make my life hard work. I want you to make your dreams come true, and I want to be the one who gets to help you get there, to stand next to you and bask in your success with you once you do. Please let me.'

He was aware of how pathetic he probably sounded, but he really didn't care. This was him taking the leap. He held his breath for the few moments it took for her to respond.

'Despite the nickname, I didn't want to cause you any trouble.'

The way she said it sounded like she thought she was a burden, and his mouth turned into a hard line with the sour taste that thought left there. Is that what she thought? Could she not see how much richer his and everyone's lives were when they had her around?

'You might be trouble, Noa, but you are the kind I want to get into. The kind I would chase no matter the consequences. You are my kind of trouble, and I want you around, now and for as long as you'll stay. Never doubt that.'

'Okay,' she muttered.

'Okay?'

'Yes, okay. I'll stay. I'll take the job, and I'll write. I don't know how to thank you. Should we talk about hours?'

He smirked. 'No, Noa. We can talk about that later. Whatever hours you want, you can have. But, right now, I can think of one way that you can thank me. I'm going to need you to crawl your little butt over here and sit yourself on my face before I fuck my new waitress for the rest of the night.'

Quickly crawling onto her knees and moving herself over, she did exactly what he'd told her to.

'Yes, Boss.'

# Chapter 41

## Noa

Placing a pint of bitter down in front of Richard Morley, Noa wiped her sticky hands on her apron and rang it through the till. This job was exactly what Noa needed. Living at home had meant that she didn't need for much and, after the small amount of rent that her mum asked for, the part-time wage was still plenty to cover what she needed it to.

She'd even been putting a little into savings for when she finally had a piece of work she was proud enough to publish. The price of that wouldn't come cheap. She'd need to hire an editor, a cover designer, maybe get some marketing help. So, the more she could save, the better. The thought had her glancing at the tip jar on the corner of the bar and smiling at how generous this town was.

Working in the evenings gave her plenty of time every day to dedicate to writing. She'd made a conscious effort to get out the house too—going on walks, writing in the park, by the lake, or anywhere pretty that would inspire her and aid in her creativity like travelling had done. It had worked so far, and she was now around eighty percent through her first novel, which tackled subjects like loss of identity, mental health struggles, and starting over in your late twenties. Basically, everything these last few months had taught her.

She was trying to write the book she wished she'd been able to read when she was struggling with these things herself, and to create something that mattered. She wanted to make relatable characters that people could get lost in and be left feeling less alone by the end of it. Doing so felt cathartic and gave Noa a sense of purpose that she'd been lacking for the longest time.

Alex did everything he could to support her, too, and she couldn't be more grateful for all his help. In the past, she had been so stubborn. She'd felt the need to prove that she could do everything on her own. Maybe because Lucas made her feel she had to and, maybe, because she didn't want to be 'that kind of girl'. The kind of girl who relied wholly on a man. The kind of girl who can't be independent or stand on her own two feet.

But, along with the other things she had learnt and let go of recently, the negative stereotypes that society had put in her head of how women should act and behave had been one of them. She still wanted to be independent, but having someone to rely on and seek comfort and support from had been nice, and knowing she could do this on her own, but didn't have to, warmed her from the inside out.

Sarah Kingsley walked up to the bar then, her warm smile on full display. She was the town's local bookshop owner. Noa had always seen her as a motherly figure, probably because she was her mum's age and had always gone out of her way to talk to Noa, checking in on her and taking a genuine interest in her life. She also had this friendly and dependable aura about her that made you want to spill all your secrets to her and let her give you her wise words of advice.

Noa fell into that again now, when Sarah pushed her wine glass onto the bar before asking, 'How are you, Lovey? It's nice to see your beautiful eyes for once instead of the top of your head as you frantically scribble into the pages of that book of yours.'

She knew Sarah was referring to the fact that Noa had been sitting on the bench outside her shop to write whenever she got chance. When the sun was out, from that bench she got a view of 'The Next Chapter', which was the name of Sarah's shop, as well as the breathtaking backdrop of the mountains behind it. They rolled and fell for miles in the background, looking like a patchwork quilt of greens, browns, and yellows. The view filled her with inspiration, similarly to how the experiences on her travels had.

Deciding to be honest and say exactly that, Noa responded.

'That bench has the best view in town. I'm surprised it's not made it onto a post card yet,' Noa giggled. 'And there's something poetic about writing a novel whilst sitting in front of a bookshop. It's inspiring, looking up at the books and thinking, maybe, I could be there one day.'

This was the first time Noa had said those words to anyone outside her family, that she was writing a novel. But she didn't want to let fear dictate her life anymore, and it felt good to tell her.

Sarah's grin spread even wider.

'Oh, Noa, that's so exiting! I can't wait to see it on my shelves. You can count on me to have the biggest Noa Drake window display in the whole country.'

Her words warmed Noa, and she was reminded of what was so special about Freymoor. This community was more like one big family. She could travel the whole world, but she would never get this anywhere else.

The telltale sound of Albert clearing his throat told Noa that open mic night was about to start. She scurried over to the end of the bar where Tes sat waiting for her.

Tes had been coming to the bar to spend some time with Noa every Friday night. Open mic nights had always been their guilty pleasure, and she loved having her best friend there to keep her company as she worked.

Or, at least, made it look like she was working whilst she put the world to rights with her bestie. Although Alex hadn't said anything about her lack of commitment on those nights, he had conveniently brought in an extra waitress to help out when Noa worked on Fridays, like he wanted to allow her that time with her friend. He really would do anything to make her happy.

It's true that it really does pay to date the boss. Because that's what it seemed they were doing now—dating. Not in public, of course. But even so, the time they spent together still felt so perfect.

She knew her feelings for Alex were growing exponentially and, at some point, she was going to have to confront them. Alex didn't deserve all the sneaking around and, truthfully, the way he made her feel about him, she didn't want to sneak around, either. This didn't feel like just a short term, casual fling anymore. She wasn't entirely sure it ever had, but it felt easier to think of it that way at first. It felt like she could justify moving on from Lucas so quickly that way. Now, she was sure that she wanted everyone to know that they were together. Even if they hadn't actually said that yet. In her head, they were exclusive, and, at some point, she would make sure Alex knew that, too.

It was a typical Friday. She and Tes chatted at the bar, like she wasn't there to do a job.

'Do we need to have a talk?' Tes asked.

'Sorry?'

'Well, I've been talking to you for the past ten minutes, and I don't think you've heard a word I've said whilst you've been staring at the man wiping those tables over there with hearts in your eyes. Which, I'm pretty sure, is your job by the way, not his. So, I guess we know who's wrapped around who's finger.'

As Tes said it, she silently clapped in Noa's direction in a teasing sort of praise.

'Stop it,' Noa laughed, fighting the urge to fake a bow in response.

'I'm just saying, if you have feelings for him, like the ones I can see plastered across your face, you need to tell him sooner rather than later. You told me recently that life's too short to not go after what you want. Didn't your trip teach you not to sit around and wait for things to come to you? Doesn't that apply here? Alex has been a player up until now, but people change, Noa. You've seen that. Don't wait until it's too late... grab onto the man and hold tight.'

The thought left a bitter taste in her mouth. Noa knew Tes was right. Her friend could be frustratingly wise sometimes.

'I know, you're right. It just feels like things are so good right now, and I don't want to rock the boat. Once I tell him and, if things get serious, it'll mean it's finally time to tell Ryan. I just... I don't want to ruin it. I like our perfect bubble, you know?'

Tes nodded, and then responded, 'I hate to break it to you, but the way you two spend every spare second together and the way you both look at each other... it's already serious. You just need to put your big girl pants on. Grab life by the boobs and take what you want.'

Noa's eyes drifted to Alex then, who was laughing with Terry Finch, owner of Finches of Freymoor, the local food market, as he carried in crates of sundries for The Brew. She felt her heart beat faster seeing him in these moments, effortlessly happy and completely at one with the town they grew up in. It was contentment and belonging written across his face as other locals joined their conversation.

*Home*, she thought, with her eyes glued to him. It had taken her too long to figure out, but he was home. Tears pricked behind her eyes as an overwhelming urge to go and wrap herself up in him gripped her. She wanted to bask in the scent of tobacco, vanilla, and spice until it was all she knew.

Sighing in acceptance, and knowing what she needed to do, Noa nodded in response to Tes without even looking at her.

Her eyes remained on him, cataloguing him. The wrinkles at the sides of his eyes looked more pronounced recently. She didn't know if it was just that she noticed him more now, or that he was genuinely happier and his face wore the evidence. She suddenly realised she wanted to bank every change from this point onward. She didn't want to miss any of it, or wonder when it happened. She wanted to know exactly when his tan started to fade and the exact number of days it took for that five o'clock shadow to develop into something more. She wanted to be there for every wrinkle, and know the source of every scar. To be a part of all his big moments, and the small ones, too.

'The two of you have wasted too much time, Noa. It's time to be brave for the both of you,' Tes voiced quietly, as if in response to Noa's thoughts.

After their conversation moved on to less profound topics, they spent the rest of the night chatting in between Noa serving and clearing tables like she'd been supposed to all along. When her shift was over, she grabbed a stool next to Tes and decided a few drinks with her best friend sounded like just what she needed.

It wasn't unusual for men to flirt with her whilst she worked, and she had gotten quite good at either ignoring them or fighting them off. Tonight, though, there was a new group of men in, on a stag night judging from their questionable shirt choices, and were very obviously from out of town. They had clearly drunk too much and, as a blond-haired guy persistently vied for her attention, she became increasingly aware of his green eyes that kept flying in her direction. The guy seemed harmless, though. So, choosing to ignore him and shrug off the feeling of having eyes burning the back of her head, she continued to put the world to rights over a gin or two with her best friend.

Her skin started to feel a little too tight with the feeling of being talked about, as the same man who'd been staring all night continued to do so, his chin lifting in her direction as he spoke to his friend. The feeling was uncomfortable, but not wanting to make an unnecessary scene, she picked up her drink and refocussed on Tes, who spoke in detail about her most recent date fail with a girl from one town over.

Tes was a serial dater, on her quest to find 'the one', and this was just another one of many disappointing dates with the men and women she came across online. She had a rule against dating people who lived in Freymoor, and Noa often had to bite her lip against saying that the Tinder pool didn't appear to be much better.

An hour passed and, when the two of them were appropriately buzzed for a Friday night, Tes's attention was soon stolen by a beautiful redhead at the other side of the bar. Typical. She was always one to be easily distracted by a pretty face.

With her friend's barstool now empty, the blond-haired guy from earlier filled the spot and continued his blatant, unapologetic flirting. She was just about to shut him down when he reached out, resting his sweaty palm on her bare thigh, sending a shudder through her body with the contact.

Tingles spread up her legs, but not the good kind that she got whenever Alex touched her like that. No, this didn't feel right. She brushed him off, but that only caused him to lean in so that he was able to whisper in her ear. His alcohol-soaked breath filling the tiny bit of space between them had her instantly recoiling.

She pulled back in time to hear Tes whisper-shout, 'Hot and angry boss alert. Hold on to your panties.'

Noa turned her head quickly to see what Tes was referring to, but there was no need. Before she had a chance to even turn fully in her seat, Alex was there. She swore that if they were in a cartoon sketch, he would have a bright red face and steam coming out of his ears, as he not-so-politely demanded the guy leave.

'You... you can't do that man.'

'I can and, more importantly, I am. This is my bar. Get the fuck out before I kick all your buddies out with you. Wouldn't want to spoil the party, would you?'

The drunk guy scoffed, muttering under his breath, 'She wasn't even worth it.'

Noa's spine straightened, knowing that was not the right thing to say in front of a livid Alex who looked like he was about to explode any second. The guy didn't get far before Alex had his fist closed around his bicep, tugging him back. The guy stumbled but managed to catch himself before he fell. Not that she thought Alex would care much if he did.

'Apologise,' Alex warned with a snarl.

Noa could have sworn his eyes went black as night then, and she would have curled up in a ball if she was the other guy. Despite the discomfort she'd felt only moments ago, there was something exciting about seeing Alex like this. That protective side of him that once filled her with rage now sent arousal thrumming through her. It was insanely attractive to see him sticking up for her like this. Maybe it was how safe she felt around him, or the intense look in his eyes that had a fire burning in her core.

The blond guy didn't seem to share the same sentiment as he scoffed, 'You've got to be joking.'

He gaped at Alex.

Alex raised his eyebrow, almost daring the guy to test him.

'You sure you want to find out? I've not had to swing my fists in a while, but there is always an exception.'

Looking at the ground, the guy muttered a hardly-noticeable, 'Sorry.'

Alex pushed him toward the door, saying things to him that she couldn't quite hear as they left. When Alex returned, Noa went to speak, whether to apologise or to get angry she didn't know. She was currently in too much of a daze from how hot the man in front of her had been. But before she could do either, he was flinging Noa over his shoulder and taking her to his office behind the bar.

To hell with whoever saw, apparently.

The carnivorous look in his eyes sent chills through her body, but this time it was the kind that set her body alight with anticipation. Every place that his eyes touched felt hot, and her inner thighs grew damp with how aroused he made her feel with nothing but a look. A look that felt like a gentle caress and a wicked promise all in one. She wanted to squirm under the intensity of it. It was as if he was undressing her with his eyes, like she'd noticed he'd been doing all night, but this time it felt like a warning of what was to come.

For a moment his expression turned soft.

'Are you okay?' he asked, cupping her cheek with his calloused hand.

She leaned into it, her lips gently brushing his pulse point.

'I am now,' she whispered.

And she meant it. As long as she was with him, she would be.

Alex's eyes searched hers for a moment and, once he was satisfied with what he saw there—the truth, maybe—his eyes glazed over with lust once again.

He turned her around so that her cheek and chest were pressed against the office door and moved so his lips grazed against her ear. His rough hands came around to pin her own to the door on either side of her head. She looked at them, imagining those inked arms snaking lower, his fingers going to the place where she ached to feel him.

She was breathy, panting with her need for him, when he whispered, 'You sound flustered, Noa. Who made you like this? Me, or him?'

His nostrils flared as he said it, and Noa arched into him in response.

'You,' she whined. 'Always you.'

She heard a rumble from his chest, then he reached down as she pushed her hips back to meet his rock-hard bulge. He slid his thumb along the inner seam of her leggings, not quite giving enough pressure to cause any pleasure. It was frustrating, to say the least. She knew he could feel how wet she was, and that he was just testing her.

'And this?' he questioned. 'Is this for me?'

'Y... yes,' she panted, as he cupped her.

She ground her hips against his palm, eliciting an eruption of shockwaves throughout her entire body until he ripped his hand away.

In the most demanding tone that she had ever heard from him he said, 'Keep your hands there. Don't move them, got it?'

She nodded. Words failed her right now. She was so turned-on as he prowled around her, taking her in. Her chest heaved and her legs trembled. She felt naked despite her clothes, and it was an effort to remain standing up straight.

'I'm trying to be a better man, Noa. To be the man you deserve. A man who thinks first and uses his fists later. To let go of that angry boy I was and be the man you need and deserve. But it's so hard when I see you with pricks like that. When all I want is for us to belong only to each other.'

'Alex, I am...'

She wasn't able to finish when his hands came up to cup her face and he inhaled her in a desperate, all-encompassing kiss that had her toes curling. He swallowed her moan as he devoured her, pouring so much emotion into what felt like one earth-shattering kiss.

He pulled away, resting his forehead to hers as they both caught their breath. Then, his eyes met hers, as if in question, and it looked like his restraint was causing him physical pain. She loved seeing him like this, knowing she caused it and that he felt every single bit of what she felt for him. Despite all his possessive nature, *that* made her feel powerful. In control.

She nodded at him, electricity coursing through her body in anticipation. The second she gave him the green-light, Alex's lips found hers again. His hands came to the front of her, pinching her already hard nipples through her top. They'd felt so sensitive lately, but when he pinched and kneaded them, it made her feel wild.

She went to move her hands, to grab him whilst he played with her, but he clasped them against the door.

He'd done this before and knew she loved it. Knowing he had taken the effort to learn what made her feel good only turned her on more.

'Does it make you crazy being unable to touch me like this?'

'Yes.'

'Good. Now stay still. This isn't going to be slow or gentle. I'm going to fuck you hard enough so that you feel me there for days. And every time you do, you'll remember who you belong to.'

For the first time, she wanted to belong to someone other than herself, to surrender control and submit to him. So, she did exactly that, enjoying every second as he fucked her relentlessly until her legs gave out and he had to hold her up. Until the strength of both their orgasms crashing through her had her seeing stars and screaming out, his fist coming up to cover her mouth.

'Save those pretty sounds only for me, Noa. I plan on being the only person who gets to hear them from now on, because you are mine.'

'Yours.'

# Chapter 42

## Noa

Noa sat at the long oak dining table that had served countless family dinners and celebrations over the years. Tinks purred contently in her lap as Noa stared out the window with her hands wrapped around her favourite polka dot mug, letting the contents warm her fingers. Even in the summer, the high ceilings and thick walls meant the Drakes' kitchen was always cool. She quite liked it, though, gazing out at the rich variety of plants, lovingly potted by her mum, whilst also avoiding breaking out in a sweat.

She'd sat gazing out at the same view for most of the day whilst the rest of the family were at work. It had given her space to work on her novel in peace and quiet before they all returned for their typical Friday night dinner. A banditry of blue tits flew past the window before landing on the berry tree at the bottom of the garden. The movement made Noa realise she hadn't been writing for a good twenty minutes but had, instead, been lost in her daydreams of Alex. Except, they weren't daydreams. They were her reality now.

She wiggled her mouse and her laptop whirred back to life, her manuscript once again filling the screen. It had been four weeks since she had started working for Alex, and she was surprised by how motivated and inspired she'd been with her writing in that time. But then, she supposed, it'd be hard not to be inspired when you are getting railed by a sexy as sin man six ways to Sunday every single night. Because that's what it had turned into. They might be moving quick, considering, but they now spent every single night together and the whole thing just felt right.

Tes, the true best friend that she was, had been covering for Noa by corroborating the story that she was staying at her house most nights since she'd still not found the right way or the right time to share the news with her family yet.

When she was at his place, Alex still liked to watch Noa write and, sometimes, when she'd exceeded the word count she had set for herself, he would even reward her with an orgasm or two. And, boy, did he know lots of different ways to do it. It wasn't a bad way to end a day and, sometimes, she couldn't believe she ever went without him.

She flushed at the thought. Even though no one was around to see it, her eyes bounced around the kitchen, as if confirming there was no one to hear her inner thoughts.

A family photo caught her attention amongst the many that were pinned to the gallery wall. Alex was in it. It was the night of her nineteenth birthday, and they all looked so young. One thing she hadn't noticed before, though, was that Alex wasn't looking at the camera in the photo. His attention was fixed on her.

Noa stood from the table, her chair scraping against the linoleum floor as she moved to take a closer look. The expression on Alex's face was adoring. Maybe more, even. Something inside her ached at the sight.

She thought back to that night, the night she had lost her virginity to a man she'd now lost her heart to, and she wished she hadn't run away like she had. Wished she'd given the whole thing a chance, because it felt like they had wasted so much time.

But then, she also felt like everything happened for a reason and, maybe, this was how things were meant to turn out. Maybe, things wouldn't have worked back then. That's one of the reasons that she had left in the first place, to protect Ryan and Alex's relationship, but also because she was young, and she knew the likelihood of a relationship at that age lasting in the long run was slim. Long distance made those chances even slimmer. It didn't feel worth risking their relationship back then for something that wouldn't last. But things felt different now. So, maybe, she should thank her younger self for making the decision she did back then.

The front door burst open and Noa heard bags crashing to the floor and boots being flung off. She cleared her throat and blinked rapidly to dissipate the emotion that had just taken over her before Ryan walked through the door.

No one but him would make that kind of entrance, and she didn't want to answer any questions that would follow as a result.

After Ryan had arrived at their parents' house, followed by her mum and dad, Noa cleared her writing materials and set the table for dinner.

Tonight, after so much time spent with Alex recently, she was spending the night at home. Ryan had been busy with his presentation at work, so he, too, had been spending more time at his cottage, meaning the two of them had barely seen each other.

As her mum cooked her homemade beef stew and dumplings, Ryan spent the night quizzing Noa on why she'd been MIA, and it was getting harder and harder to lie to him.

'Seriously, I feel like I saw you more when you lived five hours away with that douche of a boyfriend,' he complained, his tone mirroring that of a whiny toddler.

Noa rolled her eyes, exasperated at how dramatic he was being and praying he would let it go soon.

'One, despite us being together for six years, you barely even knew him. And two, you've had your head down working your ass off for the pastoral lead role, so how am I being accused of being the MIA one?' she countered.

'Exactly, you two were together that long and he rarely ever came around. So that's all I need to know,' Ryan responded, completely ignoring her argument that he had been equally as busy, too.

His words stung. She felt like someone had slammed into her gut, but only because of the undeniable truth to them. But, Ryan continued his probing, so she couldn't dwell on them long.

'So, do I need to have a word with Tes for hogging all your attention, then? Between her and this next bestseller of yours, I'm feeling very neglected.'

She was lucky her brother had been so distracted lately with his presentation. She was sure they'd have been busted a lot sooner if he'd had more time to think on the sheer amount of time she was 'staying at Tes's'. But with his mind elsewhere, he hadn't yet called her out on how suspicious it was.

Ignoring the guilt she felt at that, Noa decided to settle into the gentle teasing her and Ryan knew best.

Sticking out her bottom lip and twisting her fists against her eyes she mocked him, 'Boohoo, you big cry-baby. Do you not have friends of your own to demand all their time from. It's not my fault some of us have a life.'

'I have plenty of friends, thank you, but sue me for wanting more sibling time. There's me thinking I got best friend rights since I've been there for you since... oh, I don't know... birth. But whatever, I guess.'

'Oh yeah, because you had a choice in that,' Noa laughed. 'Things are just crazy right now, and I am trying to get settled. But I will make a mental note to make more time for your needy ass. I thought we had grown out of needing dedicated "sibling time",' she said whilst crooking her fingers in the air to make quotation marks. 'But I was wrong, and I will remember that in the future.'

Ryan slouched down in his chair like a petulant child, folding his arms over his chest.

'Thank you. That's all I ask.'

Her dad, who had sat reading his newspaper, unfazed by their playful bickering, just looked up and winked at her. It was like his version of a pat on the back for placating her brother.

Whilst Ryan spoke, her mum kept giving knowing looks, but Noa just focused on trying to ignore them. She averted her eyes, looking down at the table, her fingers tracing the very obvious groove she had once tried to hide after she'd sliced into the oak during an evening of pumpkin-carving.

They'd been watching a scary movie on her laptop at the time, as was tradition before Halloween. At the height of a scary scene, Ryan had jumped from behind her to shout in Noa's ear. With a shriek of fear, she'd cut straight through the pumpkin and into the table. Alex, who usually loved to take part in Ryan's pranks and teasing, had taken this one badly and berated him for a solid five minutes about how risky it had been whilst she was holding a knife. He then got to work trying to help Noa try to hide the mark from her mum.

The memory made her realise that he had always been protective over her, and maybe she had missed so many signs. Despite their best efforts, Noa had never been able to hide anything from her mum, and she saw straight through them. Like Noa was sure she could now.

Instead of getting angry at them about the slice, though, her mum had pointed to the doorjamb where height markers were drawn throughout her childhood, then to the colourful family portrait in the corner of the skirting boards and said, 'This house is a home, Noa. It's the memories littered throughout that make it.'

Lifting her head from the table and taking in the loving family that surrounded her, Noa suddenly felt intense guilt that she had let this thing go on for so long whilst lying to her brother. If her mum knew without her telling her, then it was only a matter of time until Ryan would figure it out. She owed it to him to be the one to tell him directly. They would tell him soon. She just needed to find the right time, and over family dinner was not it.

After a very draining family dinner, Tes arrived unannounced at their door, much to Ryan's joy. Noa had never felt so glad to be saved by her best friend. Physically pulling her from the kitchen and up the stairs to her bedroom, she closed the door and fell back onto the bed, letting out a long breath.

'Well, you look tense,' Tes observed.

'Understatement of the century. I can't lie anymore. Ryan needs to know, but I need to talk to Alex and make sure we are both on the same page. He might want to be there when I tell him, so I just need to give Ryan a wide berth until then.'

'Good luck with that,' Tes laughed. 'I don't know if you've noticed, but your brother is like a very intense, very badly-behaved golden retriever, begging for all the attention in a room all of the time.'

'Thanks. I am aware, but avoidance has been my tactic so far and it seems to be working just fine. Anyway, I am so drained right now. I don't want to deal or even think about this right now. I feel like I could sleep for a week, and it wouldn't be enough. Fancy not talking about life for a bit and just watching some TV?'

'Music to my ears.'

There were unsaid words on Tes's lips, and Noa could see it. She knew when Tes was struggling. There was something going on with her friend and she knew she should ask, but she felt like she needed some quiet time as much as Noa did, and she didn't want to push.

So, ignoring any elephant in the room, the two of them bedded down under her covers, somehow squeezing into her single bed, and watched re-runs of Noa's comfort TV show, *Gilmore Girls*. Noa had lost count of the number of times they'd done this together. The predictability of it had always settled something in her and, right now, she needed that.

Tinks squished between them comedically, with only her head popping out from under the covers, enjoying the strokes they both offered her. Noa sometimes wondered if her cat fancied herself more human than feline, but she wouldn't change her for the world. The comfort her presence brought was like her own personal anti-depressant wrapped in fluff.

Not long into episode two, as Tinks' light snores filled the room, Noa could feel Tes becoming increasingly restless as she tossed around the bed, letting the odd groan passed her lips.

'What's up?' Noa asked.

'Oh, just my stupid period. I feel like my uterus is trying to claw its way out of my body as we speak, and I will not thank her for it. Hurts like a bitch.'

'Hot-water bottle?'

'Oh my god, yes please.'

Noa flung her feet over the side of the bed and padded downstairs to the kitchen. She stared at the colourful tiles behind the kettle, mindlessly filling the hot-water bottle until suddenly the sight of it had her stomach falling.

*What date was it?*

When was the last time she had needed this for her own period? She couldn't remember. Rushing to pull up her period tracking app on her phone, her heart sank when she realised she was two weeks late. Rushing back up to her room with more urgency than when she came downstairs, Tes sat bolt upright as she barged in, as if sensing her panic.

'What's up? What happened?'

'I'm late.'

'What? You're late? As in late-late, or late to be somewhere?'

'As in late-late. Two weeks late to be exact.'

'Okay, okay. Let's not panic. There might be a perfectly reasonable explanation for this. Stress, maybe, or the pill messing with your cycle. How many times have we stressed like this only to buy all the tests in the store that turn out negative each time? Which, you could say is irrational for me, considering I mainly sleep with women and, most of the time, it's not even possible. But I swear this fear of yours rubs off on me and we lose our heads every time our periods don't show up.'

'You're right. We have been through this countless times. There is no reason this will be any different. But you know the drill, right?'

Without even having to be asked, Tes was out of the bed, pulling on her coat and boots and heading for the door.

'Yup. Let's go get you that test.'

Rushing to the store in record time and finding the pharmacy aisle without any issues, Noa pulled three tests from the shelf, looking over at Tes for reassurance.

'Seriously?' Tes asked.

'No, you're right, that's definitely not enough,' she said, picking up two more and a large carton of apple juice.

The two of them were at the counter and paid in no time. The nerves that felt like a whirlwind taking over her entire stomach meant Noa couldn't settle until she knew for sure.

‘I need to do this now,’ she blurted, stopping dead in her tracks in the middle of the supermarket.’

‘Now? Like here?’ Tes asked, looking around.

Nodding, Noa turned, heading straight to the customer toilets with Tes hot on her heels. Patience had never been Noa’s strong suit, no matter how much convincing Alex had tried and, right now, three minutes had never felt so painful.

Bouncing her leg, Noa perched on the counter by the sinks whilst Tes stood next to her, waiting for the moment that could spin her entire world off its axis.

A jarring noise rang in Noa’s ears, bouncing off the tiled walls of the small room they had locked themselves inside. Realising it was the timer Tes had clearly set, having done this with her many times before, Noa turned the sticks until the truth was glaring up at her. Two pink lines taunted her from all five tests in her hands.

Tes turned to look at her, wide eyes filled with what Noa could only assume was sympathy.

‘You’re pregnant,’ she stated after several minutes of them both standing silent and stunned.

She repeated the words again, because Noa was pretty sure she looked like she was malfunctioning. She just nodded, unable to find any words for the clusterfuck she somehow found herself in.

She was pregnant.

*Well, shit.*

# Chapter 43

## Alex

Ryan was at the bar for their usual Sunday night lock-up and catch-up. Although these had been less regular since they'd returned from their holiday, avoiding his friend altogether would've given away that something was wrong. Alex couldn't afford for Ryan to ask any questions, especially until Noa gave him the go-ahead to tell him. And despite not wanting to lie to his friend's face, for her he would.

'She's seemed so much brighter since she came back, you know. I hate to admit it—and if she asks, I will deny this—but, maybe, I was wrong. I think it was what she needed. The trip seemed to be good for her.'

Ryan continued talking about Noa and how different she'd been since her travels. He supposed this was better than the prior conversation, which had also centred around Noa, but regarding the fact that she'd been so MIA since they got back. 'Conversation' was probably not the best way to put it. It was mainly Ryan talking and failing to notice Alex's lack of contribution as he necked his beer and silently nodded along. He couldn't be accused of lying if he didn't open his mouth, right?

'That reminds me. I know I've said it already, but honestly man, thanks for going away with her like I asked. Maybe it was a bit dramatic of me, but she's my little sister, and she seemed so vulnerable when she came home. I just needed her safe from any creepers.'

*Yep, no creepers pursuing your sister here. No, sir. Just your so-called best friend.*

God, Hell should just swallow him up right now, because that seemed like where he was inevitably going anyway.

'Was she with anyone whilst you were away?' Ryan casually asked, causing beer to spew out of Alex's nose as he coughed and spluttered in his shock.

'No, you're right. Don't answer that. I mean, like you'd know anyway, right?'

'Right,' Alex muttered.

He tried to keep his face straight, but his skin burned under the pressure of lying to his best friend. His chest felt so tight it was almost concerning.

*Was he having a medical event?*

'And she told me that you offered her this job so that she could really make a good go at the writing thing. That was real nice of you, man. You're a good friend, and I don't say it enough.'

Alex sunk farther and farther into the leather wing-back chair he sat in at the back of the bar, hoping he would either become a part of it, or that the several beers he was chugging would numb the increasing sense of guilt right out of him.

'You're quiet tonight. Everything alright?'

The genuine concern in Ryan's eyes made Alex feel even worse. He needed to get it together, or else it was game over.

'Yeah, I'm fine. It's just been a long few days. These beers are helping, though. Going down a treat and, at least, I have a day off tomorrow.'

Ryan perked up even more at that. 'You know what that means, right?'

Alex just stared at him, waiting for him to fill in the blanks.

'We haven't gotten drunk together in so long. Let's have a lock-in like old times.'

'It's hardly a lock-in with the two of us. We do that most weeks,' Alex grunted.

'Potayto, potahto,' Ryan shrugged, his voice a sing-song.

'Fine, but if we're doing this, then we're doing this properly. We need a bottle of whiskey and a bucket of ice.'

'No other way to do it,' Ryan agreed as he headed behind the bar.

*Was he skipping? He was definitely skipping. Christ.*

'No, we need the good stuff I reserve just for me. It's in my office. I'll go.'

Alex went to move from his chair, deciding a breather in his office to gather himself was probably a good call.

'I got it man,' Ryan called, holding his hand up before Alex could even advance from his seat.

As the door banged behind Ryan, Alex let out a long breath. Yes, whiskey sounded like a great idea indeed. He sat, deep in his own thoughts, waiting for Ryan to return. He tried to muster up a plan in his head. What was the best plan for telling Ryan about him and Noa? Every time he tried to picture it—the perfect way to tell your best friend that you've been secretly dating his sister—he came up short.

Should he take him out for food? Do it in public? No, that didn't sound ideal. Too many prying eyes and ears in this nosy town.

Maybe, they could break it to him at one of the Friday night dinners at the Drakes'? Bethan and Isaac were reasonable people. If Ryan jumped to any conclusions, something that wouldn't be entirely out of character for him, Alex was sure they'd make good buffers. Or, at least, settle him enough so Alex and Noa could explain.

Yes. That's what they would do. The second he could talk to Noa and update her on his plan, he would. And he was sure she'd be all for it.

A second later, doors slammed again but, this time, it wasn't the office ones. Instead, they came from behind him. Turning around to see who the hell was coming into his bar at this time past midnight, he was shocked to see a breathless Noa in the doorway.

Her hair stuck to her face in a matted mess from either the drizzle of rain outside, or time spent running her hands through it. He could see the faint smattering of sweat above her furrowed brow.

She looked like a woman on a mission as she stalked toward him, and he couldn't quite work out the emotion on her face. Anger mixed with fear, maybe?

Whatever it was had panic instantly flaring in his gut, and he wanted to capture her in his arms. But Ryan was here, so he remained still as she continued across the room. She bit her lip, in the way he knew she did when she was worried, and stopped in front of him.

Alex opened his mouth to tell Noa her brother was here, but was quickly cut off by words flying from her lips at a rapid pace. Frantic, nonsensical words that he struggled to keep up with. He tried to gesture in the direction Ryan had gone, hoping it would be enough for her to understand. But she kept on going, looking only confused by his attempts at silent communication.

Eventually, he just sat there and listened as she untactfully blurted out the words that he never thought he would hear. Words that had his ears ringing and his knees almost buckling.

If he wasn't sitting, he was sure he'd have lost a few teeth in his nosedive toward the floor. He stared right at her, focussing on trying to keep upright whilst, in the space of seconds, she flipped his entire world upside-down.

And, in those seconds, too many contrasting emotions ping-ponged around his brain, and he was unable to settle on just one. Relief and fear, confusion and understanding, excitement and trepidation. He flicked from one to the other faster than he could even process. None of it made sense, and his head throbbed as a result.

This woman had changed his life forever, in more ways than one. And, knowing who remained in the bar with them, he might not be the only one who knew it.

# Chapter 44

## Noa

This was the first time Noa had ever felt intimidated by the thick wooden doors guarding The Brew, though it was likely what sat behind them that had her heart racing. Or, more like who. Her gut churned as she thought about the conversation that needed to be had.

The door served as the band-aid that she needed to rip off to see what was lying beneath, but the longer she stood there, staring up at the metal sign that said, 'Welcome to The Brew', the worse her anxiety got. She'd tormented herself over this discussion for the last twenty-four hours. Suddenly, she wished Tes was still here to hold her hand through it.

Last night, Tes, sensing Noa's trepidation, had spent all evening and way into the early morning being her rock, talking through her options for the pregnancy without judgement. Her best friend was exactly the person Noa had needed to help her process the new revelation. She had slipped straight into practical mode, printing pamphlets she found online and, together, they'd researched pregnancy advisory services.

Noa didn't know what she wanted to do right now. At least, sometimes she thought she did, but then she changed her mind every five minutes. Despite knowing that she was in a position other people would kill for, and that she was at a time in her life when people did have babies, she couldn't help thinking about the times she still felt like a baby herself. She didn't feel like a grown-up capable of making grown-up decisions. She could barely decide which cereal to buy on her weekly shop.

But this?

This was the biggest decision she would ever have to make, and the enormity of it felt like a lead weight on her shoulders. She didn't know what the right decision was and kept wishing there was some kind of 'ask AI' way of making it.

When she thought about abortion, she couldn't tell how much of her reaction was just a knee-jerk to shock and fear. Because, despite all the 'what ifs' and reasons she might not be ready for this, she kept finding herself instinctively pressing her hand to her non-existent baby bump. It was irrational, considering the baby was likely the size of a raspberry— at least, that's what the internet had told her—but as she stroked her stomach, she felt like the baby growing in there connected her to Alex.

This hadn't been in her grand plan. Actually, kids never had been. But look where not going with the grand plan had gotten her recently. Letting go of it had allowed her the freedom to be happy in a way she never had been before.

Noa had never specifically thought she didn't want kids, she just hadn't been sure, and she'd always thought that, if it ever did happen, that she would be. She thought it would be black and white. She'd have a husband and a house, and it would be planned. They'd both tell their families and they'd all be crying, ecstatic for their growing little family.

She never expected to be doing a test in the supermarket with so many mixed feelings, fear being the overwhelming one. But life was messy, and it wasn't black and white like the younger version of herself had once believed. She'd realised that messy didn't have to mean bad, and some of her most memorable experiences had come from living in the grey areas. So, as she stood outside The Brew and stroked her stomach, again, she knew that this could be really good. A happy surprise. And she hoped Alex would see it that way, too.

She was terrified, and had no idea what she was doing, but she couldn't help but ask herself, 'Did anyone?' Or was that, again, just a social construct? Tes told her not to judge herself for the array of feelings she switched between, to let it happen and give herself time and grace to sort through them to decide what's right for her.

She knew she didn't need to tell Alex if she didn't want to, and she didn't need to include him in the decision. It was her body to have autonomy over, and she had the choice of what to do with it. But telling him felt right, and she wanted his help in deciding what to do.

She knew he had complex feelings around his own dad, and had even heard him talk about the fact that he didn't want kids a few times, but she also knew him. He had become her best friend over the last few months. She knew he would try his best to be impartial and help her work through this. Maybe it was selfish of her to ask him to do that, but all she knew was, even if she didn't need him, she wanted him and his comfort right now.

So, like Tes had suggested, Noa had sat with her feelings all day. Going through her options over and over in her head, she finally decided to go with her instincts, and they had led her here—standing alone on a very empty Main Street at midnight.

As soon as she had gained an ounce of courage, knowing Alex would be locking up and they could sit and talk, she'd basically flown out the door to get here without a second thought.

If only she could make it past the doors now. She willed her feet to move. She had never felt so scared to have a conversation in her whole life. For a people-pleaser who continuously avoided confrontation, this was her worst nightmare. Had she got it all wrong? Would he be angry? Would he cut and run at the first sight of any adult problems instead of them facing it together? The more she stood there, the more she questioned it. She wished she could turn off this anxious part of her brain, the part that overthinks and spirals.

This was ludicrous. She was a grown-ass woman, and she should just come out and tell him. It takes two to tango so, if he wanted to be mad at her, then he could just go ahead and fuck right off. With that thought giving her more courage than when she'd arrived, Noa burst through the doors and let the words come tumbling out before she could second-guess herself.

'So, yeah, it's not ideal, but turns out the pill isn't one hundred percent accurate. Who knew right? Okay, well, maybe everybody knows, but they really should put that on the packets in bold letters for when hormones get the better of people. Or, maybe they do, and I just didn't look hard enough...' trailing off she stared into the distance for a minute deep in thought before realising she'd gotten distracted.

Alex's chin jutted out repetitively.

He looked like one of those nodding dogs people put on their dashboard, or a chicken roaming his coop. Eyes bugging, arms flailing, he looked like he was trying to convey some kind of secret without words. She ignored whatever he was doing. It would have to wait, because she was on a roll and couldn't get deterred from what she came here to say.

With a heavy sigh, she pressed on, a rambling mess intent on really following that band-aid analogy.

'What I meant to say was, I'm pregnant, preggers, knocked up, up the duff, bun in the oven, fertilised.'

She heard it as she blurted it out with all the composure of a toddler on a sugar high, but couldn't seem to stop herself. She cringed at her own words. The pitch of her voice seemed to go up an octave with every absurd pregnancy synonym she came up with. She'd spent hours mulling over this very conversation, and this was the best she had?

Her arms started waving around her belly in some ridiculous attempt to gesture a pregnant bump, just in case he hadn't already got the picture.

The weird hand gestures and head bobbing suddenly stopped. Alex stood still and stared at her, blinking rapidly, looking like a deer in headlights. He didn't say anything for a few minutes, and the silence felt heavy around them. There was no sound but the roar of her heartbeat in her ears and the ticking of the old grandfather clock, reminding them that time had, in fact, not stood still. Noa started to question whether she'd imagined she'd told him at all until Alex seemed to return to reality.

His eyes suddenly doubled in size, and he cleared his throat in a weird staccato she assumed she was meant to understand but just didn't. His hand came up to rub at his stubble aggressively, his features scrunching, but he still wasn't using his words.

Okay, what was going on? Had she broken him? Was he having some kind of technical glitch and needed a reset?

'Noa, I...'

Alex had finally started to respond when he was cut off by the door of the back office behind him flying open. Noa whirled around and was paralysed by a pair of stormy eyes, the same colour as hers.

*Shit.*

It was suddenly clear to her that she had fucked up. Alex had been trying to tell her something with all his weird signalling, if that's what you could even call it. In her haste to get out of the house, there was one very important detail she had forgotten. It was a Sunday night. And Alex was doing the same thing that he did every Sunday.

Which meant Ryan was here, and he'd heard the whole thing.

# Chapter 45

## Alex

Charging toward Alex, Ryan wound back his fist and clocked him straight in the jaw. Alex heard Noa shriek before she lunged forward, but he didn't move. Instead, he let Ryan take another shot.

He deserved it. He'd seen it coming, actually. He'd been lying and sneaking around behind Ryan's back with his little sister, the sister he'd always acted for first and thought later when it came to protecting.

The next words, though he'd feared them all these years, he did not expect.

'Like father like son, I guess,' Ryan spat, utter venom spewing from his tongue.

And hell, if those words didn't cut Alex deeper than any knife ever could. Ryan could've gutted him, and it would have hurt less. Alex had no words of defence, though. He could only stand there motionless, still letting the words sink in, both Noa's from earlier and Ryan's now. He reeled at the possibility that he was going to be a dad.

*I'm pregnant*. She really had said that right?

He didn't have to question whether he'd heard right for long because the rage pulsing from Ryan said it all. His shoulders were so tense they were almost touching his ears. His eyes, usually bright, icy blue like Noa's, now looked dark cobalt and twitched furiously as he tried and failed to contain his anger.

Alex didn't blame his friend for lashing out. It wasn't like he and Noa had given him any reason to suspect they had feelings for each other. And, with Alex's dating history, he knew what his friend thought.

Fuck.

How had they gotten this so wrong? They thought they were protecting themselves and Ryan by keeping this a secret, but all they had done was feed into the belief Ryan now had that this was something to hide, that Noa was another woman Alex would sleep with and walk away from. But this time, leaving behind more than just fun memories just like his dad had done to his mum. How was Ryan to know that this was so much more than that? That Noa was everything to him.

Ryan's fists pulsed at his sides like he was trying to restrain himself from any further violence.

'Noa, in the car now!' he barked, aiming his fury at her now.

His eyes were still locked on Alex, though, even as he pointed at the door he expected Noa to leave through.

'Ryan, just stop for a second and listen. You're not being fair,' Noa whispered, her voice sounding so small as it cracked with the plea.

Alex didn't want her to plead for him, and hearing it both filled him up and cracked him wide open.

Unfortunately, all it did was fuel Ryan's rage. Coming out of his daze and seeing the snarl Ryan was giving Noa was enough to make Alex snap. Ryan was angry and acting on that emotion alone. He'd regret it tomorrow, but like hell was Alex about to let him speak to Noa in that way.

'Do not...' he growled, taking a step toward him. 'Talk to her like that.'

'I told you to take care of her, Alex. I trusted you. I told you she was vulnerable and needed you to look out for her and, as always, you thought with your cock and took advantage of that. But I must be the fool for thinking you'd behave any differently.'

*And the hits keep on coming.*

That's okay. Alex could take it if it kept them from being directed at her.

'So, do not start trying to play the hero and look out for her now. You slept with my sister, damn it!'

Ryan turned away like he couldn't even look at him. He was almost vibrating with his rage.

Alex looked to Noa, who he could visibly see starting to retreat into her shell, to shrink herself like she had when she first came home, and he would not have it. Not after seeing her bloom into herself.

'Your sister is a grown woman, Ryan. Treat her that way. I did what you said, followed along to protect her but, guess what? Noa does not need protecting by you, me, or anyone else, for that matter. She is strong and fierce and a force to be reckoned with most of the time. If only you would wake up and see it, then, maybe, you would truly see her. She's got a sharp tongue, just like you, and makes for the toughest sparring partner. She's not weak and does not need to be wrapped up in wool like you seem to think. When I learnt that, I backed off and watched her come alive out there. And, turns out, even though she didn't need me there, she still wanted me, and so I stayed. Not for you. And not because of your need for protection. But for her. Always for her.'

Ryan stepped back, clearly at a loss for words. His expression morphed into a whole spectrum of emotions—shock, realisation, anger, hurt, resignation. His eyes snapped from Alex to Noa, who now stood there slack-jawed, and Alex wondered if he had said too much. But Ryan needed to hear it.

Maybe, Noa did, too. Because he meant every single word.

# Chapter 46

## Noa

'She is strong and fierce and a force to be reckoned with'. Those words rang in Noa's head over and over as the bar around them zoomed in and out of focus. Never had she felt as seen as she did when she was with this man. And, deep down, she knew that had always been true, even if she didn't want to see it in the past. Even if it was easier to keep the peace than blow up their whole world.

But, looking around her, it was clear that their world somehow blew up anyway. Ryan's face was a picture of so many emotions—confusion, anger, hurt. Alex's nostrils flared with the rage he had turned on her brother, storm clouds taking over his irises. The sound of the grandfather clock seemed even louder now, painfully so, in the tense silence that felt like it was strangling her.

This stand-off was exactly what she had always feared. But what she hadn't expected was that, in all the mess, all she wanted to do was go to Alex. Because, despite every time she had shown him her weaknesses, he believed in her strength.

She'd been feeling so many things for this man for weeks but, right now, in this moment, she knew what she felt was love. So, without glancing at her brother, she went to him.

'Can I stay with you tonight?' she asked, voice barely above a whisper.

The words came out wobbly, emotion coating her throat and gripping her entire body tight.

Ryan needed to go home. He had said some hurtful things tonight. She knew he didn't mean them. He was just shocked, angry, and lashing out. But nevertheless, he had chosen his words deliberately to pick on Alex's biggest insecurities.

She knew she and Alex needed to talk about the pregnancy alone, and that Alex would need her tonight more than ever. She didn't want him to spiral. She also hadn't expected Ryan to look at her with such anger and disappointment in his eyes, and it stung.

He needed some space, and Noa needed to be far away from him until he could have an adult conversation, because she didn't need this right now. No one needed to be happy about the pregnancy other than her and Alex and, until she worked out how she felt about it, she would not let Ryan influence that. It was too important.

Ryan's shoulders fell, and he looked like the wounded little boy he once was. Sadness formed a band around her chest, heavy and debilitating.

'Ryan. if you'd just let us—'

Explain. That's what Alex was about to say when Ryan turned his back to them. Without a word, he slammed down the bottle he was holding and stormed out of the door.

*Mature.*

Now she turned her gaze back to Alex. His eyes were so comforting, the colour of some of her favourite things—tones of coffee and caramel, and the changing leaves in autumn. Despite the rugged, dangerous look and aura this man had always had, his eyes were kind. She never wanted to look away.

Feeling safer than she had since seeing those lines on a stick, she finally broke. She let the tears fall, and she fell into him. Alex's sturdy arms held her tight, and she cried and cried until she had no more tears left and his top was completely soaked. He placed small kisses on the crown of her head, stroking down her hair, whispering 'You're okay' in her ear.

She wanted to believe him. Somewhere deep inside her, she knew with him she would always be okay, but as he ushered her up the stairs towards his flat and she thought about how out of control the night had gotten, she knew she just wasn't there yet.

# Chapter 47

## Alex

Having managed to coax her up to his flat, Noa curled in a ball on Alex's sofa, almost like she was trying to make herself as small as possible. He hated seeing her like that. She gripped his baby blue blanket in her hands, like an infant clutched a comfort blankie. He watched her fists tighten and release over and over like she was using it to ground herself.

He knew Noa better than he knew himself sometimes, and he knew this was a sign she was becoming overwhelmed in her own head. But the fact that Ryan had caused the war likely raging inside her right now when he'd flown off the handle made Alex want to tear the world down.

Tears streamed freely down her cheeks. He itched to catch them with his lips and see what they tasted like, to wipe them away, along with that scared look in her eyes. He needed her to know that he had her, no matter what. He walked toward her slowly, allowing her time to ask for space if she needed it. He would give her whatever she needed.

'Noa,' he whispered.

Her chin dipped down, and she stared at the carpet. So he got to his knees in front of her.

'I've messed it all up,' she choked out in a sob. 'He was so angry. I've never seen him so angry, Alex.'

'He'll live,' he said.

Noa's chin tucked even closer into her chest.

'I've let everyone down again. I've let everyone down,' she sputtered and cried.

This time, Alex didn't hesitate, and cupped her chin between his thumb and forefinger, bringing her face up so her eyes met his. She looked shocked for a moment, but she didn't fight him, like she was resigned and there was no fight left in her. She looked at him through tear-soaked lashes.

His wild girl, who had always managed to don her mask of confidence, who he'd always seen as self-assured and larger-than-life, had let the mask slip. He could see it in those eyes, the deepest cerulean blue, like the sky on a crisp, autumn day. She looked lost. And, fuck, if that didn't wreck him.

He wanted to fix it. And he realised he would give this girl anything she wanted to do it. To see that spark that could only be her.

'Hey,' he said in as soothing a tone as he could muster with his heart galloping in his chest. 'You have done nothing wrong. Do you hear me? Nothing. Your family loves you, and there is nothing you could do that would make that any less true. You have not let anyone down, Noa, but you are failing to see one really important thing here. None of this is about them. This is about you. How do *you* feel?'

Her eyes went wide, and she blinked at him with a look of utter shock on her face, like he'd just asked her the most obscure of questions.

'I...' she trailed off and swallowed hard.

He followed it with his eyes and had to force himself to keep the indecent thoughts that the sight elicited on a leash at this moment. God, this girl was beautiful. Even now, with mascara coating her face and snot falling from her nose, she was the most beautiful woman he had every laid eyes on.

After a beat where Alex could see she was mulling over his words, Noa looked up and said, 'Is it crazy that when I saw those lines on that stick, after the initial shock, for a moment I was happy? Before I thought about all the mess. I've done nothing but panic ever since, and mulled over every possible option in my head. But I don't know, the thought of doing this... with you... it just feels like it was meant to be. I didn't think we would end up here. Hell, nothing in my life has gone to plan lately, and I never used to think I wanted to be a mum. So, the feeling of happiness shocked me, too, but in that moment, I felt like I'd found purpose, and that brought me peace. Then I spiralled again, and it's been a whole thing but, you know... that's the gist of it.'

Suddenly, Alex felt as if he couldn't catch a breath as he stared at her, in awe of how strong and beautiful she was. She'd always been a force to be reckoned with. He meant what he'd said to Ryan. She was fierce and, despite everything she'd been through, all the battles she fought in her head, that had never changed. Looking at her, all he wanted to do was stoke the embers that he saw burning in her eyes until she set him alight, too. He would dance in her flames, because this woman had owned his heart since they were thirteen years old; since the day he had met her.

Ryan had brought him to the Drakes' house for his first-ever Friday night dinner. His eyes had found her immediately. She was tucked under a blanket on the sofa, a Michael Morpurgo book in her hand and she had looked entranced, completely lost in a fictional world.

She'd barely even noticed him, and he'd watched her—how her tongue slipped out of her mouth in concentration, her brow furrowing with concern, and the little gasps that occasionally escaped as she read. When Ryan flopped onto the sofa next to her, she finally looked up and Alex felt like he was drowning in the swirling pools of her bright blue eyes. His heart had been hers since that moment.

Right now though, she had his heart, body, and soul, and he was ready to show her exactly what that meant. He would be everything she needed, no matter what it took. He would not make his dad's mistakes, because even the thought of ever walking away from her and his child growing inside her shredded Alex's heart apart. He had never been so sure of anything in his entire life.

He nodded and, with that, gave her the only words that he could find, 'Then nothing else matters.'

# Chapter 48

## Noa

The next morning, Noa awoke to the smell of fresh coffee and bacon wafting through the generously-sized flat. She hauled herself out of Alex's comfy-as-hell king-sized bed and tugged on one of his old hoodies, preparing to go and investigate.

The living space was light and airy compared to the dark cave of his bedroom. She hadn't realised she'd slept so long. She took in his space as she made her way toward the kitchen.

When Alex first brought her to his flat after they'd returned to Freymoor, she'd been shocked at its size, as well as the lack of bachelor pad vibes. It was nothing like what she had expected.

The flat was three bedrooms and took up the entire footprint of the bar and, although the place was immaculate, it still had a homely feel to it. Picture frames dotted the walls and throws and cushions decorated the sofa.

The photos actually looked like a mini version of the gallery wall at her parent's house, and that made Noa smile for what felt like the first time in over twenty-four hours as images of Alex trying to decorate this place, picking out colour schemes and furniture and trying to make it into a home, came to her mind.

She wasn't surprised he'd drawn inspiration from one of the homiest homes that she knew. Her mum had put so much tender love and care into making it that way. It was years of memories and laughter shared under one roof, the kitchen cabinets painted her mum's favourite colour by her dad, art projects like pieces of their childhood scattered throughout, and it didn't take much for Noa to imagine this place being that way, too. She smiled wider, imagining that future where she got to help Alex make it that way.

Always one to follow the smell of coffee, despite her best effort and failure to cut down, Noa dragged herself toward the source of the smell. Her legs protested, body aching, likely exhausted from the adrenaline crash she'd had in the early hours of the morning. The events of the night still filled her with dread, but she felt comforted knowing that, despite it all, she was still here with Alex.

Stepping into the kitchen, her mouth began to water, but it wasn't from what was cooking. Alex stood there in nothing but a pair of tight, white boxers, broad shoulders on display, the tattoos that decorated the expanse of his arms, shoulders, and back making him look just a little bit dangerous. He was glorious to look at, and her brain really did turn to mush every time she saw him.

But she couldn't get distracted this morning. They had too much to talk about.

Clearly sensing her presence, Alex turned with a mug of milky coffee, just the way she liked it, and slid it across the granite island towards her.

'Sit,' he commanded. 'Breakfast won't be a minute.'

'Alex, we need to talk.'

'Noa, it is nothing that can't wait until you are fed. Eat first and talk later, okay?'

She knew it wasn't really a question, so she just sat and silently sipped her coffee. She was anxious to have the conversation, worried about how he would react but, searching his face right now, she felt comforted by the lack of anger or sadness on his face. The reassuring smile he gave her allowed her to relax, the fear dissipating a little, and she contentedly watched him from where she sat at the island.

She was enjoying the view of his corded arms moving around the kitchen effortlessly to make her breakfast. His muscles pulled and flexed, the artwork across them pulling tight as he lifted plates and set them out in front of her.

Getting lost in him, she decided a little daydreaming was okay. Until they'd had breakfast, at least.

Breakfast eaten and dishes washed, Noa and Alex sat face to face, nestled amongst the cushions on his sofa. She didn't know where to start but, luckily, he went first.

'I know you were in no state to make big decisions last night, so I want you to know that I won't hold you to anything you said. But, whatever comes next, I'm here and I support you.'

Noa put her hand on his to stop him.

'I may have been upset, Alex, but I did mean it. And if you mean what you said, and really want to do this with me, then I'm in. I'm all in. I don't know what the hell I'm doing, but when have I, really? We have each other and that's more than many can say. We can work the rest out.'

'I need to make one thing clear before we talk anymore about this baby stuff, because I don't want you to get it twisted that that's the only reason I'm saying it.'

'Okay...' Noa said, shifting in her seat.

'I've waited years for the moment I would get to call you mine, Noa. I'm not a patient man, but for you I would wait however long it takes. But please don't make me wait anymore. I don't want to share you. I want you to be mine, really mine. I've thought of nothing else for months. Baby or not, I want us to be together, all in. I want you here with me all the time, because I feel sick when you're gone. I want your cold feet on my back when I fall asleep every night. I want to hear every racing thought that you have when it comes into your mind and help you work through them like a team. I want all of it. All of you. And, if we are having a baby, too, then I'm all in for that as well because, even though I'm scared as hell, making a family with you sounds like a gift I don't deserve but am selfish enough to take anyway.'

Noa felt her eyes grow damp, tears coating her eyelashes, but she didn't move to brush them away, she couldn't. She was paralysed by his words. He was all in.

'So, will you have me?'

'You want to hear my racing thoughts now?' she asked, and he nodded.

'Always.'

'I love you,' she blurted out with as much tact as a sledge barrelling through fresh snow. 'God, I've wanted to tell you that for weeks. I've probably always loved you in some way, but now I love you in a way that it makes my heart physically hurt, Alex. So yes, I'll have you. I'm all in, too.'

She was fully crying now, and she should've been embarrassed about the number of tears she had shed over the last twenty-four hours, but nothing embarrassed her in front of Alex. She felt more seen and safer than she ever had. He accepted every messy and imperfect part of her. She knew, because of that, even if he needed some convincing, that he would make an amazing dad.

He grabbed either side of her face then, kissing her cheeks, his lips soaking up her tears. They were warm and soft, and she revelled in it.

'I love you more than I ever thought possible,' he choked out, his voice so full of emotion. 'And I will fight every day to be the man deserving of your love. Deserving of our family.'

She put her cheek to his chest, letting the steady rise and fall settle her. They sat like that for a while until Noa righted herself again and looked at Alex.

'You know Ryan was wrong right?'

Alex just looked away and swallowed.

'He was hurting and lashing out. You are the furthest thing from your dad. There is no part of you that would ever leave me and whoever this is in here,' she said, pointing at her belly. 'And if you don't trust that you are not him, then that's okay, because I have enough trust for the both of us.'

A single tear fell down his cheek. Emotion was swimming in his eyes, making her feel like she could drown in them.

'The only thing I know, Noa, is I will spend my entire life working to be better, to be a man that you and our baby are proud of. I'm not perfect, but I will do my best for you. Always.'

'We don't need perfect. We just need you.'

Alex cupped her chin, such reverence in his gaze, as he took her in like he was seeing her for the first time. His eyes felt like a gentle caress as they moved over her until her words slowly sunk in and she saw he believed them.

'And I need you, Trouble.'

Those words wrapped themselves around her body like silk, and she thought of every other time he had called her that. There was a question she had been meaning to ask, but had never been brave enough to. But now, in this moment of openness and vulnerability, she let it come tumbling out.

'Why did you call me that when we were younger? Trouble, I mean.'

He didn't even hesitate before he replied, 'Because I have wanted you every minute of every day since you walked into my life. Back then, I was thirteen and stupid, and then, as we got older, I wasn't man enough to do anything about it. To see past the complication of you being Ryan's sister and fight for what I wanted. I saw you as trouble waiting to happen and the name was a reminder that I needed to stay away because we couldn't be anything else.'

Her uvula felt like it had swollen ten sizes as it obstructed her entire airway. She gasped both at his words and wanting to gulp in the air that felt thicker than it ever had.

'I really hope there's a but coming...'

'But...' he added. 'I won't make that mistake again. I wasn't man enough then, but I am now. And I will fight for you, Noa. I will go to bat for you again and again, even if I'm on my knees, broken down and bloody, because you are worth it. I don't want to play it safe anymore, not if it doesn't lead me to you.'

She didn't let him say another word. She launched herself into his arms, wrapping herself around him and, quite literally, climbing him like a tree. Just like Lola had suggested months ago.

What came next was the result of years of yearning and pent-up emotion. They weren't graceful as they found their way back to the bedroom. They frantically fumbled through his flat, bumping into every wall and piece of furniture in their wake, but not once did they break their kiss. He bruised her lips with the intensity of it, marking her as his in the best way possible. They clawed at each other with a desperate need to be closer, and rid each other of every item of clothing that separated them.

'Off,' Noa demanded, tugging at Alex's boxers.

Her entire body shook with her need for him. A storm of desire whirled around them as Alex rid himself of his boxers and removed Noa from his T-shirt, strewing them on the bedroom floor.

Once they were undressed, Alex carefully laid her down on the bed, cupping the back of her head and peppering delicate kisses down the base of her neck. It was such an opposition to the frantic way they had made it in here. He moved himself on top of her and her legs instinctively wrapped around him, keeping him close. She felt him against her wet centre, and she sucked in a breath, anticipation driving her higher. She knew it wouldn't take much to get her there.

He knew it, too, but for a moment he didn't move. He just hovered above her, drinking her in.

Alex looked at her with such tenderness and said, 'You are perfect.'

He eased his way inside her, not once removing his eyes from where they were locked on hers. A hiss escaped his lips as he bottomed out inside her, and Noa loved the way the muscles in his neck tensed with his effort to remain in control. He rolled and pumped his hips so painfully slowly that she thought she would cry with the need for more. Yet, the moment felt so perfect. She wouldn't ruin it by rushing. This wasn't fucking like they had done up until now. No. This was 'making love' in every sense of phrase.

Alex continued to move, kissing his way down her body and making her feel truly worshipped. He nipped and sucked at her collarbone, kneaded her breasts in his hands, and played her body like a musician playing their instrument. He was skilful and knew exactly what she needed to get her where she needed.

'First, I am going to take my time with you, explore and worship every inch of your body, so there is no question who loves you.'

Noa threw back her head in euphoria as the pleasure coursing through her took control of her body.

'A... a... and then?' she managed to choke out in her delirious state.

It was a wonder she could communicate at all. Her mind and body didn't feel like hers. They felt like his, and nothing had ever been more freeing.

'And then... I am going to fuck you so hard that you're going to be screaming my name for the entire town to hear.'

'I... oh... I... Fuck yes, Alex. Don't stop, please,' she whimpered.

He touched just above where they were joined, creating purposeful circles that made her toes curl and her back arch. She pushed at Alex as the sensation building inside her became too much, but quickly pulled back, not wanting the space she was creating between them. She was greedy to have every inch of him touching every inch of her, until there was no way of knowing where she ended and he began.

Wrapping her legs around him and digging her ankles into his back to anchor herself to him, Noa continued to rock her hips, chasing her release. Alex met every one of her movements with a thrust of his own and she felt him everywhere and, yet, it still wasn't enough. It would never be enough.

In her frenzied state, her internal thoughts must have accidentally slipped free, because there was a satisfied rumble from Alex's chest in response. She could feel it in her core before he picked up his pace, not relenting with his fingers still pressed between them.

A delicious ache that she felt from her head to her toes pulsed through her in waves until she was nothing but raw need. It was agony. It was incredible. It was a build-up of everything that had come before—chanced glances and suppressed feelings, years and years of yearning and hiding from feelings bigger than either one of them. It was too long running from what was always meant to be. It was a new beginning.

Their movements were clumsy and uncoordinated as they both tumbled further towards the edge. And then, she fell. Her vision blurred, lips parting in a whimper. She gripped Alex's shoulders like he was her life raft, as if she was shattering into a million pieces. She was on the precipice of sweet oblivion, and all she could do was cling on for dear life, keeping him right there so that the moment would never end.

The stars behind her eyes started to fade, quickly followed by Alex grinding out her name in a tone that she had never heard before, but would never get enough of. She wanted it burned into her brain so she could pull it out on lonely nights and remember this moment forever. Her body vibrated with the aftershocks of what had just happened. She knew she had always craved more from sex, but she had never even imagined it could feel like that.

They curled into one another under the covers, bodies limp and slick with sweat, satiated in a way Noa had never felt. The sound of heavy breaths and pounding hearts filled the room as they both remained cocooned in each other, coming down from a perfect night. And all Noa could think was, 'I could do this forever.'

# Chapter 49

## Noa

Walking into her family home, Noa felt her gut twist. She didn't know what her parents' reactions would be, but if Ryan's was anything to go by, then she had every reason to be as nervous as she was.

Tinks came trotting towards her the second she arrived and meowed loudly, an order to be picked up. Noa lifted her and buried her face in her fur, letting her soft rumbles ease her nerves slightly.

When she was younger, her parents had warned her about avoiding accidental pregnancy. In fact, her mum had sat her down several times, using Ryan's surprise conception as an example. A mental image that she could have done without, but Bethan Drake was not a coy woman, and no topic of conversation had ever been off-limits to her.

And those were the conversations that played on Noa's mind now, as she worried that they, too, would jump to conclusions just like Ryan. That they'd assume this was a hook-up gone wrong and be disappointed that she'd ignored everything they'd taught her. She tried to tell herself that she was catastrophising, *again*, and that it was nothing a simple conversation wouldn't fix. But, sometimes, rationalising was easier said than done.

Alex had offered to come with her after they'd spent the morning talking about the logistics of having a baby, but she told him that she needed to do this herself.

Right now, she was questioning her decision. She wished she had the soothing feel of his hand on her lower back to ground her. But, big girl pants in place, she stepped into the house, ready to face the music.

She also owed it to Ryan to explain. For all he knew, this was just a one-night fling, not his sister and best friend falling madly in love. Granted, he'd chosen to fly off the deep end without allowing either of them time to explain. But she hoped that her parent's presence would diffuse the tension, allowing her the time she wished she'd had on Sunday to explain everything to her brother.

To Noa's surprise, telling her parents went off without a hitch. Her mum was a blubbering mess, pulling her into her arms, surprisingly excited by the news. And her dad gave her one of his most supportive smiles before quickly moving into rambles about what kind of grandad he was going to be and what he'd have the baby call him.

It seemed Noa's sneaking around had not been as stealthy as she thought, and her mum very much knew about her relationship with Alex, even if she didn't know the extent of it. When Noa told them the depth of her and Alex's feelings for each other and the decision that they had made to move in together and make a good go of it, her mum cried some more. Apparently, she'd been waiting for this moment since they were young, and Noa tried to bite her tongue to fight from saying 'well, thanks for telling me that'. All that was in the past, though, and the only thing she wanted to focus on was their future.

The feel of her mum and dad's warm hugs brought tears to Noa's eyes, too. The unwavering love and support they had always given her felt more comforting than ever as she thought about embarking on her own journey to parenthood. She had role models like no other and, even if she could be half the parent they were, she thought she'd be doing okay. They'd set the example, and she would follow, trusting that they would be there to catch her if she stumbled. It was like the storm inside her settled at the thought, the waves stilling, creating a silent calm and allowing her to see more clearly. They were her village. They'd be there to fortify the foundations of this baby's family life. And that made her want to hold onto them and not let them go.

As Noa finished telling her parents, Ryan walked in, a sullen look on his face as he avoided eye contact with her. She was relieved to see him attending family dinner and not hiding away in his cottage, because it meant he was ready to talk instead of avoiding her like she'd feared. He did that once when they were kids. She'd broken his PlayStation, and it had been one of the longest weeks of her life.

This was better. Even if he was determined to look anywhere and everywhere but at her. Minutes passed like that but then, taking a long, soothing breath, Noa took the first step to break the tense silence that engulfed them.

'Hey, Ry. Can we talk?'

He nodded and, clearly aware that they needed their privacy, their parents left the kitchen without a word.

Noa beckoned Ryan over to the dining room table that was littered with mugs and trays of biscuits from her earlier conversation with her parents. Ryan followed her over as she sat, but he remained standing, leaning against the oak kitchen counter-top as he dropped his head to look at the floor.

'Noa, I don't know what to say I—'

Noa cut him off. He'd already said enough and now it was her turn. Raising his eyes to look at her, his lips pressed into a hard line as she spoke.

'Well, that's good, because I have a few choice words for you. The Ryan I saw Sunday night, I don't even know who he was. I didn't recognise him as my kind and caring brother, that's for sure. And that disappointed look you gave me? Well, join the damn club! You were so quick to jump to conclusions, so quick to demonise Alex, your own best friend, that you didn't even stop to consider our feelings. The things you said about his father, I wouldn't be surprised if he decides that they are unforgivable. And, to be honest, I won't even blame him.'

'I'm sorry, Noa, but I'm not currently looking for his forgiveness. He took advantage of your vulnerability, all so he could get another notch on his belt, with you of all people. That is unforgivable.'

'This isn't one drunken night between the sheets, Ryan. We love each other. And if you'd taken a minute to listen to us instead of flying off the handle, then you would have known that.'

Ryan staggered back like she had hit him.

'You what?' he spluttered.

His brow furrowed as he clearly tried to make sense of her words before a look of realisation crossed his face.

'He has been your best friend for two decades. Has he ever given you reason not to trust him? Ever given you reason to think he would do bad by me? God, you trusted him enough to send him following me across the world. Which I'm still pissed as hell about, by the way, but it gave me the man I love, so I'll choose to forgive you.'

'I...'

'Why did you trust him then but don't now? And why don't you trust me to be a grown woman and make my own decisions?'

She was shouting now. She didn't mean to, but her brother had hurt her when he'd gone behind her back months ago, and he hurt her again at the bar.

'Of course, I trust you. I'm sorry, Noa. Maybe I haven't gone about this in entirely the right way, but you're my sister and I love and worry about you. I just want the best for you.'

'Well then, trust that he is the best for me. Surely you couldn't think of anyone better to own a piece of your sister's heart than the man you yourself have loved as a best friend most of your life.'

'Well, when you put it like that...'

He grinned at her. A wide, dorky grin.

'What?' Noa questioned, knowing that look meant he had something he obviously found extremely funny to say.

'This is such a Ross and Monica moment,' Ryan said proudly.

*Of course, he had a Friends reference for the situation they were in right now.*

But, if it rid them of the horrible energy that had been circulating between them, then she would play along.

'"The One Where Everybody Finds Out",' she agreed, and Ryan just laughed at his own joke, bouncing on the spot.

With all the difficult conversations over, Noa felt a huge weight lifted off her shoulders. It felt good. After lots of questions from Ryan, who demanded all the details of their relationship, how they got here, and what their plans were now that she was pregnant, Noa was exhausted. She'd left out certain details that she didn't think her brother would appreciate but, in the end, he genuinely seemed happy for them.

Needing to get back to Alex's and crash into bed before she did so exactly where she was standing, she decided to call it a night. As she was leaving, Ryan pulled her into a familiar bear hug.

'Congratulations, by the way,' he whispered, kissing her head.

She looked up at him with watery eyes. Apparently, she was a blubbering mess now. She could definitely blame this on the pregnancy, right?

'Thanks, Ry. It's crazy, but I can't wait for this next adventure.'

'You're going to do great. And this kid is going to be the luckiest kid in the world.'

'You think?'

'Hell yeah! With me as an uncle? I'm going to smash it.'

Noa rolled her eyes as she chuckled, enjoying how normal this felt after how tense they had left things. Feeling much more optimistic, Noa left the house she'd thought was home to head toward the man she now knew to be the meaning of the word.

# Chapter 50

## Alex

Walking into the Drake's house, hand in hand with Noa, felt like a remarkably big step. Alex was trying not to let his nerves show on his face and could only hope that Noa hadn't noticed his clammy palms. At least, if she had, she'd been gracious enough not to mention it as she guided him through the entryway.

You could say that this was a crazy thought, worrying about the step of 'meeting the family' when less than a month ago he had found out that he was going to be a father, something that he'd never once considered was going to be a part of his future. But now, doing it with her, it felt so obvious, like this was always meant to happen, and their journey was always supposed to lead them here.

But the three heads that turned to face them as they walked into the kitchen-diner had been as much of a family as his own mum for much of his life. He owed so much to them. But that also meant that they knew him more than anybody, the good and the bad, all the seedy family history and childhood trauma. They might not want him with their daughter because of that, and the thought had his skin prickling like he was coming out in hives. They might have loved him like a son, but he knew full well that he wasn't good enough for their daughter, but he still wasn't sure he was ready to hear that from the people he loved. Because, regardless, he wasn't giving her up.

The expressions directed at him didn't look like anger or disappointment, though. Bethan wore the same kind and compassionate smile he'd seen a thousand times growing up. Isaac sat looking more confused by his crossword than like he wanted to kill Alex for getting his daughter pregnant. And Ryan's face was an unreadable mask, which was an improvement from the last time he'd seen him.

A shoulder nudged his, and a throat cleared as Alex realised he'd been deep in his own head. Noa looked up at him expectantly. Realising he'd likely missed a whole load of greetings, he stepped forward and said the only thing that came to his head.

'Hey,' he croaked, his throat tight and mouth dry.

*Hey? Really? That's all you've got?*

As if trying to make things worse, he waved his hand awkwardly in their direction. He wanted to roll his eyes at himself.

*Pull it together, man.*

He didn't have chance to berate himself for much longer, though, because Bethan put down her spatula from where she was preparing tonight's dinner and barrelled toward them, pulling both Alex and Noa into a hug.

He felt the tension in him ease slightly, but knew it wouldn't dissipate completely until he'd come face-to-face with his best friend. Despite Noa reassuring him that Ryan was fine after their conversation, the two of them hadn't yet spoke since the night at the bar. He'd decided Ryan could probably use a cooling off period in order to avoid round two. His actions the other night were based on heightened emotion in the moment, and the only way to avoid that again was to let him come to terms with the news first.

Bethan released them from her grip before grinning widely at them both, 'I am so glad you two finally came to your senses. Your dad and I have been biting our tongues and waiting for the day you'd finally realise you had feelings for each other since you were in high school.'

'Mum!' Noa whined.

'Hey, I just said I've been biting my tongue for long enough. Don't go asking me to do it any longer.'

Alex saw movement in his periphery and then Ryan was next to them, poking at his mum.

'Speak for yourself,' he said. 'Some of us were very much in the dark.'

He didn't sound angry when he said it, but Alex felt guilty all the same.

'Oh, hush you. It's not our fault you chose not to open your eyes, either. You're as bad as they are. God, you young ones, it's a wonder your generation gets anything done.'

This kind of easy conversation felt natural, like they had stepped back in time. Like, despite it all, their dynamics didn't have to change all that much.

'I guess we know where you get your dramatics from,' Alex joked, speaking to Noa, who sniggered.

'No second helping for you tonight,' Bethan said, wagging her finger at Alex as she walked back to continue chopping.

Because, to her, that was it. There was no anger, no disappointment, no scolding words or warnings to stay away from her daughter. No. She just carried on like she wasn't fazed in the slightest, like this was small news. How could he have expected any different?

Maybe she *had* known this was inevitable all along.

As Bethan once again busied herself, Isaac just slapped Alex on the back before his deep, raspy voice travelled through the room like it always did, 'Looks like you really are stuck with this family now, kid. If only you'd thought that one through.'

He winked and walked back to where he'd been reading the newspaper at the dining room table.

Alex turned to Ryan then.

'Hey man...'

'Look, I'm a dick...' they both blurted out at the same time and then stared at each other for a minute before Ryan broke the silence.

'I owe you an apology. I'm not going to pretend that you lying and sneaking around didn't hurt me. But, after speaking to Noa, I will say that I understand.'

Alex's throat felt heavy as he tried to get the next words out.

'I wish I could apologise. But doing that would mean I was sorry that this happened and, for that, I never will be. But what I will say is, I have loved your sister in secret for the best part of fifteen years, and the second she showed any reciprocation of those feelings, I was done for. I would tell every lie, keep every secret over and over if it meant I'd have her at my side. But I didn't mean to betray or hurt you in the process.'

'I know. It just took me a minute to get there. But that is all I needed to hear. She deserves commitment. You put her above all else, including me, and that means something. Actually, it means everything,' Ryan's voice broke for a second before he cleared it and continued. 'I love you both and have always wanted nothing but happiness for you both. If you find that together, then I'm not going to stand in your way, and I will be okay with it.'

'Thanks, man,' Alex managed to choke out.

Ryan held out his hand to shake his, and they both pulled each other into a bear hug, pausing briefly for Ryan to drag in his sister to join.

'Wait, don't squash the baby,' Alex shouted, looking panicked. Both Noa and Bethan burst out in hysterical laughter.

'What?' Alex asked, confused.

Stepping toward him and resting her hand on his chest, Noa said, 'Oh, my love, if you think I need to be wrapped up in cotton wool this entire pregnancy, we have a long nine months ahead of us.'

'And I, for one, cannot wait to see this,' Ryan said, sporting a shit-eating grin.

Alex felt all the weight he'd been carrying fall away. He had all the people that mattered to him, and he was adding one more to the mix. Life had never been better.

The rest of the night went by without a hitch. It was a typical Drake family dinner like Alex had been to many times before. Bethan made a delicious home-cooked meal of roast beef stew, and they all sat around and talked about everything and nothing until it was time for the board games to come out.

Noa was competitive as usual, and she and Ryan went at it the whole game of Ludo. Typically, because the rest of the family found it easier to let it happen, one of the two of them won. This time it was Ryan, and Noa took on the role of the sore loser, demanding he cheated. The whole scene felt so familiar, despite all that had changed, and Alex knew in that moment that these were his role models. They always had been. Not his deadbeat dad. And if he could be half the parent his mum and the Drakes had been to him, then he might just do all right.

# Chapter 51

## Alex

As the sonographer shook the bottle of jelly and dolloped some on Noa's belly, Alex watched her flinch from the cold before letting out a shy giggle.

'Sorry,' the sonographer smiled. 'I should have prewarned you it was cold.'

Alex took Noa's hand, giving it a gentle squeeze of reassurance as they sat in the small, dark room, waiting to see their baby on the screen.

He glanced around at the photos of cute, squishy babies that he could just make out on the wall, a reminder that he would have his very own soon. A whooshing sound swept throughout the room as the sonographer began her checks, and Alex couldn't stop his knee from bouncing with both nerves and excitement.

They were at the hospital for their anatomy scan. Unlike the previous scan, this one would tell them a lot more about the wellbeing of their baby. They'd also been told they'd get a much clearer picture than the first one they'd attended at around twelve weeks.

So much had changed since then. At twenty-one weeks, Noa's little bump was showing now. He stared at it in utter bewilderment, unable to deny that there was a whole tiny human growing there, one that might have her eyes—he hoped—and his nose and be the perfect blend of them both. Though if he were honest with himself, he couldn't really care less if this baby had only her features. Then he knew that they would only have the best part of the two of them, because she was his better half. She always had been, but it just took them a while to figure it out. As Noa stared enraptured by the screen, he watched her. She glowed from the inside out, and pregnancy had only magnified that.

How did he get so lucky? He still got this surreal feeling like this was all too good to be true, like he would wake up and it would've all be a dream. But, when she kissed the back of the hand that he held hers with and he stared into those beautiful blue eyes, he was brought back to his reality, and he felt like the luckiest son of a bitch alive.

As he was starting to get lost in just staring at her, the sound of galloping hooves filled the room. Both of their heads whipped to the screen in front of them. A monochrome, changing picture filled it. Alex squinted at what looked like a large peanut, just like it did last time, hence their new nickname for baby. This time however, they could make out long legs, feet and toes, two arms, hands and fingers. The flickering of something on the screen. They were told that was baby's heart beating steadily.

Alex felt his own grow five sizes at the sight. Next to him, Noa sniffled. He looked down at her as she smiled at the screen. She had a fierce look of love and adoration in her eyes. Probably the same look he was wearing, because he knew that neither of them had felt anything quite this strong, especially not for someone they'd never met. He leant down and peppered little kisses across her forehead before brushing her lips with his.

'I love you,' he whispered.

'I love you, too.'

After the scan they walked through the hospital heading toward his car. Noa gripped an envelope in her hand that felt like a hot potato. Towards the end of the scan, the sonographer had asked if they wanted to find out the sex of the baby. Alex had wanted to, and Noa had not. Not that it mattered what they were having, but Alex liked to prepare and had never been a fan of surprises. So, to him, it felt like a logical thing to do.

He knew, however, that Noa was working hard to give up an element of control in many ways over the last few months so as not to feed her anxious habits. And, despite all the life changes, she'd been in a good place lately, even after the awful pregnancy sickness she'd experienced, which seemed to have settled now. Keeping the sex a secret seemed to be one of the ways that she was demonstrating this, so as was always the way, he would give her what she wanted, because he never could say no to her.

Now that she was carrying his child, it had gotten worse. He was deluded if he thought he would ever say no to her or get his own way again. Just the other morning, he'd been due into work, but as he moved to get out of bed, she had pouted in that sexy way she did, and demanded that his 'baby mama', as she put it, needed an orgasm or two. She'd even batted her eyelashes, just to seal the deal. And how could he deny that? So, he'd gotten to work giving her exactly what she wanted, and the bar had ended up 'closed for maintenance' that day as they'd been unable to take their hands off each other. It was a hard life he lived.

As they reached the car, Noa tucked away the envelope in her bag, shooting him a playful smile. They'd come to the 'compromise' that the sonographer could write down their baby's sex, and they would keep it hidden in case they changed their minds later.

And, if Alex knew his girl, she wouldn't be able to keep a secret like that for long.

Finishing up with some last-minute paperwork in the office, Alex glared at the clock like it had caused him physical harm. It had only been four hours since he'd left Noa in what was now their flat to have a meeting with her new editor. She'd sat at the dinner table, a mug of decaf coffee in hand—to her dismay—with Tinks curled up in her lap as she spoke animatedly with a woman named Vanessa about her near-completed book.

The shoe was now on the other foot and, instead of helping other writers with their books, Noa was finally getting her own time to shine like she had always deserved.

These four hours of invoicing and spreadsheets, however, had felt more like fifteen, and not because of the mundane tasks, but because Alex was counting down every rotation of the clock until he'd be tucked up in bed beside her. He balanced his pen between his thumb and forefinger, impatiently tapping it against the mahogany wood of his desk. Time had been a bizarre construct ever since he and Noa found out they were having a baby. Five months had never been known to go by so slow and, yet, so fast in equal measure.

Noa still hadn't broken when it came to finding out the sex, despite his various persuasion methods. And every moment seemed to have been filled with some sort of planning, whether that be implementing the insane amount of baby-proofing the internet recommended in the flat, or needing some kind of instruction manual to navigate the baby aisle in the shops they now regularly visited.

Luckily for him, his baby mama was in her element when it came to planning, and though she'd let go of control in many ways since their travels, this was a time they both welcomed that side of her personality. And when they'd been talking about everything they needed, Alex suggested 'making a list', and Noa's response had very quickly been 'don't threaten me with a good time'. To which Alex had almost definitely shown her a very good time.

But, after picking up practically two of everything anyone could ever *potentially* need when having a baby, Alex was tasked with preparing The Brew for his planned paternity leave.

He sat, scrolling through all the 'how to' guides he'd developed for Bella when she agreed to take over running the place. He'd included everything he could think of, despite the fact that she'd been working for him long enough now and could probably do his job better than him.

Maybe Noa was rubbing off on him, but The Brew was his first baby and, despite knowing it was in good hands, he wanted to be prepared. Because there was one life-changing event that he knew nothing could prepare him for. And that was stepping into the role of 'Dad'.

Alex's initial fears of becoming a father had ebbed recently, proving the cliché that time really did heal old wounds. Every day that he was the receiver of Noa's beautiful smile showed him that he deserved to be. And every day he made her laugh, or held her whilst she cried, every way he showed up for her, had gradually began to silence the voice that for too long had convinced him he would one day step into his father's shoes.

He knew now that he would never become him, because there was nothing in this world he wouldn't do for Noa or their child growing inside her. Noa had helped heal that part of him, and he would forever be grateful to the strong, tenacious woman he now got to share his life with. She loved him in a way he never knew he needed.

The hinges of his office door squeaked as they opened and closed, followed by hurried footsteps. Alex glanced up from his laptop to see Bella leaning against a bookshelf, biting her lip in that way Noa did when she was nervous about something.

But he'd never seen Bella nervous about anything. She usually wore cold indifference on her face more than anything else. Occasionally irritation. Or exasperation.

Never worry.

Alex had employed her because he'd connected to this woman who wore a front for the world to see. Who hid her emotions in a locked box after a lifetime of feeling like there was no other way.

She'd never directly told him that, but he'd recognised it, as someone one and the same. The guarded look in her eyes had told him everything he needed to know, and he'd wanted to give her a place to fall. After all, before Noa, The Brew had been that for him, too, for a while.

'What is it?' Alex asked, shuffling in his chair as he awaited her answer.

'Hi, Boss. I know I said I'd look after this place and all, and you're counting on me, but I needed to check something first.'

'Okay...' Alex replied, now nervous himself.

*Oh god, what if she left him hanging?*

*How would he find someone on such short notice?*

*He was supposed to be changing nappies soon, not pouring pints!*

'Well, it's more like a stipulation,' she continued, straightening her shoulders and seeming to remember herself. Then she blurted, 'Answering to Ryan isn't part of the job description, right?'

'Huh?'

Alex was completely confused. Had he not gotten enough sleep last night?

'He is *relentless*. When you were away, he came in here like a cow in a china shop...'

'A bull,' Alex corrected with a chuckle, before reaffirming at her confused expression, 'It's a *bull* in a china shop.'

Instead of acknowledging the correction, Bella continued, 'I know he's your friend, but he thought he owned the place after you told him to look after it. He was walking round like a cock in a henhouse.'

Her continuous use of incorrect similes to emphasise her point was endearing, but he wasn't sure she'd want to hear that, so Alex just let her continue.

'That was the longest eight weeks of my life. I thought he'd cool his jets when you got back, but he's just as irritating as ever, and I can't take him questioning me when you're off work again. I might actually kill him. I've been dreaming of how I'd do it.'

Alex rolled his eyes, internally berating his best friend. Alex had, in fact, not put Ryan in charge of anything, or told him to keep an eye on things. Ryan had suggested and taken that upon himself, even after Alex told him it wasn't necessary.

But, looking at the woman with ruffled feathers in front of him, he had a good clue as to why. He stifled his laugh, knowing by the state of her serious face, it would not be very well received.

Bella could be scary at times, and Ryan might like to poke the bear, but Alex did not. Not when the bear had agreed to take care of his livelihood for six months so he could dedicate that time to learning to be a good dad. That was all that mattered.

Zoning back into the conversation, Alex realised Bella was still talking, more like ranting, about his best friend.

'... he is self-centred, egotistical, could flirt with a blow-up doll... oh, and don't get me started on his man-child behaviour,' she groaned, as if in pain. 'So, whilst this is a great opportunity for me, I need to know that The Brew is for me to look after alone. Without interference.'

Ryan was the interference she was talking about, and Alex didn't know how to tell her that he could control his friend just about as well as he could control a feral cat.

But, opting for something more encouraging, he kept his next statement simple.

'The bar is yours whilst I'm away Bella. I'm grateful for everything you did for me whilst I travelled, and everything you have done for me since. You have total control going forward. What you say goes. I don't mind who you have to remind of that.'

Bella perked up at that, an almost-smile showing on her face. Her red hair was ruler straight. Her eyeliner flicked up at the side to make her look cat-like. She looked like a woman who meant business, and Alex was glad she'd be caring for his.

But, as she offered him a firm nod before turning to leave his office, all he could think was, *good luck to the man who crosses her. And may their balls forever rest in peace.*

# Chapter 52

## Noa

The Brew was packed full of all the people nearest and dearest to Noa and Alex. Glancing around, Noa felt extremely grateful to have such amazing people in their lives. They say that it takes a village to raise a baby and, well, they definitely had no issues there. They had a literal village, or town or whatever. Even Lola had made the trip for their baby shower-come-sex-reveal.

Yes, Noa had caved when it came to keeping the sex a secret until the very end but, in her defence, she was doing this as a surprise for Alex. He'd always wanted to find out and had been patient enough with her throughout the pregnancy. So far, that had meant putting up with a lot—pregnancy sickness, mood swings, hysteria, identity crises. Noa knew that she had been the pregnancy equivalent of bridezilla, and Alex had just taken it in his stride.

So, now that they were finally at thirty-six weeks, it felt like a great time to announce the news, with all their friends and family present. She just couldn't wait to see his face when he found out.

It had been a very long road getting here, and Noa felt like a final celebration was important before baby finally arrived and two became three. Shortly after they had found out they were pregnant, Noa moved in with Alex in the flat above the bar. Even though people thought it was fast, it felt like the right thing for them. They had wasted so much time, and knowing each other for over two decades and still harbouring feelings for each other for all that time, meant they definitely weren't worried about getting sick of each other or finding any scary skeletons in their closets. So, they took the leap.

Plus, with the baby around the corner and a new chapter in their life that they were both excited to start, being under the same roof to prepare and then parent together made sense.

Although Alex insisted that they would move out and get a bigger place soon and that above a bar was no place to raise a baby, Noa kind of liked it, for now, at least. It meant, even when Alex was at work, he was never far, and she had such fond memories there now—the day they found out they were going to be parents and admitted they loved each other and all those nights that followed, thoroughly christening every room.

It was their first home together, as well as the place where Noa had both finished her first novel and found out she was getting a book deal with a large publisher. It was where they'd spent many nights, curled up together in front of the fire, falling even deeper in love. So, for now, they would remain in the flat, and she knew they would make many more memories there.

Noa waddled over to where Lola and Tes chatted at the bar. Fairy lights now hung above them, one of a few new décor alterations that The Brew had seen, that Alex said were inspired by their trip. There was even a small paper lantern they had brought back as a memento hung above the till. Alex said he liked to look at the memory whilst he worked.

She smiled at the girls who sat huddled together by the bar, as if plotting something devious.

Oh lord, help her if these two became friends. Though, there was something in the picture of them that had Noa assessing whether that was all it was. The way that Lola slapped Tes's arm and fluttered her lashes as she laughed animatedly at something her best friend had said. It looked flirty, almost. As did their posture. They leaned into each other, knees almost touching.

Noa shook off the idea. Clearly the hormones and the sexy man she got to go home to every night were getting to her and now she saw romance everywhere.

Lola had finally finished her year-long travelling stint and was back in her hometown. She and Noa had kept in touch and remained close, so when she had mentioned the baby shower to Lola, she had practically begged her to let her come and visit for it. Noa got the impression that Lola had outgrown her tiny village whilst she was away and was itching to leave again.

'So, I see you two have met.'

Lola suddenly sat up, almost unnaturally straight, as she turned in Noa's direction.

'Yeah, no thanks to you, little miss hostess with the mostest,' Tes quipped, her teasing tone causing Lola's shoulders to relax a little.

Noa rolled her eyes and stuck her tongue out at Tes as she leaned in to embrace Lola in a hug. The hug proved a little more difficult than it had when they'd said goodbye nine months ago, with what felt like a whole watermelon strapped to her front. But Lola only chuckled, then held Noa at arm's length, scrutinising her.

'Hell, you are the best-looking pregnant woman I have ever seen. I bet all the others just hate you for pulling off that bump so well.'

Noa just scoffed and brushed her off. Her and her ever-changing body had a love-hate relationship, but she wasn't going to get into that here.

'I know,' Tes responded. 'I've been saying this the whole time. It's just a pity you're insistent on carrying on batting for the other team, because my best friend is hot and we could have been so happy together,' Tes mused, batting her lashes at the sky as if imagining some alternate reality.

'You couldn't handle me,' Noa joked, pushing her shoulder before starting to step away from where the two were perched. 'On that note, Lola, look after Tes for me, will you? She likes to get herself into trouble. Now, I don't know who's worse than who and this town can only take so much drunken debauchery, so please don't corrupt each other whilst I'm gone.'

'Where are you going that's more important than here?' Tes grumped.

Noa just looked over her shoulder, winking, 'You'll see.'

Noa made her way over to the hunk of a man that stood deep in conversation with her dad and Ryan, hooking her arms through his so they surrounded him from behind, meeting at his middle—or, almost. Again, this baby bump was a pain in the ass, and she would be glad when she could go back to being as close to her man as humanly possible.

'Hey, Trouble,' he drawled in that sexy voice of his.

Noa was amazed that she had gone so long without having this man in this capacity, and yet, now that she had, she couldn't get enough of him and didn't think she would ever get tired of having him close to her.

'Hey, you. I think it's time we go make a speech and thank our guests, don't you?'

Alex gruffed. She knew he hated public speaking, but he followed after her to the band-stand where a microphone was positioned. When they got to it, she let him take the lead. He cleared his throat to get everyone's attention, tapping the microphone for good measure.

'So, boss lady over here...' he began pointing his thumb in Noa's direction where she stood by his side, her hand in his. 'She says that, apparently, it's customary at these things to make a speech and thank all your guests for coming. Now, I know that in this town, no one says no to a party or free food and drink, so I think I should be saying "you're welcome".'

Noa elbowed him and tried to hold in a laugh.

'But, on a serious note, we appreciate all of you for coming out today, for being a part of our journey, and for all your help and support. We are about to embark on our biggest adventure yet, and I am a lucky son of a bitch for getting to do it with this incredible woman by my side. So, whilst I'm here, I just wanted to say thank you to you too, Noa, for choosing me, loving me, and making me the happiest man alive. I can't wait to watch you become a mum. Me and that baby in there are so lucky to call you ours.'

Noa swiped at the tears free-falling down her face.

'You know my emotions are all over the place. Were you trying to make me cry?'

Alex kissed her in response, only a peck, but it meant the world as he poured all his love into that one brush of their lips, here in front of everyone they knew.

Noa looked back up at him as he pulled away, remembering what she had planned to do. He had a tendency of turning her brain to mush every time he kissed her, plus with her baby brain, it was a wonder she remembered at all. but, as Alex went to step down off the band-stand, Noa grabbed the mic.

'Just one more second. I have a little speech of my own before you go back to your conversations, if that's okay?'

The room fell silent again, and Noa pulled an envelope out of her back pocket, handing it to Alex.

'What's this?'

'Guess you'll have to open it and find out.'

Tearing open the envelope, Alex pulled out what looked like a boarding pass. The confusion on his face made her chuckle involuntarily. The whole room waited on tenterhooks to find out what was going on, so Noa decided to give him a clue.

'Looks like you'll need a penny to scratch that,' she said, pointing to the window where a scratch card was visible at the corner of the ticket that read, 'The destination is irrelevant, but the journey is where the adventure begins.'

Pulling a two pence coin from his wallet, Alex scratched at the card to see what it revealed underneath. Then, he looked up at her with such joy and adoration in his eyes, she felt like her chest might explode.

She nodded at him excitedly before choking out, 'Now, I don't actually know what that says, so you are going to have to clear it up for the both of us.'

Alex's words were raspy, thick with emotion as he whispered into the microphone, not taking his eyes off her for a second, 'It's a girl.'

Noa fell into his embrace with a sob as the whole room erupted with cheers of celebration. Alex held her and brushed her hair as she let all her emotions wash over her.

'A mini you,' he whispered in her ear, 'God, I don't stand a chance do I?'

Noa looked up through waterlogged lashes.

'Oh, she's going to have you wrapped around her little finger.'

'I can hardly wait.'

# Epilogue

## Noa

Noa had been lost in deep pools of blue for the last hour as she gazed into the most perfect eyes she had ever seen. Any love she thought she knew seemed so incomparable right now as she held her daughter in her arms, including her love for Alex. It wasn't less than, just different. Like seeing your heart physically living outside of your chest.

The intensity of this love she now knew threatened to tear her apart but, luckily, she had the man of her dreams holding her together. Both physically and emotionally.

Noa inhaled Leyla's perfect baby smell, wanting to remember every minute detail of this moment forever.

A rainy beach scene still played across the ceiling of their bedroom, the relaxing sound of waves, mixed with Tinks' purrs, acting as background noise, just like it had throughout labour. Alex had been the best birthing partner, guiding her through her breathing with each contraction, rubbing her back and whispering positive affirmations, just like they'd practiced at their home birth evening.

Now, he held her in his warm embrace as she cradled their tiny human, one who was a perfect mix of the both of them, in her arms.

'I was praying she'd have your eyes,' he cooed at her.

The way he'd fussed over her since the second she made her entrance into this world just over an hour ago was almost too much for her heart to take.

'You do know lots of babies have blue eyes, right? I'm still praying for your amber ones,' Noa said, turning her head to look up at him.

Alex's face was cast in the flickering light of the projector, highlighting every familiar feature, his amber eyes glowing warmer. Her love for him had grown and reshaped itself again and again over the last nine months, until it became as much a part of her as the lungs that gave her breath. And since holding their baby girl in their arms, her heart ached with the depth that love had taken.

'Well, she is perfect no matter what, and I will spend my every breath making sure that she knows it.'

'I have no doubt,' Noa whispered.

The look of pride and devotion she saw swimming in his eyes as he stared at her caught her off guard. She still struggled to believe that the thing she had been missing from her life for all those years had been there all along.

'What?'

'I am so proud of you. You absolutely kicked labour's ass, and you are a natural with her,' he responded, stroking his hands reverently through her hair.

Noa had struggled a lot through her pregnancy. First with morning sickness, which did not only happen in the mornings, and then as her body had started to change. She'd struggled to feel confident in her new and changing body. She had also struggled when that motherly bond people said she would feel as she felt her baby grew did not arrive. But now, looking at her darling girl, she wondered why she had ever worried. But like Alex always did, because he knew her every insecurity, he soothed her worries without her even having to say a word.

He'd even been the one to research home birth in the first place. He'd found leaflets and told her that the experience could not only optimise oxytocin, but that staying in their safe space, where they could have the privacy they were getting now, could help them bond with their baby girl.

As they continued to sit, silently observing their daughter Leyla, Noa felt like she was in a blissful bubble. One they'd created. The flat they'd soon filled with Noa's collection of books and trinkets, now felt like home. Tinks remained curled up at the bottom of the bed, tired after spending the whole night by Noa's side through her labour. Forever Noa's comfort animal.

Her soft half-purrs, half-snores mixed with their birth playlist now, and Noa felt a deep sense of belonging and purpose. One she'd found in the family she had created.

Their photos that now hung on the walls were filled with the memories they'd made on their travels and in the months since. They felt like a promise of the future to come, and she imagined the ones they would add: photos of Leyla's first birthday, family Christmases, and the holidays they'd promised they'd take.

Alex caressed her arm, catching her attention again before he spoke, 'Remember that list of yours?'

Noa had let all thoughts of her '30 before 30' list slip from her mind over recent months. The whole thing seemed unnecessary now. She looked up at Alex, confusion likely clear on her face.

'Well, you did say you wanted to give Tinks another sibling. This is probably not the kind you had in mind when you wrote it, but you are forever the overachiever.'

She laughed.

'I forgot all about that.'

In her arms, Leyla made a content gurgling sound and Noa wanted to bottle up the feeling forever. Nothing could make this moment better. She felt like she was flying high in the clouds and never wanted to come down.

'Well, I didn't. Hey, why don't you pull it out now so we can see if you've managed to do everything on there...'

'It hardly matters now. We have more important things to focus on,' she said, kissing her daughters head and breathing in that indescribable baby smell.

'Humour me.'

With a huff she pulled out her phone, where her list was now kept on a shared note that they could both access. When she found out she was pregnant, Alex suggested setting it to share so that he could help her finish it before she had Leyla.

As she opened the note, Alex insisted she read it out loud to him. So, she began doing just that. She didn't remember adding the last few things on the list, so it looked like Alex had done it for her. As she finally got to number thirty, her eyes widened and her mouth fell open as her head flew up to gawk at him.

He was smiling as he said, 'Go on. Read it.'

Noa could barely see through tear-filled eyes, something that had not gotten any better through the pregnancy. Her words were shaky and barely audible.

'N... number thi... thirty,' she started, clearing her throat to remove the huge lump that seemed to be growing there. 'M... marry Alex.'

She looked up at him then and, without her knowing, he had quietly retreated from the bed next to her and was now on his knees, a red, velvet box in his hand.

'Noa Drake, you have owned my heart since the moment you walked into my life as a sassy and dorky teenager with the biggest stubborn streak I have ever known. Our journey may not have been the most straightforward, and we may have been too stupid to see what was right in front of us for the longest time, but I wouldn't change a thing if it would get me right here, now. You have given me the greatest gift in life, and I will live the rest of mine working to be worthy of the love of my girls. You are everything I have ever wanted but couldn't have dreamed of having, and I would be the happiest man on this earth if you would agree to be mine. Forever.'

Noa let out a sob, lost for words. She wouldn't change a thing either, because she was wrong when she thought nothing could make this moment better, because this moment right now was perfect. She could not love this man any more than she did, and she knew that she would love him until her dying breath.

She nodded frantically, using her one free hand to grab his shirt, pulling him up from the floor and into her until his lips crashed to hers, passionately kissing her hard enough she was sure her lips would bruise.

She pulled away, looking at him breathless.

'Of course, I'll marry you, because forever isn't long enough.'

THE END

## AUTHOR'S NOTE

Thank you for choosing to read *My Kind of Trouble*. This has been a work of love over the last year, and a lifeline when I needed one. Noa and I are similar in many ways, and so this was a love note to myself when I felt like I needed the words. I hope this book finds the readers it needs too. Those struggling through hard times who can't see past them. Those who believe if they stray from the path they set out on, that they have achieved less. Those who have had their heart broken, and to those who know what it's like to feel like their brain is constantly working against them. I see you. You are nothing short of amazing. Hard times do not define you, and neither does your mental health. It's the person you are throughout it all, and I bet you're pretty great! The fact that you get up and face every day is enough, and in case you haven't heard it lately, I am proud of you. But guess what? I hope this book shows you that you get to choose your own life path—no one else. And it is not linear. So let go of that idea, along this crazy, winding road and try to enjoy the mess. Don't be tempted to compare, or let the world around you dictate what gives you your sparkle. Just shine unapologetically bright the best way you know how. Go out and find your happiness. Because wherever it lies, it is out there.

The topic of pregnancy is discussed in this novel, and I felt it integral to explore Noa's feelings towards her pregnancy and choice. It was important for me to include Noa's conversations and her internal thoughts regarding an unexpected pregnancy and the dichotomy of emotions that stirred up.

In the world today, not all women are in the same position as Noa—a woman in the UK, able to consider her options for abortion. At a time when women's choices and rights over their own bodies are constantly being called into question, I couldn't ignore the conversation. I hear it all around me and wanted Noa to demonstrate that in considering her own fundamental rights, she is making her own choice. And that is hers and hers alone. As it feels like it becomes increasingly less safe to identify as a woman, I want people to know that they are safe with me.

I hope you enjoyed their journey and I can't wait to see you in book two!

# ACKNOWLEDGMENTS


Writing my acknowledgments means that the journey of creating my debut novel has come to an end, and that feels too insane to think about. One day in September 2024, I found myself at another author's launch event, daydreaming about writing my own novel. I'd buried this daydream for years, a nasty habit I've learnt we have as adults. I convinced myself that authors were mythical, divine beings and something I could simply never be. Listening to Lucy speak about her writing journey really humanised those I have looked up to for years and inspired me to step out of my comfort zone.

Who would have known I'd have found such comfort in doing so? You could say I had an epiphany very similar to Noa's, that some of the best and most rewarding things come from being brave and stepping into the unknown.

I started this book to heal myself, and in the process found the healing I sought, but also so much more. Thank you for reading my book and making my dream come true.

Whilst there are so many people I want to thank, I feel like a special shout out should go to all the exes that led to me being twenty-six, single, and living with my parents. I couldn't have done it without you.

Those heartbreaks shaped who I am, and really found their way into who Noa became in this story. The experience of that quarterlife crisis, or 'the panic years' is a truly humbling one, and for all those still in the trenches of it, I see you.

Thank you to my Beta readers, Laura, Imi, Sophie and Sophie—you're rockstars!

This book would not be in readers hands if it wasn't for my soulmate, best friend and lifelong cheerleader, Niamh. By being my own personal hype girl, you single handedly talked me into publishing this book, when it was only thirteen rough chapters intended for my own eyes, and in doing so, you gave me something to focus all my efforts on during one of the toughest years of my life. You helped me find my safe place and I will add it to the endless list of reasons why I am grateful for you. You truly are one of the best humans in this world!

Lindsey. God where to start? Thank you so much for hearing my voice and never once compromising it. You understood my vision and have been instrumental in revising and polishing my novel into the version everyone sees today.

Laura, you are, and always will be, one of my closest friends and my go to encyclopaedia for all things bookish. I think I owe you and Rachel a special thank you for putting up with my incessant yapping over the last year about my writing. I'm surprised I wasn't evicted, but your patience did not go unnoticed. I swear I might manage to find another topic of conversation sometime soon. But until then, I want you to know that allowing me the space to feel supported and never 'too much' has soothed my soul in a way I never knew I needed. I will love you both always for this.

Nina and Alyssa, thank you for lending me your fabulous creative brains. My cover and art genuine still make me giddy and you both did that! Absolute queens!

And finally, to my parents. All four of them. Thank you for always teaching me to be my unapologetic, authentic self. For showing me that your struggles do not define you. And that I can achieve whatever the hell I want to.

## CONTENT WARNINGS

Mental Health Representation
Parental abandonment
Conversations around unplanned pregnancy and choice
Explicit sexual scenes

Printed in Dunstable, United Kingdom

67174400R00228